THE BEGINNING....

I went back to my hotel. As soon as I opened my door I realized that the gentlemen from AVTOUR were playing for keeps. The room had been completely demolished.

The mattress looked as though someone had gone at it with a butcher knife. The drawers from the bureau hung like swollen tongues. My suitcase had been slashed to ribbons. I let my eyes scan the room, searching for something to use as a weapon. Nothing.

I slipped out of my shoes, my eyes riveted on the closed bathroom door. I padded across the room, pausing to listen. Breathing? Or the wind outside? The sound of my heart was like thunder. I winced as a floorboard creaked like a rifle shot and I froze. Nothing from behind the door. Another step. Still nothing.

I closed my eyes, took a deep breath, and lifted my leg. I kicked at the door, hard, and it slammed back. Nothing. I stepped into the bathroom and suddenly realized that my legs had turned to rubber. I sat down on the toilet and waited for my heart to slow and my muscles to stop twitching.

I whirled around just in time to glimpse a slashing arm slice down through the shower curtain, eight inches of gleaming steel grasped tightly in its fist....

The Icarus Seal

Christopher Hyde

BANTAM BOOKS
TORONTO · NEW YORK · LONDON · SYDNEY

FOR MARIEA WHO STOOD BY ME THROUGH THE TOUGH TIMES.

FOR NOAH AND CHELSEA WHO GET PEANUT BUTTER ON MY TYPE-
WRITER KEYS.

AND FOR MY BROTHER TONY WHO GAVE ME THE IDEA AND THE
TITLE, BLESS HIM.

*This low-priced Bantam Book
has been completely reset in a type face
designed for easy reading, and was printed
from new plates. It contains the complete
text of the original hard-cover edition.*
NOT ONE WORD HAS BEEN OMITTED.

THE ICARUS SEAL

*A Bantam Book / published by arrangement with
Houghton Mifflin Company*

PRINTING HISTORY
Houghton Mifflin edition published October 1982

Bantam edition / December 1983

ISBN 0-553-23785-3

Published simultaneously in the United States and Canada

---

*Bantam Books are published by Bantam Books, Inc. Its trade-
mark, consisting of the words ''Bantam Books'' and the por-
trayal of a rooster, is Registered in U.S. Patent and Trademark
Office and in other countries. Marca Registrada. Bantam
Books, Inc., 666 Fifth Avenue, New York, New York 10103.*

PRINTED IN CANADA

COVER PRINTED IN U.S.A.

U   0 9 8 7 6 5 4 3 2 1

Acknowledgements

I would like to thank the Cromemco Computer Company, Computer Innovations Limited, and Thomas Whiteside, author of *Computer Capers* for information concerning computers and computer crime. I would also like to thank Cyril and Angelika Levitt for correcting my German.

Author's Note

The technological material contained in this book is accurate and there is a great deal of circumstantial evidence which leads me to believe that something very much like the Icarus Contingency Plan already exists. The names of the various pieces of hardware, including aircraft and computers, have not been changed.

The characters, however, are fictitious, and any resemblance to persons living or dead is entirely coincidental, which should greatly please the guilty parties involved.

PART ONE

·

G.I.G.O.

G.I.G.O.: Acronym for Garbage In/Garbage Out; the principle that the results produced from unreliable data are equally unreliable.

Chapter One

The telephone rang once and then the answering machine cut in.

"This is Peter Coffin. I'm not available right now. Please leave your message at the sound of the tone."

The machine pinged.

"Damn! Hello, Peter. It's Sam Underwood. Look, this is quite urgent, can you get back to me . . . No, that's no bloody good!"

I rolled over and hit the override. Somehow I managed to find the phone and get the receiver to my ear.

"Sam? Peter." I grunted.

"What? Oh, then you are there," said Sam, his Oxford cadences rising and falling from four thousand miles away.

"Of course I'm here. Sleeping." I yawned.

"Good God, what time is it over there?"

I let my head flop to the left and squinted at the digital clock on the bedside table. "Five," I said. "In the morning."

"It's just noon here."

"Peachy. We have just verified that the concept of time zones really works." I let out another yawn. I'd hit the sack at a little after two. An evening spent drinking successfully and seducing unsuccessfully. A production assistant for a local television station I'd just done a piece for. Small mind, great legs, and a total immunity to Singapore Slings. On top of it all I was flying out of the country in another twelve hours or so. I groaned.

"What's up?" I asked, groping for a cigarette and lighting it.

"I need information," said Sam.

"Uh," I said, dragging on the Camel. My mouth tasted like the last foot of a roller towel in a Vic Tanny's men's room.

"About an airline," added Sam.

"You're doing fine, Sam. In another hour I'll have the whole story." Through the bedroom window I could see the

3

first painful attempts at a Toronto sunrise. Rosy-fingered dawn my foot—it looked more like an old bruise.

"Don't be tiresome," said Sam. "This is important."

"Nothing is important enough to wake me up at five in the morning, Sam."

"This is," he said. I sat up against the headboard. There was a note of excitement in his voice that cut through my grogginess. Sam was onto something. The fair-haired boy from the *Observer* sounded wound up like a spring.

"So give it to me," I said.

"Not a chance," he answered. "Not on the phone at any rate."

"I leave tonight," I warned.

"The Paris Air Show?" he asked. "That's not for another four days."

"I'm going to London first. An interview with Chatsworth for *Omni*. I kill two birds with one stone. *Aviation Month* is paying for the Le Bourget show, so I get the Chatsworth *Fusion* article for free," I explained.

"Shit," said Sam.

"What's the problem? We can get together in London."

"I'm flying out of here this afternoon," said Sam. "New York via Mirabel and Toronto."

"What time do you get in here?" I asked.

"Four."

"So, my flight leaves at nine. We'll have five hours. That should be enough unless you've found Adolf Hitler alive and well in Upper Tooting."

"Better than that," said Sam.

"You mentioned an airline," I prompted.

"Know anything about a charter company called AVTOUR?" he asked.

I sighed. In all the years I'd known him Sam had never answered a question directly. He defended himself by saying that the longest distance between two points might not be the fastest, but it was usually the most interesting. I stubbed out the Camel and let a few shreds of information seep into my slowly unfurling brain.

"They fly Tens," I said, after a moment. "They took a bath after the big crash in '79. Just like everyone else who flew Tens. As a charter company they should have folded, but somehow they managed to keep afloat. They do multiple destination charters on the transatlantic run, I think. Head office in Paris if memory serves. If you want anything more I'll have to consult the Box." The Box is my Cromemco Z2H home computer. It put me up to my ears in debt when I first got it, but the 12 Megabyte system has given me the edge on more than one story.

"So ask the Box," said Sam. "You won't have this story on file."

"Give me a hint."

"Do you remember I once told you about my Great Aunt Cecily?" asked Sam. Another circumlocution.

"Vaguely," I said.

"She had a certain vice," supplied Sam.

It clicked. I lit another cigarette. Sam's great aunt had been left a basket of cash by her ducal husband but she was an incorrigible smuggler. In her heyday she'd jacked anything from diamonds to orchid cuttings.

"AVTOUR," I said. "They're pulling an Aunt Cecily?"

"It looks that way," murmured Sam. "Into Mirabel."

"Go on," I said. Outside the pigeons were waking up. I was going to have a hell of a time getting back to sleep.

"No. I can't say any more now. I'll give you the details when I arrive."

"I'll be here."

"Good show. I'll be arriving on AVTOUR 360. Mirabel at three-fifteen, Toronto International at just past four. I should get to your place around five or so. We can have a quick dinner before you head out."

"All right. Sure you can't give me anything more to chew on?"

There was a long pause.

"Gambetta S.A.," said Sam.

"Spell it," I said. He did.

"That's it, then. See you for dinner."

"Right."

"Remember. AVTOUR, and Gambetta S.A. Cheerio." There was a click and then the line went dead.

I hung up the phone, pulled a pillow over my head, and tried to ignore the pigeons and the early traffic noise. I don't think I stayed awake more than thirty seconds.

I never heard from Sam Underwood again.

* * *

These days most journalists have degrees; I never even came close. My career began when I was eighteen, and not by choice. I was attending a small upstate New York college, taking Liberal Arts, dreaming of being in advertising and dipping my youthful wick into all that sixties fervour. With the Canadian citizenship I inherited from my mother I could do it without fear of being drafted. They were great days; I divided my time unequally between taking flying lessons, writing bits and pieces for the college paper, and taking classes. It was the writing that got me into trouble. I stumbled across a story concerning the suspect morals of the dean of men, and instead of giving it to the school rag, I tried it on for size at the local paper in town. They loved it. The college booted me out. The editor of the paper in town felt responsible and gave me a job at the rewrite desk. I discovered, much to my surprise, that I was good at newspaper work. One thing led to another, and after a couple of years I'd become something of a specialist in technological feature stories, writing for a variety of papers and magazines. Most of the stories were about aviation and the military. I also managed to edit a two volume Inventors Encyclopedia for a major US publisher and wrote two books of my own; one a history of alternate energy resources, the other a poorly received pot-boiler about a cocaine smuggler who used radio-controlled model airplanes to transport his goodies. As well as that I got my pilot's licence, edited a short-lived magazine about archaic weaponry, and worked as a free-lance pilot guide in the Canadian Rockies. I'm a pack rat by nature, and any information I thought was useful, or even vaguely interesting, I stored in the Box.

At thirty, I suppose you could call me a reasonable success.

At eight-fifteen the bedside clock shouted at me with its familiar high-pitched buzz and I awoke for the second time that day. I opened my eyes carefully, letting them adjust to the bright sunlight that filled the room. The bruised dawn had turned into a third degree burn that was threatening to referment the booze I'd taken in the night before.

I tapped off the alarm and let my senses take their own

good time gearing up for the day. In the distance I could hear the dull hum of the air conditioner that was keeping the baking July morning at bay, as well as the erratic bubbling of the coffee percolator. The percolator is switched on automatically by the alarm clock—one of the more humane labour saving devices that you can find in the Heathkit catalogue. I waited until I could smell the coffee before I made a move. Then I crawled out of bed, lit a cigarette, and shrugged into my knee-length kimono—a present from a more successful evening than the one I was recovering from.

I wandered into the bathroom and adhered to my morning ritual: no coffee until I complete the basics. I found out a long time ago that if I allow myself the life-giving jag of the coffee before the regular bathroom routine I'll never really get up. I just lie around all day making excuses for not buckling down to work.

Finally, showered, shaved, and dressed in a lightweight suit minus jacket and tie, I staggered into the kitchen and poured myself a huge mug of Medaglia d'Oro. Ten minutes after that, drinking a second cup and munching on a cracker larded with Boursault cheese, I went into the front room, my combination living room and office.

That room is my pride and joy. Large, lined on three walls with bookcases floor to ceiling, with the fourth wall taken up by a picture window that looks out onto the dubious pleasure of the Don Valley and the sepia hazed towers of the Toronto skyline beyond. In front of the window is my desk; seven hundred bucks' worth of teak topped by an IBM Selectric and the Box. The computer, printer, keyboard, and all, takes up less space than the typewriter. Every time I look at that room I pat myself on the back—it's a long way from the cluttered, cramped, and stifling confinement of the Rougeville *Leader-Post* City Room.

I crossed the deep-blue Kazak carpet, finished off my cracker, and sat down at the desk, lighting up another cigarette. I switched on the Box. The CRT screen glowed green, blank except for the small white rectangle of the cursor in the upper left hand corner.

I tapped out a set of instructions, accessing whatever information I had on AVTOUR. The screen cleared itself and the cursor began blipping back and forth as the information unfurled.

AVTOUR/Division Charters International Ltd. H.O. / 32
Avenue de l'Opéra Paris France. Subsid/Aviom Indust. (ref:
AV MANU. CO.) Operates multiple dest. tours loading
from—
Amsterdam
Frankfurt
London
Paris . . .
Dest. N.A.—
Mirabel/Que./Can.
TorInt/Ont./Can.
JFK/NY/NY
Aircraft type—
DC-10/9 in service 3/2/79
Br. Off.
Amsterdam
Frankfurt
Berlin
London
Marseille
Istanbul
Tel-Aviv
Tokyo
Toronto
New York
endit.

I scanned the material, trying to find some hook that might
have interested Sam. There was nothing earth shattering that
I could see. I hit the Memory-hold and banged in a new set
of commands. This time I tried a run on Gambetta S.A. I
wasn't sure that I'd have anything, but I finally found a code
for it under Air Freight / Europe.

GAMBETTA S.A.
H.Q. / 234 Rue de la Grande St. Mande France. Short
haul air freight company special. in exp. service for small
parcels and valuables—specif. bullion. Bonded for—
France
England
Germany
Italy

Turkey
Israel
Aircraft type—
GAMOS 12 (ref: AV MANU. CO.)
          (ref: DeHavilland DASH-7)
Br. Off.
TXL
BRU
DUS
FRA
IST
LHR
OAS
CDG
LBG
MIR
YYZ
endit.

The list of three letter combinations stood for various airports. Gambetta S.A. had branches in every major airport from TXL/Berlin to YYZ/Toronto. There didn't seem to be any connection between AVTOUR and Gambetta, but it was hard to tell. The air freight company was an S.A., a Société Anonyme, and as such didn't have to list its affiliations. I sat and stared at the screen for a moment, trying to put the puzzle together. Finally, on a hunch, I hit a third set of commands. I searched under AV MANU. CO. and then from there to GAMOS 12, the aircraft used by Gambetta S.A. I hit paydirt.

The reference was right out of Janes' *All the World's Aircraft*. "GAMOS 12—Long Range Turbofan manufactured under Patent contract with DeHavilland Canada. Near copy of DeH. DASH-7." There was a whole list of technical specifications for the plane, and then the corporate background. "Manufactured by Aviom Industries Inc. Head office 332 Rue Victor Hugo, Paris France."

Bingo. AVTOUR was a subsidiary of Aviom Industries, and Aviom Industries manufactured the GAMOS 12, the aircraft used by Gambetta S.A.

I leaned back in my chair and dragged on my cigarette. So there was a connection. Big deal. The corporate connection was obviously completely above board. I had it on file, and the stuff I had on aircraft companies all over the world was gleaned from regular sources like Janes' and the standard aviation journals. Nothing sinister there. I put out the cigarette and sighed. I'd have to wait for Sam to get any details. I hit the "copy" key and the information on AVTOUR, Gambetta, and Aviom Industries began rolling out of the printer beside the screen.

By six o'clock that evening it was clear that Sam wasn't going to show up. I looked up the AVTOUR number in the Yellow Pages and dialled.

"AVTOUR, may I help you?" The voice was smooth, pleasant, and male, surprisingly. Most of the airline people use women to staff their reservations desks.

"I wonder if you could give me some information about one of your flights," I asked. "Flight 360 out of London."

There was a pause. "Just a moment, please," said the voice. There was another pause. I could almost see him punching into his computer terminal. The voice returned. "May I ask who is calling, please?"

That was odd. "Why do you want to know?" I asked baldly.

The voice on the other end laughed nervously. "We have been advised to request the names of anyone calling about Flight 360," he said.

I felt my heart thud. Something was wrong. "What's the trouble?" I asked.

The man laughed self-consciously again. "Nothing serious, sir. The flight was delayed due to mechanical difficulties at Heathrow and now we seem to have lost our link with London. If you'll give me your name and number AVTOUR will call you to advise you of the flight's arrival time."

"Forget it," I said. "I'm flying out myself in a few hours. I'll be out of the country. Thanks, anyway."

"I'm sure we—"

I hung up. I'd wasted enough time already. An hour later I was in a taxi en route to Toronto International. By eight-thirty I'd run the gauntlet of ticket check, baggage loading, and immigration, and by eight forty-five I was boarding Air Canada's flight 720, a Boeing 747 flying the Great Circle route to Heathrow Airport.

It was the height of the season and the gigantic aircraft was full. I'd managed to get a window seat, and settled down comfortably, trying to ignore the babbling of voices around me. A few minutes later we began to taxi and I closed my eyes. I'd done a hundred stories on pilots, airports, and air traffic controllers, and I could visualize every step of the procedure the Jumbo was going through.

Taxiing out, the pilot was ordering 10 per cent flaps to give the optimum wing surface for takeoff. Once in position, I could feel the deep vibration shuddering gently down the fuselage as a full two hundred thousand pounds of thrust was applied by the four Pratt and Whitney JT9D-7W engines. Slowly, almost ponderously, we began to move. At one hundred and fifteen knots the pilot was easing back on the control column, lifting the nose into the air. At one hundred and sixty-five knots we reached the point of no return. The pilot would be hauling back on the column. There was a brief moment of vertigo and we were airborne. A moment later I heard the dull thud as the wheels came up, followed almost immediately by the almost unheard hydraulic whine as the flaps were drawn back into the root of the wing. In flying language the Jumbo was now "clean." We were free to climb to our cruising height, altitude and speed both preselected by the IBM 9020 D computer that had originally printed out our Flight Progress Strip.

High up in the darkened Air Traffic Centre at Toronto International, fading fast now behind and below us, the Sector Officer would be watching as AC720 climbed away, heading north. As we moved farther and farther away our FPS would wend its way down the holder in front of him, quickly losing priority. Finally, when we crossed Gander, Newfoundland, into the Gander Control area, the strip would have reached the bottom of the holder. Gratefully, the Sector Officer would toss the strip into a wastepaper basket, glad to have one less flight on his mind. For him AC720 would have ceased to exist, now it was someone else's problem. We were merely a jumble of coded electronic signals on a computer tape.

At forty-two thousand feet, heading towards the tip of Greenland and pursuing the darkness as we ran away from the sun, I called the hostess and bought a set of earphones. Half the passengers were crowding to the windows, staring out at the eternal dance of the Northern Lights. Not me. I clamped the headphones on, and with the strains of Bach in my ears I slept.

Chapter Two

The London Hilton is a little bit of North America crowbarred into Olde England, complete with deep shag and reasonably soft toilet paper. It looms over Hyde Park like a gigantic concrete tombstone, and it is one of the few places in London where you can get really cold beer. The first several times I'd come to London I'd tested out the "quaint" hotels, but after a while I learned that although the Hilton has absolutely no character, it does have comfort. At a hundred bucks a day. If you have a high enough floor, it also has a magnificent view.

From thirty floors up I gazed out at late afternoon London, nursing a Heineken and wondering what to do next. I'd finished the Chatsworth interview yesterday and I still had a day to spare before hotfooting over the Channel to France. I took a sip of beer and squinted down. On the street below, hundreds of cabs were beetling around Hyde Park Corner and the sidewalks were clogged with humanity. They say the population of London doubles during the tourist season, and if the hordes below were any indication the statistic was right. Getting to Chatsworth's place in the West End had been a nightmare the day before, with every cab full and the big, red, double-deckers swaying, top heavy with Nikon-toting Nipponese and Leica-wielding Germans. I'd eventually taken the tube.

It was tempting to turn on the television for a spot of closed circuit soft-core, and get an early night's lead on the next day's rush to Heathrow, but Sam's no-show still nagged at me. I swallowed the last of the Heineken and got out my address book.

My first call, to Sam's office, drew a blank. As far as they were concerned Sam was in New York and wasn't expected back for ten days. His home number rang without being answered. I was about to give it up when I saw a small smudged notation under Sam's name in my book—George/ Mayfair.

The George was Georgina Underwood, Sam's baby sister. I'd never met her, but Sam carried around a photograph of her in his wallet. Stupendous was the only word you could use to describe her. The snapshot showed her standing beside Sam in front of the family seat in the Scilly Isles. She was three or four inches shorter than Sam, and her hair was about a yard longer—a blonde waterfall that slid over perfectly tanned shoulders down to the cups of the bikini top she filled out so admirably. She was eight or nine years younger than Sam, which would make her about twenty-one or two. The last I'd heard she was about to graduate from one of the Polytechnics in London. I seemed to remember something about her being in photography. The difference in our ages probably meant we'd have zip in common, but I figured it was worth a try.

I looked up her number in the book and dialled. There was a snarling crackling interlude and then a dour voice informed me that the number I had dialled was temporarily out of service. I checked my watch. It was just past five. According to the address in the phone book she lived only a few blocks away in the maze of Mayfair streets tucked in behind the Hilton. I decided to flip a coin. Heads I'd stay in my room and watch television, tails I'd drop in on Sam's sister unannounced. It landed heads, so I tried for two out of three. Georgina won. I had a quick shower, and then, twenty minutes later I hit the street.

By twentieth century North American standards, Mayfair shouldn't exist. The neat, well-groomed rows of townhouses should have fallen to the wrecker's ball decades before, to make way for high rises like the Hilton. The National Trust, however, had decreed that Mayfair, like the Whooping Crane, was an endangered species, and was thus protected. The fact that the National Trust was drawing monstrous rents on ninety-nine year leases probably had something to do with the community's continued existence as well.

I consulted my tattered A to Z, relic of my first trip to London ten years previously, and began making my way through the winding puzzle of streets. Every second door boasted a small brass plaque, discreetly announcing a private club, a gallery, or one of those infamous London casinos that can strip you of your life savings in a matter of minutes.

By the time I reached Georgina's street I was having

second thoughts about seeing her. My rationale for dropping in on her was pretty thin, and I didn't want to wind up spending an embarrassing half hour sipping tea with nothing to say. The chances of her knowing anything about Sam's whereabouts were almost nonexistent, anyway.

On the other hand, what did I have to lose? Even if she didn't know where Sam was I might be able to get her to come to dinner, and if we had nothing in common I could still sit and gaze at her for a couple of hours. I gave in against my better judgement, and with a muttered what-the-hell I went up the short walk to her door and banged the cupid's-head knocker. While I waited for someone to answer the door I turned and looked around. The parked cars on both sides of the street gave fair idea of the kind of people who frequented the area. There was everything from a Berlinetta Boxer to a Rolls Corniche. The car in front of Georgina's was a mint Austin Healey 3000 in blood red.

"Yes?"

I turned at the voice and my jaw dropped. She was much better in real life than the picture had suggested. She came up to my chin and the upturned face was flawless, huge deep-brown eyes framed by the golden wash of hair. I felt about twelve years old.

"Uh, hi. My name is Peter Coffin. I'm a friend of Sam's."

"Yes?"

I began to shrivel. My name wasn't ringing any bells, that was obvious. "I'm trying to track Sam down," I managed. I began to get furious with myself—tongue-tied by a woman who was barely past being a teenager.

"He's not here," she said. Her voice was deeper than her looks would have suggested. There was a hint of toughness in her tone.

"I know. He was supposed to see me in Toronto, but he never showed up," I said. Clearly the whole conversation was going to take place on her doorstep.

"Toronto? He said he was going to New York." She frowned. I was losing credibility fast.

"He was going to stop off on his way," I said.

"He didn't tell me anything about that," she said.

Well, la-de-da, I thought. Does Sam tell you everything he does? My anger transferred to her. "It was a last minute thing," I said, my voice stiffening. "He wanted to consult with me about a story he was working on."

"Well, perhaps you should come in, then," she said. She stood aside to let me pass and I squeezed by, making absolutely sure I didn't even brush her. Any ideas I'd had about a romantic evening withered on the vine.

The floor of the narrow hall was cherry parquet, and the walls were white, lit by track in the ceiling. They were hung with dozens of stark black and white photographs. Hers probably, I thought. She stepped past me and led me down the hall to a large living room in the rear that looked out onto a vest pocket garden backed by a high stone wall. The dusk sun barely lit the room. She turned on the overhead light and gestured towards a huge fan-back wicker chair.

"A drink?" she asked.

The look on her face made it quite clear that she didn't want me to take her up on it. I gave her my best smarmy journalist smile and nodded. "Scotch," I said, "if you have it."

She returned my smile coldly. A twenty-one-year-old bitch through and through, I thought.

"Chivas all right?" she said.

"Fine," I said.

She disappeared through the door. I sat back in the chair and sighed. She was Sam's antithesis. Sam was friendly, outgoing, and willing to engage anyone in conversation. He could spend an afternoon drinking with a coal miner and have a hell of a good time. Georgina, on the other hand, had all the earmarks of a snob. Apparently my Levis and Hudson's Bay Company broadcloth didn't quite come up to scratch in Mayfair.

She returned with my Scotch and what looked like Perrier and lime for herself. She slumped down on a short sofa opposite my chair. *Her* jeans were Sassoon, and the shirt looked like silk. It was blood red, like the car outside. She sipped at her Perrier, glancing at me over the glass. I didn't touch the Scotch.

"So you're a colleague of Sam's?" she said.

"Friend," I said. "And you're Sam's baby sister." I leaned hard on the "baby" and she scowled.

"I don't think Sam has ever talked about you," she said. It was an attack. I ignored it.

"I knew him back in the old days, when we were both

doing enough dope to pay off the Lebanese national debt." I grinned, remembering. "Sam was busy finding himself by backpacking through the Rockies and I was working as a tour guide."

"And are you still a tour guide, Mr. . . ."

"Coffin," I said. "As in funeral. No, I'm no longer a tour guide. Sam found himself somewhere outside of Kitimat British Columbia and I got back into journalism."

"You're a writer, then?" She made the word sound poisonous. I kept on smiling.

"No, a journalist," I said. There was a long, cold silence.

"How can I help you, Mr. Coffin?" she asked, finally.

I shrugged. "Sam told me a little about a story he was working on. He said he was going to drop in on his way to New York. He never showed up. I phoned the airport and they told me his flight had been cancelled. I just wondered where he was."

"His flight was cancelled?" asked Georgina. I nodded. She frowned, her forehead wrinkling.

"I just wondered if he got another flight, or what. It seemed strange that he didn't get in touch with me, that's all."

"I drove him to the airport," said Georgina, still frowning.

"And he didn't get in touch?" I asked.

She shook her head. "No. He seemed very preoccupied though, as though there was something on his mind."

"There was," I said. "The story he outlined to me was pretty hair-raising."

"Dangerous?" she asked.

"Possibly. Why?"

"Nothing," said Georgina. "Just a feeling." She looked down into her drink.

"He probably got onto another flight," I offered.

She looked up at me. "I suppose," she said. "But he didn't telephone. When he goes off on one of his jaunts he always telephones."

"Really?" I said. It sounded more like husband and wife, not brother and sister.

"I'm rather afraid of flying," she explained. "I get terribly worried. Sam always telephones me as soon as he gets to his destination, so I know that he's safe."

"And he didn't this time?" She shook her head. I shrugged.

"Maybe he couldn't get through," I said. "I tried to call you and got a recording."

"Yes. That happened the day after he left. They're coming to fix it tomorrow. But it was working before that."

"Do you know where he was going to stay in New York?" I asked.

"The Park Plaza," she said. "He always stays there."

"So we'll phone the Park Plaza," I said. "And since your telephone is out, why don't we call from a restaurant?"

"Pardon?" she said.

I smiled. Dinner with a block of ice was better than dinner alone. And she was still stunning. "We'll go out to a restaurant, have something to eat, and make the call."

It took more convincing, but finally, she agreed. I let her choose the restaurant just to keep her happy, and we wound up at a place called The Stars, just off Regent Street on Soho Square. As soon as we walked in it was clear why they called it The Stars—every square inch of free wall space was covered with photographs of celebrities, and in almost every one a smooth-faced man in a tux was present—beaming behind The Beatles, grinning over Mick Jagger's shoulder, bowing beside Tom Jones' table. At one time or another it appeared that every performer in the world, or at least in the UK, had eaten at The Stars. The maitre d', who could have been the brother of the man in the tux, sat us by the stairs and slid menus in front of us before shimmering off.

"I wonder what they called it before," I asked, looking around the large, dimly lit room on the main floor.

"Before what?" asked Georgina.

"Well," I said, "when they first opened, no stars had eaten here, so there wouldn't have been any reason to call it The Stars. So it must have been called something else, right?"

She gave me a strange look and went back to the menu. The few moments of humanity she'd exhibited worrying about her brother and admitting to a fear of flying had faded quickly. We were back to square one.

"Did Sam tell you anything about the story he was working on? I asked, after we'd ordered.

Georgina gave me a long look. "No," she said. "He mentioned about it being *really* big, and that was all. He even thought he was being followed. He kept looking back over his shoulder all the way to the airport."

"I wish I had his notes," I said.

"Why?" asked Georgina, her face hard.

"Relax," I said. "I don't want to steal his story. But if I had his notes maybe that would give me a lead on where he went. The chances are pretty good we won't find him at the Park Plaza."

"Why do you say that?" she asked.

"Because he always stays there, or so you say. If you know that, then other people might know it. And if he's worried about somebody being on his tail he'd tend to change his normal patterns. I've done that kind of thing myself on a story. It's a bit melodramatic and James Bondish, but it works."

"Maybe he was worried about you being on his tail," said Georgina.

I stared at her. She wasn't joking. She was dead serious. I took a deep breath.

"Look," I said. "I've had just about enough from you. I'm an old friend of your brother's and you're treating me like hell. You've been right on the edge of rudeness ever since I knocked on your door. I'm as interested in finding Sam as you are, and if you don't believe that, sweetheart, you can go take a flying one at yourself. You are young, you are immature, you are a snob, and quite frankly, Miss Underwood, you are a bitch. Make your own goddamn phone call."

I hauled out my wallet, dropped two five pound notes on the table, and left. Half an hour later I was back in my room at the Hilton eating a soggy club sandwich and watching a Linda Lovelace acolyte do her thing on the telly.

At two in the morning, unable to sleep, I placed a call to the Park Plaza in New York. The reservation clerk checked his computer terminal and came up empty. There was no record at all of any reservation for Samuel Underwood.

Chapter Three

The next morning I took a shuttle flight across the Channel, landing at Orly just before noon. My brief run-in with Sam's sister still rankled, and three quick gins at Heathrow and another pair in flight didn't even begin to take the edge off. I've got a football player's frame and according to my doctor I have a metabolism that defies description. Liquor has almost no effect on me, and it's a vice I rarely partake in except when confronted by people like Georgina Underwood.

When I got off the Air France flight I was still irritated, annoyed, frustrated, and generally in a lousy mood—which is just perfect for Paris.

Paris is one of the oldest cities in the world, and is certainly in the running as the most beautiful. It has incredible galleries and museums, magnificent architecture, and vast parks. It also has about six million Parisians, each desperately out to maim, infuriate, and outdo his neighbour. Every taxi driver is a Fangio, every store clerk a Cardin, and anyone with enough education to sign his or her name feels capable of talking endlessly about politics, art, literature, and the state of the Parisian sewage system. Paris is a city of Ego; if Freud had been raised there psychiatry would have been stillborn. His patients would have wound up analyzing him, and then conning him out of his hourly fee.

In the late sixties I'd lived in Paris for almost a year, which gave me a leg up on the fourteen-day tourist confronted with the horror of trying to rent a car or ask directions to the Louvre. So when the taxi driver who drove me from Orly to my hotel informed me that there was a new rule about doubling the amount showing on the meter I jumped right in and started yelling at him at the top of my lungs. He backed off quickly, taking the five franc tip I tossed in through the window of his Maserati Citroën and giving me the finger as he tore off, wheels screaming.

I toted my one bag into the narrow lobby of the Left Bank pension, showed my passport to the sour old concierge behind the counter, and went up six flights of rickety stairs to my room.

It was classic: bed, bureau, and bidet. The bed was cast iron with a mattress so soft it almost hit the floor. The bureau had survived both world wars, and the bidet was poised in an impossible position—beside the bathroom door, and next to the window. In the high season every decent hotel room in the city is booked, so I hadn't even tried to get anything better. At the French equivalent of twelve dollars a night, forty-eight francs, it would look good on my expense account though.

I dropped my suitcase on the bed and went to the window. It looked out on a scene as classic as the room itself—layers of rooftops and battered chimneypots stuttering away for a couple of blocks to the foot of the Seine, with a view of the Île de Paris and Notre Dame tree-shrouded at its far end.

I left the window and went back to the bed. I unpacked, whistling "Rule Britannia" under my breath, and changed from my regulation jeans and T-shirt travelling gear into the plain blue serge suit which I kept purely for covering the Paris Air Show. To walk the streets of Paris in jeans, or in anything even faintly informal was to announce your foreignness. At six feet two inches I was already an oddity in the City of Light, but in my blue suit I could pass for a visitor from Lyons or Marseille at least.

Properly outfitted, I slipped my passport into a button down inside pocket and distributed the twenty-eight dollars' worth of francs I'd picked up at the Bureau d'Echange at Orly: ten francs in each trouser pocket, ten in each suit pocket, and ten in the breast pocket of my shirt. With the money spread out that way the most a pickpocket on the métro would get was ten francs, and I knew from experience that the subway wire artists would be out in full strength at this time of the year. I took a deep breath and headed out the door. I felt like I was going off to war, but I knew that survival in Paris required constant vigilance.

Her shortcomings aside, Paris is exciting. The Left Bank, all its tourist wares hung out like a hooker's wink, still has an unbelievable smell—a dozen odours from fresh baked bread to frying fish, compounded by dust a thousand years gone and the garlic breaths and wine sour belches of the people who live there.

It hit me as soon as I stepped out the front door of the pension, and instantly, and infuriatingly, it got my pulse moving a little faster. I even felt myself smiling. Paris does that to you. You hate her, but at the same time you have a hell of a good time meeting the challenge the old bitch has got waiting for you around every corner.

My hotel was on Rue de Latran, a backwater just off Boulevard St. Germain, the Left Bank's main drag. I bought a hot sausage roll from a hole-in-the-wall vendor, took a handful of clanking change in return for one of my ten-franc notes, and wandered up to St. Germain, heading nowhere in particular. The Air Show didn't open until the following day, and coming to Paris was more or less a retreat from my strike-out with Sam's sister. Rather a day seeing the sights in Paris and reliving old times than a day brooding in London.

St. Germain was in its full summertime riot gear—half the store windows announcing "Grande Vente" to lure in the tourists, and the rest of the windows filled with merchandise of every conceivable kind. Here and there the iron grates were up and small signs announced "Fermeture Annuelle," the classic Parisian July-August closing, but most of the merchants weren't about to toss away all those tourist dollars so lightly. I didn't bother going into any of the stores; watching the ebb and flow of the people on the streets was enough. In the space of two blocks I saw a dozen or more identifiable nationalities and heard twice that many languages. Predominantly, though, the faces were blond and nordic or dark and oriental, the languages either German or Japanese. The deutschmark and the yen had triumphed where panzer and kamikaze had failed. By the volume of people coming out of stores laden with packages it looked as though the Parisians had surrendered willingly.

I left St. Germain and went down Rue de la Harpe, heading towards the Seine. The shops and restaurants were less tourist oriented, but the narrow sidewalk was choked with gawkers, out to discover the "vraie Rive Gauche." I knew they wouldn't find it. The real Left Bank had disappeared with Hemingway and Picasso, and the remnants only came out for air during the off season. Still, it was a grand show, complete with striped jerseys, berets, early Citroëns, and "les flics," the smiling pillbox hatted policemen playing games with their nightsticks and caressing the nasty little automatic pistols they wore. Here and there, in alcoves, Moroccan beggar women, veiled, and usually with a ragged child asleep beside them, begged for alms, giving the whole scene a cinema verité quality. Once upon a time the beggar women might have made me pause and dig into my pockets, but I'd seen that kind of poverty too often and in too many places for it to have much effect. Being a journalist, even one with a specialty like mine, means you have to give up part of yourself. No matter how hard you try to hold on to all your principles and sensitivities, the business robs you eventually. You live for the story, and anything beyond it is nothing but local colour. A lot of my colleagues in the business call it professional cynicism, but it's more like a slow rape that leaves you violated and lonely, somehow cut off from the people around you.

Eventually, I reached Quai St. Michel and the Seine. To the left was the Pont St. Michel, to the right, the Petit Pont. Ahead of me, across the narrow strip of brown water was a ten-storey rococo building that could have come off a postcard. I knew better; the building behind the line of trees on the Île de la Cité was the Préfecture de Police. I'd become quite familiar with its less than pleasant interior while I was covering the riots in 1968.

I shook my head and smiled at the harsh memories the sight of the building had been so quick to bring to the surface, and turned away. I walked along the quai, the rush of heavy traffic booming past a yard away. It was then, as I passed the Petit Pont and headed towards the Pont au Double and Notre Dame, that I realized I was being followed.

I'd only been under surveillance twice before, but if it has happened to you once you can feel it in your bones the next time it happens.

I didn't see him at first, I felt him. As I made my way over the narrow pedestrian bridge to the little park at the rear of Notre Dame I sensed his unseen focus. It's much the same as that vague sense of unease you feel the first time you appear in your bathing suit on a public beach. I did the only thing I thought was reasonable under the circumstances; I sat down on one of the wrought iron benches and pretended to be taking in the flying buttresses and the big circular stained glass window of the cathedral. I lit a cigarette and let my eyes wander to the end of the bridge, watching the people crossing over onto the island. They all seemed like bona fide tourists, even the singles. I sat there for a solid ten minutes, tagging each of the men I thought were possibles, memorizing some detail to make sure I'd recognize each one if he showed again. Then I stood up slowly, yawned, and drifted off.

I tried to make some sense of it as I went around the side of the cathedral and then down Rue d'Arcole, past the Hôtel Dieu.

On both occasions when it had happened to me before the tails had been police. Once it had been the Royal Canadian Mounted Police, when I was working on a story about industrial espionage that involved a Canadian government aviation corporation; and the second time, here in Paris, I had been followed for a week by the Sûreté while they made sure I was just a roving journalist and not one of the bomb throwing kids who were so plentiful back then.

What was the reason now? The Le Bourget Air Show attracted hundreds of specialty writers each year. The aircraft and weapons systems on display were public. I hadn't done anything even vaguely political in at least a year. But the feeling, the lingering itch at the back of my neck, hung on.

I crossed the Pont D'Arcole to the Right Bank, pausing at the far end to look down at the express lane of the Georges Pompidou thoroughfare as it dove under the bridge abutments, keeping one eye on the pedestrians crossing the bridge. Four of the possibles I'd scanned were coming my way—a pair of gays who were just a tiny bit too flamboyant to be real; a tall German type in jeans and a T-shirt, but without the requisite camera; and a hippy type with too much grey in his beard to be carrying a bedroll and knapsack.

I was laying odds on the greybeard hippy.

There were two approaches. I could either stay where I was and see who lagged, or I could keep walking and try to weed him out of the crowd. Both ways had their drawbacks. If I hung around the bridge whoever was following me could simply go right past and wait for me farther on, and if I kept moving he could hang back far enough to be unnoticed. My only real advantage lay in the fact that I knew I was being followed, or at least assumed it, while the tail would be thinking that he was still covered.

I glanced down at my watch and tried to look surprised, as though I'd just remembered that I had to be somewhere, then I started off at a good clip, dodging the traffic on the Quai de Gesvres, then quick-marching around the mass of traffic whirling in front of the gilt and gingerbread of Old City Hall. I turned down a narrow side street and started beating my way towards the main métro stop at Chatelet, a couple of blocks deeper into the Right Bank.

I reached the métro entrance and went down the steps quickly without trying to check behind me. I bought a "carnet" of the yellow, magnetic-striped tickets at the glass-enclosed booth on the main level, pushed one into the slot on the turnstile, and headed into the tunnels. Four major subway lines cross at Chatelet, and so does the ultra modern high speed express, the RER, so the Chatelet métro station is a rabbit warren of passages, gates, and sliding sidewalks, each leading to an appropriate platform. I followed the signs to the Port de Neuilly line, the route that bisects Paris east and west from the Bois de Boulogne to the Bois de Vincennes.

There was a sprinkling of people waiting on the harshly lit platform, mostly tourists. The yellow tiles of the curved walls made the station look like a huge men's room. I sat down in one of the formed plastic chairs set into the wall and kept my eyes on the entrance to the platform. A deep rumbling echoed faintly from the half-moon mouth of the tunnel, and the people on the platform edged forward expectantly.

It was the German without the camera. He came through the entrance onto the platform, trying to look unconcerned, but I could see from the quick darting of his eyes that he'd been worrying that he had lost me. I ignored him and stood up, moving towards the edge of the platform and watching the tunnel mouth. I could feel a cold sweat oozing out all over me. My paranoia had turned to outright fear. There's nothing exciting about being followed by someone. It's terrifying, pure and simple. And whoever this guy was, he wasn't a cop; from his looks he wasn't even French.

There was a hammerblow of noise as the train thundered into the station, its big rubber wheels setting up a vibration in the rails that eventually found its way into my body. The doors on the high sided beige cars slid back and I climbed into the half empty car, taking one of the pull down jump seats on the far side. Fifteen or twenty chattering people climbed on with me, including the German. He put his back to the chrome plated pole in the centre of the car and let his eyes lock onto the ads above the window. He was placed so that he could get off the train at any stop without having to fight his way through the people standing in the aisle. I began to feel like a bug in a killing jar. I did my best to relax, closing my eyes and crossing my arms as though settling down for a long ride.

Why the hell was I being followed? My mind raced along with the pounding of the train through the tunnel, the constant buzz of conversation among the passengers alien and apart; as far as I was concerned there was only him and me—a hideously intimate arrangement in the midst of a crowd.

Why, and for what purpose? He wasn't a cop, I was sure of that. He didn't have any kind of official aura about him. He didn't even look like a private dick. And was it simple surveillance—follow me and find out what I do and who I do it with, or did he have something more sinister in mind?

The train pulled into the Louvre station and three quarters of the people in my car got off. The horn sounded and a few seconds later we hummed out of the station. Palais Royal was next, which would let me up onto the Rue de Rivoli. I could easily make a break for one of the side streets going up to Pyramides or the Madeleine and lose him in the crowds that were sure to be milling around.

I groaned to myself. What the hell did I know about losing tails or any of that? I was a reporter, not a spy. The other big question was, did I want to lose him at all? Unless the guy was a psycho, or hot after my body, I was being followed for a specific reason which probably had something to do with a recent story, or my expected presence at Le Bourget. If that was the case I wanted to know what that reason was, and losing my blond pal with the dead eyes wasn't going to provide any answers. I took a deep breath and tried to get hold of myself. There was still a chance that I wasn't being followed at all, and his presence in the métro was purely coincidental. After all, I thought to myself, Chatelet was a main stop, and the line I was on was undoubtedly the most popular for tourists—the sightseeing spots were lined up like beads on a string from Bastille to L'Etoile and the Arc de Triomphe.

We swept through Palais Royal, barely stopping, and pulled into the Tuileries a few moments down the line. A swarm of Americans got off, jabbering about the Tuilerie Galleries, the Jeu de Paume and the Orangerie. They were obviously hellbent on seeing all those Van Goghs and Matisses. Had I been feeling a little more charitable I might have told them that they were getting off one stop too soon, and all they'd find would be some brown grass and a long walk down to the galleries which were at the far end of the gardens. Not to mention the fact that the best paintings would probably be on tour somewhere else.

I decided to play the game straight. I'd be a tourist for Fritz and see what he did. We pulled into the station at Place de la Concorde and I got off slowly, giving him plenty of time. I went up to the surface, climbing the exit stairs onto Rue Royale. I headed towards the Parthenon shape of the Cathedral of the Madeleine a few blocks away, taking it easy and checking out shop windows as I went. After a hundred yards it was clear that the German's presence on the métro had been no coincidence. He was on the far side of the street, keeping about twenty yards behind, pausing when I paused, speeding up when I did.

I kept going straight up to the Faubourg St. Honore and zigzagged my way across the square to the front entrance to the Madeleine. I paid my two francs, took the steps two at a time and made it into the cool shadows of the giant cathedral. I tagged myself onto the end of an organized tour and let my body go into neutral. I needed time to think, and as long as I was in the church my Germanic friend wouldn't get upset. I tried to put a studious expression on my face as the group meandered through the interior of the lavishly decorated cathedral, and started putting together a plan.

I was being followed, but by an amateur, not a cop. If it had been a cop there would have been more than one tail anyway. The only way of finding out just what the hell was going on was by turning the tables. Follow the follower. And the only way to put myself in that position was to get mein herr to head back to where he came from. I figured there were two ways of doing that. I could either keep up my tourist act for a while, then go back to my hotel and pretend I was taking a mid-day break, or I could lose the tail and force him to report in. Neither way was particularly good. If I went back to the hotel there was a good chance the tail would sit himself down in the café across the street and wait for me to come out; and if I lost him, he might get upset and whoever was interested in me might wind up doing something rash. I looked up at a huge gilded Virgin Mary and sighed. The thought of being cooped up in that hotel, knowing that I was under surveillance and *not knowing why* went against all my journalistic instincts, not to mention my curiosity. I swore at myself silently. The last time I'd let my curiosity get the better of me I'd wound up ten miles behind the Viet Cong lines with a Sony cassette machine and a Nikon as my only weapons.

"Idiot," I whispered. I took a deep breath and started off. I cut myself out of the herd and started back through the gloom to the main doors. I picked out my friend almost immediately. He was lounging against the wall pretending to be consumed by a notice warning the public against "unsuitable acts" within the cathedral. I ignored him and headed out into the sunlight again. I prayed that I could lose him without him twigging to the fact that I knew he was on my tail. I made for the métro entrance on the Boulevard de Capucines side of the square, quickening my pace. Losing him on the métro was tempting, but I knew it wouldn't do me any good. I had to make him lose me without me losing him, and the only way of doing that was on foot.

I crossed Rue Duphot and headed back down towards the Rue de Rivoli and the Tuileries, trying to put some distance between me and the tail. The sidewalks were crowded with tourists staring into shop windows as they moved, and I did a lot of elbow prodding as I threaded my way through the pack.

I reached the intersection of Duphot and the Faubourg and cut to the left, fast, ducking into the first shop I came to. I slipped out of my jacket, rolled up my shirt sleeves, and put on my aviator sunglasses. I looked out the shop window, past a display of brassieres and underwear. Fritz came around the corner at a trot and stopped, no more than twenty feet away from me. I moved deeper into the store and watched. He looked up and down the street, trying to pick me out.

"M'sieur?"

I jumped about a foot in the air. I turned to face a middle-aged clerk with her hair done up in a severe bun.

"Puis-j'aider, M'sieur?" She probably thought I was some kind of pervert who got his kicks from watching women choose their undergarments. She looked like a teacher I'd had in the second grade.

"Avez-vous un sac?" I asked, frowning.

"Pardon?" asked the woman, trying to figure out what I wanted a bag for.

I leered at her. "Un sac, Madame. Un sac, vite, vite! " I leaned over her and began breathing noisily.

The woman backed off, pasting a weak smile on her face. "Oui, M'sieur, un sac." She fled to the back of the store.

I checked on my friend. He was still looking up and down
the street, unable to locate me. He was definitely upset. He
kept running a hand through his hair. His lips moved in a
curse. He turned away and stepped into a phone booth on
the corner. I watched as he fumbled for a "jeton" and placed
his call. I tried to see the number but his shoulder was
blocking me.

Suddenly I became aware of the silence in the store behind
me. I turned. Half a dozen customers and the bunned clerk
were watching me nervously. I smiled, snapping my fingers
at the matron with the bun. "Le sac," I demanded. She
nodded, clearly terrified and stepped forward, a shopping bag
clutched in her hand. "*Ici!*" I boomed, and stamped my foot.
The clerk with the bun edged a little closer and held out the
bag. I took it from her, nodded my thanks, and stuffed my
jacket into it. I looked out the window. Fritz was coming out
of the booth. He waited for the "Pietons" light to flare green
and then crossed the street. I turned back to the store,
saluted with my shopping bag, and nodded. "Pour la
République!" I called, and headed out the door. Fritz was
halfway up the block, heading north towards the Opéra on
Rue Cambon. I went after him. I hoped that my appearance
was changed enough to survive a casual glance if he looked
back.

I maintained the half block lag and managed to keep him in
sight. Five minutes later we reached Place de l'Opéra, the
square dominated by the rococo bulk of the marble and gilt
Opera House with its statues and twirling staircases. For a
minute I thought he was going to cross the square to the
métro entrance on the traffic island, but he turned right onto
the Avenue de l'Opéra, disappearing. I speeded up, hoping
that I wasn't falling into the same kind of trap I'd laid for him.
I reached the corner and slowed to a walk. I swung right and
caught a glimpse of him as he went through the doors of an
office building. I jay-walked to the other side of the avenue
and sat down at a table in front of a café, making sure that I
was in the shadow of the awning. I ordered a café crème and
waited. Unless he used a back exit I had him cold. The coffee
came, and feeling pleased with myself I tipped the waiter five
francs. He sneered at me and went back into the café. I
sipped the scorching drink and kept my eyes glued to the
entrance of the building, ignoring the to and fro of frantic

traffic. There was a familiar tug deep in my mind ... something overlooked ... I tried to pin it down but nothing came. I waited.

Forty minutes and two more coffees later Fritz came out of the building. Before I had a chance to stand up he'd forced a cab to stop by standing directly in front of it. The battered Peugeot came to a screeching halt. Fritz climbed in and an instant later the car was swallowed in the dense traffic heading south towards Palais Royal and the Louvre.

"Goddamn!" I snarled, cursing myself for a fool. I hadn't even considered a taxi. Now he was gone and I didn't have a hope of discovering where. All I had was the building. It was nine storeys high, eighty feet wide, and at least one hundred and fifty years old. It was probably a rabbit warren of offices. My chances of finding out which one he'd reported to were less than zero.

I went up to the corner, crossed with the lights, and came back down the other side of the Avenue de l'Opéra. With the tail gone I was back at the beginning. It was reasonable to assume that whoever was interested in me would have my hotel staked out so all I had to do was let myself get tailed again. But if I tried another turnabout like the one I'd pulled on Fritz they'd undoubtedly become suspicious. As I headed down the street it occurred to me that my initial fear about being followed had been replaced by anger, both at myself for being such a klutz, and at the amorphous "them" who had me under surveillance. I also realized that I was enjoying myself. Doing story after story on the newest in masers, lasers, and missiles that could do anything but the laundry had put me into a deeper rut than I'd imagined. Blowing it with Fritz was a sure sign that I'd gotten soft.

"No more," I muttered to myself. Peter Coffin, scourge of injustice and dean of investigative reporters, was back in the saddle. I pushed in through the swinging doors of the office building and looked at the directory. Visions of the American Newspaperman's Guild Award of Excellence, the Governor General's Award, and the Pulitzer fled. Coffin the Clod returned. There were about five hundred names on the ancient spaghetti board, not to mention at least twenty blanks beside office numbers that could hold a multitude of businesses. I scanned the directory hopelessly. And came up ace high.

Thankfully the board was arranged alphabetically, a logical

approach to things you don't often find in Paris. The name was third from the top, right after "Abijanian, T.S./Bijoux," and "Association Octogénaire de Paris." It read AVTOUR n. 723.

Bells rang in my head and I began to panic as synopses opened and closed in my brain trying to come up with something to hook onto the name. Then I had it, and also the source of the familiar twinge I'd felt in the café: 32 Avenue de l'Opéra, AVTOUR. I could almost see the printout from the black Box and hear Sam's voice. *Remember. AVTOUR, and Gambetta S.A. Cheerio.*

It was too much for coincidence. Sam gets onto a hot smuggling operation and then disappears. I arrive in Paris and find myself followed by someone who reports to the company Sam figures is a front for the smuggling operation. Neat and tidy.

And dangerous.

Chapter Four

I went back to my hotel, stopping once to buy some petit fours. If anyone was watching the hotel, as I was sure they were, the bakery box and the shopping bag from the lingerie store would give me a reasonable cover. I wanted to make it look as though Fritz had simply lost me through his own incompetence. I needn't have bothered. As soon as I opened my door I realized that the gentlemen from AVTOUR were playing for keeps. The room had been completely demolished.

The mattress looked as though someone had gone at it with a butcher knife; there were shreds of ticking everywhere and the floor was covered in feathers. The drawers from the bureau hung like swollen tongues, vomiting bedding and my few clothes. My suitcase had been slashed to ribbons, its lining torn out, and the remains of my camera lay on the floor in front of the yawning door of the closet. I felt a surge of nausea and closed the door gently behind me. The door leading to the bathroom was closed. I let my eyes scan the room, searching for something to use as a weapon. Nothing. I looked at the slashes in my suitcase and thought about the instrument that had done it. A knife; a very sharp knife. I put down the bakery box and the shopping bag and gently took out my jacket. I wrapped it tightly around my arm and slipped out of my shoes, my eyes riveted on the bathroom door.

I padded across the room, pausing to listen. Breathing? Or the wind outside? The sound of my own heart was like thunder. I winced as a floorboard creaked like a rifle shot and I froze. Nothing from behind the door. Another step. Still nothing. I waited. There were probably ten people within hailing distance but I had never felt so alone. My mouth was like cotton wool.

I could make out every detail in the door now: cracks in the paint revealing dry, ancient wood; rust around the old-fashioned balltop hinges. I stood stock still two feet in front of the door and closed my eyes, trying to imagine myself in the bathroom. I'd used it once just before going out. Toilet to the left, claw foot bathtub on the right with a suspended shower rail and curtain. A narrow, frosted glass window set high in the wall directly opposite the door. Just enough space between the doorframe and the tub to hide. Christ!

Sweat had popped out all over my face, running down to sting my eyes. I brushed it away and swallowed, trying to keep down the lump of fear in my throat that was threatening to suffocate me. I reached out my unwrapped hand and let my fingers touch the knob. Delicately I turned, praying that it had been oiled recently. There was a faint click. Now what? Fast or slow? Judgement told me neither. Anyone with any brains would run like hell, screaming for the cops.

I closed my eyes, took a deep breath, and lifted my leg. I kicked at the door, hard, and it slammed back. Nothing. A flush of nicotine light hazed through the slit window, puddling on the grey linoleum floor. Empty. I stepped into the bathroom and suddenly realized that my legs had turned to rubber. I sat down on the toilet and waited for my heart to slow and my muscles to stop twitching. I unwound my jacket and rummaged in the pocket for my cigarettes. Lighting one, I dragged deeply, thankful that there was no history of heart disease in my family. Obviously Fritz or one of his colleagues had gone through the room looking for some connection between Sam and me, then left—doubtless taking the damning evidence of the computer printout. I knew I didn't have much time. Anyone watching the hotel would have seen me return and would have called in for reinforcements by now. I had to gather my things together and get the hell out fast. I also had to pee—badly. I stood, turned to the toilet and unzipped, giving myself up gratefully to the simple pleasure of taking a leak.

A lot of people will tell you that they do their best thinking in the bathroom. The thought that struck me as I stood there came to me clearly and logically. "The last time you were in this bathroom the shower curtain was bunched up on the rail. A few seconds ago it was drawn all the way around the tub, which means that . . ."

I whirled around, leaping to the side, just in time to glimpse a slashing arm slice down through the curtain, eight inches of gleaming steel grasped tightly in its fist. The knife razored past within an inch of my shoulder and I ducked low, throwing myself at the curtain, colliding with the figure behind it. The unseen knife-wielder shoved back and I hit the floor, rolling away towards the door. My head slammed on the doorframe and I lay dazed for an instant. I stared up as the curtains parted. Fritz, all blond, blue-eyed, and muscular, like a piece of satanic beefcake. Absurdly, I wondered what he was doing with all his clothes on, considering that he was standing in a bathtub.

He stepped out of the tub slowly, adjusting his grip on the knife, holding it underhand, delicately poised on three fingers. He began to whistle softly, the Peer Gynt Suite. Fritz was lousy at being a tail, but it didn't take much guesswork to understand that this kind of thing was his profession, and by the look on his face, a pleasure as well.

I scuttled through the open doorway on my back. Fritz came after me slowly. I took a chance and rolled, presenting my back to him. He lunged, sweeping his arm down low, trying to get the knife in under my ribs. I got to my knees just as he reached the upswing and clasped my hands together in a hammer, arcing my paired fists into his crotch. He screeched and dropped one hand between his legs, falling back and giving me enough time to get to my feet. I dove over the bed, trying to reach the door, but I got hung up in the remains of the mattress. I struggled and then he was on top of me, the knife stabbing into the mattress beside my neck. He straddled me, his free hand coming up under my

jaw, pulling my head back. Terror took me and I bucked
frantically. We rolled and Fritz slammed into the wrought
iron end of the bed, his knife hand snagging between the
bars. I dropped my knee into his cheek and put my weight on
it. There was a cracking noise as his jaw broke and a muffled
scream. I reached over the top of the bedstead and pressed
up his arm, pulling it back until the wrist was almost doubled
over on itself. The knife dropped and I jumped off the bed,
scrabbling for it. I came up with it in my hand and turned
back just as Fritz lumbered off the bed and staggered towards
me. His jaw hung loose and I could see the shattered stumps
of several front teeth. He spat blood weakly and his eyes
burned. He was down, but he wasn't even close to being out.

In my hand, the knife was slippery with sweat. I backed off
as he approached. I didn't know the first thing about knife
fighting. Circling, I tried to move towards the door, but Fritz
kept putting himself in front of me. I felt like screaming but
my throat was glued shut with fear. Fritz and I were matched
for height and weight, but he had a lot more muscle and a lot
more experience, not to mention the fact that he was probably a psycho.

My eyes kept swinging from his hands to his eyes and back
again as we circled, and I knew I was doing it all wrong. I was
afraid of him, as well as being afraid of the knife in my hand.
I was on the edge of panic and he knew it. He lifted the hand
I'd nearly broken and flexed it. It was the size of a dinner
plate, the outer edge rough and brown with calluses. I knew
what that meant. Fritz didn't need a knife at all. The side of
his hand looked like it could cut through concrete.

I once knew a film editor who'd been doing a job in New
York. It was one of those double-rush urgent assignments
common to the business, and he was working sixteen hours a
day, usually finishing up about three or four in the morning.
The problem was that his hotel room was on the far side of
Central Park and there were never any cabs at that time of
night. By cutting through the park he could save himself a
two mile walk. Central Park at three in the morning, however, is like a muggers' convention. He solved the problem in a
typical New York fashion. Every night when he finished work
he'd take a copy of the New York *Daily News*, tape individual
pages to his arms, legs, and hat, then go running across the
park in the darkness, waving a flashlight and screaming

"Gobble! Gobble!" at the top of his lungs. The lesson being that sometimes insanity is the best defense.

I started jumping up and down, waving my arms and rolling my eyes like crazy. It stopped Fritz dead in his tracks. His eyebrows knit and if his lower jaw had been in any shape he would have frowned. A low growl formed in his throat. I tarantella'ed to one side, trying to make for the door, keeping up a continuous chicken squawk and for a few seconds Fritz just stood there. By the time he figured out what I was doing I was almost at the door. He staggered around and threw himself on me. I turned as he pinned me, my arm coming up to fend off the scythe blade of his upraised hand. The stiletto went in under his chin right up to the hilt, the point lodging somewhere in the region of his brain stem. He gave a single gurgling sigh and I watched from six inches away as the light went out of his small blue eyes. He slid down, his weight pulling the knife out of both my hand and his throat. His arm dropped in slow motion, the hand touching the side of my neck almost gently as he sank to his knees. He fell forward, his head resting against my leg, and the room was filled with the tang of tin-snipped copper as his blood drained out onto me and the floor. The last faint mist of life dissolved and his body voided, the smell of his wastes adding to the abattoir stench.

I stepped aside, shuddering, and his head fell off my leg and thumped once against the door. I moved back and stared at him, his head bowed, judgement day come and the verdict given. I walked backwards to the bed and let myself drop, my eyes watching him for any signs of movement, even though I knew he was dead. I felt my gorge rise and I only barely made it to the toilet. I vomited and then stood. Only then did I realize that my fly was still down. I zipped up and looked at myself in the mirror above the sink. I was death white, but not as pale as Fritz. I ran my hands under the tepid tap water, rinsed off my face, and waited until my breathing returned to normal. Then I went back into the bedroom.

It took me a good five minutes to gather enough courage to rifle his pockets. I found his wallet and went through it. Nothing except one hundred francs in notes. No ID, no personal material at all, not even a driver's licence. Then I found a small brown leather folder in his hip pocket. I flipped it open and found myself staring at a colour photograph of

Fritz on a plasticized identity card. Except his name wasn't Fritz. According to the card his name was Hans Helmut Kroeger, and, God help me, he was a cop after all. That meant I was in deep, deep trouble.

I sat down on the bed again and tried to figure it out, staring at Hans Helmut Kroeger's corpse as though it could give me some answers. Hans, uncooperative to the end, didn't say a word.

I had just killed a policeman in a city renowned for its hard-nosed cops and their hatred of the press. Somehow, Sam's investigation of AVTOUR had bypassed the frying pan and dropped him—and me—directly into the fire. But why had Kroeger tried to kill me? Tearing up my room I could rationalize, almost; but coming at me with a knife was something else again.

It also left a lot of questions unanswered. If Sam had got himself mixed up, say, in some kind of anti-terrorist thing, why didn't the cops just tell him to buzz off? And in my case, all Kroeger would have had to do was to get me kicked out of the country, or threaten me with all sorts of dire consequences if I didn't keep my nose out of their setup. The whole thing was awfully clumsy for a high-level police operation.

The real question I was faced with, though, was what to do right then and there. Report the body and take my lumps, whatever they were, or follow the story through?

I decided to go for broke. There was no way I was going to talk my way out of Kroeger's corpse in my room, and if I kept on with Sam's investigation I had at least half a chance of coming up with something. I wasn't going to find any answers sitting in a French jail. Sam had given me two names— AVTOUR and Gambetta. The printout was gone, and it wasn't on Kroeger, so I had to assume that he hadn't been alone when he ransacked the room. That meant two things: there was someone out there waiting for him to reappear; and that someone knew that *I* knew about Gambetta. It was going to be tense.

I stripped off my bloodstained clothes and stuffed them into the lingerie store bag, to be disposed of later. I put on my jeans, changed shirts, and emptied the pockets of my blue serge jacket. I found my wallet under the bed. Anything else I needed I could buy on the run—and running was just what I'd be doing.

Pulling on my glove-leather bomber jacket, I went to the door and took a last look at Kroeger. I knew that I was at a turning point. Step through that door and damn myself? Or give myself up and let justice take its course?

I'd stopped believing in justice when Ford pardoned Nixon. I eased Kroeger away from the door and let myself out, taking the lingerie bag with me.

I went around the stairwell and walked quietly to the end of the hall. A window overlooked a narrow courtyard behind the hotel, blocked on all sides by the rear of three other buildings. There was a porte cochère leading out of one of them, probably emptying out onto the next parallel street. True to form, there was no fire escape on the side of the hotel. There probably hadn't been a fire inspector in the place since Napoleon's day. I went back to the stairs and down to the first floor. It was identical to the one my room was on. I repeated my steps to the end of the hall and looked out the grimy window. It was a fifteen foot drop to the roof of a small shed-like construction—probably a garbage bin. I was vaguely surprised that the window opened so easily until I realized that opening the hall windows was probably the hotel's equivalent of air conditioning. I tossed out the lingerie bag and eased myself onto the soot-covered sill. I twisted, holding my weight on my elbows, and then let myself down until I was hanging by my hands. I looked down between my feet. I appeared to be about six or seven feet above the flimsy looking roof of the shed. I closed my eyes and let go, remembering to bend at the knees when I hit. Thankfully, the roof held.

Jumping off the shed, I retrieved the lingerie bag with my bloody clothes and looked up. The window gaped open—a dead giveaway to my escape route. There was nothing I could do about it though. I looked around. Apparently no one had noticed my rather unorthodox exit from the hotel. I crossed the courtyard, eased open the door of the porte cochère, and went down the dark cobblestoned corridor. Thirty or forty years ago it had probably been used as a service entrance for horse drawn wagons. Dust was thick on the blank walls and it looked as though it hadn't been used since. The far set of doors was locked from the inside with a monster bolt. After a minute or two of tugging at the rusted bar it slid back noisily. I cracked the door and looked out.

People were walking along in the sunlight as though nothing at all had happened. For them, of course, nothing had. It was just a touristy day in summer. The narrow street was awash in Keds, blue jeans, and University of Fort Lauderdale T-shirts. A fugitive with a bag of bloody laundry was about to join them.

I stepped out onto the pavement, closing the door behind me and trying to look as ordinary as possible. I began to empathize with the man in the Poe story about the Tell-Tale Heart. I was sure everyone knew that there was a dead man in my hotel room.

Nobody paid the slightest attention to me. I steered myself into the general flow of people heading towards the Seine. When I'd gone three or four blocks I stuffed the bag into the first trash can I saw and speeded up my pace. Ten minutes later I reached the Pont Neuf and crossed.

I reached the Disneyland castle of the First Arrondissement city hall and sat down on a bench to think for a moment. So far I had no plan. I was just putting distance between myself and the mortal remains of Hans Helmut Kroeger. On the far side of the street a continuous stream of people was going through the Cours Carré entrance to the complex of columned buildings that made up the Palais de Louvre. I watched them, jealous of their normalcy. Their day would end with an orgy of steak bien-cuit, Perrier, and Pepto-Bismol. God only knew where nightfall would find me. I shivered slightly as a vision of the interior of the Sûreté's endless grey-walled corridors oozed into my mind. And that was the *best* I could expect. I lit a cigarette, closed my eyes, and leaned back, letting the hot afternoon sunlight bake into my brain.

The concierge at my hotel had my name and my passport number. When Kroeger's friends got tired of waiting they'd go to my room and find the body. At that point all hell would break loose. Twenty minutes after they discovered the body my description would be tucked under the pillbox hat of every flic in Paris.

"Screwed, blued, and tattooed," I whispered, recalling the RAF lingo I'd learned in childhood. It was hopeless. The only intelligent thing to do was to go back and turn myself in. At least I'd have that in my favour. If I waited until there was an all-points out on me I'd probably wind up with a hole between my eyes from one of those wicked little automatics. Your average French beat-pounder wasn't about to be polite to a man wanted for sticking an eight inch knife into a fellow cop's brain, even if the fellow cop was a German.

But there was no point in wasting my time thinking about that kind of thing. I wasn't dead and I wasn't in the hoosegow. I *was* a reporter with a lot of questions. It was time to get them answered.

Sam had given me two names: AVTOUR and Gambetta S.A. I'd been to the AVTOUR office; it was time to take a look at Gambetta. I sat up, flicked away my butt and stretched. With a what-the-hell shrug I got up and headed for a string of phone booths at the corner. I looked up Gambetta S.A. in the book. It was in St. Mande on the extreme eastern edge of the Twelfth Arrondissement. There was a métro entrance for the Number 1 line right beside the booth. I went down, took out a ticket from the carnet I'd retrieved from my jacket, and went through the turnstile. The sign on the tile wall of the tunnel told me I was in the Palais Royal station. I looked for the "Direction" arrow and steered myself to the "Direction Château de Vincennes" side of the track. The château was the last stop on the line. St. Mande Tourelle was two up from it. I was killing two birds with one stone—getting my ass even farther away from the centre of the city as well as drawing a bead on Gambetta S.A.

The train hammered into the station and I climbed on. The car was crowded with tired looking civil servant types. I checked my watch. Three o'clock on a workday afternoon. These people were going home. A long loaf, a "baguette," was sticking out of a woman's shopping bag across from me, and I realized I hadn't had a meal since the breakfast I'd eaten on the flight from Heathrow that morning. God, it seemed like days since that flight and I'd been in Paris less than four hours!

Stop after stop whirled by, and at each one I stiffened, watching for the blue uniform of a gendarme on the platform. There was nothing, just tired people getting off and tired people getting on, all of them blank-faced and bored.

The car I was riding in was almost empty by the time we hit St. Mande Tourelle. I got off with the last trickle, the horn sounded, and the train whirred off into the dark echoing tunnel. There were two exits. I chose the Rue Royale gate at the end of the platform and rode the escalator up alone.

I surfaced a dozen yards away from one of the inevitable Stella Artois beer awnings over a corner café. Gambetta S.A. was on Rue de la Grande. I walked to the café and asked a white-aproned waiter for directions. He jerked his thumb around the corner.

"La deuxième rue," he snapped, clearly annoyed at giving me something for nothing. I thanked him and followed his thumb onto a tree-lined street heading east. A sign high on the corner of the café informed me that it was Avenue Foch. I wondered how often people got it confused with the famous Avenue Foch just off the Arc de Triomphe: the street had probably been named by a real estate developer trying to cash in on a prestige address.

Avenue Foch St. Mande was clearly a good, solid, middle class place to live. Each side was an unbroken line of the classic, faintly Edwardian looking apartment buildings that are so common in Paris, butted end to end. Here and there on the stone and wrought iron fences protecting the entrances I could see brass plates announcing the names and hours of doctors and dentists. Evidently, Avenue Foch was a good place to be sick. In two blocks I saw everything from urologists to denture fitters.

Rue de la Grande crossed at the end of the second block. There was only a single block on the street before it hit the main drag of Rue Royale, so I turned right.

The building stuck out like a sore thumb, or more precisely, a dirty one. Gambetta S.A. was hidden behind a high, rundown wall of stone and plaster, sandwiched in between two buildings like the ones I'd seen on Avenue Foch. There was only one opening in the wall—a narrow wooden gate of solid planks, just wide enough to get a car or a small truck through. There was a smaller pedestrian access door set into the centre of the main one. I turned the handle and took a quick look.

Most of the space was occupied by a fleet of vans, all Citroën 2CV's, each bearing the name Gambetta S.A. on their blue corrugated side panels, the lettering in yellow. At the back of the narrow courtyard, a set of mechanics' pits had been installed, and riding above them on heavy beam stilts was a rickety loft-like office that went from one side of the court to the other, flush with the buildings on either side and behind it. A set of narrow stairs ran up one side to a door in the side of the loft. I caught a glimpse of light and movement and heard the sound of voices arguing. They weren't speaking French, but it wasn't German either. The office door at the head of the stairs crashed open and a figure appeared, dressed in the grey lab coat that is the uniform of the Parisian blue collar worker. He turned to yell something into the interior of the office and the thin coat opened to reveal a most unworker-like shoulder holster. I closed the small door slowly and headed back down the street, hoping like hell that he hadn't spotted me. I reached the corner of Rue de la Grande and Avenue Foch and went back the way I'd come.

I rested at the café. The same waiter who'd given me directions eventually served me, taking my order for a paté sandwich and a beer. When the food came a few minutes later, I wolfed it down. Then I ordered another beer and lit a cigarette; and as I sucked the welcome smoke into my lungs I tried to put things together.

From what I remembered of the printout, Gambetta S.A. was an air freight company. That explained the fleet of trucks, but not the shoulder holster. Something stank at Gambetta S.A. The only way of finding out anything more would be to get into that loft and see just what Gambetta's *real* business was.

If I was going to add breaking and entering to my list of crimes committed in a single day, I knew I'd have to wait for nightfall, and that presented a problem. What did I do between four in the afternoon and midnight? I sipped my second beer and watched the answer being served up to me on a silver platter.

On the other side of Avenue Foch, about six doors down from the lights at the corner, a man in his early thirties was loading a pale-blue, late-model Peugeot. The trunk was filled to overflowing and he was starting on the roof rack, building a precarious pile of suitcases and cardboard boxes. He was dressed in grey flannels and a white shirt but he was showing a casualness you don't often see among Parisians: he wore no tie, his sleeves were rolled up, and instead of shoes he was wearing open-toed sandals. Obviously, he was going on vacation. A door in one of the buildings opened and a woman appeared with three young girls in tow. Two of the girls were carrying a suitcase and the youngest of the three had hers wedged into a doll carriage. There was a brief argument over the carriage, the man making wild gestures indicating the lack of space for non-essentials. The youngest girl began to cry, the second youngest joined in the argument, and the oldest, a pale, thin girl of about twelve stood by with a bored expression on her face.

Eventually the argument was settled, the last of the cases stowed, and the doll carriage was riding the top of the pile like a crown, roped around the rest of the luggage and the roof rack. There was a confused milling around on the sidewalk as seating arrangements were discussed. The smallest girl burst into tears again and bolted towards the door of the apartment building, but a drill-sergeant call from her mother stopped her. "Marie Claire Allard! Venez ici *im-méd-iate-ment!*" Head bowed, the girl shuffled back, and with a final prod from her older sister climbed into the back. The mother got into the front and the father slid behind the wheel. The starter whined and a cloud of blue smoke erupted from the tail pipe. There was a grinding of gears and then the Peugeot pulled away, heading east, out of the city.

I grinned. The one act domestic comedy had lifted my spirits, even if it was for only a moment. I raised my glass for another sip of beer and stopped with the foam at my lips. I put the glass down.

La famille Allard had left, en vacance. By the looks of the luggage it was for more than an afternoon jaunt. And if la famille Allard was on vacation and out of the city, that meant that la maison Allard was, by definition, empty. All I had to do was walk into the building, find out which of the apartments belonged to the Allards, and let myself in. There hadn't been anyone on the street waving goodbye, so the chances were better than good that I wouldn't find the Allard mother-in-law in the kitchen. It was better than taking a chance walking the streets at any rate.

I ordered another beer and let it sit. I waited for a full hour, just in case Monsieur had forgotten his best pipe, or Madame had neglected to turn off the stove. Then I got up, dropped some coins on the table, and crossed the street.

I walked down Avenue Foch and turned in at the gate of Number Twelve, trying to look as though I knew precisely where I was going. I shut the gate, climbed the short flight of steps, and opened the door to the building, letting it swing closed behind me.

The mailboxes were on the right hand wall, lit by a clear glass bulb. I bent down and peered at the name plates. I swore. There was no Allard. I straightened. So much for the best laid plans. A creaking noise startled me, and I turned to locate it. A breeze was gently moving a second door at the end of the hallway. The door had a panel of frosted glass with what appeared to be natural light behind it. Another porte cochère?

I went down the hall and opened the door. I stepped out into a vest pocket garden with a flagstone path that led to another gate. Beyond the gate, squeezed into a tiny walled courtyard was a stone house, flanked on all sides by the shuttered windows of apartments. Once upon a time the house had probably been the only 12 Avenue Foch. My imaginary real estate developer had convinced the owners to sell the surrounding property, enclosing the original house with a canyon of apartments. From the street you would never know the house existed.

I went through the gate and up a pea-gravel walk to the front door. The door was made of solid oak, deeply carved in decorative squares. The keyhole was ancient, big enough to hold an index finger. I could have opened it with a nail file. I didn't have to. On a hunch I stood on tiptoe and ran my fingers along the lintel. They soon hit something, and I pulled down a big cast iron key. I fitted it into the lock and turned. The lock let out a satisfying "clunk" and I pushed the door open. I stepped into a cool, marble-floored hall and shut the door behind me.

For the moment, at least, I was safe.

Chapter Five

The house at 12 Avenue Foch was a far cry from the austerity of my hotel room. To the left off the hall there was a large panelled library, complete with a giant antique globe on casters and two solid walls of books. A large colour television sat on a low chrome and glass table in front of an expensive

looking leather couch, and there was a massive oak desk
underneath a row of shuttered windows that looked out on
the tiny garden and the wall outside. The late afternoon light
trickled in between the shutter slats, throwing bars of pewter
light across the deep green Persian carpet on the parquet
floor. A quick shuffle through the papers on the desk told me
that M. Allard was a Professor of French Literature at the
University of Vincennes while his wife's correspondence was
addressed to Dr. Claire Allard.

On the other side of the hall there was a good sized dining
room furnished with a mixture of modern and antique, while
a small galley kitchen was wedged in close to the foot of a
curving staircase leading to the upper floor. There was a
bathroom and four bedrooms upstairs. The three small bedrooms were crammed with the toys and implements of youth,
while the fourth and largest was outfitted with a giant brass
bed and an armoire that was at least a couple of hundred
years old.

All the windows were shuttered like the ones in the library,
and the diffuse light cast an eerie glow over everything. I had
no sense that I was trespassing; instead I felt as though I was
walking through a family museum, reading the signs and
clues that together made up the Allard family's history. The
oldest girl's room was filled with ethnic dolls and bookcases
heavy with adult editions of Sir Walter Scott and Elizabeth
Barrett Browning in translation, and a case at the foot of her
bed was filled with neatly stacked classical records—a lot of
Bach and Mozart. A framed water colour on the wall told me
that her name was René Jeanette. The other girls' rooms
were less romantic; the middle one was a clutter of Barbie
dolls, doll furniture, and comic books; and the third was
awash in stuffed animals.

A check of the medicine cabinet informed me that M.
Allard was interested in natural medicine—there were dozens of bottles and jars of herbal this and organic that.

Slightly embarrassed by my intimate knowledge I went
back downstairs to the library and lay down on the couch.
Except for the gentle rustling of a faint breeze against the
lilac trees outside the windows the house was silent. I tried to
stay awake so that I could formulate a plan of action but the
events of the day had taken their toll. A few minutes later I
was asleep.

*   *   *

I woke in pitch darkness, my heart jumping out of my chest
and my clothes damp with sweat. My dreams had been filled
with blood and the fading light in Hans Helmut Kroeger's
eyes. I brought the glowing face of my watch up to my face,
half to find the time and half to convince myself that I hadn't
gone blind in my sleep; it's the same mild strain of paranoia
that makes me worry for a second when the lights go down in
a theatre.

It was ten o'clock on the nose. I sat up, dragging limp
strands of hair away from my forehead. I dug into my pocket
and pulled out my lighter. Holding it like a beacon, I stood
up weakly and crossed the room. I got in behind the desk and
pulled the drapes across. Then I closed the doors leading to
the hall. Only then did I switch on the lamp beside the
television.

Sitting down again, I lit a cigarette. Smoking was clearly a
vice that M. Allard and I shared. There had been ashtrays all
over the house, in all shapes and sizes. Here, in the library,
there was also a half empty carton of Boyards, a foul tasting
cigarette I'd tried the last time I was in Paris. They tasted
like burnt out firecrackers, smelled like Lebanese hashish,
and had a tar and nicotine rating that went right off the
scales. It was a good thing M. Allard was married to a doctor.
He was going to need her if he smoked a pack of those a day.

I turned on the television and when it warmed up I trotted
around the dial until I found a République Télévision channel
broadcasting news. A knife-nosed commentator in a shiny
grey suit was droning on about a union problem in Rouen.
He was followed by a general weather forecast for France and
then they got on to local news.

I had expected to find myself front and centre, perhaps
with an artist's rendition, or even a passport photograph.
There wasn't a whisper. The bland, dark-haired woman behind the news desk went through the day's news rapidly,
going from the demolition of another block of slums to a bank
robbery in Montparnasse with equal dispassion in her voice.
She reported on two murders—one a crime passionnel in the
Eiffel Tower restaurant, the other a gangland slaying of a

dope dealer up from Marseille. Nothing about a dead German in a Rive Gauche hotel.

I had to assume that the news had been kept quiet for some official reason. Kroeger's death was being kept under wraps. As far as the world at large was concerned, Peter Coffin wasn't wanted for anything.

It was a relief of course, but it was also confusing. More than six hours had passed since Hans Helmut had gone to meet his maker. Surely the body had been found. If that was the case, then why weren't they searching for me? I sat back on the couch and lit another cigarette. It didn't make any sense; none of it made any sense. Every step I took was raising questions that seemed to have no logical answers. My only real hope lay in finding something at the Gambetta S.A. offices a few blocks away. I stood up and began pacing back and forth across the room. I swore under my breath as I wore a line in the carpet. If I hadn't gone off the handle with Sam's sister I'd have his notes, and maybe a few answers. The way things stood now, I knew that that was out of the question. The lack of news about the killing might be nothing more than a lure to put me off guard. If I tried to catch a flight out of the country I'd probably find the airports crawling with plainclothes dicks. Gambetta was the only lead I could act on and the prospect of breaking in to that loft was making my palms sweat. Using the Allards' house while they were away on vacation was one thing, getting by the lad with the shoulder holster was another. In the space of a single day I'd gone from being a reasonably successful, reasonably respected journalist to a killer and B-and-E artist. It was like the dope scenario they used to give us in high school—smoke one joint and it would inevitably lead to the babbling needle-pocked life of a smackhead. I was trapped in an inexorably deepening well of crime. One thing led to another as I used the next crime to cover the last.

Every bone in my body was screaming for me to give myself up, while my brain pulled in the opposite direction. I had a deep mistrust of cops that had been forged in the sixties and honed to a fine edge as a practising journalist in the seventies. These were the eighties, and nothing had changed. If I was in a well it was up to me to find a way out. I was following Sam's cold trail, but it was better than nothing.

I went into the Allard kitchen and dug through the refrigerator. An hour later I had eaten enough cheese and stale bread to keep me going for a while. I made a pot of filter coffee and drank down two cups of the strong brew, black. By eleven-thirty I was ready.

The streets were empty. At the corner, the café was dark, its awning furled, tables and chairs stacked against the wall, chained and padlocked to a thick iron ring. Every dozen yards down Avenue Foch tall lamp standards threw down puddles of sulphur light. As I walked down to Rue de la Grande my boots clicked hollowly on the sidewalk and bounced ringing echoes off the blank walls of the apartment buildings on either side. Hardly any lights showed through the shuttered windows. St. Mande was asleep.

I tried to keep a slow pace to give the illusion of a man out for a late night stroll, but the empty street made me feel terribly vulnerable, and within a block I was doing a quick step. I reached Rue de la Grande and turned, slowing. Halfway down the block a gooseneck bulb shone over the gate leading into the Gambetta S.A. forecourt. The far side of the street was barren, the sidewalk giving way to a high link fence overlooking a railway cut. On the far side of the tracks there was a purple-dark wall of trees: the edge of the Bois de Vincennes, home of the Paris Zoo.

Nothing moved on the street. There was no traffic, except an endless line of parked cars, squeezed together bumper to bumper. I crossed my fingers against the thought of midnight lovers in one of the cars and headed towards the gate. I reached it and paused. I couldn't afford to loiter so, holding my breath, I thumbed the latch and stepped through, quickly shutting the small door behind me. I waited, nerves humming, until my eyes adjusted to the gloom.

Nothing had changed. The 2CV's were still parked on the cobbled court. A light shone weakly through the grimy panes of the windows in the loft. Nothing moved. Directly in front of me the mechanic's stalls loomed darkly. I kept looking around, peering into the darkness for some sign of life. Still nothing. I moved forward slowly, keeping up on my toes, shifting my position so that I stood in a deeper pool of shadow cast by one of the vans.

Someone sneezed.

I froze, my back against the corrugated side of the van, legs weak. The sound seemed to have come from one of the mechanic's stalls. As if in answer to the sneeze I heard the office door above me open. A shaft of light hit the cobblestones in front of the van like a searchlight, then abruptly cut off. The sound of clattering footsteps boomed as someone descended the stairs. I flattened myself against the side of the truck. There was a flaring sound and then an arc of light as the unseen figure tossed away a match.

"Pierre?" The voice was raw with a thousand cigarettes. There was a muttered reply from the mechanic's stall ten feet in front of the van I was using for cover.

"Quoi?" came the second voice sleepily.

"Je vais au tabac, desirez-vous de chose?"

"Rien, Gérard, merci."

"Bon nuit, Pierre," laughed Gérard, the man who'd come out of the office.

"Allez, allez!" Pierre snapped, irritated, still half-asleep. Gérard's bulk passed in front of me and I followed his back across the yard to the gate. He opened it and stepped out into the street, outlined for a second in the light. Gérard was the man I'd seen that afternoon—the one with the gun. I shivered, still flattened against the truck, my brain whirling. There were two men on night duty: Pierre, dozing in one of the stalls, and Gérard, the man with the gun, who'd just stepped out for cigarettes. The café on Avenue Foch was closed, so the closest café-tabac still open was probably on the Rue de Paris, five or six blocks away. Figure ten minutes each way, or less. I didn't have much time, and there was still the problem of Pierre.

That problem solved itself. Less than a minute after the other man had left I was treated to a broad snore from the mechanic's stall. I waited another minute, then unglued myself from the side of the van. Sweating in the darkness I slowly climbed the stairs leading up to the loft, pausing after each step to listen. Pierre seemed out for the count. I reached the top of the stairs, turned the doorknob, and slipped into the loft.

The place hadn't been cleaned in a decade. The main office was about ten feet wide and twenty long. Four or five large metal bins stood along the far wall, filled with small parcels. A desk in the corner was piled high with invoices and crumpled sheets of carbon paper. In the centre of the room, a tattered couch and a few wooden folding chairs had been

arranged around the shrine of a coffee machine. The drivers'
lounge, no doubt. A single naked bulb putting out no more
than twenty watts dangled from the rafters. The entire office,
walls, windows, and furniture, was covered in a layer of dust
and body grime. It smelled of sweat, tabac noir, and harsh
coffee.

A partition wall had been run across the office with another
door set into it. I crossed the room, bending low to keep my
shadow off the window. I eased open the door and found
myself in a second office, clearly occupied by only one
person. It was no cleaner, but at least it was relatively neat.
There was a desk, two telephones, and a row of filing
cabinets. This was what I had come for. Just enough light was
being cast by the bulb in the outer office for me to see what I
was doing.

I checked the filing cabinets first and came up empty.
Nothing but invoices again, most of them relating to packages
long since in the hands of their owners. Not that I really
expected to find something incriminating out in the open like
that, but it didn't hurt to check.

Desk next. There were three drawers on either side of the
kneehole and one drawer below the top. The side drawers
were crammed with more relics of the shipping business, as
well as some Gambetta S.A. letterheads and envelopes.

The drawer in the desk top was locked. I stopped for a
second and brushed the sweat from my eyes. I checked my
watch. Gérard of the shoulder holster had been gone for
eleven minutes. It was getting tight. I'd need at least four or
five minutes to get clear. There was no time for subtlety.

There was one of those thick bladed letter openers on the
desk. I picked it up and had a bad moment as I remembered
the feel of a similar instrument a few hours before. I shrugged
off the memory, fitted the blade into the crack between the
drawer and the desk top, then levered up. Something snapped
and the drawer came open. I pulled it wide and looked in
past the splintered lock. The drawer was empty except for a
single sheaf of paper stapled together. I took it out and
looked. A list of names topped by a number underlined at the
head of the first page: 360. The number meant nothing to
me, and neither did the first page of names, most of which
had been crossed out neatly with a marking pen. What did
interest me was the paper and the way it had been typed.

The paper was a heavy bond stock, far more expensive than the letterhead I'd seen in the other drawers. The typing was interesting, too. The list had been done on a word processor—there's a certain "perfectness" with those machines that is unmistakable. It had also been done in English. The first name on the list was Mr. John Adams, not M. John Adams.

I stuffed the list into the inside pocket of my jacket, pushed the drawer closed, and headed out of the office. I checked my watch again. Thirteen minutes gone. If I didn't hurry I was liable to run into Gérard coming up the stairs.

I let myself out of the loft and crouched down on the landing at the top of the stairs. I looked down into the courtyard. Nothing stirred. As quickly as I could I went down the steps. I'd gone about three quarters of the way across the yard when I heard the outer gate open. There was no truck handy this time—I was caught out in the open. I turned myself into a statue and willed myself into invisibility. I was standing in the shadow of the courtyard wall, and if Gérard was still night blind from the streetlights I had a chance.

He came in through the gate and jockeyed a paper bag into the crook of his other arm as he turned to close it. He crossed the courtyard, his eyes on the top of the stairs and the light dribbling through the window. He gave a snort as he passed by Pierre's ad hoc sleeping quarters, and went banging up the steps. He let himself into the loft and slammed the door behind him, clearly in hopes of waking his sleeping colleague. Pierre, bless his sleeping heart, didn't wake up.

I tiptoed the last few feet, slipped open the door, and let myself out onto the street. I was shaking all over. I was still shaking ten minutes later as I barred the door of 12 Avenue Foch behind me.

I gave myself a solid hour to relax. I sat and smoked and let the amateurish burglary run through my mind again and again. I was quite pleased with myself; I'd managed to get in and out without being seen and with luck the lock-snapped drawer wouldn't be discovered until the morning. Gérard wasn't the administrative type by the looks of him, and the chances were good that he'd spend the night flaked out on the couch in the outer office. The burglary itself had been successful all right, but I wasn't entirely sure I'd accomplished anything by it except the loss of a good five pounds to simple fear.

When the shakes and the self-congratulation stopped I studied the list, smoothing the pages flat on Professor Allard's desk.

It was more than a simple list of names. After each name there was an address and what looked like a five character computer code. As far as I could tell, the names were in alphabetical order and numbered from 1 (Mr. John Adams) to 226 (Mrs. Ruth Zwicker). Mr. Adams lived at 10 Oxford Place, Liverpool, and his code read wwT-3/2. Mrs. Zwicker lived in London with a code wsN-3/3. There were five pages, each with about forty names and addresses. The first twenty-five names on page one had been stroked out, from Adams down to a Mr. Jason Baldwin of Shepherds Bush.

I lit a fresh cigarette and leaned back in my chair, staring down at the list. What the hell was it? And why was it in the Gambetta office? More importantly, did it have anything to do with what I was involved in? Maybe it was simply a list of destinations for packages being handled by Gambetta. But that didn't make any sense either. Every one of the names and addresses I'd checked on page one were in England, which was reasonable enough, but why would Gambetta have lists of addresses outside London? If they were like any other air freight business I'd heard of, the point of delivery would simply be Heathrow Airport. If you wanted your package you came and got it, or made other arrangements to have it delivered. And if this was a list of consignees there should have been a point of origin address as well.

So what else could it be? I started going through the list name by name, trying to find some kind of connection, either in the names, the addresses, or the codes. By one-thirty in the morning I'd reached the bottom of page four and the end of my rope. Unless the whole list was some kind of crypto-gram there were no connections that I could see. I flipped to page five and the name on the top of the page burned into my retinas: SAMUEL G. UNDERWOOD.

Suddenly it fell together. The number underlined at the top of page one was a flight number—it meant AVTOUR 360, the flight Sam was supposed to be on from Heathrow to Mirabel, then on to Toronto and New York. The capital letters in the codes were destinations—T for Toronto, M for

Mirabel, N for New York. The list was a passenger manifest!

So why had it been in the Gambetta office? Smugglers or not, they'd be interested in cargo, not passengers. It looked like I'd opened another can of worms. The fact that Sam's name appeared on a scrap of paper in the Gambetta office in Paris wasn't anything to go charging off to Interpol about. AVTOUR and Gambetta were corporately tied; there was no reason for the list to be in their offices, but they had every right to have it there. It certainly wasn't evidence of any crime.

I pushed myself away from the desk and stood up, dizzy with fatigue and too many cigarettes. My head ached with a thousand conflicting hypotheses and theories.

It was time to pack it in, for the night, if not permanently. I was up against the wall and fresh out of leads. Somehow Sam, Gambetta, AVTOUR Flight 360, and the body of Hans Helmut Kroeger were tied together in some kind of pattern, but for the life of me I couldn't decipher it. The only thing left to do was risk trying to get out of Paris and back to Sam's flat in London. If I could find his notes perhaps I could make some sense of it all. But first I needed sleep. I staggered upstairs and went into the first room I came to. Within seconds I was fast asleep, surrounded by the sightless eyes of a dozen Barbies and a Kissing Ken.

Chapter Six

At any other time it would have been a fairy-tale awakening; slabs of warm butterscotch sun slid through the shutter slats and in the lilac trees a mourning dove was cooing. The only trouble was, I felt like a piece of meat that had been left out too long. My skin seemed greasy, my stomach was gurgling acidly, and my mouth tasted as though I'd been eating fur balls in my sleep.

A check in the medicine chest mirror confirmed the worst. My hair was lank, there were bags under my eyes, and I had a sooty growth of five o'clock shadow. I looked like a bum and felt the part. I checked for mouthwash, found a bottle that looked like a French version of Listerine, and took a swig. It tasted like hell, but it was a start.

A box on the far side of the foot-deep cupboard gave me the germ of an idea. Madame Allard was vain enough to cover the grey in her hair with a tinting kit. I took out the box and tried to decipher the contents. My hair is normally a run-of-the-mill dirty blond; the colouring solution was for people with black hair. The rest of my colouring is neither light nor dark, so black hair wouldn't be too bizarre. I figured out the instructions and got to work.

An hour later my hair had gone from dusty bronze to a completely nondescript dark brown. I used a safety razor that had seen better days to take off the five o'clock shadow and then went in search of the rest of my disguise.

None of the clothes in the Allards' armoire came even close to fitting, but I found a prize tucked away in the underwear drawer of their bureau—a spare pair of reading glasses with a prescription weak enough to let me navigate. I'd read enough spy novels to know that the best disguise was not something that changed you very much, but rather made you as invisible as possible.

Feeling a little cleaner and somewhat safer behind my minimal disguise, I went down to the kitchen and switched on the radio that sat on the refrigerator. I twisted the dial until I pulled in a commercial station and waited for the news. I listened at both ten and eleven, but there was still no word out on the Rive Gauche Ripper.

At eleven-thirty, after a quick breakfast of more stale bread and cheese I headed out, exchanging the security of my quiet courtyard house for the bustle of traffic in St. Mande.

I walked up towards the café, but instead of crossing to the Rue de Paris I went to the left and found myself on a narrow but long street, lined on both sides with every kind of store. The sign on the wall of the corner branch of the Banque Nationale de Paris said Avenue de Vincennes. Half a block down from the bank I found a Prisunic, the French version of Woolworths. The two-level store was packed with late morning bargain hunters, mostly women, almost all of them with children. The audio level was set on high—a continuous babble of questions, directions, and "Oui Madame, Non Madame." Cash registers popped, ticked, and rang. No one gave my artificial hair colour a second look.

I zigzagged through the matrons, eventually finding the men's clothing section. There wasn't much in my size, but I bought a drab, dark-blue poplin windbreaker and an orange T-shirt with the legend "Kiss Me" in six inch high black letters. A pair of Adidas from the sports department completed the ensemble. Next I went to the camera department and bought a cheap Polaroid with a carrying case. I finished off with a vinyl flight bag in yellow, spray painted with an outline of the Eiffel Tower. I took my purchases back to the Allards' and changed into my tourist outfit, cramming the list, my leather jacket, dirty shirt, passport, and wallet into the flight bag. I put on the professor's glasses and went out again, this time heading for the métro.

The train wailed into the underground station, three quarters empty. I climbed on with half a dozen other passengers and settled myself down, careful to avoid the seats with the signs on the windows reserving them for senior citizens, pregnant women, the blind, veterans, and amputees. A few stops later we hit the main interchange at Place de Nation and the train filled up quickly. I knew I looked like an idiot the way I was dressed, but it was precisely the kind of idiot Parisians expect during the summer months. I got a few sneers but that was all. All I needed was a wad of bubblegum to finish off the image of the classic American that the French seem to see in anyone over five foot six.

I rode the train for almost half an hour, barrelling along below the choked streets of Paris. We went through Chatelet, Concorde, Fr. D. Roosevelt, George Cinq, and Charles de Gaulle-L'Étoile, the train alternately emptying and filling. By the time we reached my destination, Porte Maillot, we were back down to the regulars. I was the only tourist left.

Porte Maillot is on the eastern edge of the Bois de Boulogne. Its biggest claim to fame is as the main terminus for shuttle buses and taxis running out to Charles de Gaulle airport, which was where I was headed. I rode the escalator up to the main level and went through a pair of automatic glass doors into the terminus. I found a ticket window selling seats on the next shuttle bus, bought one, and went to stand in line at the appropriate gate. I began to sweat. If there was heat, it would begin here.

A trio of flics, two in blue and one wearing an officer's white cape, came sauntering by within a few feet of me and I

felt my stomach go through the floor. The white cape looked
right at me and raised an eyebrow. I think the T-shirt got to
him. The three passed by, one of them cracking a joke,
probably at my expense. I didn't care. I had passed the test.
Either my disguise had worked or there was no bulletin out
on me. It didn't matter which as far as I was concerned. All I
wanted to do was make it to the airport. The same line kept
on repeating itself over and over in my head, a talisman:
"One step at a time, one step at a time." I knew I still had a
long way to go.

The compact, high sided Mercedes bus finally arrived, and
I clambered on with twenty or so others. The bus sat for
another fifteen minutes for no apparent reason other than to
fray my nerves. Then we were off, coming out into the bright
sun on the Avenue de la Grande Armée. We went around the
circular swatch of park in the centre of Place de la Porte
Maillot, gathering speed as we bullied through the cars and
trucks going past the huge modern ziggurat of the Palais de
Congrès and the Centre Internationale de Paris. We slotted
into the ramp traffic for the Périphérique, the six lane expressway that circles Paris, and headed north towards the AI
and the airport.

Like a lot of places in Paris the airport has more than one
name. Depending on who you talk to it can be l'Aéroport de
Paris, Roissy en Laye, Charles de Gaulle (CDG), or Roissy-
CDG. A reporter for Paris *Match* told me that the multiple
naming of Parisian transportation centres even confused the
natives. He'd once spent two months looking for a suitcase
that had been inadvertently sent to a non-existent train
station.

The confusion surrounding its name aside, Charles de
Gaulle is one of the largest and most efficient airports in the
world. It occupies more than a thousand acres of what was
once farmland, just beyond the sleepy village of Roissy about
twenty kilometres north of Paris. There are lots of access
roads, plenty of taxis, and once inside the giant circular
concourse building things move swiftly.

Half an hour after leaving Porte Maillot the shuttle dropped
myself and my fellow passengers at the main departure gate
on the west side of the terminal. I walked around the outer
ring of the building until I came to the British Airways

counter. I bought a ticket and was assigned a flight number and a "satellite." It is this "satellite" system that makes CDG work. The central core of the main building is a crisscrossing maze of plexiglass tunnels with moving sidewalks instead of floors. After being assigned a number you locate the appropriate tube and ride it up, down, or sideways to the appropriate waiting area. Instead of a swarm of passengers all trying to get to different gates you are shunted off with only those taking the same flight you are. Riding the tubes always gave me the slightly queasy feeling that I was a tiny blood clot in some huge brain, but other than that I found the system gratifyingly workable.

I slid up to satellite three, scanning the tube exits at various levels for any signs of especially heavy police activity. Being the size it is, CDG always has a lot of police around, but they're generally the standard Paris gendarmes. I was keeping my eyes peeled for the "specials," the white helmeted boys with the two foot long riot sticks and the Fabrique Nationale grease guns. If they were expecting trouble at the airport the "specials" would have been called in.

I didn't see any on my way up, but that didn't mean much. They could have spotted me as I'd come in and taken up defensive positions somewhere. I felt my paranoia cranking up again and the alarms started ringing in my head. I could feel my hands going clammy.

I hit the top of the tube and got off, looking around with what I hoped was a neutral expression. It's even dangerous just to *look* nervous in an airport these days. No matter where you are, local cops, airport cops, and the feds are all on the lookout for creepos, bomb plotters, and people buying too much insurance at the machines.

My satellite was a small area just across the way from the duty free shop and right beside the smokeshop and cafeteria. I had twenty minutes before my flight to London so I bought two fresh packs of Camels and the *International Tribune* at the smokeshop, stood in line for a cup of coffee and a plastic covered pastry, and sat down at a wobbly green plastic table that gave me a clear view of the loading gate and the security enclosure. I munched on the pastry, smoked, drank my coffee, and pretended to read the paper, all the while keeping one eye on the gate.

A few passengers were already lining up in front of the

metal-trellis arbour of the metal detector, but there was no one official on hand. I squinted through Professor Allard's glasses and tried to make out the letters on the video display bolted to a support column a dozen yards away. My flight was still two down and the yellow blinking boarding light was dark. From the looks of the line-up the plane was going to be "light" as they say in the business. That was fine with me—it meant I'd get aboard quicker. That is, if I got on board at all. There was still customs and immigration to go through. I hid behind my paper. From somewhere outside a whine began, spooling up to a full scale banshee wail that managed to make itself felt through the ten foot thick walls and bulletproof plexiglass of the terminal building. There is no sound in the world like it—terrifying or an adrenaline rush, depending on whether you like flying or not—the sabretooth howl of a Concorde cranking up its gigantic twin Bristol turbines. I closed my eyes and listened. I began thinking seriously about trying to astral travel myself on board. It was a nice fantasy while it lasted, which wasn't long. I was interrupted by the mundane scraping of a chair beside me. Someone sat down.

"Mr. Coffin?"

My legs turned to water and my stomach to ice. A cicada buzz of fear threatened to deafen me. I stared blindly at the paper.

"Please, Mr. Coffin."

The voice was soft, but cold. I tried to turn myself into a Polish gymnast.

"Tak?" I said, dropping the newspaper slowly. I put on a confused expression and stared at the man. He was in his forties, salt-and-pepper haired, wearing an Aquascutum raincoat. He was big. So was the man standing behind him, blocking my way out from around the table.

"Dowidzenia!" I smiled. I had used up two thirds of my Polish.

"It really is no use, Mr. Coffin. You're just being silly now."

I gave it one last shot. "Dziekuje bardzo lubie." I grinned hard.

The man smiled back. His teeth didn't show and there was no humour in his pale grey eyes at all. He reached into the pocket of his raincoat and drew out a small leather folder of the same type I'd found on Kroeger. He flipped it open and dropped it on the table in front of me. I stared down at it.

Different face, same card. This one's name was Brandt. Frederik Carl, Kapitane. I looked up at him again. He shook his head slowly, then reached over and delicately took Professor Allard's glasses off my nose. He slipped them into his raincoat along with the folder.

"We found Kroeger," he said. I looked over his shoulder. The boarding light was blinking beside my flight on the video display, and people were going through the metal detector. I watched them go, my mind completely blank.

"You were lucky," continued Brandt. "Hans was very experienced." Brandt's English was perfect. He didn't have any accent at all. I told him so. He smiled. "Thank you. About Kroeger. . ."

"It was self-defense," I said slowly. "I thought he was a psycho."

"There are some who would agree with you," said Brandt, "but that's beside the point. Kroeger's dead. You killed him."

"He should have told me he was a cop," I said dully. "I came back to my hotel room, find it torn apart, and then some jerk come at me out of the shower."

"The shower?" asked Brandt.

"That's right, the goddamn shower," I answered. "He tried to skewer me with that pig sticker of his. I got him first. It was an accident . . . Anyway, I'm not saying anything else until I see a lawyer."

"Of course," said Brandt. "You will come with us now." He stood.

I looked up at him, a flame of anger riding above my panic and fear. "What the hell are German cops doing working out of Paris? Aren't you a bit outside your jurisdiction?" I said.

Brandt gave me that lightweight smile again. "Please, let us have no arguments." He crooked a finger and the second man took a step towards me.

I lifted a hand. "Relax," I muttered, standing up. The last of my flight was boarding. The man operating the metal detector was yawning. I wondered what would happen if I tried to make a run for it.

"Don't be silly, Mr. Coffin," said Brandt, reading my mind. He took my elbow and we began moving towards the exit tube. A few minutes later Brandt and his friend loaded me into the back of a large black Mercedes that was idling at the curb outside the domestic arrivals bay. I sat between them, flight bag on my lap, looking for all the world like a truant kid being taken back to face the music in the principal's office. If only, I thought to myself. The driver flicked the wheel and we moved off, heading back to Paris. Neither Brandt nor his friend said a word throughout the entire trip.

I didn't notice it until we hit the Périphérique and started circling east. I'd been too busy feeling sorry for myself and trying to remember the name of anyone I could count on in Paris. At first it was just a vague feeling of something being not quite right. Then it clicked.

The car. There was no radio. I hadn't noticed any Police Band aerial on the roof or trunk, and there was no sign of any radio or microphone up front beside the wheel. I leaned forward slightly to check. Nothing. Not only was there no radio, but the whole car was wrong. Even without the radio it could still be a cop's private car—but there was no cop in the world who could afford a top of the line Benz complete with air-conditioning, not even in Paris where M-B's are a dime a dozen. I dug a bit.

"I assume we're going to Interpol headquarters," I said.

Brandt nodded. "That's right."

Bull. Interpol is in St. Cloud, on the far west side of Paris. We were still heading east. If St. Cloud was our destination we were sure as hell taking the long way around.

The big sedan swung into the far right lane and we went shooting up an off ramp. I had a brief flash of the sign: Porte de Vincennes. Christ, we were going back into St. Mande. I tied the knot, just to make sure.

"Du bist kein Bulle, sondern ein Krimineller, nicht wahr?"

"Excuse me?" he said, then his face fell, realizing what he'd done. I could accept cops in luxury cars, and German cops not knowing their way around a strange city. But German cops who didn't understand their own language were neither Germans nor cops.

With Brandt on one side and his goon on the other there was only one way to go. We were coming off the traffic circle and heading down Avenue de Paris. I lifted my flight bag and swiped it across the driver's face as hard as I could. His head smashed against the side window and his hands came off the wheel for a second. The car veered out of control. I put both hands on the seat ahead of me and threw myself over, falling in a heap, my rear end jammed in the leg well. The driver had his hands back on the wheel, struggling to straighten out the car. I heaved forward and kicked, catching his wrist. At least one bone cracked and the driver screamed. His foot went down on the brake and we swerved, hitting something. Whatever it was gave with a splintering crash. We came to a rocking halt and I managed to twist myself around, one hand grabbing for the flight bag. I hit the door release and somersaulted out of the car.

I hit a pile of cabbages. Scrambling to my feet, I began to run blindly away from the smoking ruin of the Benz. It took me a second or two to figure out where I was.

We had managed to jump the curb on the right side of Avenue de Paris about a block from the Stella Artois café at the corner of Avenue Foch. A regular market had been set up, complete with hawkers, booths, and piles of food and other cut-rate items. The Benz had come to rest in the centre of a gardener's stall, demolishing the poor man's stock.

I kept running, smashing into shoppers, sending bags of groceries flying. Hands reached out to grab me but I twisted and turned and managed to keep on. There were shouts from behind me and the sound of running feet. It was a fox hunt with me in the leading position. For the first time since I'd arrived in Paris I found myself wishing for a cop—a real one.

The temper of the chase changed in a single instant. There was a flat cracking sound from behind me and the flight bag jerked in my hand. Brandt or his pal had a gun. Suddenly the way ahead was clear as stall owners and their customers dove for cover.

The market came to an end, the last stall run by a news vendor. His stall backed onto the rear of the métro entrance railing. I swerved around the stall, brushing aside a suspended string of *L'Express*, and vaulted over the métro rail. I hit the ground ten feet down, banging my ankle on the bottom step as I impacted and scaring hell out of a little old lady and her poodle coming up out of the tunnel.

I hobbled down the tunnel as quickly as I could, scrabbling around in my pockets for a métro ticket. I found my half used carnet as I reached the turnstile, tore off one of the tickets, and rammed it into the slot. I pushed through the gate and headed down, making sure I was getting to the "Direction

Pont de Neuilly" side of the tracks. The other side dead ended three stops down. I'd be caught like a rat in a trap.

I hit the platform just as a train was pulling in—the first piece of good luck I'd had since noticing the Allards taking off. I sat down, my heart pounding and my breath coming in wracking gasps. A few of the other passengers gave me funny looks but that was all. Paris is the biggest mind-your-own-business city in the world.

Brandt and his buddy reached the platform just as the horn was sounding. I was in a car at the far end of the train so they were forced to get in a dozen cars up or lose me completely. The doors hissed shut and we were off. I nursed my ankle with both hands and tried to get my breath. There was no time to think about anything except staying out of Brandt's clutches, so the Gordian knot of questions that rose into my head had to be banished for the moment.

I had a fair idea of what they were going to do. With both of them on the train, one could get off and stand guard to make sure I didn't get off while the other moved one car down. The second man could take his time searching each car between stops.

The theory was proved at the next stop, Porte de Vincennes. I peeked out the window and looked up the platform. Brandt's goon was standing guard. I saw the tail end of Brandt's coat disappearing into a car three or four up. Whatever I was going to do I had to do quickly, or they'd have me. I checked the route map over the door. Nation, Reiully-Diderot, then the Gare de Lyon. That's where they'd nab me. I had to make a move before then. Nation was the only place that made sense. It was a "correspondance" stop with a couple of other lines running through it. The question was, how did I swing it without getting hooked?

I stood up, leaned against the chrome pole in the centre of the car, and thought fast. The doors were automatic with a little spring latch and rubber bumpers to keep you from getting your clothes caught. There would be about a three second pause between the sounding of the horn and the closing of the doors—not enough time. Brandt's nasty-looking colleague would wait until the doors were actually moving closed before he stepped back onto the train.

Suddenly we were in the big, dome ceilinged station, the yellow tile walls rushing by, the waiting crowds at the edge of the platform a blur. The train stopped smoothly and the doors slid open. The car was instantly filled with the chatter of oncoming passengers. Seats were found and the noise level fell to a dull whisper of conversation. I stared out through the doors, gazing blindly at the vacant platform, waiting for the horn.

It sounded at last and the doors began to slide shut. I jumped forward and stuck my arm between the rapidly closing bumpers. The rubber closed over my arm tightly, and for a second I thought I was trapped. I put my shoulder into it and pushed, manually spreading the doors a foot apart. I slipped through, and the bumpers thunked together. The train began to move and I caught a glimpse of Brandt, his face pressed against the window of the car ahead of mine. Then the train was gone and I was alone on the platform.

I needed some time to think so I headed for the correspondance exit and another line. The pain in my ankle had subsided but it was still enough to make me limp. I went up the first tunnel I came to and a minute later I found myself on a Number Six line platform. I checked the métro map on the wall. The Six line went away at right angles to the one I'd been on, twisting back and forth in a long meander beneath the city. The last stop on the line was Charles de Gaulle-L'Étoile, which was also a stop on the Number One line. It didn't matter; I'd be off the train long before that. A couple of minutes later a train came into the station; one of the old-fashioned ones with little fretwork decorations in wrought iron along the roofline. I unhooked the latch on the manually operated doors of one of the cars and climbed aboard, sinking gratefully onto a slatwood seat. A few seconds later we were off. At Picpus, the next stop on the line, the train came above ground and we began swinging through the southeastern suburbs of Paris, the tall stuccoed apartments bright in the afternoon sun. I stared out the soot-freckled window and tried to relax.

Brandt was no policeman, and that meant Kroeger hadn't been official either. Which accounted for the lack of news on radio and television. It also meant that I wasn't wanted by the French police—I could leave the city and the country any time. All I had to worry about were the people from Gambetta and Brandt, who, I was beginning to suspect, were one and the same.

There was no getting around the fact that even without the flics on my tail I was still in hot water. The Gambetta people obviously swung a lot of clout. Kroeger's ID had looked real enough and so had Brandt's. An organization that could put that kind of cover together was powerful. I'd managed to get by Kroeger and escape from Brandt, not to mention lifting the list. The next time I wasn't going to be so lucky. Brandt was going to be out for my blood and balls.

I still wasn't any closer to finding out what it was all about, but that was beside the point now—all I cared about was plain animal survival. And that meant I had to stay away from airports. Brandt had been posted to Charles de Gaulle, the obvious exit point. There'd probably be others at Orly and Le Bourget. Maybe even the train stations were being watched— which left me in a bit of a bind. The only other way out of the country was by car. They'd assume I'd make for the UK so there would probably be somebody at both Calais and Dunquerque. I shuddered involuntarily; I could almost feel the noose tightening around my neck. There were too many factors to consider, too many alternatives. Choose the wrong one and I was a dead man.

I swallowed the panic. I was in a no-win situation but that didn't mean I was going to give up. I'd beaten them twice now, I might as well try for three. If they expected me to head towards the Channel coast I'd fake them out and head in the opposite direction. Belgium was the closest border, no more than three or four hours by car. I could cross somewhere up around Arras and head for Brussels. There I could either fly into London, fly into Prestwick, or even catch a flight to Ireland and come into England through the back door. They couldn't cover every route. I felt a surge of elation. Maybe I could pull it off after all.

I checked out the window. I'd vaguely noted before that we'd been underground for a while, but I had no idea where we were. It was time to get my act together. We rolled noisily into a station and I checked the sign: Place D'Italie. I consulted the route map over the door. The next main stop was Denfert-Rochereau, then Montparnasse. I could catch a line up to St. Germain from there, and rent a car from one of the Europcar terminals on the Boulevard St. Michel. If things went well I could be across the border by nightfall.

Cars on the Paris métro, whether old or new, first or

second class, are designed alike. Each car holds about eighty-five seated and one hundred standing. There are double doors on either side of the car, large windows that open on the old cars and are sealed on the new ones, and a half-glass connecting door above the couplings between each car. At St. Jaques, a minor stop just before Denfert-Rochereau, I turned in my seat and began rummaging through the flight bag, looking for my wallet. I found it, checking to make sure that I had enough cash for the car rental. I had just placed the wallet in the pocket of my windbreaker when I caught a small movement out of the corner of my eye. I glanced back over my shoulder and found myself looking through the glass of the connecting door into the car ahead. Halfway up the car, seated beside the doors was Brandt, Frederik Carl, Kapitane. As I stared at him, the blood draining from my face, he turned and our eyes locked. He looked startled for an instant and then his mouth thinned into a hideous grin. I sat back quickly and squeezed myself into the corner of my seat as though turning away could somehow make him vanish. How had he done it? My eyes went up to the métro map above the doors. Shit!

A thin blue line ran up off the green of the Number Six line, connecting back with the orange of Number One at Bastille. Brandt had figured out what I had missed. He'd known it was useless to wait for the next green line train so he had stayed on the orange for another three stops, getting off at Bastille. From there he'd taken a Number Five line, the blue, down to meet the green at Place D'ltalie. There were only two or three stops on that line to the ten or more I'd travelled through since Nation. He'd waited until he spotted me and then climbed aboard in the next car. The son-of-a-bitch was playing with me!

I gathered together the few shreds of courage I had left and turned back to the connecting door. Brandt was gazing back at me, still smiling. I did a quick check of his car. The goon wasn't with him. Brandt had likely sent him back along the Number One line to stand guard at Nation in case I decided to double back the way I'd come. The bastard had a computer for a brain!

I watched as Brandt stood and went to the doors. The train roared into the station at Denfert-Rochereau and the doors swung open. I jumped up with the flight bag clutched in my hand and sprinted out of the car. I had nothing going for me except my age and my Adidas running shoes. Brandt might have a computer brain but that wouldn't add any speed to his run.

I bypassed the crowded escalator and took the parallel stairs three at a time. There were three flights, a wide opening at the turnstile, and then a short tunnel and a flight of stairs leading to the surface. There were too many people clicking through the turnstile so I swerved and vaulted over the gate instead. I turned up the tunnel, aware of someone running behind me. I waited for a shot, every vertebra tensing, but it didn't come. I hit the last flight to the surface and then I was out into the sunlight. There was no time to take my bearings. I just kept running—right into the street, and against the lights. A Big Saviem flatbed came within a foot of me and I pirouetted, dodging a madly braking Renault taxi. I charged on across the street followed by the squawk of blaring horns. I hit the other sidewalk and turned, chancing a look back. Through the blur of traffic I could see Brandt, his deep chest heaving under his raincoat, watching me, waiting for the light to change. I looked around.

I was in the middle of another of those interminable park and traffic circle combinations, probably Place Denfert-Rochereau. A low, windowless building squatted ten yards away at the edge of the fenced-in park. People were going into it through a narrow doorway and turnstile. It wasn't a métro station, and there was no time to figure out exactly where they were going. I sprinted down the sidewalk and joined the last of the line as it disappeared into the mausoleum-like building. If there was a big enough crowd there was a chance I could lose myself in it before Brandt got across the street.

A narrow-faced guard in a blue uniform and peaked cap stood at the turnstile dispensing tickets with one hand and collecting money with the other.

"Cinq francs, M'sieur," he droned. I dug into my pockets and slapped a ten franc piece into his hand. Methodically he thumbed the change-maker on his belt and gave me back five one franc pieces. Furious with his snail-like pace I rammed through the turnstile and found myself in a dimly lit ante-chamber. On the far side of the stone floored room there was a well-like hole. A trio of tourist types were on their way down the opening. It was a circular staircase. There was no sign of Brandt but he'd obviously seen me go into the building, whatever it was. I had no choice. I followed the people down.

The temperature began to drop almost instantly, but my shiver wasn't just due to the cold emanating from the dank, sweating walls of the hole. Like a fool, I'd done the worst thing possible. I'd gone to ground. Literally, by the looks of it.

I kept on down the worn steps. Small bulbs on a frayed cable that twisted around the stone core of the stairway lit my path. I started counting the steps. I hit bottom at two hundred and thirty-four, dizzy from the roundabout walk. A marker cut deeply into the stone wall of the corridor ahead informed me that I was sixty-nine metres underground— more than one hundred and eighty feet. Terrific, I thought to myself, buried in more ways than one. I looked around for some place to hide, but there was nothing—just the corridor ahead, the narrow walls bouncing with the shadows of the people ahead of me. I'd been the last one through the turnstile apparently; there was no one behind me. I stumbled forward on the loose gravel floor, trying to catch up to the others. The last thing I wanted was to find myself alone with Brandt in this foul place. As I ran forward I realized that I was probably part of a tour of the Paris sewers. It seemed like a hell of a place to die.

I reached the tail end of the line and slowed my pace. There was a bit of nervous whispering going on ahead, but other than that the only sound was the regular crunch of our footsteps in the gravel.

The tunnel seemed to go on forever, and I felt a clutch of claustrophobia in the pit of my stomach. Normally, small spaces don't bother me much, but this one seemed endless— an infinite grave. I kept looking back over my shoulder down the tunnel, but there was no sign of Brandt behind me. I put out my hand and touched the wall; it was cold and damp, the surface crumbling under my touch. After a few more minutes I began noticing a slight change in the way gravity was affecting me. It took me a few seconds to realize that the tunnel was beginning to slope down. I gritted my teeth. We were going deeper. The only thing keeping my claustrophobia in check now was the fact that we were still moving.

A hundred yards farther on the tunnel began to widen

slightly, and then it made a sharp turn. The people ahead of me began to slow. If we stopped I knew I'd scream. The tunnel turned one last time and then broadened into a spacious and—thankfully—well lit vestibule. The ceiling was still no more than a yard above my head. The room was an oblong, with a pair of Egyptian style obelisks at its far end guarding a portal cut through the rock. The obelisks were white with rectangular inserts of black. The tour was moving between them, shuffling through the rough hewn gate like figures in some hideous nightmare by Hieronymus Bosch. Above the opening, etched into the stone and picked out in black, was a warning in French: "Silence Mortals, you are Entering the Empire of the Dead." As I read it, the last of the crowd disappeared, and for a moment I was left alone in the chamber. Slowly, I walked forward and went through the doorway, bending my head. As I came out on the other side I straightened and looked around. I took a step backwards, recoiling.

Stretching away in all directions, stacked like cordwood in piles twenty feet thick and head high on both sides of me were bones. Yellowed, human bones. Layer upon layer of thighs, ribs, arms, legs, and skulls—tens of thousands of skulls, their shadowed eye sockets leering blindly across the rows at each other, jaws and teeth locked together in perpetual grins of final horror. The damp air was filled with a sweet musty odour, and there was no sound except for the whispering footsteps of the people ahead, now out of sight.

I wasn't on a sanitary sewage tour. I was in the Catacombs of Paris.

Chapter Seven

As a city, Paris has been in existence for almost two thousand years. It started off as a tiny village on the Île de Paris, where Notre Dame now stands, then began spreading outwards, benefitting from its protected location inland and its easy access to the sea via the Seine.

Like all rapidly expanding urban centres it was faced with two very large problems: garbage and dead people. At first they dumped the garbage anywhere and buried their dead with the same kind of abandon. By the Middle Ages their ad hoc garbage solution caught up with them in the form of the Black Death, which in turn upped the case load in the dozens of cemeteries that had sprung up beside every church.

The cemeteries didn't really bother anyone until Bonaparte's time, a few hundred years later. By then there were more than two hundred burial grounds in the Paris area containing the remains of slightly more than six million ex-Parisians. There were more people dead in Paris than alive.

Bonaparte's urban renewal plan for Paris was supposed to turn the city into the greatest capital in the world. Thousands of slums were demolished to make way for the master plan. Magnificent monuments were erected, those dozens of "Places" constructed to haunt future generations of automobile insurance agents; and statues sprang up all over the place. So did corpses.

Almost every time a foundation was sunk, skeletons appeared. Parisians had been burying their dead for so long they'd forgotten just where they'd been put. Within a year or so the situation became critical. France was still a good Catholic country, so they couldn't just ignore the remains of all those people. Something had to be done. Napoleon himself came up with the answer. A central depository for all the skeletons planted over the last millennium and a half. An ossuary patterned after the catacombs of Rome. There was even an ideal location—a series of worked over lime pits on the edge of the city. Properly stacked, the bones would all fit. A few monuments here and there, the odd group epitaph, a quick blessing from the Cardinal of France, and you were in business.

It took years, but eventually the six million skeletons were transferred from the hundreds of cemeteries to the lime pits, and a bylaw was passed. From that day on you only had one hundred years of peace in any of the six major cemeteries that had just been established. Beyond that time, the city had the right to dig you up and cart you off to the Catacombs. This hundred year rule was eventually picked up by every major city in the world.

The Catacombs served another purpose one hundred and fifty years later. They were used as the headquarters of the Paris Resistance during the Second World War. The maze of

passageways and tunnels through the stacks was a death trap
for anyone who didn't know exactly where he was going. The
few squads of Gestapo agents who went down into the pits
were never seen again.

And now, here I was, two hundred feet underground with a
killer coming up behind me and death's waiting room in
front.

I pelted down the loose floored passageway, trying to rejoin
the main body of the group, peering ahead through the
gloom. Every few yards along the main passage there were
side tunnels ending in wrought iron barriers that had been
dropped over pins set into the stone walls. It was clear that
major sections of the Catacombs had been blocked off for the
purposes of the tours. It was also clear that the place was still
in operation; I passed a wheelbarrow left in an alcove, piled
high with assorted bits and pieces of what had once been
human beings.

I turned down another bend in the passageway, looking
back over my shoulder to see if I could spot Brandt. As I
turned, my bad ankle slid out from under me on the gravel
floor and I fell, my leg twisting. A bolt of pain shot through
the ankle, and I yelped, in spite of myself. I waited for a
second and then stood, weaving slightly. I shook my head,
trying to clear the fog of pain, and put my weight down on
the foot. Another spear of agony went through me. At the
very least it was sprained. There was no way I was going to
outrun Brandt now, and he must have heard me fall. I
listened. At first there was only silence, then I heard it; a soft
rodent-like scuffling noise that grew louder with each passing
second. Running footsteps on the gravel floor.

"Brandt!" I whispered aloud. I slumped against the wall
beside me. The bones gave slightly, held in place by nothing
but the weight of the ones above. The sounds were coming
dangerously close. I straightened, reaching up to grab the
knob of one of the bones in the stack. I wrenched it out with
a grating sound. It was about a foot and a half long, knobbed
heavily at both ends. I swished it through the air. No match
for Brandt's gun. It wasn't going to be enough. I looked
around. There was a side passage a few feet away on the other
side of the main corridor. If I couldn't run I'd have to hide. I
staggered across the corridor into the shadows of the side
passage. The footsteps were much louder now.

I stopped at the wrought iron barrier. Behind it the darkness was impenetrable. The echoes of Brandt's approach whispered darkly from around the last curve of the low ceilinged gallery. I grabbed the barrier and lifted it off its pins, heaving upwards. The pins groaned out of the eye-bolts in the wall and the barrier came free on one side. I slipped behind it quickly and turned, setting the grate back on the bolts. I pressed myself into the darkness and stood, waiting.

There is probably nothing in the world more obvious than a bright-yellow vinyl flight bag with an Eiffel Tower spray painted on it in black. It's the kind of thing that once seen is never forgotten, like your first glimpse of a three hundred pound woman in a supermarket with her hair in pink rollers and her buttocks squeezed into matching pink capri pants. I must have dropped it when I fell. It sat there in the corridor, a gleaming beacon of bad taste that was going to hang me. Automatically, I lifted my hands to the cell-like bars of the grate, then stopped. There was no time to retrieve it.

The footsteps rounded the last corner and I saw Brandt, shadows cast off him like shrouds in the weak light of the ceiling bulbs. He stopped dead when he saw the bag on the floor and turned slowly, trying to find me. I shifted back into the darkness. Two things happened. First the barrier settled slightly on its pins with a tiny metallic click. Brandt went into a crouch, one arm sweeping back his coat, the other digging for the gun under his jacket. His gun hand came out, a short-barrelled pistol growing out of his fist like a questing snake set to strike. He rotated slightly on the balls of his feet, trying to locate the sound. That was when the second thing happened. The damp and mouldy dust of the Catacombs had been fighting with my sinuses for the past ten minutes; my nose chose that precise moment to give up the battle. I sneezed. I gave myself the luxury of a single whispered "Shit!" as Brandt whirled, gun arm extended. Without trying to be quiet, I stumbled further into the darkness of the side passage, heading deep into the blackness, one hand on the wall of bones, the other groping out in front of me. I could hear Brandt struggling to lift the barrier behind me.

I collided with another wall of bones and turned blindly. I could hear Brandt coming up behind me, his steps slow and methodical, his rasping breath echoing off the bones. I hit another turn and went right, knowing that if we kept this up

for long enough both of us would be lost. From the sound of
it Brandt was no more than a hundred feet behind me around
the last corner. It was time to stop and fight.

I'd left my knobby club back at the barrier. Now, I felt
along the wall of bones beside me until my fingers touched
the smooth curve of a skull. I slid my thumb and forefinger
into the eye sockets, hooking them into the nasal cavities. I
pulled. The skull came loose. I hefted it. A couple of pounds
at least. I vaguely remembered that the skull was the hardest
bone in the human body. If I ever actually connected with
Brandt at least it wouldn't shatter at the first blow. I listened.
Brandt had stopped; there were no footsteps. I reached into
my windbreaker pocket, coming out with the battered Zippo
I'd been using since I was sixteen—my only other weapon.
What was Brandt doing?

I tried to put myself in his place, a trick a hunter I'd
guided in the British Columbia bush had taught me. Think
like the quarry, put yourself in the animal's body and
mind . . . But I wasn't dealing with a mule deer or a wolverine
now.

Brandt was a professional, that much I was sure of. The
stance when he'd heard the barrier move was classic. He was
no spy movie killer. The gun looked like a Smith and Wesson
Police Special. A .38. Nothing out of the ordinary, but lethal.
Brandt would take no chances. He'd aim for the middle torso,
the largest target and the one with the fewest bone obstruc-
tions. Gut-shooting. I could almost feel my stomach trying to
squeeze up under my ribs in expectation. I had to lessen the
target.

I slid back against the wall, flattening myself along the
passage, then waited. An age passed, then Brandt began to
move. I waited until I could hear his breath directly in front
of me, then flicked open the lighter and thumbed the wheel,
tossing the lighter towards him down the passage. Even
before the flame blazed I was moving, pushing off the wall in
a low dive that I hoped would get in under his gun, or at least
his aiming point.

The lighter arced over Brandt's head, the sputtering flame
throwing the walls of bone on either side into nightmare
relief. I had a brief stroboscopic view of Brandt's contorted
face above me before I crashed into his knees, toppling him

backward. Then the lighter went out and we were in the dark.

Brandt's gun went off twice, the concussion blasting my ears and one of the bullets searing past my cheek before it crashed into the wall, sending bone shrapnel showering into the air. I clawed my way up his body, trying to get a hand on his wrist. I managed to straddle him somehow and brought the skull down where I hoped his head would be, hammering with all my strength. There was a crunching noise and the skull fell apart in my hand. Brandt slumped. I didn't wait to see what damage I'd done. Pulling the gun out of his hand, I staggered back down the passage. A few moments later I was at the barrier, now completely off the wall. I stepped out into the main passage and started off in a limping run, pausing only to pick up the Judas flight bag.

I followed the twisting passage through walls of bone for almost half an hour, ignoring the pain in my ankle, my mind intent on nothing but the steady movement of my feet. I'd hit Brandt hard but the chances were good that he wasn't badly hurt. With hindsight I realized that I should have put a bullet in the bastard's brain, but it was too late for that now.

I went through another portal like the one at the entrance, and found myself running up a sloping corridor that was a twin to the one at the other end, eventually coming to the exit. It was another spiral staircase, this time with a small desk at its base and a woman behind it selling postcards and slides. There was also a uniformed guard, probably put there to make sure that people didn't try to walk out with the bones of their Tante Louise hidden in their knapsacks. He ignored me except for a brief look of annoyance that I was so far behind the rest of the tour. It was probably closing time. I headed up the stairs.

I reached the surface, stepping out into a bleak whitewashed room with an open door facing the street. A light spattering rain had sprung up from somewhere, slanting across the doorway in finely etched grey lines. I stuck my free hand in the pocket of my windbreaker and looped my finger around the trigger of Brandt's gun. I stepped slowly to the door. Directly across the narrow, alley-like street I could see a shop window filled with skinned rabbits on hooks. Apparently the Catacombs exited unceremoniously on a back street. I waited in the doorway, thinking.

There had easily been enough time for Brandt to call for reinforcements before he'd gone down into the ossuary. Brandt was no fool—he'd almost surely have someone at the exit, or close to it.

I peeked out the doorway, hand tight on the gun in my pocket. The street was deserted. There was nothing to see except cars parked on both sides and rain-wet store windows. The tables beneath the awning of the café at the end of the block were empty. Maybe Brandt hadn't been so smart after all. I stepped out onto the street, the rain falling on my face with a welcome coolness.

With perfect timing a bright-red, battered Peugeot taxi turned the corner and headed down the street towards me. His roof light was extinguished. He was off duty. "Not for long," I muttered under my breath. I slipped out between two parked cars, and stepped directly in front of the approaching taxi, waving the flight bag. The taxi came to a jarring halt and the driver, a bull-necked man in his fifties, leaned out the window and started yelling a stream of abuse.

And then there was a screech of tires behind me. I whirled, the hand with the gun in it coming out of my pocket. A large black Mercedes leapt out from behind a van halfway down the block and careened towards me. Blinking the rain out of my eyes I levelled the gun and started squeezing the trigger. The gun bucked in my hand time after time, but the car kept on. Beside me the taxi driver had fallen into terrified silence.

I finally hit the Mercedes. Its windshield shattered, sending a million shards of safety glass spinning wildly into the rain filled air. The car swerved, slammed into a parked van, and stopped. I ran to the Peugeot, stuck the gun through the window, and gestured at the cowering figure of the driver.

"Votre taxi s'il vous plait," I said.

"Absolument!" stuttered the driver. He slid away from the wheel and out of the passenger side. I climbed into the car, put it into reverse, and did a tight turn in the street. Slapping my foot down on the gas, I took off, heading away from the dumbfounded driver and the wreckage of the Mercedes piled behind him.

I headed north, running up every one way street I could find, doubling back and cross-hatching my way beyond the big military cemetery at Montparnasse, then east towards the

Jardin des Plantes and the Seine. I knew I had to get rid of
the taxi, and fast. The driver would have reported it stolen by
now. I wondered how accurate his description would be and
then grimaced as I squinted through the sweep of the Peugeot's
worn wiper blades. The "Kiss Me" T-shirt was about as
inconspicuous as the gun I'd shoved into the man's face.

The gun. It was a liability now. I drove one-handed, almost
taking out a 2CV in the process, and dug into the pocket of
my windbreaker. I took out the gun and shoved it down
behind the backrest and the seat. It wouldn't get me off a
weapons charge if I was caught, but at least I wouldn't be
tempted if I was cornered.

I swooped and swerved the grumbling car through the
erratic late afternoon traffic, finally managing to cross the
Seine at the Pont d'Austerlitz, getting myself onto more
familiar ground. I hadn't driven in Paris for a long time and
my brain was in no condition to unravel the complexities of
the dozens of conflicting road signs. The situation was complicated even more by the fact that I didn't have the slightest
idea where I was going.

Things were getting worse with each passing minute. Ripping off the taxi had multiplied my pursuers a thousand fold.
Up until Brandt's flub with the German I'd assumed that the
gendarmes were on my trail. Now it was a fact. I knew that I
had to do more than simply get rid of the car, I had to get out
of Paris, tout de suite. Any bulletin put out would have me
listed as "armed and dangerous" or whatever the French
equivalent was. I wasn't going to have the time for the luxury
of a car rental, and I'd already discovered that Brandt's men
had the airport sewn up tight—probably all the airports. I
was going to have to take a chance on a railway station . . . even
though there was no guarantee that the going would be clear
there, either.

In Paris there is a train depot for almost every point of the
compass, depending on your destination. If I wanted to get
back to London it was the Gare du Nord. I checked my
watch. It was just past five. If schedules hadn't changed too
much I still had time to catch the night express to Dover, the
one the dope smugglers of the sixties used to call the Full
Moon Train.

I swung the car around Bastille and the Juilliet Column,
then arced to the west up the broad ribbon of Boulevard

Beaumarchais, its shops and cafés greyed by the strengthening rain. I whirled around République and kept my foot down, crossing Boulevard Strasbourg, then Lafayette. I went up and down a few back streets, finally tucking the car into an almost impossible parking spot on the Rue d'Alsace, next to Gare de l'Est. If I was lucky, the cops wouldn't find the car for quite a while, and when they did they'd assume I'd taken a train from there rather than Gare du Nord. It wasn't much of a decoy, but it was all I could come up with.

The rain was coming down strongly now, and I was soaked within one hundred yards, but I was glad of an excuse to keep my jacket zippered and the T-shirt out of sight. I hoped the taxi driver hadn't noticed the flight bag; the bloody thing had got me into enough trouble for one day.

Only a dozen or so blocks separate the Gare du Nord from the Gare de l'Est and a few minutes later I had reached the squat, grime-encrusted building. There was a scattering of people huddled under the wide stone portico by the main doors. They were mostly kids in their late teens and early twenties, armed to the teeth with crisp nylon knapsacks, L. L. Bean sleeping bags, and freshly laundered pre-shrunk and ready-faded Levis. It was a far cry from the bedrolls and beads of the old days.

The scene jogged something in my mind though, and the germ of an idea began forming. I walked slowly down the sidewalk, squinting through the rain, trying to find a likely prospect. There were two or three who might have fit the bill, but they had the wrong look—too clean and too secure. A solitary figure smoking a roll-your-own beside the luggage room entrance caught my eye.

He was my size and weight and a little less well-dressed than the others. More important was the expression on his face. He was scared shitless. It was a look that I'd seen a thousand times on my travels, the look of someone who was strapped, broke, tapped out, with nothing left but his passport and parents who weren't about to spring for two bits let alone plane fare home. He was on his own and afraid. Well, he was about to meet his Guardian Angel or the Devil's footman, depending on which way you looked at it.

I approached slowly and moved in beside him under the protection of the canopy. I pulled out a cigarette and pretended to be looking for a light. It was true; my lighter was somewhere down in the Catacombs. I spoke to him, keeping my voice as friendly as I could. "Got a light, man?" I asked.

He turned and looked at me. The beard on his face was wispy and there were still a few holdover pimples from adolescence. He was about twenty, big and strong, but thinning out the farther he got from home. He handed over a damp package of matches from a Wimpey bar in London and scrutinized me.

"How'd you know I spoke English?" he asked.

There was a wire in his voice, a tension that I couldn't place for a minute. Then I had it. The kid was on speed. Probably diet pills. "It shows," I said, smiling. "Not to mention the fact that you're wearing Topsiders, which are pretty hard to get in this part of the world. You're also over six feet. Nobody in this city ever breaks five-five."

"Sherlock Holmes," said the kid, turning away.

"No," I said, "just been around a lot." I paused, telling myself that things had changed over the years. Peace and Love were no longer operative conditions. Paranoia ruled, especially in the mind of a speed freak, even a pill popper like him. "You just get in?" I asked. The kid nodded, staring out into the street. I waited for another few seconds. There was no time to be subtle.

"You want to make some money?" I asked. He turned to me, eyes flaming. I put up a hand quickly. "Relax pal. I'm not going to bite you. We can help each other out."

"I'll bet," said the kid. He smirked. "My mother told me about guys like you."

"Fuck off," I smiled.

He frowned. That wasn't the right comeback. "So what's the deal?" he asked.

"You're broke aren't you?" I asked.

"I suppose that shows, too," said the kid, annoyed.

I shrugged. "I've been in the same space," I answered.

"So?" said the kid.

"I'm hot," I answered. There was no point in lying. It was the only explanation that made my idea reasonable.

"How heavy?" he asked. The kid was not a complete fool. He wasn't about to get himself tied into something really bad.

"Hot enough, but nothing I couldn't beat," I said. "It's an immigration thing. I want to get lost for a while."

"What's that got to do with me?" said the kid.

"I want to buy your clothes. Everything, knapsack and all."

"You're crazy," said the kid.

I pressed it. "Two hundred bucks." His eyebrows rose. The carrot was irresistible. He nodded. I looked around. On the far side of Rue de Dunquerque there was a public toilet, the entrance marked with a round blue WC sign. I pointed it out to him. "I'll meet you in there. Two minutes. We can change."

The kid nodded briefly, then gave me a long, hard look before he headed across the street. "You so much as touch me and I'll break your fucking head," he said, his voice low.

"I told you not to worry," I said. He turned and walked out into the rain. I watched him go, feeling a twinge that surfaced above my own problems. My two hundred bucks wasn't going to do him any good at all. He'd wind up in some jail over here before long. I took a last drag on my damp cigarette. The kid was a ghost from my past, trying to fit himself into the patterns of a time he'd never known and never would. I stubbed out the cigarette and followed him.

Ten minutes later, dressed in the kid's stained and odorous jeans and his lumberjack shirt, with his knapsack on my back, I went through the doors into the Gare du Nord. We'd transferred the contents of flight bag and knapsack. I was still wearing my Adidas because our feet were different sizes.

I skirted the stairs and escalators leading down to the métro stop below the station, and headed towards the "Billets International" window. A sign above the glass enclosure informed me that the ticket sellers spoke German, Italian, Spanish, French, and English. I spoke to the woman behind the counter in German.

"Ein Zimmer für Dover, bitte," I asked.

"Ein Zimmer?" she answered. I realized I looked a bit scruffy to be asking for a compartment rather than a coach seat, but the thought of sitting up all night was too much to bear.

"Jawohl, ein Zimmer," I said. I brought out my wallet and dropped a pile of one hundred franc notes on the counter. She shrugged and started making up the ticket. I asked her, in German still, when the train left. She told me an hour, but that with a sleeping compartment I could load right away.

I made some light conversation with her as she worked at the ticket, then counted out my change. The German I'd picked up at all those industrial trade fairs over the years was coming in handy. It wasn't much, but it would put just a little more distance between the Peter Coffin who'd highjacked a taxi and the one who was getting onto the boat train. If anyone questioned her about a tall American with a lousy French accent wearing a T-shirt that said "Kiss Me," I wouldn't fit the bill. I was the German hippy with enough money to buy a compartment. In twenty-four hours she wouldn't remember me at all. I picked up my change, crammed it into my new/old jeans, and with the ticket in my hands I went to the gate for the train to England.

I crossed the floor of the big, vault ceilinged concourse, doing a casual survey of anyone loitering around. There were a few "flics" doing their strolling act for the pickpockets, but no one who looked like Brandt or one of his cronies. I reached the gate, showed the official my ticket, and went through the barrier.

The train was a long one, a mixture of green Société Nationale de Chemin de Fer coaches, and blue British Rail cars. I found the sleeper number I wanted and climbed up into the gleaming SNCF car. A porter gave me a nasty look until I showed him that I really did belong among the rich folks; then he guided me to my room, handing me over the buff envelope with my customs forms in it. In rather formal English he advised me to fill out the forms, put my passport into the envelope and give it back to him before we pulled out of the station. It would be slipped under my door sometime during the night, after the customs and immigration men who travelled on the train had a chance to go over it. He gave me a salute, then ushered me into the narrow room.

I closed the door, locked it, and dropped down onto the plaid blanket that covered the bed. The room was no more than six feet wide, fitted with an upper and lower bunk, a small sink and mirror in one corner, and a window that looked out onto the platform beside the train. The carpet was the same dull-green plaid as the blanket. Everything else was done in mud brown enamel. Below my feet I could feel the wheeze and click of machinery and I felt the rush of excitement I get every time I board a train, even if it's only the Amtrak connection from Toronto to Buffalo, New York.

I located the switch panel over the sink, flicked on the ceiling light, and pulled down the blind. I filled out the forms with the ballpoint they provided in the envelope and inserted my passport. I buzzed for the porter, handed over the package of documents, and then locked the door again. I lay down on the bed, lit a cigarette, and waited. I didn't really relax until the first load of current hummed into the rooftop connectors and we pulled out of the station.

I turned off the light, opened the blind, and watched Paris roll by in the slanting rain for a few minutes. Then I lowered the blind again, pulled off my clothes, and sank down onto the bed. I fell into an exhausted, dreamless sleep.

Chapter Eight

I woke only twice during the trip: once as the train was broken down to be loaded on the ferry in Calais, and then again as we went through the reassembly process in Dover. I barely opened my eyes in Calais, but in Dover I awakened fully, got up, and dressed. The porter brought a horrible tasting but piping hot styrofoam cup of coffee half an hour later, and as we rocketed up the line to London I watched out the window, sipping the foul brew and smoking. The weather in England was overcast but it wasn't raining, and the sunlight, muted by the thin clouds, gave the pastoral scenery of rolling sheep meadows and thick oak woods a crisp, almost surreal look. Unlike the pale artists' light of France it had a Winston Churchill air of solidity. The change was vaguely comforting.

As we sped through the countryside, interspersed now and again with small commuter stations, I tried to formulate some kind of plan.

I had made it back to England, but the safety was only relative. I could forget about the Paris gendarmes, but Brandt and his men were still a factor. Brandt, or whoever his boss was, would assume that I'd slipped by them. They'd also assume I'd head for England, I was almost sure of that. They'd figure I had the missing list, and they would also assume, given that it contained Sam's name, that I'd figured out what it was, even if I hadn't fathomed its meaning.

The meaning of the list was probably contained within Sam's notes, which I knew he kept meticulously and in

duplicate for every story he worked on. I also knew that Sam
never kept them at his apartment—what I wanted from there
was the key to his basement locker. I was banking on the fact
that Brandt's people had undoubtedly gone over the apartment with a fine tooth comb, but that they'd just as surely
overlooked the locker key. The last time I'd been in Sam's
place, his study had enough papers littered around to choke a
horse. On the surface Sam gave the impression of being the
standard messy newspaperman, but I knew him better than
that. Anything important he filed. The locker in the basement of his building was clean enough to do open heart
surgery in. He kept the key in the same place he hid his
grass—behind a false switch plate on his kitchen wall. It was
a technique he'd learned after reading a hilarious little manual called *The Stash Book*.

I was betting that Brandt's people had different reading
habits. If I could get into Sam's apartment unseen I'd be able
to retrieve the key and then the notes.

And that put me back into doublethink, one of those Len
Deighton "they know that I know that they know" conun-
drums. It was terrific in Deighton's spy novels, but it was
driving me crazy. I lit another cigarette and looked out the
window again. The rolling fields were giving way to the
serried chimneypots and television aerials of London's suburbs. The sun was breaking through the clouds, sending
down thick pillars of gold. A real Billy Graham sky.

I built up a tower of items, shakily. I had the list. They
knew it. They knew I didn't know what it really meant. They
knew the key to it lay in Sam. So did I, and they knew that I
knew. They knew that I'd have to come back to Sam's
apartment, so they'd have it watched, but I knew that
too . . . What it really came down to was the fact that I didn't
have any choice. I *had* to go to Sam's place if I wanted to find
out just what the hell was going on. And they'd be waiting for
me.

So I decided on a delaying action. I had a few facts to work
with, even without Sam's notes. I could do a bit of checking
on my own. After that, I would make my move. London is a
gigantic city. If I kept away from any of my own or Sam's
usual haunts, I'd be safe. I hoped.

It sounded good, but I was still worried. I had killed one
man—maybe two, if Brandt hadn't made it. I was locked in

with a Cosa Nostra kiss. I knew enough to be a threat to Brandt's people. I wondered about Sam. Had he gotten in too deep as well? I had a brief vision of Kroeger and his knife and felt a swell of angry pleasure. If Kroeger had succeeded in doing to Sam what he tried to do to me, then I was happy to be Kroeger's killer. But I still hoped it wasn't true.

How about the police? That didn't wash, either. What did I tell them—my Paris interlude? Breaking into Gambetta? Blowing up a Mercedes because I thought it was full of bad guys, then confiscating a taxicab at gunpoint? Hardly. Murder, missing journalists, and men pretending to be German cops. Christ! They'd have me in a straitjacket before I could blink.

"Face it," I told myself, "you're all alone in this one, with no cavalry to come to the rescue."

The train pulled into Victoria Station.

I got off the train, went through customs without a hitch, then made my way through the crush of early morning commuters out of the big red brick building and into the sunlight, now shining fully through the last of the breaking clouds. It was going to be a good day. For some people, anyway. I wasn't so sure about me.

I checked my wallet. I was still flush, with both pounds and the now useless oversize franc notes. I could easily afford the Hilton, even without using my credit card, and I yearned for a nice hot bath. But it was too risky. Any manpower that Brandt's people had in London would be centred around places like that. I needed something a little less conspicuous.

I found it. A four floor narrow walkup hotel tucked away on a sidestreet off the Vauxhall Bridge Road, about half a dozen blocks from the station. Six pounds a night, loo at the end of the hall, pay in advance, no cooking in the rooms. The man behind the desk looked as though he'd died of syphilis a decade before and had a voice to match. He chewed peppermints that made him smell like the inside of a funeral parlour. I took my key and climbed the stairs to my room, suffering from déjà vu as I went up. It was like a repeat of Paris. I went into the room and again felt someone walk over my grave. Even the room was the mate of the one in Paris. I shuddered and dumped my belongings on the swaybacked bed. I went to the mirror over the washstand and looked at myself. What I needed was another change of image. The

ersatz hippy look wasn't going to work in the places I wanted
to go.

I left everything behind except my passport and wallet,
tucking the list under the bedsprings before I went out again.
I looked into a few shops and was surprised to find them all
closed until I realized that I hadn't turned back my watch. I
adjusted it by an hour and then nosed around until I found a
fast food restaurant. The food was on a par with the railway's
morning coffee, but at least I was full again. I picked up a cab
on Buckingham Palace Road and went to Selfridges on Oxford
Street. The American Express people would have been proud.
None of the clerks did more than raise an eyebrow at my
appearance. I went the whole route: an off the rack Cardin in
charcoal, four shirts (two pearl grey, two light blue), underwear, a pair of Calvin Klein jeans, two shetland sweaters, a
Hardy Amies tie, and an old-fashioned canvas and strap
suitcase to carry it around in. At the last minute I remembered
to add a new lighter. I slipped them the little green card, had
them put everything in the suitcase, and went back to my
hotel.

The bathroom at the end of the hall on my floor was light
years away from the lush and lavish Hilton, but an hour's
scrubbing in the tepid water from the overhead cistern did
the trick. I went back to my room, changed into one of the
grey shirts, put on the suit, and went back down the stairs
again. The attendant did a double-take, trying to figure out
where I'd come from. I was pleased by the reaction. I was
becoming a chameleon and that was just fine by me. I walked
up to Victoria Street and spent ten minutes trying to whistle
up a cab. I finally found one that wasn't crammed with
incoming tourists and their baggage and told the driver to
take me to Heathrow. I sat back in the seat feeling pleased
with myself. The old juices were flowing; I was on the trail.

By most definitions, Heathrow International Airport is the
largest in the world. More than 200,000 international flights
arrive and depart on its three runways each year. It handles
an average of 46,000 international passengers a *day*—which
adds up, when you include domestic travel, to slightly more
than twenty-four million passengers a year. Fifty-eight different airlines operate out of Heathrow, and the airport employs
53,000 people full time, including a special unit of men and

jeeps whose only job is to scare away birds. The approach lanes, taxiways, and runways are so complex that there is a guide book for pilots who find themselves lost between landing and getting to their proper "stand." There is a huge customs and immigration area on the north side of the terminal, and on the south there is a cargo terminal that is effectively an airport in its own right, handling and storing more than half a million tons of goods per year. The cargo area is also used for security flights and state visits. Close to Heathrow Terminal Two, a recent major addition, the control tower looms over the airport. Here more than 150 air traffic controllers work on rotating shifts in green-lit privacy, tensely going through the necessary rituals required to land or send off an airplane. Directly below the tower is the main computer centre, and beside it is the airport administraton wing.

I went through four different security checks on my way to the administration offices, and my press card and courtesy card didn't get me any further than the outer lounge even then. I gave the blonde receptionist my best smile and asked for Garth Young, the assistant general manager of the airport and a man I'd run into fairly regularly on the aviation beat. The receptionist returned my smile times two and buzzed for him. A few minutes later he came into the lounge. He was in his late fifties and balding, but he still had the swagger and the squinty-eyed look of a pilot, which was what he'd been for years prior to catching the brass ring as assistant general manager at Heathrow. Young had flown everything from Spitfires in the Battle of Britain all the way up to Jumbo's. When the Concorde started making the transatlantic run at Mach 2 he figured it was time for the younger kids to take over. Fifty thousand a year and a free Bentley didn't hurt either.

He shook my hand and guided me through to his office, a big one, ankle deep in pale-gold pile with a slab of tinted glass overlooking the runways. He could have rented it out as an observation platform. He sat down behind the big mahogany desk that lay in front of the window. I let myself slide into a perfectly sculpted leather and chrome armchair across from him. There was still room to have a cocktail party for seventy-five in the area behind us.

"How's the Bentley running?" I asked. It was a long

standing joke that the Bentley had been the key clause in his contract for the job.

Young grinned, a dozen capped teeth gleaming in his Côte d'Azur tan, every inch the man who'd made it. "Traded her in," he said happily, his English accent flattened by years of stopovers around the world. He had the ultimate midatlantic tone; which was reasonable, considering that he'd spent a good deal of his time in midatlantic. "She was a bit stodgy, really," he added, frowning. His smile snapped on again. "Bought a Ferrari."

"And your wife?" I said politely.

"Still drives that idiotic Mini," he said, then realized his mistake. He looked flustered. "Beth, oh, she's fine, fine. Kids, too. Andrea's at Neuchatel now. Eighteen."

There was a long pause. He looked at his watch. I got the message. I'd written some nice things about Heathrow in my time, but I wasn't VIP by any stretch of the imagination.

"I need some help, Garth," I said, leaning forward in the chair and putting the emphasis on his first name.

"Anything I can do I shall." He smiled; but the smile was a bit thinner.

"I need some information on an airline that flies out of here. A charter company."

"Oh," he said. I felt an undercurrent. I was a reporter and that usually meant something bad to people like Young unless I was doing a picture piece. Airports and airlines are tender about PR these days. Too many crashes and too much hanky panky.

"A company called AVTOUR," I said.

"Never heard of it. Why do you want to know about them?"

"A rumour," I said. I needed Young and I didn't want him upset. "There might be something to it, and then again there might not."

"What kind of rumour?" asked Young. All the friendliness had gone out of his voice now. This was straight business.

"The rumour is that they're trying to jump the green." Jumping the green is a term referring to the green colour of the customs walkway. Young stiffened.

"I don't believe it," he said.

I looked at him. "Why not?" I asked. "I thought you said you'd never heard of them."

"I haven't," he replied coldly. "But we've beaten every smuggling racket that has ever sprung up here. It's impossible, especially for a company. Individuals might get through with a bit of goods now and again, but that's all."

I sat back in my chair. What he'd told me was a complete crock, but it was a standard line from airport management. The truth is, any airport is a sitting duck for smugglers and thieves of all kinds. A gold smuggling racket out of New Delhi worked Heathrow for over a year without being caught, individual couriers bringing through as much as $150,000 at a time. Corporate smuggling was no different. It was easy enough to forge or alter a customs invoice or a bonding seal. And Young knew it.

"Look," I said eventually, watching him cool a bit. "I said it was a rumour. If they're working a number they're doing it out of more than Heathrow. If I find out they really are jumping I'll play your backyard down, all right?" There was no way he could refuse.

"What do you want from me?" he asked. I took a deep breath.

"I want the run of your computer centre, or at least a few minutes at the keys."

"Explain," snapped Young.

"I just want to do a very basic run on AVTOUR and see what comes up. Frequency of flights, seats filled, cargo manifests, that kind of thing."

"Cargo manifests?" he asked.

"How else do you find out what people are smuggling?" I asked.

"When do you want this information?" he asked. I could see a stall coming from a mile off.

"Now," I said.

He waved a manicured hand vehemently. "Impossible. It would interfere with necessary work, and besides, you're asking for what amounts to classified information. No, I don't think so, Mr. Coffin." Mr. Coffin. No more first names. It was time to trump his ace.

"You were flying Great Circle to Tokyo in '71," I said calmly. "It was your last year as a jock. You wound up in a geisha house and got plastered among other things. According to my sources, who have pictures to back it up, you went through seven of the house's best and they almost had to drag you onto the plane. You deadheaded back here when you should have been at the controls but you were still too ripped. Your second and your crew covered for you. Neither your wife nor the airline knows about it. Neither do the chiefs here." I sat back in Young's perfect chair. He'd paled under his tan. His face looked like ashes.

"That's blackmail!" he sputtered finally.

"No, it's not," I smiled. "It's duress. Reporters do it all the time. If we weren't the stalwart honourable fellows we are, we'd do it more often and we'd do it for money, not information." In some ways it was true. I didn't know anyone in the business who didn't have enough bits and pieces of dirt to crucify a lot of contacts. I was pressing Young hard, but what I wanted was no big deal. Just a few facts.

"You have pictures?" said Young.

"I don't, but my sources do," I said. It was a lie but he'd never know. I'd picked up the item a few years before when I was doing a story on Sex in the Sky for *Penthouse*. The source was a stew who'd seen Young being poured onto the plane. She'd wormed the details out of the co-pilot who'd flown them back. She was having a fling with the number two at the time. Journalism is a strange business.

"All right," he said. He stood up. I followed him out and walked behind him all the way to the computer centre. He never said another word to me. He introduced me to a fresh faced young man at a console in the main control area and told him to give me anything I wanted. Then he turned and walked away. I sat down beside the young man and explained what it was I wanted. He looked a little confused at first but then he shrugged and started punching the keys. The VDT, video display terminal, began to pop and the information unravelled on the screen before me.

According to the computer, AVTOUR ran an average of two flights a month out of Heathrow, always on the same tour through Mirabel, Toronto, and New York. The computer indicated that there were other flights run by AVTOUR on international routes but rang up an ID, or insufficient data code when I queried. I asked the young man to punch up AVTOUR's last ten flights on the board, homing in on passenger units.

The whole idea of a charter is to fill as many spaces as you can on the plane. Most companies have a breakoff point. If they can't attract that many passengers, the tour is cancelled. On all of its last six flights, AVTOUR was flying way low. A DC-10 can take almost three hundred passengers. AVTOUR was flying out with as few as sixty-five. It didn't make any sense. They should have gone bankrupt.

"Interesting," murmured the programmer. He'd spotted the same thing. He gave me a quick look. He obviously figured I was an official of some kind. I didn't do anything to destroy the illusion.

"Let me see the passenger lists," I said. He tapped the keys. We got a DE, Data Expired.

"Common enough," he said. "Most airlines can't afford to keep that kind of data on hand for very long."

"Okay, give me their Flight 360." I did some quick calculations and came up with the time and date of Sam's flight. DE again. The tape had been wiped.

"Anything else?" asked the young man.

"Cargo," I said. "Listing for the flight previous to the one we just got the DE on." He did a search and came up with it. There was nothing spectacular listed. A lot of specialty store orders, some hard to get car parts, and then a long list of bonded orders of machine tools.

"Can you get me point of origin for those?" I asked, pointing to the bonded orders. He checked the code numbers and searched. Every number he punched came back with the same pair of words: Aviom/Paris.

"How about the carrying agent?" I asked. The man tapped some more: Gambetta/Paris.

"Destination?" I asked. It was getting interesting. The young man entered the question. The reply was immediate: Alpha/Mirabel.

I had a new word to add to Sam's list. Alpha. Whatever was being smuggled eventually found its way to them at Mirabel. I was willing to give odds that Alpha was a freight forwarding company or a trucker. But it didn't make any more sense than it had when Sam called me. With an eventual destination of New York why drop whatever it was at Mirabel? I put the question on hold—for now it was detail work. There had to be a logical reason. I just couldn't see it. I was in an insufficient data position.

There was one other thing I wanted from the computer.

"Can you get London Air Traffic Control information on this terminal?" I asked.

The man nodded, looking up from the keyboard. "Some," he replied. "Nothing on line, but if it's been stored I should be able to get it."

"See if you can get me a straight departure sequence for that date I gave you." The programmer grimaced and consulted a manual of bypass codes. He spent a slow five minutes getting to the London ATC material. He keyed in the question and the screen flooded with information. The list of flights departing ran off the screen. I scanned the list quickly and motioned him to complete the sequence. He hit the "more" key and the rest of the list appeared. What I wanted was halfway down: AV360 . . . CANCELLED/LATC/NFSO.

No Flight Strip Outstanding. A clean cancellation order. The aircraft had never taken off. I could feel my eyebrows jack-knifing. If the aircraft hadn't taken off then it, and the cargo it was carrying, should still be at Heathrow. According to the previous information there had been no other AVTOUR flights since AV360. The DC-10 was probably in maintenance and the cargo, at least the Alpha material, would be in one of the bonded warehouses on the south side of the airport.

"Can we try maintenance, now?" I asked.

The programmer sighed. "You do get around, don't you, sir," he said. "What exactly would you like to know?"

"The whereabouts of AV360—that one there." I leaned over and tapped my finger on the glass of the VDT. The programmer jotted down the flight code sequence, looked up maintenance in his book, and keyed it in. The screen cleared and then the flight code sequence repeated itself on the screen, followed by a three letter designation: NOH.

"What does that mean?" I asked.

"Not On Hand, sir."

"In other words the aircraft isn't there."

"That's right, sir."

"And it never took off."

"Yes, sir."

"So where the hell is it?" I asked. "A four hundred ton jet doesn't just get up and walk away."

"No, sir," said the programmer, getting rattled. His machine had betrayed him.

I shook my head. There was only one answer. "Could someone have fiddled with the computer?" I asked.

The programmer looked shocked. It was the ultimate violation. "Absolutely not," he said.

I sat back and thought. "How many terminals patch in here?" I asked finally.

"Directly?" asked the programmer.

"Any way," I said.

"There are about ten in here," began the young man, his face thoughtful, as though counting in his head. "Then there are another fifty or sixty at the airline desks. Say seventy for the whole building."

"And outside?" I asked, knowing the answer.

The man winced. "I'm not quite sure, sir. I suppose you could say that any of the airlines using Heathrow have access to relevant flight information, number of seats available, that sort of data. The members of the International Association of Travel Agents have access too, I suppose."

"There are fifty odd airlines using Heathrow with a total of maybe five or six hundred offices world wide. There must be five or six thousand members of the IATA. So you've got six or seven *thousand* potential accessing points into your computer. Any one of them could have gotten in."

The man shook his head and held up the blue covered book of codes. "He'd need one of these, sir," he said proudly.

I sighed. I'd been doing stories on computer scams for years. "And how many do you have in this office?" I asked wearily.

The man's brow furrowed. "I'm not sure exactly how many there are," he said.

"So you wouldn't know if one was missing, would you?" I answered. He didn't say anything. I stood up and gave him a smile. It wasn't his fault. I knew guys who could have broken into his computer from two continents away using a pocket calculator and a touch tone phone. All it needed was skill, and that was easy enough to acquire. The young programmer looked crestfallen. Obviously, he'd been a firm believer in the sanctity of computers and his own position as one of the high priests.

"Should I report this to my superior, sir?" he asked, indicating the NOH on the screen.

I shook my head. "No. Forget about it, and don't worry

Mr. Young about it, either. I'll deal with the situation myself."
The man looked relieved. He wasn't going to be the sacrificial
lamb who brought the bad news.

I thanked him again, then let him escort me out of the
computer centre and back to the reception area. We shook
hands and I made my way back to the main concourse and
out to the taxi ranks.

I headed back into London, going over what I'd learned
and still drawing a blank. Every piece of new information I'd
come up with since the whole thing began had taken me
down one blind alley after another. I was definitely going to
have to make a try for Sam's notes.

The cab let me off in front of my hotel. I paid him, then
went up the steps into the narrow, dusty vestibule that passed
for a lobby. I nodded absently to the beet-faced man behind
the desk and went up to my room. I put my key in the lock
and opened the door.

He had a pink bandage over the left side of his forehead,
and the dark glasses he was wearing didn't quite cover the
yellow and purple of his blackened eye. Silently, with no
change in his blank expression, Frederik Brandt lifted the
heavy-barrelled weapon in his lap, pointed its bulbous end
towards me, and squeezed the trigger.

Chapter Nine

I opened my eyes, which was fairly disconcerting considering
that my last sight had been the gun Brandt was aiming at me.
I had a splitting headache and my mouth was thick and
clotted. I felt consumed by the need to brush my teeth. I
knew the feeling was familiar and after a few minutes of
blearily looking up at the eggshell ceiling about twenty feet
over my head, I remembered. My appendix operation, the
last time I was in hospital, aged sixteen. The headache and
the clotted mouth were what you had when you came out
from under the anesthetic.

Brandt had shot at me with a tranquillizer gun. So I wasn't
dead, and the ceiling above me wasn't inside one of heaven's
many mansions. I pulled myself up on my elbows and looked

around. I blinked. I wasn't in heaven, but it was pretty close. The distance between the end of the massive canopy bed I lay on and the tall window on the far wall was a good thirty feet. The window was bracketed by long drapes in gold, pulled back with thick gilt ropes, the multi-paned glass covered with a pale-yellow gauze from floor to ceiling. The walls were done in a pale-green watered silk, an almost perfect match for the velvety broadloom on the floor.

It took me a few seconds to realize that there were no corners in the room. It was definitely oval, the sculpted plasterwork frieze running around at the edge of the ceiling repeated the shape of the room above my head.

In addition to the bed, the room contained a pair of light-green bedside tables, a burled oak chest of drawers, a Queen Anne writing desk, and a scattering of chairs from the same period, upholstered in light-blue Moire silk. I sat up fully. The sheets covering me were silk as well—green to match the walls and floor. It was a very expensive room. But where was it?

I felt my stomach lurch. Christ! Had they taken me back to France?

I pushed back the sheets and swung out of bed. I was still woozy and there was an angry red spot just over my navel. It stung. I'd been right—Brandt was a gut-shooter. I sat on the edge of the bed until the little flares in front of my eyes receded, then walked naked across the floor to the tall window. I pulled back the gauze curtains and looked out.

Judging from the distance to the ground below I was on the second or third storey. Directly below the window a wide fieldstone esplanade fell in broad steps away from the edge of the house to a formal garden blazing with a dozen different flower varieties laid out in ornamental beds. Beyond the flowers the ground sloped gently away—acres of manicured lawn that stretched for at least a quarter of a mile to a small lake complete with stream and a rundown looking footbridge. The stream disappeared into a thick stand of trees behind it.

Halfway to the horizon, the trees thinned out and I could faintly see the shapes of grazing cows. Between the edge of the forest and the cows I could make out a long black line. Asphalt. There was a sleek needle-nosed aircraft parked at its far end. I squinted. It was a Dassault Falcon, a French fan-jet, just about the most expensive bizjet you can buy.

I went back to the bed and sat down. My clothes had been draped neatly over one of the chairs. I got up and went through the pockets. Everything was there, passport and money included. I pulled out my Camels and lit a cigarette with the new lighter. Then I dressed quickly. I had an idea that someone would be along to see if I was awake fairly soon. Somewhere between the Catacombs and this palatial mansion they had decided to use tranquilizer darts on me instead of bullets—and they had done it for a reason. Someone wanted to talk to me.

I was right. Ten minutes later the panelled door set into the curving wall at the end of the room opened. A tall, heavy-set man in a dark-blue suit was standing in the doorway, one hand deep in the pocket of his jacket. He had a short, almost military haircut and a seamed and sunburned face that had clearly been exposed to the elements.

"Come with me," he said. His voice twanged out of the midwest. An American. I nodded and followed him.

We went down a long carpeted hall, with me three paces behind. I had a fleeting urge to jump him, but sensing it the man looked back over his shoulder. "Don't," he said, his face breaking into a split-second grin. It was almost a dare. We kept walking.

We reached a magnificent oak-balustraded stairway and we descended it. We went down two floors to what was obviously the main entrance hall, then turned left, going down another corridor. The man in the blue suit stopped in front of a wide, brass panelled door worked in an intricate design of intertwining leaves and branches. Even in my still foggy condition I was awed by the lavish outfitting of the house. There was a lot of money involved.

"Inside," said the American. He opened the door and ushered me in, closing it behind me. He stayed outside.

The room was a good fifty feet long, white marble bookcases built into the robins' egg blue walls, the ceiling arched and squared off in white plaster panels edged in gilt. The parquet floor was covered almost wall to wall with a gigantic Persian carpet in saffron and green. At the far end of the vast room a huge carved desk stood in front of a high mantelled Carerra marble fireplace. An ordinary looking man, dressed in a charcoal suit and white shirt, sat behind the desk, playing with a letter opener. Brandt sat in a high backed chair to one

side. I walked the length of the room until I stood a few feet
in front of the desk.

"You must be the chief bad guy," I said, with a bravado I
didn't feel at all. "How come you're not wearing a black hat?"
I looked at the man. From the door he'd seemed quite
young, but the dark hair had been disguising. On closer
inspection the lines in his face betrayed his age. He was
hitting sixty, or maybe more.

"Step forward," said the man. The accent was British. I
was getting a real international tour. I did as I was told and
stepped up to the desk. I glanced at Brandt. He was smiling.

The man behind the desk stood up and leaned forward
across the bare expanse of oak. Almost idly he backhanded
me across the face. I reeled back. He might have been
getting on into old age but his hand had hit like cold rolled
steel.

"I dislike impertinent young men," he said, his tone clipped.
He sat down again. He went back to twiddling with the letter
opener. Brandt kept on smiling. After a few moments the
man spoke again.

"Your name is Peter James Coffin. The fact that you are
alive at this point is a matter of my choice, as is your
continued well-being. I would caution you not to anger or
irritate me in any way. You have already caused me a consid-
erable amount of trouble and you would be well advised to do
everything in your power to please me. Do you understand?"

I nodded, swallowing the anger that rose in me at his tone.
This was no time for false heroics. Whoever the man was he
had the look of someone who disposed of people the way
other men swat flies. His eyes were grey-flecked blue and
looked as hard as ball bearings. "I understand," I said.

The man nodded. "Good," he said. "Now for a few questions. Please answer quickly and completely. Also answer
truthfully. If I detect any attempt at deception I shall be most
annoyed. You are nothing more than an anomaly to me, Mr.
Coffin. Your story can perhaps clear up a few details, nothing
more. Lie and you will be disposed of immediately. Yes?"

I nodded again. The man turned to Brandt as though for
confirmation. Brandt smiled. I wished I'd hit him harder in
the Catacombs. I had the queasy feeling that I was facing my
executioner. The man behind the desk began.

"You received a transatlantic telephone call from a Mr. Samuel Underwood on July sixteenth, correct?"

"Correct." Jesus! They'd had Sam's phone tapped. Who *were* these people?

"Two days later you had a somewhat brief dinner with Mr. Underwood's sister."

"That's right." A tail on Georgina Underwood as well.

"The following day you flew to Paris. On the afternoon of that same day you found a man in your hotel room. His name was Hans Helmut Kroeger. You murdered him."

"Killed him," I corrected.

"A semantic cleft-stick," said the man behind the desk. He continued. "After Mr. Kroeger's death, you disappeared for a period of some twenty-four hours. Where did you go?"

"I broke into a house. The occupants were away on vacation."

"Where is this house?"

I hesitated, then decided on the truth, praying that the Allards were gone for a long time. "Number Twelve, Avenue Foch, St. Mande," I answered.

The man turned to Brandt. "Note that," he said. Brandt nodded. The man turned back to me. "On the night of your first day in Paris, after Mr. Kroeger's death, you broke into the offices of the firm of Gambetta S.A. and stole something. A list. It was found among the belongings in your London hotel room. Do you know what that list represents?"

"It's the passenger list for AVTOUR flight 360," I said.

"How did you discover this?"

I shrugged. "Simple deduction. A list of names, one of them Sam's, a flight number, and computer codes. It wasn't hard."

"I see," said the man. He looked down at his hands for a moment and then back at me. "During the period you spent in the house on Avenue Foch, whom did you contact?"

It was a setup. He was checking to see if I would bluff. I didn't. "Nobody," I said.

He nodded. "After your escape from Mr. Brandt and his colleagues you returned to London, yes?"

"That's right."

"We were watching the Gare du Nord and the airports. No one answering your description was seen. I am interested in how you managed it."

I smiled. "I wasn't answering my description, either," I said.

"Don't be flippant, Mr. Coffin. Flippancy offends me."

"I exchanged clothes with a kid outside the train station."

"For money?"

"Yes."

"What is the young man's name?" he asked.

"I don't have the slightest idea," I said.

The grey-flecked eyes gave me a long hard look. "You arrived in London and booked into the Cameo Hotel on Carlisle Place."

"Correct."

"You went to Heathrow Airport and had a conversation with Mr. Garth Young, the assistant general manager. You talked about the possibility that AVTOUR was involved in a smuggling operation."

"Yeah." My mind was racing. They hadn't tapped Young's phone for that one. I'd never talked to him on the phone. If they knew about my meeting with him, then they'd got the word from Young himself. He was part of the goddamn thing! Suddenly his nervousness when I started talking about smuggling operations made sense. He wasn't thinking about PR, he was thinking about himself. I held my breath, waiting for the next question.

"What did you do after you left Mr. Young?"

That was it. That was the reason for the tranquillizer. The son-of-a-bitch didn't know. Young hadn't told them about the computer run, probably because he didn't want them to know about his Tokyo indiscretion. It sounded as though they were hanging the same kind of thing over him and he didn't want to give them any more fuel for their blackmail.

"I went back to my hotel and ran into Mr. Brandt," I said, hoping I hadn't hesitated too long. It seemed to pass him by.

"Other than Mr. Young and Mr. Brandt here, who else did you meet with while in London?" Maybe I'd spoken too soon.

"With the exception of a couple of taxi drivers, the clerk at the hotel, and some salespeople at Selfridges I didn't talk to anyone." Almost the whole truth. Was it going to be enough?

The man leaned back in his chair and tucked his hands like a priest in front of his pursed lips. He eyed me thoughtfully. Brandt was studying the knick-knacks on the mantelpiece, bored.

"Let us change our course somewhat," said the man. "We will go from facts to generalities, yes?"

"If you say so," I answered, keeping my voice even.

"I do say so, Mr. Coffin. Instead of concise answers to specific questions I now want opinions. I would be most interested in your conception of what you are involved in."

He waited. So did I, wondering what and what not to say. I let out a breath. "I wouldn't want you to take offense," I said.

The man waved the objection aside. "Feel free, Mr. Coffin. I told you that I found impertinence and flippancy objectionable, not frankness."

"All right," I said. "I think you *are* involved in a smuggling operation. Everything I've discovered ties AVTOUR, Gambetta, and Aviom Industries together with a ribbon and a bow. You've got a regular run using the AVTOUR charters and you offload whatever it is you're smuggling in North America. At a guess I'd say it's either bullion or heroin. Probably the latter. Sam had a lot of contacts in the drug business and he's done stories on smack before. I think he fell into the story that way. You found him listed as a passenger on AVTOUR 360, and you panicked. You thought he was about to blow the whistle on you. You either kidnapped him or killed him, then cancelled the flight to make sure you weren't nicked by the customs people at Mirabel or JFK. Something like that." I breathed hard. "Do you mind if I smoke?" The man shook his head lightly. I lit up, noticing that my hand was shaking. Brandt's boss scared the hell out of me. It showed.

"You did very well," said the man. "Very well indeed."

"And now I suppose I know too much," I answered.

For the first time the man laughed, a rough braying noise that was at odds with his sophisticated dress and surroundings. He sounded as though he didn't use the laugh often.

"On the contrary, Mr. Coffin," he said, recovering, "you know far too little. In the films the hero is often in mortal danger by having too much knowledge; in your case, it is your ignorance which condemns you." The man raised one hand in a dismissing gesture. "Goodbye, Mr. Coffin. I'm very much afraid we shan't be meeting again."

I stared at him for a moment and then turned and made my way across the room again, aware of Brandt's eyes on my back every step of the way—measuring me for a bullet or something equally nasty I was sure. I reached the door and opened it, wondering if by some miracle the corridor would be empty. It wasn't. I gave my fullback guard a nod and accompanied him back to my room. He deadbolted the door behind me. If I'd been five years old again I would have burst into tears. I smoked another cigarette instead.

"Condemned," that was the term he had used, and the man in the charcoal suit wasn't one to use words idly. He meant precisely that: I was going to be killed. It was only a matter of time.

I had been brooding in the lavish bedroom since my conversation with Brandt's boss. Noon and afternoon had come and gone without any sign of food or drink. I was famished, thirsty, and frightened. I found that I kept thinking of Sam. I would have liked to believe that ignorance hadn't "condemned" him. But as I concentrated desperately on my own situation, I became certain that what was going to happen to this journalist had already happened to another.

I'd gone over the room a dozen times, but there was no way out. The door remained locked and when I put my ear to it I could hear faint movements and the sound of breathing. The room was guarded. The window was painted over and even if I had been able to open it, there was a forty foot drop to the hard stone flags of the esplanade below. So, escape was impossible, but the alternative was to sit and wait for Brandt to come and have me discreetly "removed." It wouldn't be long; they were probably only waiting for darkness, and that was coming up fast. The shadows outside had deepened into dusk, and the guard and dog patrols I'd been watching all afternoon would soon begin using their flashlights.

I sat at the writing desk, smoking and pondering my predicament. I had to come up with something quick—I was down to my last cigarette. I laughed bleakly, and the sound of my own voice in the quiet made me even angrier.

I began pacing the perimeter of the room, silently cursing the soft pile of the carpet that stole away even the small satisfaction of the sound of my footsteps. Silk sheets and walls, gold drapes and ceiling frescoes. Opulent, but a prison cell nonetheless.

I smoked the last quarter inch of the Camel and butted the remainder maliciously on the windowledge. I looked out. The low sun was a blood-red blur and the forest was a solid mass of black, blending into the deepening violet of the sky. I sighed and started around the room again.

What would James Bond do, or Harry Houdini? Fleming's character would blow a hole in the door with a Braun lighter concealing a miniature laser. Houdini would have used some obscure breathing feat to squeeze himself under the door. Great for them, but I had no bag of tricks to dip into and I certainly wasn't a contortionist.

"Condemned." The word rang in my head like a tolling death knell.

"Doubledamn!" I said aloud, staring around the room. Time was running out on me. There *had* to be a way. I just had to attack it logically, Holmes and Watson style.

The room had no secret passageways. This was real, not something out of the Hardy Boys—not to mention that I'd already prodded a few pieces of moulding here and there just to make sure. The door might have been forced—except that there was a guard on the other side. So what else was there? The window and the closet. I stopped and turned.

Well, what about the closet? A penny had dropped somewhere. There'd been a closet in my room as a child. It had backed onto an identical one in my parents' room. The adjoining wall had been flimsy enough for me to listen to their arguments about whether I should go into the army or not. Flimsy enough to be kicked in? It was worth a try.

I walked to the closet, almost unnoticeable since it was covered in the same silk as the wall. I'd opened it before to make sure it wasn't a connecting door. It had been empty. I opened it again and again got a nose full of cedar. This time I noticed that the walls were done in a small-patterned floral paper. I hooked my index finger into the joint between two sheets and picked a square of it away, exposing the wall behind. Wood. Cedar, probably, which would account for the smell. I tapped the back wall with my knuckles. It sounded depressingly solid. Just to be sure I put my shoulder to it and heaved. I was doing isometrics—there was no give at all. Strike three and you're out. My head fell back wearily. I was out of ideas. I blinked up at the dark ceiling of the closet. I squinted and blinked again, not quite believing it.

Six feet above my head was an old-fashioned plank trapdoor, about four feet square. I'd seen hundreds like it before in other houses, set into top floor ceilings and closets and used for access to the upper crawlspace between the ceiling and the roof. I'd even gone through one once with my first girlfriend when I was ten or eleven years old. We'd been looking for a spot to enjoy some experimental biology and she'd taken me up to the half attic in her parents' house. It had been cramped, but it had served its purpose admirably. Maybe it would do the same now.

The crawlspace probably extended the full length of the house, and in a place of this size there had to be more than one trapdoor. All I had to do was get up there, edge along the rafters until I hit another one, then drop down into the room below. If I was lucky the room would be unoccupied and unlocked. It was a long shot but it was all I had.

I went back into the room and picked up the chair at the writing desk, grateful, now, for the muffling carpet. I carried it back to the closet and climbed up. I had just enough leverage to push on the trap. I pushed, but nothing happened. A vision of Brandt smiling at me behind the barrel of a gun came to me and I pushed harder. A sliver of black appeared around the edge of the wooden square. I stood on tiptoe and gritted my teeth, giving it one last shove. The trap moved to one side. I climbed down off the chair and took it back to the desk. I wanted to do this without leaving any trace. If they came in and found me gone I wanted them to spend as much time as possible figuring out how I'd done it. I checked that I had everything, then went back into the closet, closing the door behind me. I couldn't see a thing, so I had to do it by touch. I arranged myself with my back against the wall to one side of the door and then walked up the wall on the far side until my knees bent and my feet were almost level with my face. Then I slid my back up, bringing my feet along on the opposite wall. I think it's a mountain climbing technique. All I know is that it hurt like hell. The crouch was also threatening to split the back of my jacket.

I was up at the trapdoor. This was the tricky part. I had to get my hands up over the lip of the trap and pull myself through it without falling back. I managed it on the second try, got my elbows hooked over the sides of the trap, and hauled myself up. I fumbled my lighter out of my pocket and flicked it on. The gloom retreated and I had a look around.

I was standing in a brick chimney arrangement that was slightly larger than the closet below. The chimney went up another ten feet or so. Above that was more darkness. There were five dark metal U-bolts set into the brick on one side. I was obviously standing in a shaft representing the differential between the ceiling of the closet and the ceiling of my room. I clambered up the U-bolts one-handed, keeping the lighter on.

I reached the top of the chimney and encountered another trapdoor. I had to put the lighter aside to open it, but as soon as I came through I lit it again, taking in the small area that the flame illuminated around me. The crawlspace was about five feet high, the rafters overhead thick with cobwebs and dust. If I stooped I'd be able to walk quite comfortably. I lowered my arm and checked the floor.

It was laid out in a regular grid. Huge wooden beams running parallel with each other disappeared into the darkness beyond my little puddle of light, cross hatched at regular intervals with narrow joists. The roof's rafters were placed directly above the floor beams and braced every few feet with thick wooden uprights. Peat moss insulation filled the intersecting squares of beams and joists, the dark granular substance scenting the air with a musty smell reminiscent of the Catacombs. The similarity was enough to make me grimace.

I clambered to my feet and reached up to one of the rafters overhead. If I kept my hand on one of the rafters and used the other to light my way I'd be able to move without fear of stepping off into one of the insulating squares. I was sure that there was nothing below the peat moss except plaster and lath and the last thing I wanted to do was come hurtling through the ceiling of one of the rooms, or worse, into the hall. The lighter was beginning to heat up in my hand, so I flipped it shut. Old peat moss is one of the most flammable things in the world. If I dropped the Zippo into it I'd be a torch in seconds. From now on, I'd only use the lighter to get my bearings.

I began shuffling forward, my feet tentatively moving along the beam. I came to an upright and worked my way around it. After the third upright I stopped and flicked on my lighter again. I looked down—no trap. I kept moving, flicking the lighter on every few uprights to check for a trap.

For some reason I'd been expecting to find the next trapdoor directly in line with the one in my room. I'd been fooled by the regular grid pattern of the crawlspace floor, which, of course, had nothing to do with the shape or layout of the rooms below. Because of this I almost missed it. I was on my fourth or fifth lighter stop and was about to douse it when I spotted a square of wood about ten feet to one side, halfway between two of the narrower floor joists. I swore under my breath. To get to it I was going to have to tightrope along the joist and kneel awkwardly over the hatch while I lifted it. I'd need both hands to work up the hatch—and that meant no light *and* nothing to hang on to. I was beginning to regret all those gym classes I'd skipped in high school. I considered the idea of continuing on the same path and hoping for an in-line trapdoor, but the longer I stayed in the crawlspace the more likelihood of being trapped. It had been almost dark when I left. If my theory was right, someone was bound to come into my room soon. The idea of being up in the crawlspace with Brandt somewhere behind me wasn't pleasant. I decided to take my chances with the dangerously positioned hatch.

I took a deep breath and held it, lifting the lighter high. I edged out onto the joist, hanging on to the upright beside me for as long as I could. When I got to the limit of my reach I let go and moved inch by inch along the beam, unsupported, arms held out for balance, the lighter hot and shaking in my hand. The flame sent mad shadows gyrating around me, confusing my vision. I was horribly aware of the potential pyre of the insulation on either side of me.

Every muscle quaking I finally reached the trapdoor and knelt above it, lowering my arm to examine it. The hatch was identical to the one I'd come from: square, made of jointed planks, and framed together with moulding at the sides.

I took another deep breath and snuffed the Zippo, putting the red hot instrument into my jacket pocket. The sudden darkness threw my balance off and I swayed dangerously on the crossbeam. I was aware of sweat dripping into my eyes with a salty sting, but I ignored it. I reached out to the trapdoor and used it to regain my balance. After a few seconds to let my heart slow down I got to work.

The trap was stiff with age; obviously no one had been through it for years, if ever. I pulled as hard as I could and the trap pulled free with a loud screech. I stiffened, waiting for some response to the sound. After a full minute passed I out my hands on the edges of the hatch and pulled it away completely. I squatted on the crossbeam and took out the Zippo again. I looked down.

The same chimney as before. For a hideous second I wondered if I'd somehow managed to walk around in a circle, then dismissed it. I squirmed around until I got my feet over the edge. I found a U-bolt and eased myself down. I descended the ladder of bolts until my feet hit bottom. The lighter showed me the second hatch. I bent down and listened for a moment. There was nothing. Not that it would have made any difference—there was no way in the world I was going back up into that crawlspace and along that narrow joist.

I eased open the trapdoor at my feet and checked with my lighter. Like the closet in my room, this one, too, was empty. I flicked off the lighter and turned myself over the edge. I lowered myself down, slowly unlocking my elbows until I was hanging fully extended. Then I dropped.

Somewhere I'd made a miscalculation. I hit the floor with a jarring thud that threw me off balance and against the closet door. The door burst open and I fell, flailing arms and legs, into a brightly lit room. I scrabbled to my feet, heart pounding wildly.

"What on earth were you doing in my closet?"

It was Georgina Underwood, and she was stark naked.

Chapter Ten

My father was a philosopher, at least that's how he used to describe himself at parties. I prefer to think of him as a collector of clichés, which was more to the point in his case. He was constantly coming up with homilies of one kind or another, from crackers like "he who laughs last, laughs best," to the newer strains like "do your own thing." New for him was always at least ten years in the past. But on one of those rare occasions when he took time off from the defense of his nation and had a "man to man" chat with his only begotten son, the old man actually came up with something good.

"Peter," he said, puffing on an incredibly battered Peterson that he carried with him everywhere, even into battle, "Peter, my boy, when you find yourself in a crisis situation for the first time, be it good or bad, you'll notice that things happen fast. Success comes quickly and failure even faster. Reality ceases to exist, things get all twisted up in their own logic, and the only thing to do is go with the flow. You can run from A to Z in a split second, and it's only a very fine line between life and death."

Maybe it was the memory of that conversation, or perhaps it was just my expectation of just about anything after what I'd been through over the past few days, but whatever the reason I didn't turn a hair when I saw Georgina Underwood standing nude in the centre of a Bokara rug, a fluffy white towel dangling from her hand.

"Hello," I said.

Georgina gaped. She made no move to cover herself. She just stood there staring at me. "What were you doing in the closet?" she repeated.

I resisted the urge to tell her that I was just dropping in and got down to business. "Escaping," I said.

"Oh," she said. She looked down at herself, suddenly remembering that she had no clothes on. "I've just been having a bath," she explained calmly.

"Terrific," I said, "so get dressed."

"Why?" she asked. Reality was ceasing to exist all right.

"How long have you been held here?" I questioned.

"Since the night we had dinner together," she said. "I decided to go to Sam's place. I let myself in and there was a man there."

"Brandt?"

"Who?"

"Never mind. What happened then?"

"They bundled me into a car, blindfolded me, and brought me here."

"So we're still in England!" I murmured.

"Of course we're still in England. Where else would we be?" she said, looking at me as though I were a lunatic.

"You don't know the half of it," I snorted. "Anyway, what happened then?"

"Nothing. They gave me this room, told me that there were guards everywhere, and that was that."

"They didn't tell you why you were being held?"

"The one who calls himself Llewellyn said that they had

Sam and that I was supposed to cooperate and tell them everything I knew. I didn't *know* anything, so I couldn't tell them anything. Except about you. They asked about you and I told them what you'd said."

"Right," I said.

She flushed. All over. It was quite pretty. "They said they'd hurt Sam unless I told them!"

"It's not important," I soothed. "This Llewellyn character—he's the one with the dark hair and the really crisp accent, about sixty or so?"

She nodded. "It's dyed," she said.

"Pardon?"

"The dark hair. It's dyed. He colours it. I think he must be very vain. He was forever shooting his cuffs when I talked to him."

I'd missed that. "Has anything else happened?" I asked. "Have they tried to talk to you again, or hurt you?"

She shook her head. "No, nothing like that. They made me write a postcard to my father today. Telling him I'd had the sudden urge to visit Frankfurt and that I'd keep in touch."

"Must be harder to dispose of a Lord's daughter than a reporter," I murmured.

"Excuse me?" she said.

"Nothing. Thinking aloud." I looked around the room. It was somewhat smaller than mine, but it had an attached bathroom. I became aware of how much I needed to use it and did so. When I returned, Georgina was just about finished dressing. I gestured at the door.

"Locked?" I asked.

"No. They bring up my meals and things, but no one ever stopped me going out. Have you seen those Dobermans they have?" She shivered.

"Yes, I caught a glimpse. There's no guard either, I suppose." I was fairly sure there wasn't. He'd have to be deaf not to have heard my entrance into the room.

"No guard," said Georgina.

"That's something, anyway." I took a breath. "Okay, let's kiss this place off." Georgina looked confused. "Split," I explained. "You know, leave. We don't have much time."

"How?" she asked baldly.

It was a good question and I didn't have the answer. I tried to appear in control. "You know the layout better than I do, why don't you tell me," I said.

She thought for a moment. If she hadn't been such a spoiled little bitch she would have been great to have around. As it was she was going to be more of a burden than anything else.

"Front or back?" she asked.

"Front. I could see the back of the house from my window."

"Well," she began, buttoning her blouse at the same time, "the house has three parts to it; the north wing, the main house, and the south wing, which is where we are. There's a large coach house quite close on this side, connected by a covered walkway. I believe they use it as a garage. The guards may live there as well—there are living quarters up above. There is a parking area in front of the coach house and a circular driveway past the main entrance."

"If you were standing on the front steps, what would you see?" I asked. As she thought again, I checked my watch. It had been twenty-five minutes since I'd left my room. Outside Georgina's window it was fully dark.

"You'd be looking down the drive," she answered finally, her eyes closed, picturing it. "There is lawn on either side and in front for about a hundred yards, then trees."

"You can't see where the drive ends?"

"No. But I have a fair idea. Most country houses like this will have a stone or brick wall and a gate at the road; the trees are a privacy screen really."

"Can you take a guess at how far it is from the house to the end of the drive?" I asked.

She shrugged. "It could be quite long, or it could only be a few hundred feet. I don't really know. The trees are too thick to tell."

"What about guards? How many do you think?"

"I've seen at least three different ones with dogs. There are a few in the house as well. Other people, too."

"Other people?"

She nodded. "Once I saw a pair of men going into one of the rooms on the main floor. I peeked into the room; it looked as though it was full of radio equipment. There's a large antenna on the roof, too."

"What's the best route out of the house?" I asked.

"Down the servants' stairs I should think. A house like this is bound to have them."

"Okay," I said. There was no time for any more questions. "I start up a diversion and then you can lead us out of here."

"A diversion?" she asked.

I nodded. "It's going to be a dilly," I said.

It had come into my mind, full blown, as Georgina talked. There was no way we were going to be able to simply walk out of the house, down to the main gate, and then hail a cab. The staff in the house had to be diverted, and so effectively that we'd be able to slip out unnoticed.

So I decided to burn the house down.

The peat moss insulation would ignite like bone dry tinder. From what I'd seen there had to be tons of it up there in the crawlspace, and once lit it would be very hard to put out. It wouldn't take long for the fire to reach the upper floors, alerting the staff, and when it did and the alarm was sounded, we could make our break. I was adding arson to my list of crimes.

I told Georgina to wait by the door and keep a watch posted. Frowning, she did as she was told, biting back her questions. There was some notepaper in the desk by the window and I twisted it together into a crude torch. Then I went back into the closet, getting up on a chair to reach the trap. I struggled through the hole, then made my way up the U-bolts to the crawlspace.

I flicked on the lighter and put the flame to the spill of paper. It flared, tossing shadows up into the rafters. I held up the torch and paused, realizing the enormity of what I was doing. It was a beautiful house and I was about to destroy it. But there was no other way. I tossed the torch into the insulation and waited to see if it would ignite.

I needn't have bothered. The torch landed in one of the squares of peat moss and it exploded into white hot flame, the concussion of indrawn air almost knocking me off my perch. Within an instant it had jumped to the next square beyond the joists and the flames had begun to lick up the nearest support upright into the rafters. It was going to be one hell of a bonfire.

I squirmed back down, re-entered the closet, and jumped off the chair. Georgina was at the door.

"It's lit," I muttered. "Let's get out of here!"

Georgina checked to make sure the way was clear and then opened the door wider, motioning me silently. I followed her out into the hall. We padded along to the main staircase and went around it. From the main floor I could hear the sound of muffled voices. We hurried on, continuing along the corridor past a dozen closed doors, eventually reaching the end of the wing. I smiled with relief. She'd been right. A set of narrow stairs led downward at a steep angle. We stopped at the head of the stairs and I cocked an ear. Everything seemed quiet. Not for long.

We went down the stairs, wincing at every squeak, and eventually reached the main floor. The stairs ended in a narrow windowless antechamber, lit by a single bleak bulb in the ceiling. There were two doors out of the room, one clearly leading onto the main floor hallway, the other far larger and closed with a large bolt. Both bolt and hinges were rusted. It hadn't been used for a long time. I pointed to it and whispered in Georgina's ear. The long blonde fall of her hair smelled of Pears soap.

"Where do you suppose that leads?"

"Probably outside," she whispered back. "We're on the side closest to the old coach house."

"Good," I replied, "that's the way we go then." I stepped across the little room and tried easing the bolt back, wishing desperately for a can of oil. With a lot of tugging the bolt released gratingly. I opened the door a crack and was met by a fan of cool night air. We slipped out into the darkness and I closed the door behind us.

I found myself standing on a narrow brick path, the walkway to the coach house. Directly overhead was a low roof that swept down in open arches on either side. I peered into the night and as my eyes adjusted I slowly began picking out the brooding shape of the mansard roofed building one hundred feet away. I looked to the right. A broad curtain of light fell on the gravelled path of the drive from the main hall. The light faded short of the walkway; we'd be able to cross unseen.

We started forward but I suddenly felt Georgina's hand on my arm, pulling me back against the shadows of the wall. I turned to her, mouth open to speak, but she raised a finger to her lips. She pulled me close.

"Listen!" she hissed.

Somewhere to the right I could hear the sounds of feet crunching on gravel and the slight clinking of a chain. The roving beam of a flashlight swung across the arches of the walkway. One of the guards! I held my breath and sank into the shadows, praying that the Doberman he was leading wouldn't pick up our scent. I closed my eyes tightly and waited.

The footsteps grew louder and I could actually make out the soft sounds of the dog's paws striking the ground. An awful vision of the creature's lolling tongue and sharp gleaming fangs reeled into my brain and I tried to ooze into the wall by strength of will alone. Now I could hear the animal's hot panting breath. All the guard had to do was turn the corner and that would be the end of it. My throat filled with the acid taste of bile. I was sure that I'd be sick.

Then all hell broke loose. A loud clanging sound rose out of the house, joined almost immediately by the wail of a siren splitting the night. Instantly, lights began snapping on in the upper floor of the coach house and the sound of the bell and the siren was joined by shouting voices. Georgina and I stood frozen against the wall.

A door opened in the coach house and half a dozen figures were silhouetted in the light from the interior. They were all armed with what looked like automatic weapons. The figures began racing towards the main house, shouting back and forth to each other as they ran in front of us. When they disappeared, so had the guard with the dog. I waited for a few moments, making sure that no stragglers would appear, then grabbed Georgina's hand, pulling her away from the wall. We tore along the walkway and across the now brilliantly lit front of the coach house to the open door. If anyone from the main house looked our way we were as good as dead. We sprinted the last few feet and went through the door at a dead run. I closed it behind me. The light had come from a lamp at the bottom of the stairs, the rest of the main floor of the garage was in darkness.

"Some diversion," panted Georgina beside me. I ignored her and looked around, trying to make out details. I found myself staring at a huge car, twenty feet long at least, with a peaked hood and a squared off windshield. The massive batwing fenders looked big enough to allow the thing to take flight.

"What the hell is that?" I whispered.

"Rolls Royce Wraith, 1936," supplied Georgina, still breathing hard.

"Car buff?" I asked.

"Something like that." She finally caught her breath. "Are we going to use it?"

"Not if I can find something better," I said. "Stealing a car like that would be like driving around with a sign saying 'arrest me.'"

"There," said Georgina, pointing into the gloom. I followed her finger. Half-hidden behind the Rolls was another car. Two of them in fact. A sports car and a Land Rover.

"Healey 3000," said Georgina, looking at the sports car.

"Forget it," I said. "We need a bit of weight."

We climbed into the Rover.

"No keys," said Georgina.

"So what?" I squeezed down below the wheel, and calling up almost forgotten adolescent skills I managed to hotwire the car. The engine flared and caught. "Get the door," I said, over the sound of the motor.

Georgina slipped out of the Land Rover and crossed the floor of the garage. I gave her the high sign and she heaved the modern overhead up along its tracks. I could spot running figures silhouetted against the brilliantly-lit facade of the house. Orange flames were licking out all along the roof line. No one seemed to be paying any attention to us at all. Georgina ran back to the Rover and climbed in, banging the door shut behind her. I ran through the main set of gears once to make sure I had the sequence, found first again, and popped the clutch. We lurched out of the coach house and I turned down the drive, picking up as much speed as I could.

It wasn't enough. Someone started whacking the Rover with a ball-peen hammer and there was the sound of breaking glass behind me. "Down!" I yelled.

In the distance behind us I could hear the chatter of a submachine gun. Our escape hadn't gone completely unnoticed. Suddenly the interior of the Rover filled with the rank odour of gasoline. Georgina squinted back over the seat.

"They've hit one of the jerry cans of petrol!" she shouted.

I put my foot to the floor and prayed that they weren't using nickel-jacketed bullets. One spark off a ricochet and we'd go up like a bomb with all those fumes. We hit a bend in the drive and the house blanked out behind the screening trees. Half a mile later we reached the gate and I pulled to a stop.

Georgina had been right. A stone wall ran off on either side. It was at least ten feet high. The gates were even higher. I leaned forward and checked through the windshield. The wall was stopped by a triple strand of barbed wire and strung through the wire I could see the small white shapes of insulators. High tension. I located the headlight switch on the dashboard and flicked them on. The gate came into view clearly. Wrought iron with bars two inches thick. I couldn't see any insulators on the gate but that didn't mean anything. The gatelock was impressive. A rectangular box a foot square and without any visible keyhole. Electronic, probably controlled from the house. I also noticed a pair of squat little Sony monitors perched on either hingepost, equipped with infra-red emitters. Mr. Llewellyn, or whoever he was, believed in security.

"What are we going to do?" asked Georgina. She'd cranked down her window and was fanning away the fumes from the leaking gas can in the back.

"Break it down," I answered.

I'd been expecting something like this, which was why I'd chosen the Rover over the faster Healey. I banged the gears around until I had it in reverse and then whined the vehicle back a hundred feet. I hit the four wheel drive engage, switched to the four by four gearbox, and kicked my foot down. I had a strange feeling of otherworldliness as the gate loomed up in the headlights, almost as though I was watching the whole thing in a movie theatre. I wondered calmly whether the electric shock would kill us before the current ignited the gasoline and turned us into Roman candles.

We hit at about forty miles per hour. The heavy front end of the Rover rammed home and the edge of the steering wheel smashed into my abdomen. Then the air around us was filled with flying metal as the gates tore open and we sailed through. The rear end fishtailed, sending the car into the left side gatepost. The sidelong collision with the stone pillar jerked the wheel out of my hands and for a wild moment I lost control. One headlight had smashed. The other poked its beam up into the sky as we tore across the road and vainly tried to climb the embankment on the far side. I managed to get my hands back on the wheel and wrestled with it, turning us towards the road. We bumped down hard on the pavement, the impact knocking my breath away. I had enough sense to disengage the four wheel drive and then we were off down the narrow crack pavement highway, dark trees like clutching ghosts whirling by on either side.

I kept my foot to the floor for the next twenty kilometres, struggling to keep the top heavy vehicle on the road as we swept around curves and up and down hills. There was no one else on the road ahead of us and no headlights behind. It looked like we'd pulled it off, at least for the moment.

I caught a glimpse of a roadsign and slowed. "Where the hell is High Wycombe?" I asked.

"The Chiltern Hills," said Georgina. "Buckinghamshire. It's about forty miles from London."

I pulled the Rover onto the grass shoulder. "You drive," I said. We played musical chairs around the Land Rover, switching seats. Georgina settled down behind the wheel and we moved off.

"Where exactly are we going?" she asked, glancing over at me.

Exhausted, I let my head fall back against the seat, and closed my eyes. "Montreal," I muttered.

PART TWO

•

Execution Cycle

Execution Cycle: That part of a control cycle in which an instruction, having been accessed, is performed.

Chapter Eleven

I was born in the US and brought up in Canada. Travelling back and forth between the two countries I discovered an essential fact about the North American personality. It is bus oriented. You might see people getting on and off airplanes in films and on television, and they'll tell you that it was the railroad that tied both the US and Canada together; but the bus is far and away the people's choice. Less than half the population of North America has ever been on an airplane, and less than 20 per cent have travelled by train. Everyone's been on a bus at one time or another.

And it shows in every transportation centre I've ever been in. They all look like bus terminals. Formed plastic chairs, cigarette machines, hotdog buns microwaved to death, sleeping drunks, overflowing wastebaskets, and that single guy in blue overalls with a pushbroom coming out of his fist like a prosthetic arm. Penn Station in New York is no exception. It lurks below Madison Square Garden looking for all the world like the chrome and formica interior of a Greyhound.

Georgina was going to have another one of her quiet furies. She'd been having them all the way across the city of London, at Heathrow, in mid-ocean, and at JFK. You could tell she was having one by the way her lips thinned and her eyes narrowed. Once in a while she'd say something, just to let you know she was still mad.

She started again on the escalators down from the Seventh Avenue entrance, hissing at me vitriolically. "I still think this is insane," she said. "You carry me off on this wild goose chase to the bloody ends of the earth and then you don't even get us where you want to go. We should have gone to the authorities in London. I mean, my God, we were kidnapped, held against our will!"

"I explained that," I replied, sighing and knowing full well I was wasting my breath. "The first flight out was to New York. There was no flight to Mirabel until the next day. By going to New York and then taking the train to Montreal we

113

might shake them off our tail. Your friend Llewellyn knows I'll be heading there; he'll have someone watching every incoming flight. This way we sneak in the back door—"

She cut in. "And what about the police? They would have protected us, *and* dealt with Llewellyn. The man is a criminal!"

"Yeah, and you're a Lord's daughter. I know all about it," I said wearily. We reached the bottom of the escalator, stepped off, and crossed the low ceilinged lobby to the ticket counter.

"Well?" she demanded, as we joined the line.

I checked the screen over the ticket window. The Montrealer was leaving in twenty minutes. "Well what?" I asked; shuffling forward as the line moved.

"Why *don't* we go to the police?"

I was just about ready to let her have five in the head. "I've been over this with you a dozen times already," I groaned. "We know Llewellyn is a kidnapper, a killer, and God knows what else. Nobody else does, and the guy has got a lot of clout. I'm wanted in France already and you and I are both involved in an arson in England, not to mention car theft."

"*You* set that fire!" she snapped.

"And you're an accessory. Forget it George old girl, the cops are out. Even if we had gone to them in London they probably wouldn't have believed us and we would have been out in the street. I want to put as much distance between myself and Llewellyn as possible. If you want to hop on the next flight back to London, you're welcome to. As far as I'm concerned you're just a lot of trouble and you're probably going to wind up getting me killed. So either shut up or take a walk!"

"You're an insufferable bastard!" she snarled.

"And you're an incredible little bitch," I answered.

We moved forward in the line.

"And in the future, don't address me as George," she said icily.

"How about Lady Underwood?" I offered, turning my back on her. She made a small choking sound behind me. I reached the head of the line. There were only two kinds of seating left on the train—bedrooms and coach. The thought of spending the entire night awake and sitting up beside Sam's sister was enough to send shivers down my spine.

Being holed up in the same room with her wasn't much better, but at least I'd be able to sleep.

"Bedroom," I said. "For two. One way."

"Husband and wife?" asked the clerk sleepily.

I winced and then nodded. "Right," I said. Georgina had heard and was going apoplectic. I paid for the ticket with my American Express card and then dragged her out of the line before she made a scene, propelling her by the elbow across the concourse to the head of the stairs leading down to the Montrealer Gate. There was already a crowd waiting at the barrier.

"Relax," I muttered to her, "I wouldn't touch you with a ten foot pole."

She tugged her arm away and shot me a rattlesnake smile. "It's just the thought of you being my husband that's turning my stomach," she said.

There was no point in rising to it so I just shrugged and kept my mouth shut. The only time we'd been civil to each other was under the threat of imminent execution. I promised myself that I'd ask her why she hated me so much if we ever had the time. A few minutes later a grizzled looking man with a pot belly wearing a grey Amtrak uniform raised the barrier. We went down to the platform and climbed into the waiting train.

Amtrak bedrooms are much the same as the ones you'll find in Europe, with the exception that they all include toilets. There is the same bunk bed arrangement, the same fold down sink, and an almost identical panel of switches. There is also a small compartment for your shoes that can be opened from the corridor. The idea behind this is to have the attendant polish your shoes while you sleep, but I've never known anyone with the guts to do it.

We squeezed into the compartment and Georgina immediately sat down on the lower bunk, legs crossed, foot bouncing up and down. I stood in the narrow space between the bunk and the wall, undecided. I peeked at myself in the mirror above the sink. Once again I looked like hell. I hadn't had a bath since the one in the Cameo Hotel two days before, and I was wearing the same clothes I'd been needlegunned in. They were also the clothes I'd clambered around in up in Llewellyn's attic, and the ones I'd flown out in. The suit was

wrinkled and dusty, and my once crisp cotton broadcloth shirt
was greyed and limp. I grunted out a cigarette-scarred chuckle.

"What on earth have you found to laugh at?" muttered
Georgina.

I looked at her reflection in the mirror and actually smiled.
"It's one of those times when I really do look as bad as I feel."

She looked confused. "I don't see the joke," she said.

"That's because you look pretty good," I said. And she did,
from the cuffs of her designer jeans to the pale doeskin jacket
and grey silk shirt she wore. Her hair was neatly done in a
long single braid she'd worked at on the plane, and there
wasn't a trace of fatigue on her face. I consoled myself with
the thought that she'd climbed out of her bath and into the
fray. I had a fleeting image of her standing naked in that room
and I smiled again.

"*Now* what's so funny?"

"Nothing, nothing at all," I said quickly. She made a
grumping sound but something between us had warmed a
trifle. I went and sat down beside her on the bottom bunk.
We both stared out at the barren platform for a moment.

"Well—" I began.

"Look, I—" she said, almost at the same time.

"You first," I said.

She reddened slightly, and frowned. "I'd like a cigarette if
you don't mind."

I gave her one and took another for myself. "I didn't know
you smoked," I commented.

"I don't," she answered, puffing. "I just wanted one..."

"You were saying?" I prodded.

She coughed on a lungful of smoke. "I've been a bit of a
prig," she said, recovering. I let it lie, afraid to interrupt. If I
nodded in agreement she'd probably bite my head off. "I get
that way when I'm frightened," she went on. "I'm afraid I
sound rather like my father when his taxes go up or someone
does something foolish in the House."

"You've been okay," I inserted. I tried to keep the grin off
my face. She was apologizing!

"No, really," she said. "I didn't know what was happening.
It was all so terribly melodramatic. I felt like a kidnapped
heiress. I mean that kind of thing doesn't happen in real life
you know."

"Tell that to the Lindbergh baby. Or Aldo Moro. It's real enough."

"Yes, but that's in the newspapers. This was happening to me! So I really did my best to pretend that it wasn't happening at all..."

"And I ruined it by coming through your closet ceiling and then setting fire to the house," I said.

"Yes, something like that. You *were* a bit of a shock. You made me realize just how dangerous a position I was in."

"We're still in it," I cautioned. "This thing isn't over yet by any stretch."

"Yes," she said thoughtfully. "I'm beginning to see that." She butted her half-smoked cigarette. "Anyway," she said, looking at me, "I'm sorry if I've been awful."

"That's all right," I said. There was a long pause. The train jerked and began to move.

"Pax?" she said. "I promise to be less of a gadfly." Her eyes were large, and marvellously dark.

"Pax," I agreed. She smiled. We left the main terminal and dropped down into the maze of tunnels that would eventually take us under the Hudson River to the Jersey side. Annoyed, I realized she was getting to me.

"You were going to say something before I began...all this," she said.

I nodded. "Um," I admitted. "I was going to tell you that your fly was down."

She glanced at herself, then back at me, eyes blazing. I stood and hotfooted it up the ladder to the top bunk.

"You really *are* a bastard!"

But there was laughter in her voice. I lay back on the pillow feeling quite unreasonably happy.

It didn't last. By three in the morning sleep was still eluding me and the pleasure at my peace with Georgina was long gone. My only reminder of it was the soft sound of her breathing in the bottom bunk. I lay in the dark as we roared through Connecticut, fighting to keep the demons away.

The whole thing was catching up with me, and I felt a yawning sense of insecurity that was threatening to turn into a full fledged case of the screaming meemies at any moment. Question after question tugged me in opposing directions, and I began to lose all sense of time and space. I was out of my depth and out of my element. I was a journalist, an observer, not an active participant. The dramas and tragedies and terrors of life were there only to be noted and explained to some amorphous group I called "the public." But I was caught, trapped, hooked, anything you wanted to call it. Instead of doing the sane thing and running like hell, I was on a train that was taking me right back into the whole obscene scenario. And I had no choice. Either I discovered the source of what was going on and got away with enough evidence to prove it, or I was doomed. I'd seen enough and heard enough to know that this wasn't some mock battle or game of chess where defeat could be conceded. This was an equation as pure and unloving as the dots and dashes of current that made a computer work. It was yes or no, black or white, live or die. If we ran, Llewellyn would find us, and having found us, he would kill us.

In Vietnam I'd met men who thrived on that kind of program for life. I didn't. It terrified me, and I wanted out. But there was no way out, and that began the foul sequence of thought in my head once again; a snake swallowing its own tail. A noose of anxiety was choking me slowly, but inevitably.

Georgina's voice, ghostly in the dark and the dull, muffled sound of our passage, pulled me back from the black hole of my thoughts.

"Peter."

Christ! How long had she been awake? It was a struggle to breathe let alone talk. "Yes?"

"I'd like to ask you a question."

"Okay."

"I don't want you to get the wrong idea," she said shyly.

"I won't," I responded absurdly.

"All right. Well..." She paused. I waited. "It's silly really, but it's been bothering me."

"I said it was okay," I answered.

"When you saw me," she began. She stopped and I could hear her taking a breath. She started over. "When you saw me after you dropped into my room, what did you think? I mean, about me that is."

"The way you looked?" I said into the air.

"Yes," she said quietly.

"I thought you looked beautiful," I said. And it was the truth.

"I'm glad," she said. "Goodnight, Peter."

"Goodnight," I said. And a few minutes later we were both asleep.

Chapter Twelve

After Paris, Montreal is the largest French-speaking city in the world. The similarities end with the language, and even that isn't accurate. My French is perfectly usable in Montreal, but in France I have to repeat everything at least twice. The Québécois have fought like hell to keep culturally virgin, but over the decades every aspect of life and language in La Belle Province has been hit by creeping MacDonaldism. In Paris you'd order "un steak haché avec une portion de crudites." In Montreal it's "un hamburg avec le works." Pepsi is as endemic to Quebec as wine is to France.

The city itself reflects its North American origins and way of life. La Vieux Montreal, the Old City, is a tiny enclave of buildings dating back a couple of hundred years and looking like a failing hamlet in the Loire. The rest of Montreal seethes with huge skyscrapers, rambling suburbs, and gigantic shopping centres, sprinkled liberally with firetrap slums, a classically rundown waterfront, and the belching smokestacks of industry. Topping the whole kaleidoscope off are the science fiction installations of Expo 67 on Île St. Hélène, and the ziggurat and starship complex of the Olympic site. It is a city trying to live in its past, present, and future simultaneously; an urban centre of almost three million people that can't seem to make up its mind.

It was also boiling hot. We came up the escalator from Central Station and stepped into a steambath. Montreal was in the midst of a heat wave. Even the stodgy Victorian bulk of the old Sun Life Insurance building across the street looked wilted. The chrome and glass tower of the Bank of Montreal head office stood like a burning spear in the harsh mid-morning sun that beat down from a cloudless sky.

"Good God!" said Georgina. "I thought Canada was the land of ice and snow."

"That's the first half of the year," I grinned. "The second half is all heat and humidity."

"It's bloody awful," she said. "An hour of this and my entire body will evaporate."

"Come on," I said, pointing up Mansfield. "I know a nice cold restaurant we can cool off in." The light changed and we moved with the rest of the slow-moving assembly of lightly dressed pedestrians.

"What's that?" asked Georgina, pointing ahead. "It looks rather religious." She was staring up at The Mountain, and the large steel beam cross on its summit. The tall, tree covered hill is almost the exact centre of Montreal, with the city laid out at its feet in a massive sprawling circle.

"It's the mountain the city's named after," I explained. "Mount Royal. In French—Mont Réal. I've never been able to figure out what the cross is for, all I know is that it glows in the dark. Neon lit."

"If the city is named after the mountain, why isn't it pronounced Mont-real, instead of the way you do it, Moe-ree-all?" she asked, as we walked up the hill towards St. Catherine's Street.

"They've been debating questions like that for years," I smiled. "Language is a sore point here. That's why all the signs are in French. You won't see much English in Montreal, or anywhere else in Quebec for that matter."

"It seems rather childish," frowned Georgina.

"Only to us Anglos," I said.

We reached St. Catherine's and headed west. We could have taken a cab, but I was enjoying the exercise after so much time spent in transit, as well as the security of being on relatively familiar ground. It was good to be on home turf. For a few minutes I could forget about the problems which lay ahead.

Even in the incredible heat the shoppers were out in full force. We wove our way through the chattering swarms of people all looking for bargains in any of a thousand stores of all descriptions that lined both sides of the bustling street. After half a dozen blocks, Georgina began giving me looks.

"What's the problem?" I asked.

"We've passed at least twenty restaurants," she said.

"I'm heading for a special one," I answered.

We kept on walking for another five minutes before we reached our destination. I steered Georgina into the foyer of Pauzies, which rates as one of the top seafood restaurants in the world. At eleven o'clock in the morning it was also guaranteed to be quiet.

The decor of Pauzies is Cape Cod Motel Modern: lights recessed behind frosted glass portholes, fish nets on the ceiling, and seashells everywhere. But it's dim, air-conditioned, spacious, and friendly.

The restaurant was almost empty and the crisply uniformed waitresses were laying out the place settings for the one o'clock rush. I led Georgina to one of the big comfortable booths that run along one side of the restaurant, and she sank down onto the leather seat gratefully.

"I may never walk again," she sighed. She drained the glass of cold water the waitress set before her and the woman refilled it. The waitress left menus and then went back to her work with the knives and forks.

"They have kippers," I suggested.

Georgina laughed. "I hate to go against the mythology." She smiled. "But actually, I hate kippers. I spend the entire day smelling like the Fulton Fish Market. Seafood omelet and coffee for me."

I decided to have the same and caught our waitress' eye. I ordered, and then settled back in my seat. We sat there silently until the food came, lost in our own thoughts. Mine were a combination of admiration and apprehension.

The food arrived and Georgina brightened with her first taste of the perfectly fluffed omelet. "It's terrific!" she said.

"You sound surprised," I answered. "The days of living on caribou pemmican and spruce-bark tea are over."

Her eyes flared and she put down her fork. "Don't be so defensive," she said. "You may take all this running around without batting an eyelash, but I don't. Less than thirty-six hours ago I was in England. Twelve hours ago I was in New York. Now I'm in Montreal. I've been kidnapped and shot at and I still have no real idea why. So don't bristle like some pompous little colonial ass. I've been walking around in a fog. I'm disoriented, and anything even vaguely pleasant and normal, like this bloody omelet, is a relief. All right?" She started eating again.

"Sorry," I said. "I guess I'm a little out of whack myself."

We finished in silence. The coffee came and I lit a cigarette, leaning back. Georgina gave a discreet belch behind her napkin and sighed contentedly.

"Okay," she said. "Now what?"

"We go into hiding," I said. "At least you do."

"Explain that last bit," she said, her voice gone cold again. "It sounds just ever so slightly chauvinistic."

"It's not," I said, knowing that I was treading on thin ice. "It's simple common sense."

"Go on."

"I have a colleague here with an apartment. He spends his summers in the eastern townships: his place is going to be empty. I know where he keeps the key, so we can use his apartment as a base. We could both do with a bath and a change of clothes."

"Keep going," said Georgina.

"I want you to stay there," I said, after a pause. "There's no point in both of us getting involved with this." I looked across the table. Her whole face was freezing over. I plugged on. "Look, this is my home territory. I have friends and contacts here. I can figure out what's going on, gather some leads together, then maybe go to the authorities. But it's crazy to have both of us in a potentially dangerous position."

"So you go off, spear in hand, and I'm left to mind the cave and deal with the trash," said Georgina acidly. "Perhaps do a bit of mending on the side." Her nostrils flared. "Well, bugger you," she snapped.

"It makes sense," I insisted.

She shook her head, the single braid swinging. "It doesn't make any sense at all," she replied. "In fact, it's ludicrous."

"Why?" I asked defensively.

"You really are a bit of an idiot," she said, still shaking her head. "You said this man is a colleague of yours, the one with the apartment. What's his name?"

"Claude Carrierre, he works for Montreal *Matin*."

"And how long have you known him?"

"Seven or eight years. We've done work together from time to time. What are you getting at?"

She sighed. "I hate to sound like a first form teacher, but it should be obvious, Peter. If this fellow Claude is a friend of yours, other people are going to know about it. According to you Mr. Llewellyn has ears everywhere. What's to prevent his bully boys from coming to dear old Claude's apartment and doing me in while you're away?"

"That's a bit far-fetched," I said.

"Like hell. You said it yourself last night. Being a kid-napped heiress is far-fetched, but it happens. It happened to me. And so did that episode you told me about in your hotel room in Paris. And that fire and those bullets weren't fig-ments of my imagination either." She wagged her finger at me. "No, Peter, we'll leave Claude's place alone. A nice anonymous hotel room under assumed names, and me stick-ing with you every minute thank you very much."

"Every minute?" I quipped, unable to resist.

She gave me a withering glance. "Please," she said.

I took a drag on my cigarette and thought about it. She was probably being paranoid, but this affair was awash in para-noia. The plan that had been slowly evolving in my mind hadn't considered her as a factor but I could tell from the look on her face that I'd have to make her fit one way or another.

"Okay," I agreed.

"Many thanks, sahib," she said, her lip curling slightly. As far as she was concerned this should obviously be a joint effort; she didn't like the idea of a "boss." I was also beginning to understand that it wasn't chauvinism that had made me want to exclude her, it was the reverse. I was worrying about my own inadequacies and the possibility that some dumbass move on my part would get her hurt—which was a twisted kind of paternalism. I sighed, and for a moment I found myself wishing that Sam's sister had been a wart-nosed cretin rather than a stunning and intelligent woman with a mind of her own. The effect she was starting to have on me was confusing, and that was the last thing I wanted.

"I don't suppose you'd consider going back to England, maybe go to your father's place?" I asked, giving it one last try.

Georgina shot me one of those familiar withering glances. I was actually becoming fond of them. "No," she said, the word loaded with two thousand years' worth of Anglo-Saxon aris-tocracy.

For some reason I was overcome by an overwhelming desire to kiss her, but the sour-plum look on her face warned me off. "Well," I muttered lamely, "I just thought I'd ask."

"I appreciate your concern," she said, a little of the acid

leaving her voice. Then she actually smiled. "Just don't do it again, agreed?"

"Agreed." I smiled back. I was beginning to think there was hope for us after all.

We checked into the Château Champlain, a tall single tower hotel with half moon windows that make the building look like a giant cheese-grater. The Champlain is located a block or so away from Central Station and is connected to it by the maze of underground shopping alleys that make up Place Bonaventure and Place Ville Marie. I gave my American Express Card its head once again, and by the time we got to our room on the twentieth floor we were both outfitted. I was back to jeans and T-shirts and a new leather jacket. Georgina opted for a pair of sandals and a short summer dress. What we'd been wearing was sent to the cleaners. Georgina took her new clothes into the bathroom with her when she showered. She came out fully dressed. I did the same. I ordered a pot of coffee and sandwiches from room service and then dialled housekeeping for a pair of scissors.

"What are the scissors for?" asked Georgina. She was sitting in one of the grey velvet armchairs leafing through a copy of Montreal *Life*. I sat down across the coffee table from her and gave her the bad news.

Your hair," I said. "It goes."

She stiffened and grabbed her braid. "Why?" she said, startled.

"Because you already stand out like a searchlight," I explained. "We're going to have to do some snooping around at Mirabel, right in Llewellyn's backyard. They'll have descriptions for both of us, so we change. I bought a box of Clairol brunette while you were shopping for that dress. Your days of being a blonde are over."

"It's ridiculous!" she sputtered.

I shrugged. "It's better than nothing."

"I'll go to a beauty salon," she offered.

I shook my head. "We don't have time for that. I'm going to cut it off shoulder length. Blunt. Then you're going to turn it brown."

She fumed, but finally she agreed. The scissors were delivered and in ten minutes a foot of braid was lying on the bathroom floor. She grabbed the hair colouring out of my hand and slammed the door in my face. I sat down with a cup of coffee and waited. Half an hour later she reappeared, towelling her hair. She had changed completely. The darker hair made her look shorter and not as attractive. The cutting was fair, but still amateur.

"I'll never forgive you for this," she said, slumping down onto the edge of the bed.

I poured her a cup of coffee from the beaker. "It can't be helped," I said, trying to soothe her.

She sipped at the coffee and then frowned. "There's only one bed," she said. "Where are you going to sleep?"

I raised an eyebrow. "Relax," I grinned. "I'm not going to be sleeping here. Neither are you."

"I don't understand," she said, looking at me quizzically. I suppressed a laugh. Her hair was still damp and stood out all over her head. She looked like an overgrown twelve-year-old.

"This room was just to get our bearings," I said. "I want to get out to Mirabel this evening. We can check into the Airport Hotel. Separate rooms, separate check-in, different names. It might throw them off the track if they're looking."

"Won't it be dangerous staying there?" she asked.

"No more than anywhere else," I shrugged. "Hopefully they'll assume that we haven't even come into Canada yet. They'll be watching the arrivals gate, not the hotel lobby. Anyway, there's really no place else. I want to take a good look at the Gambetta office, and find out what this Alpha thing I told you about is. Mirabel's out in a farmer's field, there's nothing else for miles around."

"And how do we get there?" she asked.

"I was just about to arrange it," I said. I went to the house phone and dialled the Hertz number.

In terms of actual area Mirabel is far and away the largest airport in the world, covering a total of eighty-eight thousand acres of clay-based farmland an hour north of Montreal on the Autoroute. The size, however, isn't representative; most of the land is undeveloped and classified as a "buffer zone." The land around the actual terminal and runways, as well as the distance from Montreal, means that unlike most major airports Mirabel has no curfew—it can take off and land aircraft twenty-four hours a day.

During the late sixties the Mirabel project incited near riots on environmental grounds; at the time, such a huge area of land seemed unnecessary. During the seventies, when the old Montreal airport at Dorval was becoming overcrowded, attention swung away from the environmental to the economic. Scandals swarmed around the construction of Mirabel like bees around a hive, and for a time it looked as though the project would never be completed. When the airport was eventually opened in 1975, everyone said it was the biggest white elephant ever produced by the federal government. Almost no planes were landing there and the terminal was usually empty. By the eighties things had changed. More than thirty airlines were using Mirabel regularly, and it had become one of the main centres of passenger and cargo transport in North America. The Château de l'Aéroport was putting up in-transit guests from all over the world, and the duty free shops were doing a roaring trade.

We arrived at the airport in the late afternoon and checked into the Château separately. Georgina was on the third floor of the four-hundred-room hotel, and I was on the fifth. Pleading fatigue, jet-lag, and general malaise, Georgina stayed in her room while I went on a reconnaissance of the airport. I crossed the pedestrian walkway over the main arrivals roadway and entered the immense terminal building.

The design of the Mirabel terminal is simple and straightforward. It is a single, cantilevered rectangle of tinted glass, concrete, and steel one hundred yards wide and four football fields long. According to the system, you're supposed to park your car on any of three underground levels, taking a space closest to the sign for the airline you're interested in. Take the nearest escalator and you should wind up within a hundred feet of that airline's arrival gate on the main floor of the terminal.

The main floor of the terminal is divided roughly in three along its length. The arrivals zone, fronted by a fifty foot high wall of glass that overlooks the landing apron, is a kind of no-man's-land, itself cut in two by a seemingly endless row of orange customs booths. Once past customs, the passenger crosses to the baggage area. If there is any question about his or her declaration there's a further customs check here. The baggage retrieval area and its dozens of carousels is overlooked by the second floor observation deck. Baggage in hand, the passenger proceeds into the third and final area, the concourse. From here the passenger either hops a bus or cab on the main level, or heads down into the parking garage. As far as I could remember, no actual flight control was centred in the terminal; that's what I'd taken my walk to find out.

After meandering down the length of the concourse and up onto the observation level I found a Transport Canada booth and picked up a brochure on the airport. I took the booklet to the Ceil Volant bar with its open-air ceiling of dangling kites, and settled down with a pint of draft. The sun was already beginning to set, dusting the interior of the terminal with a milky deep sea light, and I had to strain to read the brochure, flipping through it until I found a general layout diagram. I ignored the constant flow of chattering people and tried to figure out the site plan.

The terminal and the hotel occupied a central position on an artificial hill or plateau, with access roads and cloverleafs on either side. The main aprons and remote gate clusters for VIP's were directly in front of the main terminal, with taxiways leading left and right to the two runways, Alpha and Bravo. The control tower was located beside the link taxiway that joined the two runways, and was surrounded by a cluster of general service buildings including the rescue centre, the central heating plant, and the fuel tank farm. Further to the northwest, parallel with Runway Alpha, was the cargo area, connected to the control tower and service complex by an interior road, and linked directly to the main road leading to the passenger terminal.

I took a slug of the now flat mug of beer and lit a cigarette. The terminal was emptying out, and the interior lights were coming on. It was the lull before the evening transatlantic departures.

I was pretty sure the answer to all my questions lay somewhere in that cargo area. The Gambetta office and the Alpha company would almost certainly be there. The problem was how to get there. Not literally, that would be easy enough in the Mustang I'd rented—but with a legitimate reason. You can wander around the passenger terminal at an airport for hours and no one will pay any attention, but a cargo area is something else. Without a reason for being there, Georgina and I would be marked within a few minutes.

Nothing came to mind, so I pocketed the brochure and headed back down to the main level. There was one other thing I could check on.

The AVTOUR ticket counter was located at the extreme end of the concourse next to Royal Air Maroc. The counter was closed for the night: computer terminal shrouded. I checked the spaghetti board behind the vacant desk. There was a flight due in the following day at noon. I had a quick look at their poster, which was displayed on a chrome stand beside the computer terminal. It showed a DC-10 in flight, from above, the sun glinting down on the slightly overweight-looking fuselage. It was the first time I'd seen the company's product: a huge jet in dark blue, a five storey high stylized "A" in gold on the tail. I turned away and headed for the hotel. Come hell or high water I was going to be somewhere close by when that flight came in the following day.

Chapter Thirteen

It was five to twelve. Georgina and I sat in the Mustang awaiting the arrival of the AVTOUR flight. I'd parked the car on the grass shoulder of the main road to the passenger terminal, halfway between it and the cargo area. We had a clear view to the north, encompassing both runways, the sunblazed glass sarcophagus of the terminal, and the windowless brick bulk of the cargo building. The only thing in our way was a ten foot high chain link fence topped by a triple strand of barbed wire. Georgina had her head out the window, scanning the hot blue and cloudless sky with a pair of binoculars.

The whole thing had been her idea, described to me that morning in the hotel restaurant over breakfast.

"There's no way of knowing if there's going to be any contraband on the flight," said Georgina, talking around a mouthful of toast and Dundee marmalade. "So why take the chance of being caught out at the cargo terminal? We can sit in the car somewhere just off the road and watch the flight arrive. If it *does* have any cargo on board it should move off to the cargo area once the passengers get off, right? If there's no cargo we won't have taken any risk." I nodded my agreement, mildly annoyed that I hadn't thought of it myself. I didn't think of the binoculars either; Georgina picked them up in one of the shops in the hotel lobby, along with a Nikon with a 500mm lens and half a dozen rolls of Tri-X black and white. The binoculars made sense, but I couldn't figure out the camera, and I told her so. She grinned.

"Evidence, dear fellow," she said. "If we get out of this alive we're going to have to come out of it with proof." Once again she'd hit on a good idea. I was both chagrined and pleased; far from being a burden, Georgina Underwood was fast becoming a valuable asset. Nailing AVTOUR on film had never occurred to me.

"See anything yet?" I asked.

Georgina shook her head without taking her eyes off the sky. "Just some small planes," she muttered.

"There's a commercial field marked on the site plan," I said. "It's in behind the cargo area. A STOL port as well."

"STOL?" said Georgina, without turning around.

"It stands for Short Takeoff and Landing," I explained, glad to be able to show off some expertise. "I think they run shuttle flights between here and Ottawa. It's—"

"There!" broke in Georgina, the binoculars steadying. "There it is!" I leaned across the seat and looked over her shoulder. I couldn't see a thing. Georgina popped open the door on her side and stepped out onto the grass. I followed her, and she handed me the binoculars. "To the left," she instructed. "Over the terminal." I put the glasses to my eyes and adjusted the focus. For a moment I could see nothing but the featureless sky. Then I locked onto her.

The wide body jet was coming in to her final approach turn, the thick slab of her wings a darker blue against the sky. She turned, and for a moment I almost lost her. Then I picked up the familiar shape of the underslung engine pods as she completed the turn, and I caught a glimpse of the giant, glowing emblem on the tail. The jet was filling my field of vision and I could even see the darker smudges on the underside of the wings and on the engine pylons, caused by the wickedly hot exhaust. She was in full profile now, dropping quickly. Her undercarriage lowered; the flaps kicked down hard. Even at that distance I could hear the beginning thunder of her approach. Then she was gone, the final moments of touchdown hidden by the terminal as she dropped out of sight. I lowered the binoculars.

"Shouldn't be long now," I said. Georgina nodded, her face

tense. A wind came up from nowhere, slapping the thin fabric of the dress against her legs and driving motes of airborne dust into my eyes.

I ducked my head against the force of the breeze and felt around in my pockets for a cigarette. I lit one in a cupped hand and stared back out across the featureless desert of the tarmac on the far side of the fence. I felt a shiver of foreboding run through me as we waited for the jet to reappear. The out of scale buildings, the broad and barren runways, the road at my back, running away to nowhere, all combined like the components of some strange Fellini dream within a dream. An abandoned nightmare, props intact but all life gone.

An airport is nowhere, a limbo trapped between home and destination. I realized that we had been travelling in that nonexistent dimension since leaving London. If the AVTOUR jet headed towards the cargo bays the limbo would dissolve and reality would begin again. The quick and deadly reality my father had described to me so long ago. Curiosity, anger, and resolve deserted me. I wanted to run.

"Scary isn't it?" said Georgina. "This waiting." I nodded and she moved a little closer to me. Then the midnight blue of the DC-10 appeared. The AVTOUR jet was on the linking taxiway, headed either for the maintenance area far to the east, or the cargo terminal.

The jet, her fuselage more than three hundred feet long, lumbered slowly along the taxiway like an ancient dinosaur, the distant whispered howl of her turbines distorting the air, while silvered mirages shimmered around her on the ground, cast up from the baking heat of the asphalt. I lifted the binoculars and focused on her, letting my eyes rake the sleek dark hull, past the tinted windows to the cockpit. Sunlight danced on the windscreen, its five-sided single eye staring blindly forward. "All right, you bitch," I thought. "What's inside your belly?"

Then the eye turned to stare at me as the jet pivoted on her nose wheel.

"It's headed for the cargo terminal!" whispered Georgina.

"Let's go," I said, and willed my legs to take me back to the waiting car.

The brochure had told me little about the cargo terminal beyond the fact that it was forty-five thousand square metres in area, could handle four wide bodies at once, and held facilities for forwarding agents like Gambetta, customs clearance, and a post office handling bay.

We drove quickly down the access road and turned down the main service road behind the blank walled blockhouse of the terminal. The other side of the road looked like it was a good sized industrial park; lots of modern commercial buildings, and a big sign at the main entrance advertising the businesses within. I turned away from it, guiding the Mustang into the cargo terminal parking lot. I found a spot close to the main doors, parked, and got out of the car.

"Now what?" asked Georgina, as we walked across the hot pavement to the doors.

"We play it by ear," I said, wishing I had a better answer.

We went in through the main doors and found ourselves standing in a bleak lobby manned by a single security guard seated behind a scarred wooden desk. He was in his fifties, paunchy, and had his dark-green peaked cap tipped back on his head. He was leafing through a tattered *Penthouse* that had obviously made the rounds of the entire terminal. He glanced up as we approached, and tried to look official.

"Oui?" he said.

"I'd like some information," I said.

The man shrugged and leaned back in his swivel chair. "About what you want to know?" he asked, his accent broad and twanging. He gave me a slow, gap-toothed smile. I knew what it meant. I was a goddamn Anglais.

"There's a jet unloading at the cargo dock," I said, trying to keep the edge out of my voice. "I'd like some information about it."

"I don't know nothing about no jet," he grinned. "Me, I just know about the front door, you know, who come in, who go out, like that."

"Who would know?" asked Georgina.

He turned his attention to her, his leer grotesquely blatant. He shrugged again, letting his wet eyes travel up and down her body. "Je ne comprends pas," he said, still grinning.

"Who would know about the jet?" she repeated.

His eyebrows lifted. "I don't know," he said. "Maybe you should ask someone else. I said before, I know about the front door, that's all."

"Where's the customs office?" I asked.

"Pardon?" he said. We were clearly the most fun he'd had all day.

"La douane," I said.

"A la main gauche," he said, waving vaguely to the left. I took Georgina's elbow and we followed his lead towards a long corridor to one side of the lobby. Ten minutes and three wrong turns later, we found the customs area behind a pair of battered swinging doors.

The large fluorescent lit room was almost totally packed with scores of metal racks filled to capacity with parcels of all shapes and sizes. A haggard-looking young customs officer was painfully tapping out some kind of form on a typewriter at a desk behind the waist high counter in front of us. He got up as we came in and smiled, looking glad of the break.

"I need some help," I said, matching his expression as best I could. It wasn't easy. Being in the cargo area was making me nervous.

"What kind of help?" he asked.

"There's a DC-10 unloading. I'd like some information about what she was carrying and where it's headed."

The man's smile wavered. "Why?" he asked. It was a damn good question.

"I'm writing an article," I said.

"Yes?"

"About cargo," I added, thinking desperately. "Air cargo."

"Oh," he said, frowning.

"So that's why I need the information." The man's frown stayed put. I kept going, trying to build some momentum. "I have a package on that plane," I said, showing every tooth I could muster. "The AVTOUR flight. I had it sent from Paris, you see, kind of a 'day in the life of a parcel' angle. I'm trying to follow its path as closely as I can."

"I see," said the man skeptically.

"Right," I said. "But now I've got a problem."

"Yes?" He was obviously trying to figure out what kind of hustle I was operating, and it had him confused.

"Yes," I answered. "I feel like an idiot, but I've forgotten the name of the forwarding agent it was supposed to get sent out with. I know it's stupid of me, but I was wondering if . . ." I let it dangle.

He rose to the bait. "You were wondering if I could find out who the forwarding agent was?"

"That's it," I said.

"Was it bonded?" asked the customs man.

"Yes."

"Who was the agent in Paris?"

"Gambetta S.A.," I said.

"And it's on the AVTOUR flight?" I nodded. He flipped open a large ledger on the counter and ran a finger down one page. "AV220," he said. "Frankfurt, Paris, London, Mirabel, JFK. That it?"

"That's it," I said. We were getting somewhere.

"Okay. Now what's the waybill number?" he asked, looking up expectantly.

"The waybill number?"

"Can't tell you anything without it. The whole thing's logged by the waybill numbers. All on computer in the back." He jerked a thumb over his shoulder at the maze behind him.

"I lost it," I said lamely.

"I've got fifty thousand pieces of goods coming in today, and you don't have a waybill number?"

"No," I said.

The man sighed, then stood up. "Hang on a minute," he said. He headed into the aisles of merchandise and disappeared. I lit a cigarette and rested my elbows on the counter. Sweat was pooling in my armpits; fear sweat. If someone from Gambetta—someone like Brandt, or anyone who had our description—walked in to pick up a bonded package, we were dead. Literally.

"God!" whispered Georgina beside me. "A day in the life of a parcel! I thought I'd die!"

"I didn't notice you coming up with anything better," I snapped.

"Well, I'm terribly sorry!" she said, hurt.

I gave her a lopsided smile and apologized. "Sorry," I said. "But I'm a bit tense." She nodded, softening. We waited silently in the harshly lit room. Ten minutes later the customs man reappeared, just as I was about to bolt.

"Took a while, but I got you something on the computer," he said, giving me a strange look.

"I appreciate it," I said heartily.

His brow had furrowed. "Now, you're sure it's on that flight?" he asked.

I nodded. What the hell was wrong? "Positive," I said. "Why, is something the matter?"

He shrugged. "It's weird, that's all. According to what I have on file, that whole flight is under special seal."

"Pardon?" I said.

"Special seal. It's bonded okay, but it never comes in here. They've got authority to take it right through to destination without inspection. You don't see that kind of thing too often. It's usually currency stuff going to Ottawa or Toronto, but who the hell has ever heard of Pendleburg, Ontario?"

I decided to jump in with both feet and grinned insanely. "That's my home town!" I said.

"Well, then. Maybe your stuff is on the plane." He seemed pleased with himself. "Anyway, the forwarding agent is AAS. They've got an office in the park across the road. According to the computer, all the stuff from Gambetta is handled by them at this end."

"AAS?" I said.

"Sure," he said. "Alpha Air Services."

Bingo!

"That was a stroke of luck," said Georgina, as we headed back to the Mustang.

"It wasn't luck," I answered. "It was youthful incompetence you might say. That kid in customs would've had his stripes pulled if his supervisor had overheard. Not that I'm knocking it. At least we've got a lead, now." We reached the car and climbed in.

"What's the next step?" asked Georgina.

I thought for a moment. "We find out when AAS next has a flight out to Pendleburg first of all. You can handle that on the phone from the hotel. Then we find out just where Pendleburg Ontario *is,* and get ourselves there as fast as we can."

The stubby winged little aircraft sat in the mid-afternoon haze at the end of the short cracked runway, grass growing up around her wheels. Oil had dripped down from beneath the engine inspection hatch, forming a dark, gritty patch below the cabin. The fuselage had once been red, now it was the colour of rust. The leading edges of the wings were dented and scored from a thousand hours of hard flying, and the flaps on the trailing edges drooped tiredly.

"You really must be joking!" said Georgina, eyeing the relic. "You don't actually expect to get that thing off the ground, do you?"

"It's the only game in town," I answered, looking at the log book the owner had handed over when we rented her. None of the air services at Mirabel had anything to offer, and this field, twenty miles away at St. Magritte, was our last hope.

The aircraft before us was a Maule Rocket. The log book said it had been purchased in 1963. According to the owner, a beer-bellied Québécois named André St. Amour, "She fly and she fly damn good, yes sir!" I had my doubts. The Maule's days of rocketing were long over. She was rated at a cruising speed of one hundred and fifty miles per hour with a ceiling of eighteen thousand feet and a range of six hundred and eighty miles. It might have been true once, but now the chances of getting her over one-ten at seven thousand were slim. I could fly the crate. But it was going to be seat of the pants all the way.

We didn't have much choice. The Alpha flight had left an hour and a half ago, and they flew Skymasters. They'd be way ahead already, and I wanted to get us to Pendleburg before nightfall. Much later and we wouldn't have a chance in hell of keeping track of the Gambetta consignment. According to the road map of Ontario I'd purchased, Pendleburg was located just north of Chalk River, next to Algonquin Park, about two hundred and fifty miles away as the crow flies. Depending on the winds, it would take us at least three hours and probably more to reach the town. If everything went right, we'd hit it around seven-thirty, just as the sun went down. I didn't have a lot of experience night flying, and the thought of bringing the Maule down on some obscure field in the dark wasn't doing my nerves any good.

I climbed up onto the wing. Pulling open the door, I stuck my head into the cockpit and looked around. Four seats, vinyl split and stuffing erupting like burst pimples; dual controls, and electrician's tape wound around a crack in the pilot's wheel. The cockpit controls had obviously been cannibalized for parts years ago. The panel was full of empty sockets, and there didn't seem to be much left except an altimeter, the oil pressure gauge, and a fuel indicator. There

was no sign of a radio. On top of it all the cabin interior was
boiling hot. I sighed and went back out onto the wing.
Georgina looked up at me.

"Well?" she asked.

I shrugged. "It'll fly. Maybe. I think I can get her into the
air. After that your guess is as good as mine."

"Full of optimism aren't you?" she said. "I'm afraid enough
of flying as it is." She frowned at the Maule.

"You can stay at the hotel," I offered.

"No-o-o-o," she said, drawing it out. "Whither you goest, I
goest."

She didn't sound too sure, but I didn't press the point.
There wasn't time. "All right," I said, squatting down and
extending a hand. "If you're sure about coming we might as
well get a move on."

She grabbed my hand and I pulled her up on the wing.
The whole plane creaked with the weight, and I prodded her
into the cabin before something fell off. She settled down in
the co-pilot's seat and I wedged myself in beside her. I went
through the controls a few times, banging the rudder pedals
back and forth and checking the flaps. The plane had as much
response as a piece of damp cardboard. Finally, satisfied that
I knew as much about her as I could under the circumstances, I hit the engine switch and thumbed the starter
button. There was a dull clattering sound like coins in a
washing machine and the ancient Continental two hundred
and twenty horsepower engine spat, coughed, and wheezed
its way up to power. It sounded like an enraged lawnmower,
and sent a series of erratic vibrations shuddering through the
cabin.

"Dear God," said Georgina, clutching the sides of her seat,
her eyes firmly closed.

I took a deep breath, slewed the rudder around, and gave
the creature something to sink her teeth into. We jerked
around slowly until I was facing her into the wind and down
the rutted concrete of the single runway. In the far distance I
could see St. Amour at the door of the tarpaper shack that
passed for a control tower. He waved his quart beer bottle at
us in a hail and farewell gesture. I assumed that we'd just
been cleared for takeoff St. Magritte style. I pulled the
throttle back and we slingshotted down the runway with a
surprising amount of force. There was no groundspeed indi-

cator so I had to wait for the Maule to let herself find rotate speed. We hit it within twenty feet of the end of the runway, giving me an ominously clear picture of the line of trees fifty yards beyond. I hauled back the wheel and we climbed into the air like a panicking mallard. The trees disappeared under the wings. We were airborne. I took her up to just under a thousand feet, every rivet in her popping, and swung us west.

Chapter Fourteen

Flying has been called "the passionate affair"—and not without reason. You either hate it or love it; and while feeling one way you're never far from feeling the other. Those most terrified of flying will admit to a certain sense of wire taut excitement in the air, while million-mile pilots will tell you that they've often cursed and screamed at the aircraft they steered through the sky. One way or the other, flying is a sickness without a cure.

I grew up in the air; there wasn't a time in my childhood that I couldn't mark with some kind of flight. We were always moving around as my father climbed the military ladder, and I was as familiar with the insides of transport planes as I was with the backside of my teddy bear. I think my father always assumed I'd join Canada's RCAF, or the US Air Force, but I balked at that. Just as my father's career had little or nothing to do with actually fighting wars, I knew that the air force didn't have much to do with airplanes. The decision was made for me when I hit six feet and kept going. They don't like fighter pilots who have to use a shoehorn to ease into the cockpit of an F-5B. But the bug had a firm grip, and I can still remember the first time I took the controls of my Uncle Harry's Twin Otter. Harry was a bush pilot flying routes in northern Ontario and Quebec and I spent a lot of summer days with him, helping to crank that decrepit old buzzard onto fields in the middle of nowhere.

Harry's calmness in the face of imminent disaster was the only thing between me and panic as I guided the floundering Maule on a line that would take us to Chalk River. After the first hour I was able to ignore the pain in my back as I sat hunched over the controls, but the headache I developed wasn't so easy to throw off. Every sense was fine-tuned to the breaking point as I waited for one of the hundred different noises that could dump us out of the sky to build into something more than an isolated pop or clang. Georgina sat rigidly beside me, white-knuckled and eyes squeezed shut, holding the worn out aircraft in the air by her will alone. After two hours and roughly one hundred and seventy miles, I had enough control over the Maule to make an attempt at conversation.

"Not so bad after all," I said, raising my voice over the rise and fall of the engine noise. I had taken her to three thousand feet, and the airspeed indicator needle was just brushing one hundred and twenty knots. Below us, the wide band of the Ottawa River twinkled brightly in the dying sun, the brooding purple shapes of the Gatineau Hills on the right, the checkerboard of Ottawa Valley farms on the left.

"How much longer?" she croaked. Her eyes were still glued shut.

"Hour, hour and a half," I answered, putting the estimate on the short side. "We went past Ottawa about twenty minutes ago. That was just about halfway."

"That long?" she moaned.

"Relax, kiddo, there's nothing to worry about," I said, as lightly as I could.

She snorted. "Relax! I'm terrified in a Jumbo jet, this thing is giving me heart failure."

"Oh, come on," I said, "there's nothing to it. The engine could stop dead and we could glide twenty miles in this thing." It wasn't true. The Maule probably had the glide factor of a concrete block.

"You're lying," she said astutely. The conversation died and I flew on. I didn't speak again until almost an hour later. Chalk River still wasn't in sight and the light was fading fast. If it hadn't been for the continuous snaking arrow of the river below I would have worried about being lost.

"Almost there," I muttered.

"Umm," answered Georgina.

I squinted over the side. The ground was almost totally dark now, the horizon gone from blue to a misty mauve. We had another half hour at the most. Dead ahead the sun was a waning fireball. I cursed silently. I'd done a rough triangulation on the road map, which was our only chart. Pendleburg was about twenty-five or thirty miles past Pembroke, but off the main highway and slightly west. By lining up the town of Fort William on the Quebec side of the river, and the military base at Petawawa, I should have had Pendleburg between it and the forests of Algonquin Park. If the airport there didn't have runway lights we were going to be in real trouble.

Suddenly I picked off a huddle of lights directly ahead. We'd already gone over Pembroke so it had to be Camp Petawawa.

"Georgina!" I said sharply. "Check out the window. I want you to tell me when you see lights."

She shook her head. "I'll be sick if I open my eyes."

"So be sick!" I snapped. "Better that than trying to land this thing in the middle of a goddamn forest. Now look!"

The plane jittered slightly as she shifted her weight. I kept my eyes glued to the lights of Camp Petawawa. I heard Georgina's dull groan. "See anything?" I asked. Petawawa was going by under us. There wasn't much time.

"No," she moaned. "Not a thing. Oh! There. Yes. I see lights." I breathed a sigh of relief and tapped the left rudder pedal, pushing the yoke forward at the same time. The nose dropped too sharply and we went into a long yawing turn. I pulled back, counteracting the move, and the turn smoothed out.

"You did that on purpose, you bastard!" raved Georgina.

I didn't have time to answer. We'd swung off the river and I had no landmark now. I could see the endless gloom of Algonquin Park twenty miles ahead. If Pendleburg had lights they'd be showing soon. I eased the yoke forward another inch and we started sliding out of the sky. At that moment I would have given my left leg for a radio and a calm-voiced air traffic controller on the other end, talking me down. I still couldn't see the lights. Where the hell was Pendleburg?

I had a brief paranoid fantasy that Brandt had found out about us and arranged to have all the lights in the town turned off. And then I saw it—a weak cluster of luminosity a few miles to the left, and beyond it a single pulsing red beacon. Dusk was fully down and the ground below was dark; the sun was nothing more than a grey haze in the bowl of the sky. I concentrated on the limited display of instruments on the panel and started my approach. One thing gave me a bit of hope. The red beacon meant that Pendleburg was open twenty-four hours a day, probably as a refueling point for companies like Alpha. I was banking on the fact that the runway would be better than the rutted track at St. Magritte.

I banked slightly as we passed over the town, throttling back and putting the nose down. The beacon slid by beneath the Maule's belly as I made a pass at three hundred feet, sweat popping. The last time I'd made a night landing was in a fully equipped Piper Cherokee at a field ablaze with light and with a fully qualified IFR pilot in the number two seat. Even then my nerves had been frayed. Now I was trying to land a Model T with wings, and my co-pilot was about as useful as a sack of potatoes.

The single pass told me that Pendleburg's lighting equipment was non-existent. The beacon was it. I'd caught a quick glimpse of a single Quonset hut beside a narrow, dark strip of runway. I did a count in my head as we went over the runway's length and came out with a figure of just under a thousand feet. That was a relief, at any rate. The Maule supposedly only needed seven hundred at a stall speed of forty miles per hour with full flaps. I wheeled the tired old bird around again and went in on final.

I lined up with the beacon and dropped the nose again, throttling back even farther until the needle on the airspeed indicator was almost to the red line. The engine started making angry sounds as the fuel was choked off. The threatening black pan of the runway leapt up to meet me and the instant I felt the nose wheel touch I hit the flaps hard, bringing the tail down with a shuddering crash that rattled my teeth and forced a muted grunt of anguish from Georgina. I cut back on the throttles and hung onto the yoke for dear life as the suddenly powerless aircraft slewed back and forth down the runway. I kept my feet dancing on the rudder pedals, trying to keep us from cracking off a wing as we slalomed along the asphalt. We finally came to a stop fifty yards from the dark bulk of the Quonset hut and I sat back in my seat, weak with relief. I could feel my whole body shaking slightly and the pounding of blood in my ears. The sudden and complete silence was overwhelming.

"We made it?" asked Georgina. I let my head fall to one side and looked across at her in the gloom. She was staring unbelievingly through the windscreen.

"Uh huh," I said. The cool of the evening began creeping through the cabin. I shivered and wiped my clammy hands on the thighs of my jeans. The cooling engine ticked and whimpered. I forced my brain to get back to work and ordered one hand to go in search of my cigarettes. It found them, and somehow managed to get one to my lips. I lit it and dragged gratefully. Neither of us said a word for several long minutes, and then Georgina shuffled around in her seat, leaning close to the windscreen.

"I wonder if anyone's home?" she said, staring out at the Quonset hut. A light burned over the half moon wall of corrugated metal facing us, and a weathered sign announced that the hut was the home of Pendleburg Air Freight and Flying School.

"I doubt it," I said. "Not unless they've got a scheduled flight coming in later on, and this place doesn't look like it has many scheduled flights."

"What about Alpha Air Services?" asked Georgina. "They use this place regularly."

"But not at night probably." I groaned, flexing the knotted muscles in my back. "Anyway, the only way to find out is to go up and knock."

We clambered out of the aircraft and hopped down to the welcome hardness of the ground. Even then my legs were still rubbery from the flight. As we walked the short distance to the Quonset hut I wondered idly what André St. Amour would do about his plane. One thing was certain, nothing on earth was going to get me to fly it back to St. Magritte, PQ.

We reached the door and I knocked on the unfinished plywood panel. Nothing happened for a few seconds and then I heard the sound of shuffling feet. I knocked again. A bolt snicked back and the door opened fractionally. I found myself looking into a single squinting eye behind the thickest eye-glass lens I'd ever seen. A bushy white eyebrow rode guard above it.

"What?" said a voice. It was male, cracked with age and a lot of liquor.

"We just landed," I explained.

"No, you didn't. No one ever lands here. Haven't for years. Except for Luther and his flying school, and that doesn't count because it's only two days a week in the summer and

one in the fall and none at all in winter and spring and it's
only two Pipers anyway. You didn't land here."

"Yes, we did," broke in Georgina. The eye swivelled
behind the lens, discovering her.

"Two of you."

"And we just came in on that piece of junk out on the
tarmac," I said. I stepped aside and gestured at the Maule,
just visible behind me.

"So you landed here," he said. "What do you want?"

"Could we talk inside, please?" I asked.

"Why?" said the man. The door didn't budge. I reached
into the pocket of my jeans and came up with a ten dollar
bill. I stuck it an inch in front of his Coke-bottle eye. Like
magic, the door swung open.

"Name's Bimm," said the man, "Edgar Bimm." He extended an arthritic hand and I touched it briefly. It felt like
parchment. Bimm was in his seventies at least, with a falling
shock of nicotine white hair and a small pursed mouth that
looked like it hadn't laughed for half a century, and even then
only under duress. His body was bent and thin, the twisted
frame clothed in a pair of grimy suit pants and a white shirt
gone grey with age, frayed at pocket and cuffs. The pants
were dragged up almost to his armpits by a pair of thin
suspenders. He wore pink felt slippers on his feet and no
socks.

I looked around. Clearly this was home for Edgar Bimm.
The room was about fifteen feet long and cluttered with junk,
most of it to do with airplanes. There was a propeller
propped up against a desk made from sawhorses and an old
door, and a stripped down engine of indeterminate age hung
from the curved ceiling on a block and tackle. In among the
airplane parts there were pieces of charity shop furniture,
including a wretched-looking sofa in MacIntosh plaid, a broken lay-zee-boy rocker, and a television set with rabbit ears
made out of a twisted coat hanger. There was also a small gas
stove, a small fridge, and an old army cot. The rest of the
Quonset was blocked off by a floor to ceiling partition wall.

"Beer?" asked the old man. He looked at us expectantly. I
shook my head and Georgina did the same. Bimm shuffled
over to the rocker and eased himself down. He gave a groan
of satisfaction as he settled into the chair, and then stared up

at us. The ten spot had long since disappeared into the pocket of his shirt.

"So then," he said, "what can I do for you folks?"

"We want to know about a flight that came in earlier today," I said.

"Told you, no one ever lands here. No flights today. Any other day for that matter."

"There was a flight plan booked in for it. Alpha Air Services," I insisted.

Bimm shook his head. "Never heard of them," he said.

It was time to try a different tack. "If no one ever lands here, why the night beacon?" I asked.

Bimm shrugged wearily. It looked as though my ten bucks wasn't going to take me far. "That beacon there?" he said. "Red one?"

"That's it."

He shrugged again. "Luther had it put up. He didn't pay for it. Not Luther Ranke, not him, that's for sure." Bimm laughed himself into a choking fit. I let him recover, then pressed on.

"If he didn't pay for it, who did?"

"Flying club," said Bimm.

"Which flying club?" I asked.

"Not sure," said Bimm. "The one over to Pembroke I think. Came in one day and asked Luther if he'd mind putting one up, seeing it's his field, you know. Sure, says Luther, what the hell, I don't need no beacon, but you can put it up if you want. Then he asks them why and they tell him they have a flying club, like I said, maybe the one over to Pembroke. Anyway, they tell Luther they might want to do some night flying and it would be handy to have a beacon at the end of the regular leg, in case of an emergency. But it's never happened and it's been a year now. You're the first, you know. You from that flying club over to Pembroke?"

I blinked. Bimm's erratic switching from monosyllabic answers to the verbal runs was giving me vertigo. "No," I said. "We're not from the flying club over to Pembroke."

"So where are you from?" he asked. I didn't bother answering him. I was more interested in the partition wall. From the outside the Quonset had looked like a regulation sixty footer. This front room didn't take up a quarter of the available space.

"What's back there?" I asked, pointing at the wall.

Bimm shrugged and slid his lump-jointed hands under his suspenders. "Luther's stuff. He lets me stay here so he can get the twenty-four hour on duty grant from Transport. Luther's a mean bastard, tight you know. There's times he's—"

I cut him off quickly. "What kind of stuff?" I said, picking my way across the junk on the floor to a door set into the wall. I tried the handle. Locked. There was a big Shlage deadbolt set in above the knob.

"Just Luther's stuff," said Bimm. He wheezed up out of the dead rocker, watching me.

"Got a key?" I asked.

Bimm made a thin flatulent sound that might have been a laugh. "No," he said, "but I can get in there if you want."

"I want," I said.

"You gonna steal anything?" asked Bimm.

I shook my head. "I just want a look."

"You steal anything Luther's gonna know it was me let you in there. He'd never give me a key in a million years, but he'd figure it out and I'd be out a place, you know."

"Open the door and you get another ten," I said. I pulled a pair of fives from the pocket of my jeans and held them up for Bimm to see. His eyes lit up like fireflies behind the thick lenses of his glasses. He did a slow motion two step through the litter on the floor and motioned me away from the door. He grabbed the knob with one clawed hand and tugged sideways. The flimsy doorframe spread and the door swung open.

"Figured that out a long time ago," said Bimm proudly. I gave him the two fives. Georgina crossed to the doorway and together we peered in. It was pitch dark.

"How much is it going to cost me to find the light switch?" I asked, turning back to Bimm.

He knew it was a joke but he was still tempted. "Free of charge so long as you don't try to steal anything," he said. "Foot to the right there on the wall." I felt around until my fingers closed on the switch. I flicked it on. The rest of the Quonset lit up, half a dozen big industrial pans hanging from the ceiling pushing back the darkness.

The rest of the hut was being used as a hangar. The two Pipers squatted side by side, taking up most of the space. They were silver with Luther Caldwell Air Freight written in script along the engine cowlings. From the antique look of them I was positive they were the original PA-18 series from 1949. I walked across the stained concrete floor and tapped one wing. Coated fabric over a steel tube frame. The little two seaters had been around for a long time. St. Amour's outfit wasn't the only backwoods field flying museum pieces.

The leftover space was taken up by workbenches along one wall and bins for spare parts along the other. A pile of fuel drums were stacked up against the partition wall. Unless the whole thing was an elaborate cover, Luther's Air Freight and Flying School wasn't connected with Alpha or Gambetta. We'd come to a dead end.

We went back into Bimm's pig sty. The old man sat down again, sighing happily. I noticed a pile of beer cartons behind the chair and I had a pretty good idea where my twenty bucks was going to wind up.

"Is there a hotel in town?" I asked.

"Yup," said Bimm. "Motel actually," he added.

"How about a taxi?"

"Yup. One."

"Phone?"

"Under the desk. Number's pasted on it. Luther owns it. The motel, too. Luther owns half the town. Mean bastard."

Behind the lenses Bimm's eyes were starting to flutter. The old man was fading out for the night. I found the phone, read off the number for Luther's Cab and called in. The nasal female voice on the other end told me I'd reached Luther's Slumber Haven, which was also the home of Luther's Cab. She told me it would take about twenty minutes for her to get down to the "station." By the time I'd made the arrangements Bimm was fast asleep, his fragile snores a preview of his death rattle. I slipped another five into the pocket of his shirt and we let ourselves out into the night. The clean air was a relief after the sour interior of Bimm's den.

"Bit of a cock-up," said Georgina, shivering.

"Pardon?"

"A drag. Here we are in the middle of nowhere, with nowhere to go."

"How poetic," I said. I lit a much-needed cigarette and stared out at the shadowy shape of the Maule.

"We don't give up, do we?" asked Georgina. She swatted away an eager moth, one of the swarm collecting around the light above our heads.

"No," I said, suddenly feeling terribly tired. "We don't give up."

"So what do we do?" she asked.

I yawned. "Sleep," I said, "and figure it out in the morning."

The cab finally arrived, a well cared for Cadillac from the fin era. We climbed in and the woman driver didn't even ask us where we wanted to go. Ten minutes of fast driving on unpaved roads brought us to the outskirts of Pendleburg and Luther's Slumber Haven.

We all got out and the driver changed roles, slipping in behind the counter in the motel office and booking us in. I signed for Mr. and Mrs. Dante, and she handed us the key. I had enough foresight to ask if there was a car rental in town and she said there wasn't, but if we liked she could drive us into Pembroke in the morning and we could pick up a car there. I thanked the woman, and we headed for our room. All the parking slots in the lot were empty. By the looks of it we were the only people staying with Luther that night.

"Why Dante?" asked Georgina as I fitted the key into the lock.

"Because we seem to be going from one circle of hell to the next," I muttered.

We went into the room. I didn't even bother turning on the light. With the door locked behind me I fell onto one of the twin beds without undressing. The last thing I remembered was the sound of gargling and the flushing of a toilet somewhere. It fit my mood precisely.

Chapter Fifteen

The taxi dispatcher, taxi driver, and motel receptionist drove us into Pembroke early the next morning, chattering all the way. She called herself Mrs. Leona. In addition to her other roles it turned out she was also Luther Caldwell's wife and mother of his six children. Her opinion of Caldwell wasn't much better than Edgar Bimm's and according to her, the five boys and one girl which were his issue were cut from the same cloth. She thanked God effusively that they, at least, had moved out of the house long ago, something she wished

Luther would do as well—preferably in a pine box. After twenty minutes of family history I finally managed to get a word in.

"Does the airport get much business?" I asked, as we twisted down yet another concession road lined with scrub bush. The squat little woman guffawed and shook her head vehemently, wispy grey bun bobbing.

"That's a laugh!" she bellowed. "He gets about one person a month to go up in one of those crates of his. Any money he makes is by bringing in bootleg from the stills on the Quebec side. Sure as hell never shows up in the grocery money, though. Luther is the biggest son-of-a-bitching tightwad you have ever seen—bar none, sonny."

"So why does he keep it up?" I asked. She lifted her shoulders, manhandling the swaying Caddy around a curve. Beside me I felt Georgina stiffen. Riding with Mrs. Leona seemed almost as bad as flying in the Maule. Georgina hadn't said a word the entire trip.

"I think he keeps it going 'cause it was the first. He flew transports in the war, and when he got back here it was the only trade he knew. Late forties and fifties was good for short haul stuff, especially into the bush, Rouyn, Noranda, up there. He did okay and invested. Edgar Bimm was his mechanic."

"Kind of a nostalgia thing?" I asked.

She shrugged again. "Maybe," she said. "I don't think he'd keep on if it wasn't for the transport money and the landing fee he charges when a plane comes in."

"Mr. Bimm told me no one ever landed there," I said.

She nodded, glancing at me in the rearview mirror. "No one ever does, but he's used as an alternate sometimes by the flying clubs and once in a while by one of the commercial companies. Maybe a dozen times a year. Pays the taxes and buys a bit of gas for the Pipers."

"Bimm told us about the beacon, too."

"Yeah," she agreed, "there's that as well. They pay him a lump sum to keep it operating. Never come in that I've known, though. Must have more money than sense." She pulled up at a stop sign, then turned us onto a paved road. On the far side I could see water gleaming through a thin screen of trees. Being on pavement seemed to excite her and she floored it.

"This club that put up the beacon . . . Bimm said they were from Pembroke," I said, after a pause.

"Horse manure!" snorted Mrs. Leona. "Edgar hasn't had a working part in his brain since 1946. There is no flying club in Pembroke. I think Luther said they were from Ottawa, or maybe Montreal. Foolishness wherever they come from if you ask me!"

"You don't remember the name then?" I asked.

She shook her head. "Naw."

In the distance I could see the growing shape of Pembroke. The bush had given way to reasonably well cared for farms and the odd new house.

"How about Alpha Air?" I asked. "You ever hear of them?"

She shook her head again. "Nope. Not from around here. There's some freight haulers at the Pembroke Airport, but I never heard about any of them being called Alpha Air."

"What about other airfields?" I asked.

"Aren't none," she said. "Not that I know of. Luther's and Pembroke is all there is around here. There's one in Mattawa, but that's way up the line to Temiscaming." Pembroke had sprouted now on both sides of the road, a collection of solid looking Victorian brick buildings, mixed with weathered clapboard rural. Mrs. Leona slowed the Caddy at the first real intersection, and we began moving sedately along the main street.

"How about private strips?" I asked, as a last resort.

"Now how would I know?" she said, turning to grin at me over her shoulder. "If it's private?" She chuckled at her joke. She swung the car into a slot beside a big orange and white Budget Rent-a-Car sign and checked the meter. The charge was nine dollars and I gave her ten. She never offered change. We climbed out of the car.

"You want your room again tonight?" she asked, peering out the open window.

"Probably," I said. "Thanks." She nodded, then backed out of the slot and into the street. A few seconds later the Caddy was on its way.

"She drives the way you fly," said Georgina, speaking at last.

"Thanks a lot," I said. "Come on." I went into the car rental office with her tagging behind me.

The clerk was quick and efficient and within a few minutes

we were in possession of a Granada with less than 10,000 miles on the clock. The clerk had also given me directions to the local registry office. I found it easily enough, and we went into the small, copper roofed building.

"Why are we going here?" asked Georgina as we entered the musty interior of the building.

"Maps," I said. "If that flight from Alpha didn't land at Luther's field, it landed somewhere close by. They wouldn't file a flight plan that was too far off because they'd be picked off by one of the regional air traffic controls in Pembroke or Mattawa. It has to be a field like Luther's with no ground control."

"I don't really understand, but I'll take your word for it," she smiled.

"A little bit of faith at last!" I said, grinning back. "You're forgiven for that crack about my flying." We went down a short hall and through a door marked Central Register.

A middle-aged man in a short-sleeved white shirt was reading a newspaper at the counter. He looked up as we came in and then down at the newspaper again. I stood in front of him and waited. After a few seconds he realized we weren't going to go away and looked up again, folding the paper slowly. "Help you?" he said.

I nodded. "I'd like to see some general survey maps," I said. "The most recent you have."

"Of what?" he asked. "We got 'em for the whole of Renfrew County and farther. You got to be specific when you ask for a map." He made a motion as though to reopen his paper.

"Anything within a fifty mile circle around Pembroke," I said quickly. That would take in Luther's field with a few miles to spare. I was sure it was in that area.

"Take a minute," he said.

"Fine. We'll wait."

The man moved slowly off into the murky depths of the high ceilinged room and disappeared behind a bank of double height map drawers and file cabinets. He came back five minutes later with an armful of rolled maps, and dumped them onto the counter. "You can't take 'em away," he remarked.

Picking up his newspaper, he retired to a desk at the far end of the counter. He sat down, propped his feet up, and disappeared behind the paper. I unrolled the maps and started looking. They were all dated 1979, so it was a recent survey. I found three that included Luther's field marked as "arp't/sec." for secondary airport, and overlapped them. I let my eyes wander over the maps, trying to locate another airport.

Mrs. Leona hadn't been far off. There was another airport at Deep River, forty miles away, but that was it. Bored, Georgina sat down in a battered captain's chair beside the door. I kept on looking. It *had* to be there. But it wasn't.

"Why would they need a beacon?" Georgina asked, a few minutes later.

"What?" I turned to her, irritated by the break in my concentration.

"Why would they need a beacon?" she repeated, ignoring my scowl. "If they don't land there, why do they need a beacon?"

"What the hell are you talking about?" I asked.

She cocked an eyebrow. "Just what I said. Assuming that the beacon wasn't really for a flying club at all."

"What makes you assume that?" I asked. "It's reasonable enough. Good cautionary planning, actually."

Georgina shook her head. "But it's not logical. It would make sense if there really was a flying club here. They might fly from Pembroke to Luther's field and then back again. But there isn't a flying club here."

"I still don't see . . ."

Georgina sighed. "Luther's wife says the club is in Ottawa or Montreal. They wouldn't put a beacon in Pendleburg, they'd use the lights at the airport here, wouldn't they? They wouldn't need the beacon at Luther's."

"So you think the flying club is phoney?"

"Right. I think the flying club is part of the whole Alpha thing."

"But Alpha doesn't fly into Pendleburg. We know that," I said.

Georgina nodded vigorously. "Precisely. And that brings us back to my original question. Why the beacon? They don't land there, so what do they need it for?"

I lit a cigarette and thought about it for a minute. What she said about the flying club *did* make sense. Beacons aren't cheap. If they really were from Ottawa or Montreal they wouldn't bother with the expense. But phoney or not, it still left the problem of the beacon.

"What exactly does a beacon do?" asked Georgina thoughtfully, staring up at the ceiling.

"It's a visual guidance device," I said. "You line up with it to give you your proper approach. There are usually several."

"And how far away can you see them?" she asked.

I frowned, not understanding what she was driving at. "Ten, maybe fifteen miles if it's a clear night. Why?"

"So why couldn't the beacon at Pendleburg be used to line you up with something else?" she said slowly. "Another field ten or fifteen miles away. A private one that wouldn't be marked on any of the maps?" She looked down from her perusal of the ceiling and stared at me questioningly. I took the cigarette out of my mouth.

It fit. Especially if there was another beacon, one that they turned on only when a flight was expected. With a pair of beacons, one at Luther's, and the other at the field where they intended to set down, they'd have a perfect line of sight approach.

"Jesus!" I whispered. I turned back to the maps. Georgina stood up and came to look over my shoulder. I fumbled around in my jacket pocket and hauled out my wallet. I took out a credit card to use as a straight edge and found Luther's field on the maps. Then I put one edge of the card on Luther's and swung the card around. Nothing. The only thing the line of the card intersected with was the town of Pendleburg itself. I checked the scale. My credit card was only ten kilometres long as far as the map was concerned. It wasn't enough.

I raised my voice. "I need a ruler," I said to the man with the newspaper.

He put the paper down and eyed me severely. "Hey, now, you can't mark up those maps," he cautioned, rising.

"I don't want to mark them," I said. "I just need a straight edge of some kind."

The man grimaced, but began digging around in the drawer of the desk. He brought out a twelve inch ruler. "This do?" he asked.

I nodded. "Fine, fine."

He walked over with it and watched me as I placed one end on Luther's and started pivoting again. The ruler touched one thing within a twenty mile range. A square on the map with a letter-number classification. There were two approaches to it: a concession road, which eventually became a private one; and a rail spur leading back to what looked like a main line running to the west.

"What does Q-23 mean?" I asked the clerk.

He bobbed his head. "Have to look it up," he muttered.

"Could you please?" asked Georgina, turning on a smile.

He twitched his lips back at her and moved off. A minute later he came back with a thick file folder in his hands. He thumped it on the counter and started thumbing through its pages. Then he dropped a forefinger down. "It's an RHI 9.6," he murmured to himself.

"What on earth is that?" asked Georgina.

"Zoned for heavy industry, just about any kind. Big pollutant allowance."

"What's the name of it?" I asked.

He looked back down, squinting at the page. "Omega Electronic Manufacturing Corporation," he read.

"Cute," said Georgina. "Alpha and Omega. The beginning and the end."

"Ever heard of them?" I asked.

"Seen them," said the man. "Trucks roll through here now and again. Semi's, big ones. No one around here works for them though, to my knowledge. Trucks got a big horseshoe design on them. Sharp looking."

I stared down at the map. The whole thing was turning into a conglomerate, company within company, all linked by whatever it was Sam had turned up. Omega. Maybe it really would be the end of the line. I checked the concession road number and fixed its rough location in my mind. I thanked the clerk and we left the registry office. I paused on the steps and took a deep breath, blinking in the sunlight.

"Well?" asked Georgina.

"Well what?" I asked, still caught up in my thoughts.

"My due," she said. "I think I deserve a round of applause."

I looked at her and smiled. She was right. The solution had come from her questions about the beacon.

"You were brilliant," I said, and leaned over, planting a kiss on her cheek. She turned her head at the last second and I caught her fully on the mouth, my lips just brushing hers. She let it go on for an instant and then pulled away, smiling.

"Thank you," she said. "Credit where credit is due, you know."

I followed her down the steps to the car.

"I wonder what all this is leading to?" Georgina commented, as I piloted the Granada out of Pembroke, heading back to the Pendleburg turnoff.

"It's leading us into the most inbred yahoo territory in the country," I joked. "They could have shot *Deliverance* here and Burt Reynolds would have fit right in. Hillbilly country without the hills."

"You know perfectly well that's not what I meant," said Georgina.

"Yes. But that's as good an answer as I can come up with," I said ruefully. "This thing's gotten to the point where I'm nothing more than a bloodhound. Following the trail without knowing why. Smugglers usually don't have large industrial complexes tucked away in rural Ontario. It's got me stumped."

Georgina stared out through the windshield for a minute. "What did you mean about this being hillbilly country?" she asked finally. "It looks like perfectly reasonable farmland to me."

"A lot of it is," I admitted, then grinned. "And a lot of it isn't. My mother comes from a place not too far from here, actually. Town called Eganville. We went there once, over a summer. It was unbelievable. The town was about a hundred and fifty years old. It's on the Bonnechere River, which flows down out of Algonquin Park. The river was used to power the mills for lumber. I guess at one time it was a fairly large timber centre, but it didn't last. The whole area eventually went back to subsistence farming. The town was half Catholic and half Protestant, and they were always at each other's throats. The Catholic church burnt down once and the Papists figured it was an Orangeman's plot, so they burnt down the post office, which was on the Protestant side of the river. And those were the townsfolk. The people out in the countryside were even stranger. My mother told me all sorts of crazy stories about babies being born covered with fur, virgin sisters locked in the attic by jealous brothers, that kind of thing. I met a few oddballs myself when I was there. One guy on the street kept showing me that he had two complete sets of teeth. I had nightmares for months after that summer."

"Really, Peter!" scolded Georgina.

I shrugged. "All of it's true, I swear. The big deal in the town these days is a tourist attraction, a set of caverns about ten miles into the bush, the Bonnechere Caves."

"Well, I think it's very pretty," said Georgina.

"Maybe," I said, "but pretty doesn't pay the bills. These people are literally dirt poor. It's not a happy place."

"You're being a journalist," she said, smiling.

"I guess, but the place gives me the creeps. It's like that story, 'The Legend of Sleepy Hollow.' It looks fine in the daylight, but you can imagine just about anything going on after dark."

"Then perhaps this Omega Corporation fits in after all," she said. "It has a fairly sinister track record if its associates are any indication."

I turned off onto the Pendleburg side road. There had been no town close to the Omega outfit on the map, but I'd marked its position by a nearby lake and stream: Bisset Creek.

"Are we going there?" asked Georgina.

I nodded. "We'll stop back at the motel and ask Mrs. Leona for directions. You can pick up the camera, too."

Another half hour's driving brought us back to the motel. Mrs. Leona was at her post at the switchboard. She gave me a set of complex directions for Bisset Creek and the concession road we wanted, sketching it out for me on a sheet of Luther Slumber Haven stationery. I pocketed the ersatz map and joined Georgina back at the car. Then we headed off.

The deeper into the countryside we travelled, the more depressing it became. For the first few miles there was scattered evidence of some kind of civilization, but it thinned rapidly until we were alone with the grey-barked scrub and the endless snaking road. The road surface was parched and a rooster tail of dust followed us, spuming into the baking air. Once we caught sight of water flowing muddily at the bottom of a low, rolling valley to the west, but for the most part we travelled along a choking alley of jungle-dense bush made up of second growth and yellowing cedar interspersed with small stands of poplar and birch. In winter it would be even worse; I could imagine the ground frozen and hard, the foliage gone, the cedars half buried in snow. To walk a mile from a stalled car would be a death sentence.

"It is rather gruesome," said Georgina.

"Slash," I said.

"What's that?"

I lifted one hand off the wheel and gestured at the surrounding bush. "All this," I said. "That's what they call it. Dry as tinder in the summer, freezing cold in the winter, and a swamp in between. I bet the blackflies are thick as molasses out there in spring. Stop for ten minutes and they'd bite you to death."

"I must say you don't paint a pleasant picture of your country for the tourist!"

"It has nice parts," I allowed. "This just doesn't happen to be one of them. A couple of hundred years ago even the Indians didn't want it."

Finally, we hit the concession road marked on the map. It looked exactly like the road we'd been travelling on. I turned onto it, then pulled over and stopped.

"Now what?" asked Georgina.

"You keep asking that," I said. "Let me think."

"We can't really do much more than drive by can we?"

"I guess not," I answered. "We can't exactly turn up and ask for a tour." I put the car into drive and we moved slowly down the road. A little further on there was a narrow break in the bush. The road in front of it was a mass of ruts.

"Heavy trucks," I said, pointing. We drove by. The break in the trees was filled more than adequately by a fifteen foot high fence tipped with barbed wire. There was a gate to match. Beyond it a road twisted off between banks of trees. On the gate, a sign read:

OMEGA ELECTRONIC MANUFACTURING CORPORATION
NO ADMITTANCE
ELECTRIFIED FENCE   NO TRESPASSERS
KEEP OUT

I stopped just long enough for Georgina to squeeze off a frame. I'd noticed a pair of television cameras high on the gateposts. The setup was vaguely reminiscent of Llewellyn's place in England. I kept on driving slowly, keeping my eye on the fence. It had come in at an angle just before the gate, and after that it continued to follow the road, screened by trees but still visible a few yards in. It ran out after half a mile, veering back into the forest. We'd reached the edge of the installation. I pulled over again.

"Well," I said to Georgina, "what do you think?"

"They don't take any chances, do they?" she admitted. "The only thing missing was Beware of the Vicious Dog."

"They probably just ran out of space," I said. "The dogs are there, I'll bet. And more. Trip wires, photo electric cells, infra-red, the works. *That*, my dear, is a security installation."

"Bit extreme, don't you think?" she asked, looking back.

"There's only one way to find out." I shifted the car back into drive and started moving ahead.

"Good God, we're not going *in* there?" she said.

I turned to her and smiled wanly. "Wanna bet?"

"But how?"

"I haven't figured that out—but it's the only way. What are we going to do, develop that shot and show it to the cops as evidence? These people are heavy duty. We've got to have them cold before we try and give this to the authorities."

There was a pause. "When do you want to do it?"

I shrugged. "There's no point in waiting around for inspiration to strike. We'll have a stab at it tonight."

"I think we're both crazy," decided Georgina.

"I think you're right," I said.

Chapter Sixteen

Everything I'd seen so far had led me to believe that the people we were dealing with were highly professional, careful, and backed by a lot of money. Any group that could manipulate DC-10's and whistle up killers like Brandt and his cronies had incredible resources. So I was expecting the worst, or rather the best. Security around the Omega installation was going to be tight. But there had to be a flaw somewhere. There always was.

I had done any number of stories in the past on military and industrial security, and I knew that once a flaw had been identified, the entire system collapsed around it. And the more complex the system, the better chance there was of finding a flaw.

From the brief look I'd had of the perimeter, it seemed that the Omega installation wasn't really depending on the outer fence. According to the sign, the fence was electrified; but considering the size of it, that was doubtful. To wire a fence that high and that long would require a generating station all its own, and the chances of a fire starting spontaneously with the fence that close to the trees was enormous. I was pretty sure the sign was bluster to scare off the odd passerby or snowmobiler in the winter.

The real trouble would begin once you got beyond the wire. The infra-red cameras and trip wires I'd mentioned to Georgina would almost surely be in use, not to mention the real possibility of dogs and regular patrols. The more I thought about it all, the more depressed I became. But I knew my fears about Llewellyn's people eventually catching up to us weren't just paranoid. We had to keep going. We had to break them before they broke us. I also knew the trail we'd left was going to be easy enough to pick up. We didn't have much time left. We had to act, and quickly.

I brooded for the rest of the afternoon before I came up with anything even vaguely resembling a plan of action. What I eventually cooked up was so full of holes it was embarrassing, but there wasn't anything else. Georgina had tired of my long silence and was napping when I finally decided it was time to get moving, so I left her a note telling her I'd be back before dark and headed off to Pembroke for the second time that day. I found most of what I needed there, and the rest I managed to buy in Renfrew, twenty miles down the road. I arrived back at the motel just after six. Georgina was fuming.

"So where the bloody hell have you been all this time?" she snapped.

She was sitting on one of the beds, ankles crossed, her mouth a thin angry line. I dumped my packages onto the empty bed and closed the motel room door. "You sound like a fishwife," I said.

"Too right!" she snarled back at me. "I've been sitting here for the last two hours wondering if you'd done something stupid like go off alone to that place!"

"Sorry," I said. "I had to get some things and you were sleeping."

"Screw your sorrys!" she cried, her voice cracking. "I've been half out of my mind with worry!"

"I didn't know you cared," I said, starting to get angry myself. "I'm touched."

"Don't be! I was worried for myself, not you. I've been

dragged half the bloody way around the world to this incredible place and it's—Oh, shit!"

She turned away from me and I heard her sobbing. I crossed to the bed and sat down beside her, tentatively reaching out a hand to touch her shoulder. She jerked away from me. I sat back, not sure what to do next. I began looking for my cigarettes.

"I shall scream if you light one of those," she said, her voice muffled by the pillow. "Every time we get into a spot you light one of your bloody cigarettes!"

"What's wrong with that?" I demanded. "You'd prefer me tense, maybe?"

She turned her face towards me. Her eyes were red, there were teartracks down her cheeks, and with the short, tousled hair she looked very young.

"I quit, you know," she said, her voice still tight from crying. "I quit about three days before I met you for the first time. I used to smoke a package of Senior Service a day. I thought I was doing marvellously until I met you. I really was going to quit."

"How the hell was I supposed to know?" I asked, laughing.

"Well, why do you think I was such a bitch that night we had dinner? There I was with my nose full of your cigarette smoke and you prattling on about the name of the bloody restaurant. I was in agony!"

"You really should have told me," I said.

She started to giggle. "The Underwood pride, don't you know. And father bet me five hundred pounds that I wouldn't last a month!"

"Do you want one?" I asked, offering the crumpled pack of Camels.

She waved it off, then let her hand slide onto my arm. "No," she said, "I don't want a cigarette."

There was a long pause.

"Would you like anything else?"

Georgina rolled her eyes. "My God, are you this obtuse with all your women?" she moaned.

"I didn't think you were one of my women," I said.

"I'm not," she responded coolly.

"Oh," I said, my fantasy dying stillborn.

"Yet," she added. She reached up and wound her arms

around my neck, pulling me down. She kissed me, then let me go.

"What about the Underwood pride?" I asked. "Shouldn't you let me seduce you?"

"Peter," she whispered, shaking her head, "the Underwood pride is no match for your inability to see what is a foot in front of your face."

"I can see," I said, reaching out and letting my fingers trail down the front of her dress.

"Well, it's about time!" she smiled. And pulled me down again.

"Don't say it," I muttered in the darkness. We lay naked together on the narrow bed. By special dispensation I had been allowed a cigarette. Georgina said it came under the "eat, drink, and be merry" category.

"Don't say what?" asked Georgina, curled up beside me, her fingers trying to put the hair on my chest in order. Outside we were being serenaded by a group of particularly enthusiastic crickets. A mosquito buzzed somewhere in the room, and no breeze was coming through the screened window. It was stifling.

"Don't say 'now what?'" I said.

"Pig!" she countered, tugging at a pinch of hair. I yelped.

"Well, you were going to say it weren't you?" I asked. "I could feel it on the tip of your tongue."

"The only thing that's been on the tip of my tongue is the—"

"Okay. Okay." I peered at the window. The sky was definitely dark. "Time to get ready," I said, stirring.

"What, again?" asked Georgina, hanging on to me.

"No, not that," I said, smiling at her half-seen face. "The other thing."

"Oh," said Georgina. "I'd almost forgotten." She sighed. "And just when things were looking up."

"Don't think about it," I grinned.

"Do we have to go, Peter?" she asked. "I mean, can't we just leave. Go somewhere, wait for all this to blow over."

"It's not going to blow over," I said slowly. "We stuck our foot in it, and deep. These people obviously have a lot to protect. Llewellyn said it himself. I'm an anomaly, something that doesn't fit into the scheme of things. What doesn't fit, Llewellyn removes. That goes for you as well. It's him or us."

"But we don't have to beard the lion in his den, do we?" she asked.

"It's better than getting it in the back on the run," I said bitterly.

"That sounds a bit like John Wayne, don't you think?"

I shook my head and took a last drag on the Camel before butting it in the tin ashtray on the bedside table. "I don't think so," I said. "I'm no fatalist. If I didn't think we had some kind of chance I wouldn't be doing it. This way we might just pull it off. Run and we definitely lose. We just have to corner them before they corner us."

"And how, pray, do we do that?" she asked.

I got up off the bed and went to the pile of goods I'd picked up that afternoon. "I'll show you," I said, and started unwrapping.

It was almost ten by the time we reached the concession road turnoff to Omega. I pulled over and stopped, switching off the headlights. As the engine noise died the night sounds of swamp and forest returned; we were alone with the dark. Above us, the stars glittered brightly in the black sweep of the sky. There was no moon. We waited silently for a full five minutes, then climbed out of the car, easing the doors shut behind us. I went to the trunk and began lifting out the equipment.

"I still think this is madness," whispered Georgina as she stripped down, folding her clothes neatly and placing them in the trunk. When she was down to her underwear she began pulling on the wetsuit I'd purchased at the sporting goods store in Pembroke.

"It's the only way," I explained again. "They're bound to be using infra-red cameras, just like the ones they had at Llewellyn's place in England. Infra-red cameras see by heat. With these on we cut down on the body heat we radiate. Mylar would have been better, but these should do." I began squirming into my own suit.

"I feel like something out of one of those kinky magazines," Georgina giggled. "Running about in the forest dressed all in rubber."

"Quiet!" I hissed. "This is no game."

I picked up the knapsack with the rest of the stuff in it and motioned Georgina to follow me. If we got close enough, the camera she had around her neck could get us what we wanted. We padded along the grass shoulder of the road, our sneakers making soft whispering noises as we walked. Ten minutes later we reached the corner of the high fence.

By now, the insulated rubber had turned the suits into sweat baths. I wiped the perspiration from my eyes and set the knapsack down quietly. The sounds of the surrounding forest probably worked against the possibility that the installation used any kind of audio sensing equipment, but it didn't hurt to keep our noise down. I opened the knapsack and pulled out the small VU meter I'd picked up at a hardware store. Tensely, I approached the fence and then, holding my breath, I touched the alligator clips to the chain link. Nothing happened. I peered down at the meter. The needle hadn't moved. There was no current in the fence. I let out my breath and squatted, trying to figure out the next step. Georgina got down on her knees beside me. Even this close to the road the mosquitoes were swarming, biting at every exposed inch of flesh. I tried to ignore them and got down to the work at hand.

Although there was no current in the fence, there was a good chance it had some other form of remote sensing device connected to it. The most likely was a tension sensor: the tautness of the fence would be balanced to a particular pressure, and any decrease in that pressure would trip a switch and ring an alarm. I reached into the knapsack again and brought out a pair of turnbuckle wire and spring clip contrivances I'd put together. I attached the spring clips to the links and screwed the first turnbuckle tight, twisting until there was no more play. Then I attached the second turnbuckle a few feet below the first and tightened it as well. Hopefully the devices would take up any slack when I began to cut, bypassing the links. I took out a pair of bolt cutters and began cutting a man-sized hole in the fence, stopping every few seconds to check the tension on the turnbuckles. After five minutes, I had an opening big enough for us to use. I squeezed through the hole, keeping my eyes glued to the mossy ground, checking for trip wires. When I was satisfied the way was clear I motioned for Georgina to crawl through. We were inside. We stood up and stared into the wall of trees ahead, listening. Nothing. Georgina started to say something but I put a finger to my lips. I scanned the forest, looking for some kind of opening. Now we were faced with the most difficult choice.

There was a ten or twelve foot no-man's-land between the fence and the edge of the trees. As far as I could tell the open ground was free of trip wires. The easiest way would be to follow the no-man's-land to the gate and then simply walk down the access road to wherever it ended. That route, though, would almost certainly have the tightest security. Cutting through the forest would probably be safer, and we would be faced with fewer obstacles as far as security devices were concerned, but it would be terribly easy to make a mistake. A single trip wire running through the trees could be our undoing.

"Shit!" I said quietly. My thinking hadn't progressed much farther than getting us through the wire. Now that we were in I was stumped. Then I remembered something a security officer at a US Navy installation had told me when I was doing a story on the Tomahawk Cruise Missile they were testing. "Security is a method of channelling," he'd said. "Like herding cattle. You move an infiltrator where you want him to go. *Then* you nail him."

So the no-man's-land and the access road were the channel. The forest, by its very unattractiveness, was the way to go. "That way," I whispered, and pointed towards the purple-green blockade of cedar slash. We headed into it.

By the time we'd travelled a hundred yards our faces had been bitten remorselessly by clouds of mosquitoes and my hands were torn by the low straggling brambles that twisted through the cedars in a choking tangle. After twenty minutes I gave up searching the forest floor for trip wires. No one in his right mind would have laid them there.

We had a brief respite when we came upon a dry stream bed that seemed to be going in our direction, but after fifty yards it veered away and we were forced back up into the trees. Nothing I had experienced in the tall woods of British Columbia or the steaming paddies of Vietnam even approached the grinding tenacity of that bush. The trees, the brambles, the mosquitoes, and the spongy, deadfall-littered ground were all conspiring against us. We were trespassers; and we paid for every yard of earth we conquered.

It took us about an hour and a half to travel what I estimated was less than a mile. By then we were resting as often as we moved, kneeling in the claustrophobic welter of slash, trying to ease the chafing of the suits and the aches in our shoulders and backs. There was no extra breath for speaking, and nothing to say. The stretch of bush had become the totality of our universe; our only objective was to reach its end.

When we did it came so abruptly that we almost stumbled out into the open before we realized that the trees had come to an end. I dropped to the ground and pulled Georgina down with me. I'd never seen anything like it.

The clearing was at least one thousand yards a side, the whole area covered in undulating drapes of camouflage nets held up by irregularly placed supports. Between the lattice-work of cloth strips woven through the net I could see the stars. Below the net there was another forest—but not of trees. Hundreds of pipes, each the size of a sewer conduit and each topped with a manhole-like covering, sprouted up from a surface that was as smooth as a golf course. Each of the coverings was itself topped by a complex arrangement of pipes and dials. They looked like gas meters. The conduits were laid out in neat rows, each one separated by a space of ten or twelve yards. The paths between the ranks of pipes were as wide as a medium sized truck and paved with concrete. For some reason the clearing reminded me of a gigantic graveyard, each of the conduits a headstone. A military graveyard.

"My God!" whispered Georgina. "What is it?"

"I don't know," I said. "But take some pictures anyway."

She unstrapped the camera from around her neck, adjusted the focus on the Nikon, and began photographing. I'd picked up some infra-red film at a camera store in Renfrew, but even with it I doubted that she'd come up with anything useful. The pictures would look like shots of a filtration plant. My brain was reeling. What did this have to do with smuggling?

"Okay," whispered Georgina. "I think I have enough."

We stood up and I stepped gingerly out into the covered clearing, carefully watching my feet for trip wires. I hit one on the third step, almost falling over it. I silently pointed out the faint silvery thread and Georgina stepped across. We continued on, moving rapidly down one of the rows of pipes.

I stopped at one point and took a closer look. The dials were marked off in BTU's—British Thermal Units. It didn't tell me a thing. Generating plant? Steam pipes? But why camouflage it? I didn't understand, but at least in one way it was a relief. To an infra-red television monitor the whole area would read as one big red smudge. If there was anyone watching the installation on such a monitor, we'd be lost in the heat patterns. I kept going, looking back every now and again to make sure Georgina was close behind me.

We eventually reached the end of the conduit plantation, and we halted behind one of the last pipes. Beyond it the camouflage net ended and we could see out onto a wide paved area that looked like a parking lot. Huddled together in a rough C shape around it were a collection of dark, windowless buildings. To the right, a road turned off into the darkness—the access road leading out of the installation. There was no sign of life, but I knew that was an illusion. You didn't go to this much trouble to secure a place and then leave it empty at five o'clock each night. Somewhere in those buildings men were awake, and watching. Georgina unlimbered the Nikon and took a few more exposures. Once again I knew they'd be useless. Except for the conduit farm the place looked like any other industrial installation. We had to get closer.

I scanned the buildings facing us, looking for some way in. There was a small door set into one wall about fifty yards away. I was about to get up when a sound registered faintly on the perimeter of my senses. I cocked an ear and waited. A truck, and a big one at that, coming down the access road. We waited, crouched behind the man high pipe. A few minutes later I caught the wash of headlights running across the face of the building closest to us and heard the truck engine gearing down. The truck itself appeared, pulling into the lot. In the faint starlight I could see the ten foot high logo on its side panel: a giant flared horseshoe—the Greek letter Omega.

I heard a faint clicking sound and whirled. Georgina grinned at me and then turned back to the camera, squeezing off another shot. There was a spill of light from a long warehouse-like building at the top of the C-cluster, and I caught a brief glimpse of a forklift silhouetted against it. Then the door closed. The forklift crept towards the truck and stopped at its rear doors. I squinted at the truck, trying to pick off details, but everything was in shadow. A door slammed and I heard a brief mumble of voices. There was a short laugh and then the sound of creaking hinges. The doors of the truck were being opened. Beside me Georgina kept shooting. The forklift whirred, bringing the skid up level with the bed of the truck, and I watched as a dozen cannisters were loaded on. Each one was the size of a fifty gallon oil drum, but by the way the two men were handling them they were obviously quite light. When the forklift was fully loaded the truck driver hopped onto the back of the smaller machine and it turned, heading back to the warehouse. The light reappeared as the forklift approached and then snapped off again as the carrier entered the building.

I tugged at Georgina's arm. "Come on," I whispered into her ear. "I want to see if there's anything else on that truck!"

We stood up and sprinted across the asphalt to the truck, lowering ourselves beside one of the big rear wheels. I waited, muscles tensed to run again. We were out in the open. If anyone came out now we were as good as dead. It had taken the two men about five minutes to load the drums; I figured on about half that time to unload and return. We had to hurry. I stood up again, keeping my back against the truck, and slid around to the open rear doors. I boosted myself up on the tailgate and then turned, kneeling to give Georgina a hand. She clambered up beside me and we crept into the long trailer.

Obviously, the forklift load was only the beginning; the truck was still almost full. I looked at the barrels closely. There were no markings on them at all, not even the Omega symbol. Oddly the drums weren't made out of sheet metal—they were dull, finished, stainless steel. What the hell did you carry in stainless steel drums? Milk? It hardly seemed likely. Georgina was shooting furiously. I checked my watch. Two minutes since we'd left the cover of the pipe. Time to go. We returned to the edge of the tailgate and I jumped down. Georgina followed. A voice called out and we froze as a searchlight blinded us.

"Guten Abend, Herr Coffin," said the voice. "You'll notice that my German has improved."

Brandt.

Chapter Seventeen

The room Brandt and his men escorted us to was in the back of the warehouse housing the forklift. To get to it we were frog-marched down an aisle piled floor to ceiling with the mysterious stainless steel drums. Every few yards or so the various shipments had been marked off with serial numbers attached to the metal grillwork holding up the banks of drums.

The room itself was about ten by ten, high ceilinged and windowless unless you counted a ventilation grill far up on one side of the flat-white enamelled walls. There was no furniture. Brandt had ordered one of his men to stand guard outside the locked metal door; and the walls, on inspection, also proved to be metal. "No attic escapes from here," I said, trying to sound a lot more cheerful than I felt.

Georgina said nothing. She sat crouched against the far wall staring stonily at the door. After a while, I sat down beside her. At least we were out of our rubber suits. A few minutes after seeing us into the cell, Brandt had returned and wordlessly handed over two pairs of denim coveralls and two shirts. I tried again to coax a smile out of Georgina. "Now what?" I said.

Her expression didn't change. We sat together silently as time slowly crept past. I dozed uneasily for a while but it must have been only an hour later when the sound of a key turning in the lock brought me fully awake. Brandt appeared, carrying a simple wooden chair. He set it down in the middle of the room, then exited. I had a suspicion that the chair wasn't for our comfort, so I didn't move. I was right. A minute or two later Brandt came back, this time with Llewellyn behind him. The thin, erect man sat down in the chair and looked at us. He waved a hand and Brandt left the room, closing the door behind him.

"Well, then," said Llewellyn, smiling thinly. He was immaculately dressed in a lightweight cotton suit. He sat in the chair with his legs crossed, revealing pipe stem ankles

166

encased in pale woollen socks. He tapped the fingers of one
hand on his knee. The other lay like a coiled snake in his lap.
"You are quite an amazing young man," murmured Llewellyn,
staring at me.

I shrugged. "I try."

"Would you like a cigarette?"

He took a gold Dunhill cigarette case out of his breast
pocket and flipped it open. I sat up and took one of the
cigarettes. He offered me a light and I sat back, dragging in
my first nicotine since I'd left the car, hours before.

"Thank you," I said.

Georgina still hadn't moved. She looked as though she
were in shock. But there was nothing I could do. Llewellyn
lit a cigarette for himself and leaned back in the chair slightly,
eyeing me. We smoked in silence for a few moments, and
then he spoke again.

"For such a determined man you are quite stupid," said
Llewellyn.

"Really?" I said.

He nodded, the thin-lipped smile still in place. "Really,
Mr. Coffin." The smile flickered briefly, and I felt the coldness
emanating from him like a physical force. I had the feeling
Mr. L was doing his best to keep himself in check. "You not
only managed to make the connections that led you here,
turning my country home into an inferno in the process, but
you also managed to penetrate one of the most secure installations in this country."

He paused to tap his ash into a cupped hand, then continued. "On the other hand, you were extraordinarily careless.
You left your car parked by the side of the road for anyone to
see while you fought your way through that jungle outside.
One of my drivers spotted it, and reported to Mr. Brandt."
Now he sat forward in the chair, leaning towards me. The
smile was gone and his eyes were pale and dead. "Mr. Coffin,
you have led me a merry chase. You have forced me to
change plans at great expense. You have made it imperative
that I leave important work in England and elsewhere so that
I could deal with you personally. A merry chase indeed, Mr.
Coffin, but one, I fear, which has come to an end. For you
and Miss Underwood, that is."

"Go fuck yourself," I said, giving him the best my pearly
whites had to offer.

He smiled back. "I think not," he said. "Although your bravado is commendable."

"Screw the bravado, Llewellyn. I've never thought of myself as being the gentleman adventurer type, so maybe you're right about me being stupid that way. But I am a good journalist—and I've got you cold."

"Fluff," said Llewellyn calmly. "You have no more idea of what is going on now than you did in London. Fluff and bluster. The next thing you'll tell me is that you've sent a copy of your notes to a solicitor with instructions that he go to the press if you die under mysterious circumstances. Yes?"

"No," I said. "Not my notes. Sam's. Three photocopies, and not with my lawyer, either. Die or not, they'll come out and you're up shit creek." I stubbed the cigarette out on the floor.

"Mr. Underwood made no notes," said Llewellyn. "We searched his apartment thoroughly." He paused, and gave me a searching look. I had him worried. "Not to mention that you never went to his home. We had it watched."

"You had the train station watched in Paris, too, didn't you?" I said. "I assure you, I not only got into Sam's, but I also retrieved his notes. You didn't find them because they weren't in the apartment. They were in his safety deposit box. And I knew where the key was."

"Frankly, I don't believe you," said Llewellyn.

I shrugged. "Tough," I said. "But I do have the notes. Check behind the light switch in his kitchen. You'll find the key. But the box is empty."

Llewellyn stood up, staring down at me angrily. "A waste of time, Mr. Coffin. A few minutes added to the end of your life."

"It may be a waste of time, but you *will* check it out, won't you?" I sneered. "You can't afford *not* to check it out. You've got too much invested in your operation."

"Many millions of dollars, Mr. Coffin," said Llewellyn, nodding, his grey face tight. "As well as a great deal of time and effort. You are correct, of course. I will have your little story checked out. It won't, however, do you any good. Even if you do have these mythical notes, I seriously doubt that they would prove anything. I don't think Mr. Samuel Underwood knew any more than you." He reached into his pocket again and pulled out the cigarette case. He took out a cigarette and tossed it to me. It landed on the floor between my outstretched legs. "Enjoy it, Mr. Coffin. It will be your last."

He stared down at me without a trace of emotion in his face, then turned on his heel and went to the door. He rapped on it twice and it opened. He went out and the door closed behind him.

"Prick," I whispered, as the lock snicked home. I leaned down and picked the cigarette off the floor. I sat there, looking at the door and tossing the tube of tobacco from hand to hand. Then I crumpled it and tossed the pieces away.

"Quitting?" said Georgina.

I turned and looked at her. The glaze was gone from her eyes and she seemed alert. "Welcome back to the land of the living," I said.

"I was never gone." She smiled weakly. "But I knew that if I said anything I'd burst into tears so I just tried to ignore the world for a while. It helped."

"Good," I said.

"We're in real trouble aren't we?"

I laughed hollowly. "That's putting it mildly," I said. "I don't know how much time I bought with that cock and bull story about the notes, but it won't be much. He's going to find out pretty quick that the key in Sam's stash isn't for a safety deposit box."

"But he will find a key," said Georgina. "Won't he?"

"He will unless Sam's changed his habits," I answered.

"Well, that should make him stop and think at any rate," said Georgina. She sighed deeply.

"Cheer up," I muttered. "We'll figure something out."

Georgina nodded absently. "Peter, what do you think Sam really found?" she asked, after a moment. "And . . . and what's happened to him?"

"I'm not sure on either count," I said. "Llewellyn was right. We don't know very much more now than we did a couple of days ago. Any theories I've got would be shooting in the dark."

"I think they've killed him," said Georgina, her voice breaking as she finally admitted it. "They wouldn't keep us around if they had him to interrogate."

"We can't say that for sure," I lied, trying to be diplomatic. But we both knew that she was right. Sam had been written out of the equation a long time ago. The question was: why? What had he found out that marked him for death? If Omega Electronics was a front for whatever it was they were smuggling, it was a front on a massive and expensive scale. Nothing I could think of required such a gigantic and multi-levelled operation.

"Drugs," said Georgina.

"Pardon?"

"Drugs. That's what they've been smuggling. That's what those drums are full of. I'm sure of it."

She'd been reading my mind and she'd come up with a possible answer. I let her spin it out, trying to find the flaws. "Go on," I prompted.

"What can you put into fifty gallon drums that you can't bring into the country legitimately?" she asked rhetorically. "It has to be drugs. Does AVTOUR fly out of Turkey, or any place like that?"

I cast back in my mind, then nodded. "Yes. They've got a branch in Istanbul. And landing privileges."

"So," said Georgina. "They pick up the raw opium in Turkey and fly it to France. Don't they have big narcotic laboratories in France?"

Once again I nodded. "Marseille is famous for it," I answered.

"So they manufacture the heroin in France, load it back onto an AVTOUR flight, and fly it to Canada."

"Yes, but why Canada?" I asked. "Why not right into the US? Canada has a tiny smack population in comparison to the States."

"I've thought about that. The answer's stockpiling."

"I don't get you."

"The Middle East has always been dicey politically," she explained slowly, "and American relations with Turkey and Iraq and a lot of other opium producing countries haven't been too good in the past. Things have been deteriorating. Couldn't it be that the major distributors of heroin got together to set up a stockpile—rather like the De Boer's diamond cartel? With a stockpile of heroin like the one in this warehouse they could artificially raise the price without being dependent on shipments from overseas. And Canada makes sense. You'd have a hard time finding a better spot than here. Small shipments could be smuggled across the Canadian-US border as they were needed." She grinned triumphantly. "What do you think?"

"It fits," I said. "It's a bit on the incredible side, but this has all been incredible. There's only one thing that bothers me. It's been nagging at me for a long time, and I still can't pin it down."

"What?" asked Georgina, frowning. "I thought my scenario was flawless."

"The flight," I said softly, staring up at the ceiling of the room. "The cancelled flight. It doesn't make any sense."

"Why not?" she asked. "You explained it quite well enough to me. They were afraid Sam had blown the whistle on them."

I shook my head. "That's what I thought at first," I said, "but it doesn't hold water. They're too well connected. God! They managed to get a handle on the assistant general manager at Heathrow. And that customs clerk—he told us the shipment sent out by Alpha Air Services was all under special seal. These guys have got the customs sheds of at least three countries in their back pockets. If they can get special seals, fiddle with computers and all that, then they can do anything. They wouldn't have cancelled the flight."

"Maybe they were just being careful," suggested Georgina.

I lifted my shoulders. I was beginning to wish I hadn't trashed the cigarette Llewellyn had given me. "Maybe," I said. "But it doesn't really fit into the way we've seen them operate."

"But they *did* cancel the flight," insisted Georgina. "They must have had a reason."

"Find that out," I said, "and I think you'll have the key to this whole thing."

"So I wonder what happens next?" said Georgina.

We didn't have to wait long for an answer. Almost as soon as she'd spoken the door opened and Brandt motioned us to our feet. "Out," he said, crooking a finger at me. With his other hand he gently massaged the bandage on his head. I felt something hard form in my stomach and I winced inwardly. It looked as though Brandt was looking forward to his revenge for the clip across the head I'd given him.

We walked out of the room and into the warehouse. Two armed guards fell in beside us as Brandt led the way back down through the stacks of barrels. The guards were wearing the same pale-green fatigues and mindless expressions as the ones who'd taken us in a few hours before. Instead of going out to the parking lot we turned and went through another alley of the big tin cans, heading towards a pair of wide double doors. Brandt opened them and stepped aside. We walked out into the blackness of very early morning.

We'd exited at the rear of the warehouse, coming out onto a flat expanse of asphalt fifty yards wide, stretching out both left and right for a good three thousand feet or more. Floodlights glowed. It was the private airstrip we'd been looking for.

A hundred feet up the runway sat an aircraft—a spanking clean Beechcraft Duke in dark blue and gold. The AVTOUR colours. I looked for some ID, but there was nothing except the registration number. Even feeling the way I was I could appreciate the needle-nosed good looks of the twin engine prop plane. The six seater was one of the best in the world of its class; half a million dollars' worth of high speed, high altitude, aviation craftsmanship. I'd flown one on test the year before for *Private Pilot Magazine* and it had handled magnificently. The two big Lycoming TS-10's spun out three hundred and eighty horsepower apiece, and could boost the sleek machine over a thousand miles at twenty-five thousand feet, cruising at a breakneck two hundred and seventy-five miles per hour. It was the closest thing you could get to a jet and still take off from a strip under a half mile long.

One of the guards nudged me and I went across the asphalt, Georgina close beside me. We climbed up into the Duke, Brandt bringing up the rear. Llewellyn was already seated and strapped in to one of the two rear facing, boardroom-style seats that backed up behind the pilot and co-pilot positions. Georgina and I sat down on the forward facing bench seat, and Brandt clambered in to sit beside Llewellyn. As we strapped in I looked up the short, narrow walkway between the seats that led to the flight deck. I could see the peak cap of a pilot's head, but the co-pilot's chair was empty.

As soon as the buckle clicked on his seatbelt, Brandt reached into his jacket and hauled out a brutal-looking Colt service revolver with a barrel mouth the size of the Holland Tunnel. He set it down on his lap, keeping his forefinger on the trigger. I hoped he wasn't idiot enough to use it. A blast from a gun like that would tear through anything it was aimed at and take out a good sized chunk of the airplane besides.

Up ahead the pilot did his runup and a few seconds later the Lycomings began to throb, the stainless steel prop noses becoming a whirling blur. The pilot nicked the left hand throttle and we turned, taxiing back along the runway. We reached the far end, facing another wall of trees, then turned again to face back the way we had come. The man in the driver's seat let the engines spool up to a heavy roar before he cut in power. We began to roll, the multi-building complex of Omega whirling past on my left. Still a couple of hundred feet short of the perimeter fence the pilot lifted the nose, lining up the bottom of the windscreen with the horizon. The nose wheel came off the ground and we were airborne. He took us up in a fairly steep climb for such a heavy plane, then half rolled us in the opposite direction. There was a faint thud as the wheels came up. We were on our way to God only knew where.

Brandt wasn't enjoying it at all. There was a faint sheen of sweat on his broad, furrowed forehead, and his free hand twitched nervously, moving up to his temple, playing with the bandage. He had that stony-faced look people who are afraid of flying sometimes get; a controlled desperation that makes their eyes waver with every noise and the muscles in their cheeks twitch when the course changes by a hair. I looked beyond him to the windscreen, but I couldn't see much beyond the faint greyness of approaching dawn. I hoped the weather would be clear. Brandt had the reactions of a sickbag chronic. The slightest turbulence would probably have him puking all over the nice bronze-tinted rug at his feet, and I was a little too close for comfort. On the other hand, it was nice to see him looking uncomfortable. Llewellyn seemed unperturbed. In fact, he looked as though he hadn't even noticed the takeoff. He sat calmly, going over a sheaf of punch-edged computer sheets, making little notations every once in a while. After almost an hour in the air he finally looked up from his work and glanced at me.

"Enjoying the flight, Mr. Coffin?" he asked.

"Nice plane, but you should get yourself a new pilot," I said. I wasn't kidding. The faceless man up front was handling the responsive craft like a truck driver—too much power too soon, and a heavy foot on the pedals.

"Henri is used to flying our Falcon," said Llewellyn. "But I assure you he is fully capable of taking us to our destination."

That explained the hardass flying. Henri was the pilot for the Dassault I'd seen at Llewellyn's place outside London. There's a lot of difference between a twin prop like the Duke and a bizjet.

"I don't suppose you'd like to tell me what our destination is?" I asked.

Llewellyn showed his teeth and shook his head. "No," he said. "I am not the evil figure from a James Bond melodrama who gloatingly reveals all to his victims. I am a businessman, Mr. Coffin, and I see no point in compounding my errors. You are along for the ride as they say. Your part of the journey will be terminated when I receive word from our people in London that they have checked out your story concerning Mr. Underwood's apartment."

"By terminate I gather you mean violently," I said.

"You gather correctly. Violently, but I assure you, with efficiency and decorum. I am not a litterbug, Mr. Coffin."

Even I had to smile at that. But Georgina didn't think it was funny at all. "You really are a revolting man," she said slowly, speaking for the first time since takeoff.

His eyes swivelled to her. "Oh?"

"Yes," she said, with a look that would have shrivelled anyone except a man like Llewellyn. "When my father hears about the way you've treated us, and the things you've done, you'll wish you'd died in that fire we set."

"But your father never *will* know," said Llewellyn, folding his printouts carefully and slipping them into a briefcase at his side. "At the moment, your father thinks you are on a holiday in Frankfurt. Within a day or two he will receive a telegram from New York. The telegram will inform him that while returning from a supposed love affair with a man you met on the flight over you were involved in a terrible automobile accident in which you were burned beyond recognition. The charred remains of your passport will reflect your passing. The ashes will be returned to him from the district coroner's office in Buffalo, New York. Your father will be distraught, but the documentation with which he will be provided will satisfy him. As far as our dossier shows, you have something of a reputation for somewhat bizarre assignations with men."

Georgina coloured to the dyed roots of her hair and fell silent.

"And what have you got planned for me?" I asked.

"Something on the same order, Mr. Coffin, with a few added details. You are wanted by the French Sûreté for questioning in the case of Mr. Kroeger's heinous murder. A man of your description is also wanted in Paris for the theft of a taxicab at gunpoint. Your editors in Toronto have already been questioned by the RCMP, and they too have a warrent for your arrest, based for the most part on a supply of heroin found in your lodgings. Your remains will be found in the trunk of a rented car in the Montreal suburb of Mount Royal. Mr. Brandt here will attend to the necessary cosmetics, yes?" He turned to Brandt, who smiled broadly. "It will appear that you were involved in a drug ring operating between Paris and Montreal. Your age, your somewhat checkered background, and the amount you travel will lend credence to the story. Since you have no relatives living there will be only minor fieldwork necessary beyond that."

I turned away from him and looked out the side window, trying to quell a sickly rise of panic. He had it all worked out, and there wasn't the faintest doubt that he had the tools to pull it off. It looked as though Georgina's drug scenario had been on target. There was a grotesque irony in using dope to set me up for the fall.

The picture outside did nothing to improve my mood. It had lightened up enough for me to see that the weather was building. We were up a good eighteen or twenty thousand feet, but Henri was having a hard time keeping above the rapidly forming heads of cloud that were boiling up all around us. Almost in response to my unspoken thought I felt the nose tilt as we climbed even higher. The sky beyond the scything prop was a deep purple, etched brilliantly here and there with smaller, almost phosphorescent puffs of lower cloud. The storm mass stretched from horizon to horizon. If we stayed on course it looked as though Brandt was going to lose his breakfast. I smiled sourly at the anvil-shaped masses ahead, then glanced at Brandt and Llewellyn. We were in for a rough ride, but facing back the way they were they hadn't noticed the approaching stormline. I thought about letting Brandt in on what was in store for him but stopped myself. He'd find out soon enough.

A little less than ten minutes later we did. Henri had pushed the Duke to the limit, but it wasn't enough. We hit the front head on. One minute we were flying in grey light, the next we were enfolded in murky darkness, the windows opaqued by slashing lines of rain. Henri had held off until the last minute before warning his passengers, hoping that he'd be able to get on top of it. Now it was too late.

Brandt had gone dead white at the first buffet that hit us, spasmodically grasping the sides of his seat. Llewellyn merely looked out the window and frowned slightly. I checked on Georgina. She looked almost as bad as Brandt. She was pale and tense, lower lip quivering. At least she had her eyes open, which was a step up from her last flight.

I smiled across the cabin at Brandt. "Ever flown in a thunderstorm before?" I asked. He ignored me, staring blindly. I went on anyway, enjoying every terrified twitch of the vein that had begun to pulse in his forehead. "It's awful," I continued brightly. "You get thrown all over the sky. Sometimes, if you can't get around it, like now, you wind up flying through hailstorms. Pellets the size of golfballs. They can tear the props right off a plane like this."

"Shut up!" yelled Brandt. His face had gone green.

"No, really," I said, "it's like flying into an insane asylum. Crazy. But the hail isn't the worst, you know."

"Mr. Coffin," warned Llewellyn.

I paid no attention; I was getting a little of my own back. "The worst things," I said solemnly, "are the air currents. Wicked in a storm like this. Did you know that they don't really understand exactly what goes on in this type of weather? I bet this is the first time ol' Henri there's ever gone into some. Terrible. Sometimes it's like the earth just opened up and swallowed you."

Which, at precisely that moment, it proceeded to do.

Chapter Eighteen

During the summer months, and especially in the humid, almost stifling period between mid-July and mid-August, the area between Algonquin Park in the west and Montreal in the east is a breeding ground for phenomenal thunderstorms. Often, the storms become trapped between the upsweep of the Gatineau Hills and the Laurentians in the north, and the incoming high pressure regions along the St. Lawrence. They circulate in a gigantic cauldron of furious weather, pummelling the land below and sometimes reaching almost hurricane proportions. Because of the high temperatures and the excessive humidity present during this period, there is intense electrical activity. The surging currents of air are occasionally so severe that tornadoes are created—thin, jet-black funnels of horror that reach down out of the looming cloud masses to strike the land below.

On the whole, a thunderstorm isn't much different from an ordinary rainstorm except for the violence and speed of the moving air within it. Because of this erratic and high speed movement of currents, water, ice, and dust particles within the growing cloud mass are forced past each other, and as the cloud mass reaches its full growth—the familiar flat-bottomed anvil shape—vast electrical charges are created within it. The upper, less dense portions gather up positive electrons, while the lower area lines up negatively. The lower area also casts an "electron shadow" of positively charged particles on the ground below. When the charge becomes unbearably large, a thin layer of positively charged particles at the base of the cloud initiates a discharge, joining with the particles on the ground. These intermittent discharges are called "strokes," and are invisible to the naked eye. It's the "return stroke" that we see as lightning, and which causes all the fireworks. This return of current, a discharge from the ground below of all its stored electricity, travels up the already existing electron channel created by the initial "stroke," moving at light speed to the mass of negatively charged particles in the thunderhead. The enormous surge of current is contained in a channel only a few centimetres wide and produces heat in excess of thirty thousand degrees Celsius. In the split second it takes for the current to knife up into the cloud, the channel breaks down under the incredible forces within it, expanding with supersonic speed and producing a shock wave of deafening proportions. Thunder. Sometimes, when two major thunderclouds are in close proximity, the electrical discharges take place between the clouds with the same ear-splitting result.

Henri had clearly never flown in an Ottawa Valley thunderstorm before. Instead of turning along the weather, or even trying to drive through the cloud mass, he had opted instead for a small alleyway of relatively clear air between two of the purpled horrors. The shifting up and down drafts were almost enough to tear the wings off the Duke. We plummeted down into the air pocket between the clouds like a runaway express elevator—right into a passionate electrical embrace between the two highly charged clouds.

If we hadn't been strapped in, everyone on board the Duke would have literally hit the roof. I felt my stomach rise up into my throat as the floor dropped out beneath my feet and I had a snap impression of Brandt's face as his gorge rose, then expelled itself into the cabin interior. Llewellyn's briefcase spilled over, filling the small cabin with reams of fluttering paper, and somewhere I heard screaming. The entire aircraft lit up brilliantly for an instant and the battering blast of the shock wave threw me against the wall of the fuselage. Outside, the world had gone mad. We were right in the middle of hell, continuous crabbing bolts of lightning cracking across the sky in a technicolour nightmare. The plane seemed to pause in mid-flight and then began to tumble. We were doing a rapid wing-over, completely out of control.

The interior of the Duke was filled nauseatingly with the stink of ozone and Brandt's vomit. Both he and Llewellyn were panicking, trying to unstrap themselves. Brandt's mouth was wide with terror, but his scream was lost in the pandemonium of the storm and the gut-tearing roar of the straining engines. The wing-over flipped us onto our backs just as Llewellyn unsnapped his belt and he crashed into the ceiling, now below our suspended bodies. An instant later the plane flipped back again, sliding into a yawing turn. The flashes of lightning lit the plane like a strobe, etching my retinas with Llewellyn's jerky dance as he hit the back of Brandt's seat then bounced off the thug's thrusting body.

I managed to get out of my own belt, and staggered forward, the dropping nose of the Duke flinging me between the two forward seats and into the cockpit. Henri was at the controls, his head snapped back against the headrest, blood streaming from his nose and mouth. There was a matching smear of red against the windscreen. His arms hung limply away from the controls. The yoke had been pushed all the way forward, probably from the force of Henri's chest smashing into it.

I struggled into the co-pilot's chair and tugged on the dual yoke, trying to bring us out of the swooping, wing waggling dive. The yoke answered and the nose came up, but the pedals were like glue at my feet and we continued to yaw back and forth. Another concussion and another bolt of lightning. It threw the plane out of my hands again and the engine RPM's almost hit the pin. We were stalling. I let the nose drop and pushed the throttles on the console to the pin, trying to get power, but the pedals still wouldn't answer. I took a quick look across at Henri. His feet were entangled in the controls on his side, interfering with what I was trying to do. Ahead of me I could see another brooding bank of cloud and there were dark, lightning shot masses on either side. We were right in the middle of it all.

"George!" I yelled.

With Henri lousing up the pedals there was no way we were going to get out of this alive. I shouted again, struggling to hang onto the jerking yoke. I could feel the Duke vibrating crazily. Much more of this and she'd tear herself apart.

"George!" I screamed again.

This time I thought I heard an answer, but there wasn't time to check. The nose of the Duke sliced into another clot of thick black cloud and my vision was completely obscured. Suddenly there was a repeated smashing sound and the windshield was abruptly alive with dozens of impacting hailstones, bouncing onto the glass and disintegrating. The hail hammered at the plane like thousands of insanely pounding fists and I could feel myself blacking out. It was too much to take. Then, out of the corner of my eye, I spotted Georgina balancing herself by clutching the backs of the cockpit seats. There was blood on her forehead.

"Get him out!" I bellowed over the kettle drum clatter of the hail.

She pushed forward and tried to get her hands under the unconscious pilot's armpits. She finally managed it and began dragging him back. She disappeared from my vision and the last thing I saw were Henri's legs as she pulled him back into the cabin. I hit the pedals experimentally and they responded mushily. I let out a whoop of satisfaction. The game wasn't over yet. The plane was mine.

But what the hell was I supposed to do with it? I gave the panel a quick once over, digging into my memory for something to hitch on to, some instruction ... Climb. When you're in trouble, climb if you can. I pulled back on the yoke gently and watched the nose come up ahead of me, almost invisible through the fog-like cloud. I checked the artificial horizon. At least we weren't flying upside down. The digital rate-of-climb monitor showed us lifting steadily, and as we went up the vibrations and gyrations lessened. We were in the top layer of the storm. Henri hadn't been able to get above it, so I didn't even bother trying. I levelled out and wondered what to do next.

Then the portside engine cut out and I didn't have any choice in the matter.

Losing an engine is the kind of thing your instructor warns you about when you're going for a twin-rating; and it's also the kind of thing you never expect to happen, at least not to you. Any one-off instruction you do get is usually given on a nice clear day within spitting distance of a good long runway— not in the middle of a lashing storm eighteen thousand feet up, with no idea where the ground is, let alone a field to put down on. I hit the master switch with my thumb, trying to keep the rudder hard left to compensate for the pull of the starboard engine, but the Lycoming just sat out there, the four vane prop spinning slowly. The fuel feed was fine, the mags were fine, everything was fine, except the goddamn thing wouldn't go. I throttled back on the starboard engine, reducing the strain on the rudder. The rain was still pounding furiously on the windscreen and my visibility was nil. The only thing in my favour was the fact that we weren't falling out of the sky. I gently nosed her down and throttled back some more as another flare of lightning lit up around me, the crash of thunder that followed on its heels sending a booming shudder through every rivet, strut, spar, and pylon.

Then the *starboard* engine quit. At the same instant all the dials suddenly dropped to the pins, and the healthy glow from the LED avionics panel faded to nothing. The hail, or maybe just the battering the Duke had taken in the storm, had screwed an electrical connection royally. I was all alone.

I gave myself just enough time for a single and colourful expletive before I began to panic. In front of me, the needle nose of the plane began to fall away as we went into a steep, gliding dive towards the ground below. I felt, rather than heard, things coming apart behind me as bodies started tumbling again. I checked the console but the dials were still dead. All I knew for sure was that we were going down, and I didn't have any way to stop it. I tried to remember how far a Duke could glide in a no-power situation but nothing came to mind. Not that it mattered—I didn't know where the hell I was anyway.

I tipped up the nose slightly, trying to lessen the angle of descent, my mind burning. The chances of landing the Duke with no power were less than zero. One way or another I had to get at least one of the engines rotating again. The weather was doing its level best to distract me. The lower we fell, the worse it became. We were back into the active centre of the storm, and electrical activity was building up again, great tearing sheets of lightning rippling across the windscreen, followed by more of the mindbending thunderclaps, each concussion threatening to rob me of what little control I had left. My hands were slippery wet with sweat on the yoke, but I didn't dare try to wipe them off. I knew that if we ran into another of the downdrafts that had got us into trouble in the first place I'd spin out without any way of pulling the Duke back onto the level. The Maule would have been of more use to me then. At least her control surfaces were moved around by wires and pulleys, not hydraulics like the Duke. Hydraulic controls need power to keep them going, and I didn't have an ounce. I swore again, desperately trying to remember if there was anything you could do to dead-start a plane like the Duke. I also knew that the longer I waited the harder it was going to be; dead-starts are bad enough, but if the engine cooled too much I wouldn't have a prayer.

Get the props windmilling. Let the props turn over the engines even if the starter is out of action. Textbook stuff. But *how* do you get the props to turn over?

Easy. Dive. Straight down.

It was just about my only hope, but even knowing that I hesitated. I figured I'd lost three or four thousand feet. That still left me with ten or twelve to glide in, outreach the storm, and come out into the clear again. On the other hand there was a good possibility I was running *with* the storm by this time, rather than against it. The compass was out so there was no way of telling. I had to get power—and I had to get it right now.

"Peter!" It was Georgina, somewhere behind me. "Brandt is coming around!" she yelled, her voice almost lost in the clamour of the storm. "What do I do?"

"Hit the son-of-a-bitch!" I called back. "Then hang on!" I waited for a few seconds more, then pushed the yoke steadily away from me.

The nose fell and I felt myself slipping forward in the seat. I cursed myself for an idiot. I hadn't bothered to strap in! I let go of the yoke with one hand and fumbled with the buckles, finally managing to get myself into the harness. I could feel the pull now as we dropped. I eased back fractionally, not wanting to risk an uncontrolled roll. We steadied, but not by much. There was a sound like a shotgun going off beside my ear and I almost jumped out of the seat as the lightning exploded only yards in front of me. The shock wave took the Duke and worried it like a cat with a mouse in its jaws. Both hands came off the yoke and my head smacked squarely into the side window. I rolled myself back, groggy and seeing double, and grabbed the yoke again. Something wet was dripping into my eyes and I blinked it away. Blood.

Our descent was so steep that I could hear the harsh banshee screaming of the air going over the wings. I was running out of altitude. Now or never. I checked port and starboard. Both props were whirling. I flicked the master a couple of times, praying. Nothing happened. Then I realized what was wrong. A ghostly voice from a year before rose into my brain, the voice of the Duke demonstrator at the Abbotsford Air Show: "*Best dual tank system of any aircraft in its category.*"

I looked down at the control panel, slack jawed. If the electronics were out there was no way for the automatic fuel switching to work. The manual override was right below it. I pulled the small choke-like handle. Like magic, both the engines caught almost instantly and I felt the jerky vibrations of the cooling machines take hold again.

It was almost too late. As I began easing the nose up out of the near vertical dive I found myself staring almost straight down at the ground. It looked as though we were less than a thousand feet up, with wet, dirty-brown farmland below. But at least I could see.

I yanked the nose up, leaving myself wide open for a back-flip that would inevitably turn into a dead-stick spin, and fought with the sluggish pedals. With only a couple of hundred feet to spare I managed to get the Duke back into enough control to keep us from turning into a post hole. I did a quick check of the engines again, trying to see through the haze of spattering rain. Both engines were turning the props, but I could both feel and see that things weren't going smoothly. The sound and vibration were both ragged, and there was a long greenish slick forming above the wing. I was leaking oil or fuel, and badly. I was going to have to put down. I searched for the manual undercarriage controls and cranked the wheels down, bearing hard. There was a dull thud and then a satisfying click as they locked into place. I leaned forward and peered through the windscreen, looking for a place to put down. We were still flying at treetop height with less than a thousand yards' visibility. I prayed there weren't any hills in the near vicinity. By the time I saw them we'd be nose deep into the ground.

Directly below, a railway line appeared out of the misting rain and I veered back, following it, keeping my eyes over the side, looking for a field big enough. The engines were sounding rockier with each passing second, and like it or not I was losing power again. To the left, like a smudge in the distance, I saw the square shadow shape of a farmhouse. It was situated on a low hill, surrounded on all sides by rolling fields dotted irregularly with stacks of hay. I tucked us right and made a single pass, taking a chance and dropping a wing for a better look. As I banked into the turn I thought I saw the lights of a town blinking, half shrouded by the gusting sheets of rain. It looked like it was only a couple of miles away.

I finished the turn and came in for my approach. I kicked back the engines as low as I dared and dropped the flaps 50 per cent. The field ahead ended with the farmhouse on the hill. I'd have less than a thousand feet to put her down. I closed my eyes for a split second and then dropped the flaps to full. We sank like a stone, almost clipping the nearside fence as we angled onto the field. I felt the first touch of the wheels, and throttled back some more, leaving just enough power to keep the front end aligned when we were fully down.

Soft field landings. They tell you all sorts of things about them when you learn to land. Things like: keep the nose up and the speed down; watch out for runway tilt; beware of ground water on the grass that will skid half the runway out from underneath you. It's all good stuff, but it's like the stuff they give you on power-outs: hypothetical. Some pilots love coming in on a grass strip; they pretend they're Spits back from a quick trip over the Channel, and it gives them some kind of buzz. I'd always preferred the relaxation of a nice wide strip full of markings and a guy on the other end of the horn giving me explicit information about crosswinds over the runway. Never in my wildest dreams did I think I'd ever be landing a crippled twin on a farmer's field in the middle of a blinding rain. And I blew it.

An instant after I felt the first touch of ground at the nose wheel, the soft earth grabbed on and brought the front end to a dead stop. Unfortunately, the Lycomings, even in their crippled condition, obeyed Newton's law and kept heaving forward. I had a single brief moment of clarity as the fibreglass nose dug into the ground and crumpled. Then the world turned upside down as we turtled, and the lights went out.

I woke up with my eyes full of rain and Georgina's sopping coveralled breast against my cheek. I was soaked to the skin, and I could feel cold wetness against the backs of my legs.

"Unngh," I said, and blinked. Georgina's face swam into view. Her hair was a wet, tangled mass plastered to her cheeks, and her long eyelashes were jewelled with beads of water.

"Can you hear me, Peter?" she asked.

I nodded, and the movement sent a grinding pain down through the back of my head and into my spine. I groaned again and mumbled a reply. " 'Kay," I said, or something like it. I struggled, and Georgina caught me under the arms, helping me up. Everything hurt, but nothing was inoperative. I swayed and almost passed out. Georgina hung on.

"Are you all right?" she asked. Her voice seemed fuzzy and distant.

I lied. "Fine, fine," I managed. My eyes stopped soloing and things began looking a little more normal. I glanced around, still staggering slightly with Georgina at my side, her arm around my waist. Somehow she'd managed to drag me

out and away from the demolished Duke. It lay a hundred
yards away, shattered undercarriage poking at the surly blackness
of the ruptured sky above. We were standing in a quagmire,
the gluey soil tugging at our shoes. I would have done better
landing the Duke on her belly.

"Brandt, Llewellyn?" I mumbled.

"Still inside. The pilot's dead, I think. His neck doesn't
look right."

"Hard cheese for Henri."

"There's a farmhouse," said Georgina. She turned me
gently and pointed up the slope I'd seen on the approach.
The tall, gothic-looking structure perched on the hill two or
three hundred yards away. It might as well have been ten
miles. I was sure that I couldn't make more than ten feet.

"Come on," said Georgina. I glanced blearily at her. Except for a ragged flap of skin a couple of inches square that
had been chewed out of her temple, she seemed in good
shape. If she was willing to make a try for the farmhouse I
decided to go along with her. I wasn't in the mood for
decisions. More than anything I wanted to lie down and close
my eyes again; standing erect had become a drag. She kept
her arm around me, guiding me up the slope. Before we
started she had bent awkwardly, and scooped something from
the ground to tuck under her other arm. It looked like
Llewellyn's briefcase.

I lost track of time for a bit, and the next thing I knew we
were going through the gaping, doorless entrance to the
farmhouse. I stopped and turned, looking back down the hill
at the Duke. From the other direction the trip had seemed
impossible. I knew I must be better than I felt. Beyond the
wreck, town lights blurred in the rain. The settlement had
been closer than I'd imagined. And someone had either seen
or heard us go down. A pair of winking red lights were
moving in our direction, and fast.

"Inside," said Georgina softly. I stumbled through the
doorway into the enclosing blackness of the house.

The place had been abandoned long ago. In the weak light
coming in through the shattered windows I could see the
gloomy interior. The floor was littered with old newspapers
and broken bottles. Laths and crumbling plaster were piled
at the base of the walls in jumbled heaps. It looked as though

someone had gone at the place with a twenty pound sledge and then stopped when the booze-madness faded.

There was a kitchen chair minus its back beside one of the windows. Georgina moved it up against the far wall and sat me down gently. I let my head fall back against the wall and closed my eyes. It felt marvellous. I breathed deeply, sucking in the musty smell of the house as though it were ambrosia. I opened my eyes. Georgina had taken up a position at the window, kneeling on the floor among the garbage and peeping over the sill.

"What's going on out there?" I asked.

She glanced back over her shoulder to check on me, then turned again to the window. "A police car, I think. And there's another coming. A truck...No, an ambulance. They've stopped at the end of the field."

"What are they doing?"

"Nothing," she replied, her voice low. "A couple of men just got out of the police car. They're looking at the airplane. Talking. One of them has something in his hand. A radio. The ambulance just stopped."

"Anything happening at the plane?"

"No," she said. "The police are walking across the field now. Two men from the ambulance are going with them."

"Are they looking this way, paying any attention to the farmhouse?"

"No. They're just interested in the plane."

"Good," I said. "Let's hope it stays that way. What colour is the police car?"

"Green and yellow," she reported.

"Quebec," I said. "We're in Quebec somewhere." I closed my eyes again. "Tell me if they come this way."

"Shouldn't we go out?" asked Georgina.

My eyes snapped open. "No!" I barked. "We're in too deep. Llewellyn set me up too well. We go out there and we'll never talk our way out of it."

"One of the policemen is under the plane now," Georgina went on. "He's trying to get through the door." There was a pause. "He's coming out and he's got someone with him! I think it's Llewellyn...Yes, it's him."

"Mobile?" I asked.

She shook her head. "I don't think so. They're putting him onto a stretcher and the ambulance men are going back."

I'd had enough of the blow by blow. I got to my feet and went across to the window, keeping low. I crouched beside Georgina and looked out. They were bringing out Brandt. From that distance I couldn't tell if he was alive or dead. I fervently hoped he was stone cold. I'd had enough of him to last a dozen lifetimes. Llewellyn was a different story. I wanted to wring his neck personally.

The ambulance men returned to the field, stepping daintily through the mud with their folded stretcher. They loaded him on and began the return trip. By then the two cops had already begun pulling poor old Henri from the cockpit. From the way they were lugging him I knew he'd pegged out. I didn't feel the slightest twinge—it served the stupid bastard right for flying a prop plane like a jet. The ambulance men made the third trip out into the boggy field and took Henri back at a trot, high stepping it through the ooze. Then the ambulance took off, lights flickering, siren wailing faintly as it sped towards the town. The cops stuck around for a while, poking through the wreckage. Eventually, they left as well. They hadn't paid any attention to the farmhouse. For the moment, at least, it looked as though we were in the clear. I slid down below the window, groaning.

"Jesus!" I whispered. The shock was finally getting to me and I began shaking all over. Georgina disappeared into the dark innards of the house and came back a few minutes later with a tattered blanket. She wrapped us both up in it and we sat bundled together against the wall. My teeth were chattering and for the first time in my life I actually *craved* alcohol. I felt Georgina's hand sneak under my coveralls and unbutton the fabric of my shirt. Her hand felt cool against my chest. She massaged gently, then let her fingers trail down to my waist and below.

"Christ!" I moaned. "This is hardly the time for that."

She grinned at me in the half light. "Shhh," she murmured. "I read about this in a book once. It's accepted first aid for someone in mild shock."

"I don't believe you," I said. "But don't move your hand."

"See?" she whispered. "It's making you feel better already."

We sat that way for a long while, and I let the warmth of Georgina's hand and the closeness of her body do their soothing work. "I really did get you into a bind, didn't I?" I said eventually.

Georgina lifted her cheek from my shoulder and I glanced down at her. Dank hair and all she was the best thing I'd seen in ages. "It's not so bad," she smiled.

"Wanted by the cops, penniless, wet. God!"

"Not penniless," said Georgina. She shifted under the blanket and stood up. Going to the doorway, she picked something up off the floor. Llewellyn's briefcase. She handed it to me, settling back under the blanket again. I unzipped it.

Inside there was a large plastic-covered map folder, a credit card case, some other loose papers, and a wad of cash. I counted it. There was well over a thousand dollars. "Where the hell did you get this?" I asked, setting the briefcase aside and holding up the money.

"I went through their pockets right after I dragged the pilot out of his seat. Everyone was unconscious. I thought we might need some money if we actually made it through the storm."

"You're incredible!"

"Simple foresight." She smiled, pursing her lips and lifting her nose into the air. Then she dropped the pose and grinned. "I don't know about the other stuff. I just grabbed. The credit cards and the plastic thing came from Henri."

I picked up the briefcase again and replaced the cash. I brought out Henri's credit card case and flipped it open. Henri was Henri Martin St. Jacques. Most of the credit cards were British with a few French ones as well—Prisunic, Europcar, and a Finagaz. The Barclay card and the Carte Blanche were usable in Canada, though. I dropped the cards into the briefcase and took out the map case curiously. I opened it up. They were flight charts. I went through them one by one, holding the case up to the sulphur light of the window. Ottawa Valley, Ottawa, Montreal, Quebec City, then up to Chicoutimi in the north. I kept flipping, interested now. Why would we be going north? I'd assumed our destination was Montreal, but the charts went well beyond.

From Chicoutimi the charts laid a path northeast, to Sept-Îles on the Gulf of St. Lawrence, then headed almost due north to Goose Bay, Labrador. The last chart in the sequence was the northern match for the Goose Bay map. Someone had dotted in a point and added a few notations: 62'16" W / 54'51" N / 220 Mhtz ch.3. It was an exact longitude and latitude with the frequency and channel number of a homing beacon.

The spot was a good hundred miles or more north of Goose Bay. I'd flown into Goose Bay years before when the Americans finally decided to shut down their air base there, effectively useless since the ferry flights of the Second World War. Goose Bay was already in the back of beyond—the notation position was even further into desolation. And I was positive there wasn't any kind of settlement for miles, let alone a landing strip.

"Now that's *really* crazy," I muttered.

"What is?" asked Georgina.

I pointed at the chart. "We were on our way to Labrador," I said slowly. "And I can't think of one goddamn reason why."

"Well, there had to be one," said Georgina. "Or we wouldn't have been going there. Simple logic."

I grunted sourly and rubbed my forehead. I had a sneaking suspicion that her piece of simple logic was going to get us into even more trouble.

PART THREE

•

Interrupt

Interrupt: A break in a program or routine caused by an external source, which requires that control should pass temporarily to another routine; e.g. to monitor an event which may be proceeding in parallel to take action as a direct result of an event which has already taken place. The interrupt is made so that the original routine can be resumed from the point at which the break occurred.

Chapter Nineteen

We waited out the dawn. Or at least I did. After a while, Georgina fell asleep; and although I longed to follow her example I knew that our survival depended on getting away from the site of the crash as soon as we could. It was still fairly dark outside. The storm was still in progress, and it was only about four o'clock in the morning. But as soon as the rain eased up, and as soon as normal wake-up hours rolled around, I was sure that people would start making appearances. Policemen, reporters, the curious. Not to mention a crony or two of Llewellyn's.

I concentrated on listening to the thunder grumble its way into another portion of the sky. The darkness lifted a little; not much—but enough for me to see that the house was in even worse shape than I'd thought. The broken walls and tumbled laths all had a faint brown tinge, like dead mould; and directly above the rickety stairway that led from our room up to the second storey was a jagged hole in the ceiling. Ragged strips of asphalt roofing hung down like blackened bandages around a wound. I stared through the hole, checking the gradual lightening of the still overcast sky against my watch. Finally, I nudged Georgina, who was curled up beside me. "Rise and shine," I said encouragingly.

She mumbled something incomprehensible as I took the initiative, easing myself away from her and out from under the blanket. When I stood up, every bone in my body cracked. Things still hurt—but it was bearable. I could feel a crust of blood just at my hairline, but other than that I seemed to have weathered the crash fairly well. I luxuriated in a full-out stretch and a jaw-popping yawn, then peered out the window facing the field.

The Duke was right where I'd dropped her, nose crumpled like a paper cup, undercarriage in the air. I frowned, looking out across the field. Within a couple of hours that plane was definitely going to be getting the full work-up. Henri had died, so that meant a DOT Inquiry, the RCMP probably, and the local cops again. Both of us looked like escapees from a mental institution in our coveralls; and the blood spattered here and there didn't do anything for our credibility either— but just the same we were going to have to leave the sanctuary of the farmhouse as soon as possible. Plus I was starving. Neither of us had eaten since a sandwich snack the day before at Luther's Slumber Haven, just before setting out on our ill-fated journey to the Omega complex. The vision of a plate of bacon and eggs wafted into my mind and I almost swooned.

I bent down and shook Georgina's blanket-shrouded shoulder. She batted my hand away, but I kept on shaking.

"Leave me alone," she grumbled.

"Want to have breakfast in the local jail?" I asked.

Her eyes opened and she looked up at me blearily. "Yes," she said, after a long glance. "I'd settle for anywhere that had some kind of heat." She pulled the blanket up to her chin and her eyes started sagging shut again. I pulled the blanket right off her.

"Bloody hell!" she whimpered. But she was awake.

I gave her a hand up. "Time to press on," I said. I checked out the window again. In the distance the town was still sleeping. I wondered just where we were.

"Why can't we just stay here?" she asked, yawning.

"Because that field's going to be swarming with cops in a little while," I explained. "And if Llewellyn is fit enough, he could have told them about us. Christ only knows what story he might have told them!"

"Maybe he died," suggested Georgina, clearly quite happy with the thought.

"People like Llewellyn don't die," I said. "They always come back to haunt you. I don't want to be around when he does. Or Brandt for that matter."

Georgina looked at me carefully, her eyes scanning me from head to toe. "God, do I look anything like you?" she asked.

"If not worse," I said. Her coveralls were muddy, one sleeve of her shirt was torn, and her hair would have made a good scouring pad for an egg-crusty frying pan. She looked like hell, there was no way around it.

"That's not possible," she grimaced, still eyeing me. "You look absolutely appalling. I shall just have to wash."

I shook my head. "Later," I said. "We have to get away from here."

"And where are we going? Where are we now for that matter?"

"I don't have the foggiest idea. But it's about time we found out. We can find a gas station somewhere and you can wash up there."

"Are we heading for that town?" asked Georgina.

I looked out the window again. Still no activity there, or on the road that ran beside the field. It was chancy, but the only other choice was hitching in the other direction. In our condition we'd stand out too much if we tried to thumb it. I nodded. "The town," I decided. "It's probably the quickest way to get our bearings. It looks big enough; five or six thousand people. Maybe we can keep off the main drags..."

It didn't take us much time. Most of it was spent slogging across more fields as we kept away from the potential danger of the road. We hit the city limits at the rear of a scrap yard piled high with junked cars.

"Lovely," murmured Georgina, checking out the automotive graveyard. We wove our way through the skeletal frames and eventually came to a narrow street faced with a clutter of small frame houses done in the colours you usually associate with toilet paper. Some paint store with too much inventory of pastel shades had held a sale about ten years ago by the looks of it. I wondered what would happen if some early rising old gentleman happened to peep out his window. Even if he didn't phone the police the minute he saw us the word would spread fast enough about the two weird-looking strangers he'd seen coming out of the salvage yard. I took Georgina's elbow and hurried her forward. It was still cool enough to see our breath as we scurried along the cracked sidewalk. I began having odour hallucinations—coffee, mostly.

The street, Rue Baubein, according to a rusted sign, went on for about five blocks in a straight line, then veered to the south. The houses began giving way to seedy-looking light industrial buildings. I checked the signs, trying to figure out exactly where we were. All I could tell was that we *were* in Quebec.

The road ran out at a chipped stucco garage. A pile of old battery casings stood by a whitewashed glass door. We turned left and found ourselves in the cinder parking lot of a railway

station. I saw the rectangular white shingle hanging from the
eaves of the plum-red building and grinned.

"Well, what do you know."

"Alexandria," said Georgina, reading the sign. "Well, we
certainly aren't in Egypt."

"No," I told her happily. "Better than that. We're halfway
to Montreal on the main rail line!"

Georgina frowned. "Halfway from where?"

"Ottawa," I said. "The nation's capital, you know. Alexandria's
the mid point between there and Montreal. It couldn't be
better."

"So where are we going?" asked Georgina. "Assuming that
you mean us to take the train. Montreal or Ottawa?"

"We'll go in whatever direction the first train is going," I
said.

It turned out to be Ottawa. The train was the businessman's
special that leaves Montreal at seven-thirty and gets into
Ottawa at nine-forty. We wound up having to wait less than
half an hour. The surly little man behind the counter in the
station gave us a few hard looks as he stamped away at our
tickets, but that was all. We went outside onto the narrow
platform. A few minutes later the big blue and yellow Via Rail
diesel pulled into the station, half a dozen cars in tow. We
climbed on and found four seats together: two for us, and two
for our outstretched feet. A few seconds later the horn
blasted and we pulled out of the station. The outskirts of
Alexandria vanished quickly and the train began gathering
speed as it arrowed through the scrub lots and farmland on its
way to Ottawa.

I leaned back in my seat, ignoring a curious white-haired
lady across the aisle from us. I kept my hand securely on the
briefcase and watched the wet scenery roll by. Scraps of blue
sky were showing through the dissolving storm clouds. It was
going to be a nice day after all. I dozed, my head resting on
the cool glass.

When I woke, startled, Georgina was gone. I sat up and
looked at my watch. Only a few minutes had actually passed.
I waited until my heart slowed down, figuring that she'd gone
to the toilet at the end of the car. A moment later I saw her
coming through the connecting door from the car ahead. She
swayed down the aisle with the rocking motion of the train

and sat down across from me. She reached into her coverall pocket and pulled out a blue and white package of Players filter, flipping them to me along with a book of matches.

"Thanks," I said, ripping off the cellophane and pulling open the package. I slipped off the foil, tapped out a cigarette, lit it, and took a deep drag. Not Camels, but not bad.

"To hell with thanks," said Georgina, darkly. "I want one myself. Hand them over."

"I thought you quit," I said, tossing her the pack.

"I started again in that thunderstorm. That's how I got myself through it, by imagining the cigarette I was going to have when we got down."

I watched her light up and take a deep drag. She coughed on the smoke—just as she had when she'd tried one of my Camels on another train, the one from New York to Montreal. "My God!" she wheezed. "I *have* missed these." She took another drag and smiled happily.

"It suits you," I said. "I thought it did before."

"Before?"

"On the Amtrak train, remember?"

A bemused expression crossed her face. "That seems years ago." She looked down at the curl of smoke rising from her cigarette. "Sam used to say it suited me. Sam... never quit..."

"It's okay," I said gently.

"No. No, it's not. He was my brother and that bastard killed him!" She leaned forward and savagely buckled her cigarette in the nearest ashtray. There were tears forming in her eyes.

"Why don't you go to the women's can and I'll go to the men's," I suggested, stubbing out my own cigarette. "We can clean up and then talk."

Georgina nodded and we both got up, going to opposite ends of the car. I took the briefcase with me. Ten minutes later, feeling a little better after a dose of the liquid green soap in the men's toilet, I returned to my seat. I'd managed to get the blood off my scalp and clean away most of the dirt on my hands and face. Georgina came back to her seat a few minutes after me. She'd done even better. Except for the wrinkled coveralls she looked almost normal. She'd even scraped the caked mud from her shoes. She settled down in the seat across from me and I handed out cigarettes again.

"Better?" I asked. .

She nodded. "Much," she said. "I feel almost human."

Her eyes were red and puffy. She'd taken time to have a good cry for Sam. I glanced out the window. We were still going through a mixture of woodlots and farmland, more farm than trees. In the far distance to the north I could see the pale shadowed humps of the Gatineau Hills on the other side of the Ottawa River.

"What's our plan when we get to Ottawa?" she asked a few minutes later.

I shrugged, pulling the briefcase onto my lap. I unzipped it. "I'm not sure yet," I murmured, going through the contents. "Any suggestions would be appreciated."

"What about this Goose Bay place? Is it accessible?"

"Probably," I replied, pulling out the map folder again. "They must have some flights up there still. It's pretty much of a ghost town these days, though."

"Didn't it have something to do with the war?" asked Georgina. "I seem to remember something about it in my contemporary history course in university."

I nodded. "It was the most northerly Allied airfield with the exception of a one-laner in Greenland," I said. "It was part of the Atlantic Ferry route. The new planes off the assembly lines in the US would come up, refuel, then head out across the Atlantic for England. Kind of like a pony express station. The Americans kept a base there for years to service the Distant Early Warning line of radomes, but they shut down in the late sixties or early seventies as I recall. It doesn't have much reason for being other than that. There's a town, though. A place called Happy Valley or something."

"Have you figured out any reason why we should have been on our way there?"

"No reason at all. It's like everything else—nothing fits. Why would a dope smuggler want to go to Labrador?" I glanced over some of the loose sheets of paper in the briefcase— what was left of Llewellyn's computer printouts. "Weird . . ." I said.

"What is?" asked Georgina.

I tapped a finger on the papers in my lap. "I think the printout is in Fortran. It's nothing I can read anyway."

"What on earth is Fortran?"

"A computer language," I explained. "It stands for FORmula TRANslation. That's what's so strange. Fortran is a scientific language, all mathematical with a few straight English statements thrown in."

"And you can't read any of it?"

"Nope."

"Not much of a clue then, is it."

"Oh, I don't know," I said. "It's negative information, but it fits into a different theory."

"Which is?"

"Llewellyn has nothing to do with dope smuggling," I murmured, trying to decipher the complex equations on the pages. "I think it's something entirely different."

"Like what?"

"I'm not sure. But it's all too scientific, like this computer language. The Cosa Nostra might use computers to do their books, and they might have front companies to cover their activities, but not like the ones we've run into. It's all High-Tech. Aviom is a relatively big aviation manufacturing company. They don't need dope to keep going. And that whole setup with the special seals at customs and Alpha Air Services. It's too neat, too clean."

"Maybe it's just efficiency," put in Georgina. "From what I've read about the Mafia, it's a highly efficient organization. I think they're beyond the days of olive oil and Chicago gangsters."

"Maybe you're right," I said. "But it still seems too big, too purposeful."

"And too bloody confusing," said Georgina. She lit another cigarette and stared out the window. "And I don't really care very much anymore," she whispered.

"What?" I asked.

She turned and glanced at me, her eyes suddenly cold. "I don't give a damn about the why of it," she said. "Or the how or the when or the where or whatever it is you journalist types refer to. It's much simpler for me. I just want to find the people who killed my brother, and I want to make sure they pay."

"Llewellyn didn't *tell* us Sam was dead..." I said, uneasy at her tone.

She looked at me fiercely. "Don't be patronizing," she snapped. "You know perfectly well that he is!"

"All right," I said harshly. "He's dead. There's nothing we can do about that. But there's more to this than Sam's death, no matter how we feel about it."

"Sam's murder," she corrected.

"All right, murder. That's not the only thing we have to consider."

"It is to me," she said.

"Then you're a fool," I said, regretting the words the moment they were out of my mouth. We were both under an incredible strain, and we had been for quite a while. The unrelieved pressure was getting to us.

"Bugger you!" Georgina said, her voice low.

I lifted a hand placatingly. "I didn't mean that," I said slowly. "But I meant what I said about the extent of whatever it is we're involved in. This is a huge operation. Llewellyn said it himself, he's invested millions of dollars. And I think he's only the tip of the iceberg. An expediter. There are people a lot bigger than he is involved in this, and they're trying to hide something. I want to find out what it is."

"Yes," she said icily. "I suppose that's your job, isn't it? A good journalist always gets his story." She turned to the window again.

"Oh, Christ!" I moaned. "You really are a twit aren't you? I don't give a good goddamn about the story! I want to keep us both alive, you idiot, don't you understand that? The only way we're going to come out of this with our skins intact is by blowing the whole thing wide open, and I want to get out in one piece. With you. *That's* what's important. You—me—survival!" I sank back into my seat, frustrated and annoyed. "Damn! Why couldn't you just go back to England, and leave this to me."

"Bugger you," Georgina said once more, "you and your chauvinism. I told you not to ask me that again. Not to mention the fact that you sound ridiculous. You—me—survival. Good Lord, you could be something out of Tarzan of the Apes!"

Her voice was sharp. But the bleak look had gone from her eyes. I grinned at her. "That's right," I said. "And Tarzan care too much about Jane to lose her now."

There was a pause. Then she smiled back at me. "Jane feel same way about Tarzan," she said.

Which gave us something to think about until all the sleep we'd missed finally caught up to us. When we woke up again we were in Ottawa.

Chapter Twenty

Ottawa is located at the confluence of the Ottawa and Rideau Rivers, a little more than one hundred miles from Montreal, and about two hundred and fifty miles from Toronto. Most world capitals are located in historically strategic places; Ottawa, at least as a capital, is founded on political expediency. During the latter half of Queen Victoria's reign, both Montreal and Toronto were squabbling over which city should be capital. The dour old Queen, playing the role of Solomon, decided that neither city would win the prize, and chose a town roughly midway between them—a fly-blown and boggy little settlement called Bytown, named for the Colonel of Engineers who had built the canal system linking the Ottawa River with the Rideau Lakes. The Rideau River was unnavigable because of the large falls where it dropped one hundred feet into the Ottawa, so a set of locks was built, supposedly for military use during the War of 1812. It was never used. More than one hundred and fifty years later, the only craft to ply the canal that wends its way through the city are pleasure boats and sightseeing launches. In the winter the canal is drained down to a foot or so of its bottom and allowed to freeze, forming what the local tourist association likes to call the longest skating rink in the world.

Before Queen Victoria's decision, Ottawa was a lumber camp, its economy based on the immense stands of timber surrounding it, both on the Ontario and Quebec sides of the Ottawa River. Within a few years of being made the capital, Ottawa rapidly grew into a bastion of multi-tier bureaucracies.

But Ottawa is a pretty city, its metropolitan population of half a million gathered snugly around the stone bluff overlooking the Ottawa River called Parliament Hill—resplendent with its neo-gothic Peace Tower, House of Commons, and Senate. Ninety per cent of the city's buildings are made of either stone or brick, and there are parks and tree-lined streets

everywhere. The streets are kept clean, slums are virtually
non-existent, and the crime rate is low. It is probably one of
the few major cities in the world where you don't take your
life in your hands when you go for an evening stroll down-
town. Its only black mark is the high incidence of minor sex
aberrations—the city is home to literally thousands of flashers,
flag wavers, and Toms, undoubtedly a result of having a city
comprised of more than a quarter of a million low level civil
servants. The whole city revolves around the federal government; if you don't actually work for one of the dozens of
departments, you make your living feeding them, clothing
them, or making sure they get to work on time.

To the average tourist visiting during the summer months,
Ottawa looks like a great place to live; I spent a little less than
a year there as a wire service reporter and I know differently.
The city might be pretty and clean, but it's also almost
insufferably boring. After you hit the War Museum, the
National Gallery, and the Museum of Man, and take a quick
walk up the Sparks Street Mall, there's nothing left to do but
watch the politicians' endless gavotte while you oil your
snowblower in preparation for the six months of Arctic winter.
Thankfully, Georgina and I were just passing through.

We arrived at Ottawa Station right on time, climbing up
out of the spiral tunnels into the small, steel beam and plate
glass station. We caught a Blue Line cab outside the main
doors and a few minutes later we were speeding down the
Queensway, the expressway that bisects the city from east to
west. The cab veered off at the Metcalfe exit, and we rolled
around the squat, turreted bulk of the National Museum,
heading into the city core. The driver let us off at the Sparks
Street Mall, and headed up the hill towards the Parliament
buildings.

Georgina wanted to eat a substantial breakfast. So did
I—but first things first. We had to get rid of our less-than-
inconspicuous clothes; and after that we had to be on the
move again. The sooner we knew what lay at the end of
Llewellyn's charts the better. Within an hour the two of us
were outfitted once more, both of us going the jeans and
T-shirt route this time. I bought a small overnight bag in a
leather goods store and dumped the contents of the briefcase
into it. The empty case and our coveralls went into the first
available trash bin—and then we headed for the first available

snackbar. It wasn't bacon and eggs, but the hot dogs and coffee would tide us over until we reached an airport. We sat down on a bench to eat.

"That is absolutely the last time," said Georgina, sipping, chewing, and people-watching simultaneously.

"Last time for what?" I asked, knocking off the coffee in three gulps.

"Buying clothes," she said. "Do you have any idea how much money we've been spending making sure we have something to wear? We've left a litter of luggage halfway across the country."

"Don't worry," I said. "As they used to say in this town, I can see the light at the end of the tunnel."

"I beg your pardon?" said Georgina, looking at me with a horrified expression on her face and mustard on her upper lip. I cleaned off the mustard with the tip of my index finger and put on a stern look.

"The art of buzz," I said, lecturing. "To see light at the end of one's tunnel is a bureaucratic expression of the genus verbosa incongrua. There are others such as 'policy objective analysis,' 'in the present time frame,' and real winners like 'motivational interface integers.' How to say absolutely nothing in the greatest amount of time while wasting the most breath, paper, and money. This city is famous for it."

"But what does it have to do with us?" she asked.

"Like I said, absolutely nothing. It's a way of putting off the inevitable."

"Which is?"

"Finding out how we get ourselves to Goose Bay, Labrador," I said wearily.

Most of the major airline offices are on the Mall's five-block length or close to it. Neither Air Canada nor Canadian Pacific had anything going into Goose, but we finally found a connection at Nordair, one of the smaller regional airlines. They had a single flight each day, a DC-9 to Dorval, changing to an Eastern Provincial Boeing 737. The Eastern Provincial left Dorval at noon, and got into Goose Bay at four; a three hour flight with an added hour for the change in time zones. If we hurried we could still make it. The man in the Nordair office made out our tickets and directed us across Confederation Square to the Disneyland castle of the Château Laurier Hotel. We could catch an airport bus there. We walked back

up the Mall, crossed Confederation Square and the War
Memorial and reached the Château. Fifteen minutes later a
battered-looking Bluebird bus rattled up to the stone porch
entrance to the turreted hotel and we climbed aboard, paying
the driver as we went by. We settled down in the cracked
leather seats and after a few minutes' wait the old bus groaned
out into the mid-morning traffic around the square. We went
down Wellington Street, past the Parliament buildings, the
reflecting glass box of the Bank of Canada, and the Supreme
Court; then we turned into a maze of side streets, eventually
coming out onto Bronson Avenue. We went down the wide
artery, lined with a hodge podge of stately homes, restaurants, and gas stations, crossed the bridge over the canal, and
finally got into fourth gear as we headed by the institutional
wasteland of the Carleton University Campus. Bronson did a
hop and skip, changing abruptly into the Airport Parkway, a
two lane route through low cedar forest. Twenty minutes later
we reached the flatlands of Ottawa International Airport,
baking in the sun.

They've got a lot of gall calling Ottawa Airport international. The terminal would fit neatly into one of Heathrow's
parking lots. The building is no more than two hundred yards
long, and is only barely two-storeyed. It's so old-fashioned
that the control tower actually sits on top of it. It would be
small for any city over a hundred thousand, but considering
Ottawa's position as a national capital it is ludicrous.

We had a complete breakfast in the airport restaurant, then
got on board the waiting Nordair flight. We were barely up
before we were down again at Dorval. We spent an hour there,
wandering around the terminal of what had once been
Montreal's main airport, then boarded the red and white
Eastern Provincial 737. The small, twin-engined jet was less
than half full as we took off, and the few passengers flying
with us all looked depressed. Goose Bay, Labrador obviously
wasn't their destination of choice. I knew how they felt.

While Georgina dozed in the seat beside me I looked out.
The outskirts of Montreal dropped away as we climbed, and
within forty minutes we were high above the Laurentians,
heading on a course roughly parallel with the broad silver
band of the St. Lawrence. There were almost no clouds and I
could easily pick off the long narrow strips of farmland leading
down to the water. Hundreds of years ago, when the St.

Lawrence offered the only communication with civilization, the farms were invariably arranged with one end on the river. Ploughing the north forty must have been quite the operation.

Eventually we swung almost due north, the farmlands dissolving into an infinite, lake-dotted blanket of trees. In its own way, the land below was as much a desert as the Sahara. The flat, brooding forest went on for a thousand miles, ending at the treeline, beyond which nothing grew. No wonder Cartier the explorer had called it the land God gave to Cain. With nothing to see I joined Georgina, putting my seat back as far as it would go and closing my eyes.

I awoke to find Georgina leaning over me, peering out the window. The engine noise had lost its steady note, and as I opened my eyes we went into a smooth banking turn.

"It's quite incredible," said Georgina, staring down. "Every tree in the world must be down there. And I used to think the New Forest was big."

I lifted my head and took a look. In the distance I could see the coast and the pewter sheet of the Atlantic beyond. A spacious inlet cut in almost directly below us: Lake Melville, not a lake at all, but the sound leading from the sea to Goose Bay at its western end. We had arrived.

We did a single circuit and then came in from the west, sloping down the approach corridor to line up with the longest of the three runways sitting on top of the plateau where they'd built the airport almost forty years before. The plateau was like an oasis. There was nothing around for miles except bush, and the small cluster of buildings and roads marking the settlement of Happy Valley, slightly to the east of the airport itself.

Suddenly we were flying above the trees and there was a triple jolt as we touched down. The pilot cut in full reverse thrust and the cabin filled with the noise of the roaring engines.

It was already late afternoon; too late to accomplish anything that day. We went through the dusty, almost derelict terminal and climbed into a station wagon taxi with six or seven others. Twenty minutes later we checked into the Happy Valley Motor Hotel on the edge of the small community.

Chapter Twenty-one

We were back at the Goose Bay Airport by nine the next morning. We ate breakfast in the terminal restaurant and then went in search of transportation north. The few buildings making up the airport complex were all located within a few hundred feet of the terminal so we didn't have far to go. There were three charter companies working out of Goose Bay, and two of the offices were closed. The only signs of life were coming from a low, wood frame building sitting half screened by the trees that fringed the edge of the plateau. The sign over the door said Moonblanket Charter Services Limited. There was an old, but serviceable-looking Beechcraft Musketeer equipped with floats parked under a makeshift sunscreen next to the building.

We went through the front door and a bell tinkled. The room we stepped into was neat and tidy. Above a scuffed, vinyl couch hung an imposing homemade calendar, the days marked off in large squares, with scraps of scratch paper pinned on here and there. A desk in the middle of the office was piled high with charts. There was a tall man bending over an old-fashioned Corey coffee machine in one corner, a screwdriver in his hand. He turned at the sound of the bell.

"Morning," he said. He pointed the screwdriver at the machine. "Offer you a cup when I get the old girl pumping." He was in his early forties, big and broad shouldered with the unmistakable jet hair and intense eyes of an Indian. He was wearing a pair of faded dungarees that might have been war surplus from the US Army, and a T-shirt that had probably been white once. His broad face was friendly and intelligent.

He fiddled with the coffee machine for another few seconds and there was a hissing noise as water began to flow through it. He tossed the screwdriver down happily, and waved us into a pair of old office chairs on the far side of the desk. He sat down himself and smiled across at us. "Harry Moonblanket," he said, extending a hand. "The coffee will be ready in a minute."

We introduced ourselves as Mr. and Mrs. Baker—the first name that popped into my head. "We're looking for a charter," I said.

Behind Moonblanket the coffee machine was making noises like a leaky radiator on a cold morning. He ignored it. "Chartering's my business," he said, still smiling.

"Just the Musketeer?" I asked.

He seemed surprised that I knew what kind of plane he had outside, but he nodded easily. "That's it," he said. "Had a Twin Otter for a while, but it didn't pay. Too big. The Beech is the right size these days. Not a lot of loose charter money floating around so you have to go with the smaller planes."

"I suppose you do a lot of flying for hunting and fishing groups?"

He made a see-saw gesture with the flat of one large, grease-stained hand. "Some," he said. "Not so much as a few years ago. I do a fair bit of freight hauling up the coast, some government contracts, that kind of thing." He paused and gave both of us a long, slow look, his eyes flickering back and forth between us. "You going fishing?" he said, his voice doubtful.

"No," I said. "Looking. Sightseeing you might call it."

Moonblanket nodded, and got up out of his chair. He went to the coffee machine and poured the dark liquid into three styrofoam cups. "No milk or sugar," he said. "Black is it."

"Fine," I said. Georgina nodded as well.

Moonblanket brought over a pair of cups and then went back for his own. He sat down again, looking thoughtfully at us over the white styrofoam rim. "Expensive way to see the country," he said.

"The only way," I answered, shrugging.

"I suppose." He had eyes like a judge and jury, but he wasn't going to ask too many questions. "Hundred bucks a day, plus gas and expenses. You go up for an hour, you pay for the day."

"Okay," I said. "We'll want you for a couple of days at least. Do you know anywhere where we can get some camping stuff?"

He nodded slowly. "I've got some here. Sleeping bags, Coleman stove, that kind of thing. Nothing fancy, but you can have it cheap. Extra twenty a day."

"That'll be fine," I said. I reached into my jeans and pulled out our bankroll. I peeled off two hundred dollars and put it on the desk. Moonblanket looked down at the money, his face expressionless. The look was clear. We still hadn't done business.

"You planning on having me set down somewhere?" he asked.

I nodded. "You know where Shipiskan Lake is?" I asked. The lake was the closest body of water to the location marked on Henri's chart.

Moonblanket bobbed his head. "I know where it is."

"That's where we want to go."

There was a long silence. Obviously, Harry Moonblanket wanted to know why we chose that particular spot, but he wasn't about to ask. He looked down at the money on the desk again. He wanted more information before he made the deal. Harry was a careful man.

"You know about planes?" he asked, changing tacks.

"Some," I said.

"Pilot?"

"Singles and twins," I said. "Conditional IFR. I've done a couple of thousand hours."

It did not seem to completely satisfy him—but he nodded. "Okay," he said, picking up the money and tucking it into his dungarees. "When do you want to go?"

"Whenever you're ready."

We took off an hour later, Harry Moonblanket lifting the flat-grey six seater off the ground with practiced ease. The interior of the airplane was worn, but he obviously took good care of it. The one hundred and eighty horsepower engine purred as he took it up to five thousand and levelled off, heading west. Below us the sunlight was twinkling off dozens of small lakes scattered throughout the thick unbroken forest. I was sitting in the co-pilot's chair, watching Harry fly. Georgina was behind us, keeping the camping equipment company.

"Doing this long?" I asked, raising my voice against the throb of the engine.

"Long enough," said Harry, his hands lightly holding the yoke steady. "Almost twenty years now."

"Good business?"

"Nope," he said flatly. "Just enough to keep me going. But

it's all I know. Never was a city Indian." It was the first time
he'd made any reference to his background.

"Born up here?" I asked.

He shook his head. "No one in his right mind is born up
here." He grinned. "I'm from Niagara Falls originally."

I nodded. There was a big Six Nations reserve there,
straddling the Canadian-US border. "So why'd you come up
here?" I asked.

He shrugged. "Got some training in New York, came up
here as a mechanic. Worked on the last of the US civil stuff
up here. Put enough money together for a down payment on
a plane. Been doing it ever since." He looked across the
narrow cabin. I knew what was coming. We were in the air
now, his territory. It was time for him to start finding out
about us. "You ask a lot of questions," he said. "You're a
journalist, aren't you? Reporter?" Harry was quick.

"Right the first time," I said. "Good guess."

"No guess," said Harry. "I've been expecting someone like
you. I'm just surprised it took so long."

"What do you mean?" I asked, suspicious. Why would
reporters be coming up here? Goose Bay had ceased to have
any news value ten years before, even for feature stories or
nostalgia. Harry caught the edgy tone.

"Don't worry," he smiled. "I won't blow your cover."

"What's that supposed to mean?" I asked.

"Well, that's what you call it, isn't it? When you guys go
after a story. Investigative reporting?"

"Who said anything about a story?" I asked. I could sense
Georgina tensing behind me.

"I did," said Harry blandly. "And people don't fly to Goose
Bay in blue jeans to go for a camping trip," he added. "You're
looking into all the comings and goings the past ten days or
so."

I was alert at once. That sounded interesting. "Tell me
about it," I asked.

Harry laughed. "You know more about it than I do I'll bet,"
he said.

"Pretend I don't."

"Okay," he said. "Traffic."

"Run that by me again," I said.

"Traffic," repeated Harry. "Air traffic. Day and night. Using
the Air Force runway. Three big Sikorsky RH-3's and a

Caribou. Caribou's been making a regular run in and out
every day. Leaves around midnight, another one comes in
around four in the morning. The choppers are buzzing in and
out all the time."

"The RH-3's," I said. "Aren't they troop carriers?"

Harry nodded. "Used to have a couple here for the search
and rescue team," he replied. "But not like these. Big green
bastards, with all the windows painted out. Same with the
Caribou."

"War games," I suggested.

"Thought of that," said Harry. "Couple of times I spotted
guys in uniforms, fatigues, you know? But I don't think so.
No military markings on the planes for one thing, and no
insignia on the uniforms. And I listened in a couple of times
to Goose Air Traffic Control. They're getting a civil clearance
on Red 29—that's a commercial approach. But it sounds like
they're using military code groupings to designate the choppers and the Caribou. The Sikorskys are all called something
like DEED-L-S, 1, 2, 3. And the Caribou is always IKE-R-S
1."

"Odd," I said.

"That's one word for it," said Harry. He checked the chart
in his lap and made a slight course correction. He handled
the yoke as though he was stroking a cat.

"Deed and Ike," I said, turning the code groups over in my
mind.

"Mean anything to you?" asked Harry.

"Ike," said Georgina. "Eisenhower?"

"Maybe," I said. "American President, old US Air Force
base."

"What about Deed?" Harry went on.

"Any prospecting activity going on up here lately?" I asked.

"A fair amount," said Harry. "I've flown a couple times for
Energy Mines and Resources. Once for a US company. Lots
of old mines up here. Gold mostly. Some uranium. Mostly
people seemed to be interested in offshore oil since the big
strike in Newfoundland... You mean deed, like in mining
claim?"

"It's possible," I said. "You ever see them loading anything
onto that Caribou?"

"Not a chance," he said, shaking his head. "For one thing

that whole end of the airport is restricted, and for another all the activity goes on at night."

I thought about all those stainless steel drums in the Omega warehouse. Uranium ore? It was crazy. The few pieces of the puzzle that I'd been sure of had come apart again.

Harry Moonblanket cleared his throat and looked across at me, as if he were waiting for me to say something in particular. I grinned back at him. "You're right," I said. "I'm not Mr. Baker and she's not Mrs. Baker. My name's Peter Coffin, and this is—"

"Georgina Underwood," put in Georgina, independent to the last.

Harry nodded. "Glad to meet you." He stared through the windscreen for a moment. "Any particular reason for going to Shipiskan Lake?"

There was no point in making up a story. Harry already had us figured as a north wood's Woodward and Bernstein. "We've got a chart position," I said. "Shipiskan is close to it, but not too close if you know what I mean."

"So you want to put down on the lake and then find this place from the ground?" he said.

"That's it," I answered. "According to the chart, Shipiskan is about ten miles south."

"Long walk," murmured Harry.

"It's the only way," I said. "I don't want to attract attention."

"So we better get down into the trees," said Harry. "From ten miles they'll see us coming if one of those choppers is in the air. Shipiskan is outside Goose Control; nobody's going to get worried because we fall off the scanner."

He slid the yoke forward gently and we began to drop almost imperceptibly. Something clicked in my mind, but I couldn't quite get a handle on it. "Shipiskan is in uncontrolled air space?" I asked.

"Except for the CADIZ there's a lot of free air up here," he said. "Most of it in fact."

"What is a CADIZ?" asked Georgina, pronouncing the unfamiliar word carefully.

I turned in my seat. "Canadian Air Defense Identification Zone," I explained. "You have to identify yourself going in and out of them with an exact time and course."

"Supposed to make the Russians think twice about sending in their paratroopers," laughed Harry.

Again, he jogged the yoke slightly and we steepened our descent. We were down to less than a thousand feet. Below, the featureless glut of trees was taking shape, and I could pick out small clearings of swampy muskeg here and there among the pines. The closer we got to the ground the more worried I became. Ten miles on a chart—or from ten thousand feet—was one thing; but it was going to feel like a lot farther on the ground.

We flew like that for another half hour, continually getting lower until the floats beneath the plane were almost scraping the trees. Harry adjusted for minor elevation changes calmly. The flight was dead smooth; his experience flying the north country showed.

"There's the lake," he said eventually, pointing forward.

I looked out; in the distance I could see a long finger of silver, smooth as mercury in the mid-day sun. Harry throttled back and we fell even lower. He peered ahead, frowning slightly. He nodded to himself, then nudged the throttle open again. We increased our speed. "Glass," he muttered, annoyed.

I knew what he meant. It was something my uncle had told me about, and even demonstrated once or twice. From a distance, landing a float plane looks like fun; in fact, it's one of the most difficult things a bush pilot learns. Water's inherent instability means that you constantly have to readjust as you approach. "Glass" is the most difficult condition of all.

When water is glassy you can barely see it from directly above, so your perception of the distance between you and the water is sometimes off by as much as a foot: That kind of margin can be fatal. Hit the water too soon, with your nose still level, and you stand a good chance of digging in with the floats and turning over. Glassy water also means that there is no wind, so the heat differential between the water and the surrounding land can often be critical, the mismatched temperatures creating low level turbulence that can take you by surprise. The best thing to do in the case of glassy water is to bring the plane in close to the shoreline, or try and manufacture some ripples to guide yourself in. Harry Moonblanket chose the latter.

We came in over the shoreline, fast. Harry dropped the nose and we headed straight down the long narrow body of water, only a few feet above the surface. He tapped the rudder pedals back and forth, waggling the wings, and at the end of his run made a tight wing-up turn that forced a gasp out of Georgina. By then we were facing in the opposite direction. The wing waggling had broken the surface of the water sufficiently for Harry to judge his landing. He picked a likely-looking stretch of weedy shore and brought us down, nose up, throttling back as we hit, letting the floats "mush" safely into the water. Then he cut the engines and we coasted in to within a few yards of shore.

"Nice," I said, complimenting him. Harry smiled and said nothing. We popped the doors and climbed down onto the floats. Georgina handed out the gear and we waded to shore.

For a moment I thought I was deaf—the whole world seemed to have lost its voice. When the engine noise was gone, and when the waves we'd caused on the lake were finished, we were alone in the silence. I stood on the pebbled shore, looking into the dense mass of trees forty feet away. The scrub around the Omega installation had been impersonal, even though it had been full of small animal noises. Here, it was different. The trees beyond the shore were dark and heavy, and the only sound, a faint almost unheard buzz of insects, added to the sinister quality. The forest was a living thing, waiting to see if we would be foolish enough to enter.

"Spooky," I said, more to break the hard silence than anything else.

Beside me, Harry Moonblanket nodded. "Guilt," he said. "You feel as though you shouldn't be here at all. Trespassing." A distant expression clouded his features as he stared into the trees, almost as though he was trying to locate something he knew he wouldn't find. "This is no place for man," he said softly. "It never was." As if in answer, a last faint ripple from the lake crept along the shoreline at our feet.

Then the mood passed, and we began to set up camp.

That night, asleep on a bed of pine boughs cut by Harry Moonblanket, huddled in my sleeping bag beside Georgina, I dreamed dark dreams of falling and black forests reaching up with spiny claws to clutch at me. I dreamed of thick mosses, and of ground that sank beneath my feet as I struggled endlessly to reach Georgina, sinking before me, unreachable.

I awoke in the cold, purple light just before dawn, listening
for the half whispers of my nightmare, feeling the cool dewed
air touch the sweat that had covered me in my sleep. I
reached out and let my hand fall on Georgina's warmly
covered body. I lay that way, staring up into the fading dark,
waiting, until daylight.

Chapter Twenty-two

We breakfasted on beans and instant coffee cooked over the
portable Coleman stove. Georgina and I shared a cigarette
over seconds of the coffee, while Harry sat on a rock outcropping
overlooking the water, studying the chart taken from Henri.
He compared it to his own charts and made a few notations
with a felt-tipped pen. Then he got up from his perch and
crossed the shore to join us.

"More than ten miles," he said, taking the steaming cup
Georgina offered. He squatted on his haunches, sipping and
looking down at the maps. "More like fifteen. Not going to be
easy."

"Do you have any idea what kind of terrain it is?" I asked.

He nodded, a crooked smile creasing his face. "Muskeg,"
he said. "Summer muskeg. Going to be like walking in glue.
Bugs too. Blackflies this time of year. Good thing I brought
some repellent along. They don't go for me much, but they'll
eat you two up."

"You're coming with us?" asked Georgina.

Harry looked surprised. "Sure I'm coming with you," he
said. "You think I'd let you city slickers try and get through
that muck on your own?"

"You don't have to," I said, bristling a little. "I've done a
fair bit of time in the bush out west. I think I can handle
this."

"Sure you can," said Harry. "But you might need an extra
pair of hands." He paused, grinning. "And I'm curious,
anyway. I'd like to know what these people are up to."

"Suit yourself," I said, secretly relieved.

Harry nodded and stood up. He started bundling our gear
into the packs he'd brought along. "As soon as I finish we can

move the plane in a bit closer to shore," he said. "Moor her under that high point there. The overhang and the trees will make her pretty much invisible."

We moved the plane, wading in and pushing it under cover. Then Harry carefully daubed us with a waxy stick repellent and we set off.

At first we followed the shoreline, heading north, and the going was relatively easy. At the far end of the lake we veered west, following a track laid down by Harry's pocket compass. Almost instantly we found ourselves in a quagmire. The ground looked solid enough, but with every step we sank to our ankles. Trees grew in dense clusters on humped areas of ground throughout the swamp, but none of the islands of hard ground were much larger than a tennis court and we made no headway travelling across them. By noon, after travelling more than four hours, we had covered less than three miles by Harry's reckoning. By five, and the first failing of the light, we had covered ten. By then I didn't really care. I was only interested in the placing of one mud encrusted foot in front of the other. I had bites all over my hands, neck, and face, and I could feel huge blisters building on my heels. None of us talked; the only sound was the rasp of our laboured breathing. The swamp seemed infinite.

We paused for a cold meal of canned spaghetti, then pushed on. By seven, at dusk, I was completely exhausted. Georgina had been keeping up until then, but as the sun sank away in front of us, she also began to fade, falling back steadily so that we had to pause and wait for her. I didn't have any objections; the longer we had to wait, the more time I had to catch my breath. Harry seemed untouched by the wickedly tiring journey. The only sign of strain was a tenseness around his jaw.

At eight, with the light almost completely gone, we stopped to set up a make-shift camp on one of the pockets of dry land. I dropped flat on my back, my strength gone. I waved a hand at the cloud of mosquitoes we'd disturbed, then gave up listlessly. If the little buggers wanted me, they could have me; I was in no shape to defend myself.

Georgina was sitting beside me, head buried in her arms. Harry was setting up an ersatz lean-to made of a blanket strung between two stunted pines. "How much farther?" I asked him.

"Two, maybe three miles at most. If your chart is accurate... Not far."

"Not far!" moaned Georgina. "Not far he says."

"We don't have to go any longer today," offered Harry, indicating the blanket and the pines. "We can stay the night here and complete our journey in the morning."

"No," I said, making a sudden decision. "Tonight: We've wasted enough time as it is, and the more time we spend stumbling around in this swamp the more dangerous things are going to get."

"You sound like you know something you're not telling," said Harry.

I laughed dully. "You might say I've brushed up against these people once or twice," I said. "Not friendly at all."

"You want to let me in on it?" asked Harry.

I rolled my head negatively. "No," I said. "The less you know the better. If we get nabbed then you can play the innocent tour guide."

"Sure," said Harry. He didn't sound convinced. Without bothering to finish the lean-to he came and sat down beside me. I got up on my elbows and looked out across the swamp. There was still a faint light in the sky but the swamp was deep in shadow. I couldn't see more than a couple of hundred yards across the deceptively smooth surface of the sawgrass-covered morass. Harry picked up a twig and began chewing on it, spitting out little pieces of bark now and then.

"Go or stay?" he said finally.

"Stay," said Georgina, head still in her arms.

"Go," I said.

"Bloody hell," said Georgina.

We moved off again.

There were times during the last part of that agonizing trek when I wasn't sure I was going to make it. Georgina and I had been living on borrowed energy for too long, and there wasn't much left to draw on. We began stopping more often, urgently drinking water from our canteens, desperately trying to replenish our rapidly dehydrating fluids. My mind began slipping in and out of time, dancing into tight, almost nause-ating dream-states in which Paranoia was king. The bugs, the sucking ground, the tearing twigs, and the lancing roots were all Llewellyn's agents, each obstacle placed there with the single purpose of bringing us down. I discovered how long eternity was; eternity was a single horrifying mile of Labrador.

Eventually, the ground began to slope gently upwards, and walking became easier. The gluey swamp miraculously began to fade, replaced by rocky ground, thinly treed, covered sporadically with a thin layer of mossy topsoil. It was completely dark by now, and we were guided solely by the glowing rose of Harry Moonblanket's compass.

"We should cross your location pretty soon," murmured Harry, as we paused for a brief rest stop. "But we're going to have to be careful. Depends on how exact that compass bearing on the chart was. If it's off much we could miss by a couple hundred yards and never know we'd passed it."

"We won't miss it," I answered, panting for breath. "If they're flying helicopters in and out they must have a base camp or something like it."

"And just what do we do when we get there?" asked Georgina, breathing hard beside me.

"I was kind of wondering that, too," Harry said.

I shrugged. "Play it by ear," I said. "Take a look and then decide."

"Take a look at what?" asked Harry. "Just what is it you expect to find?"

"Harry, old pal, if I knew that I wouldn't be here."

We kept going, climbing steadily upward, the trees becoming more dense, swarms of mosquitoes mushrooming around us as we went, filling our mouths and nostrils. My legs seemed made of lead and my back and shoulders were stiff and aching. Georgina was keeping pace now, having worked into her second wind. Harry had never faltered. He kept on setting the pace, slipping through the shadows within shadows ahead of us, bending back snagging boughs to make our passage a little easier.

The moon was well up when we hit the clearing. It was just before midnight. Harry stopped at the edge of the trees, waving us silently to a halt. I came up beside him and looked.

"What the hell is it?" I whispered.

"Looks like somebody's building a highway," he said, voice low, staring out at the bizarre sight.

The clearing wasn't really a clearing at all. It was a wide path at least two hundred yards across, heading away at right angles, fading into the dark distance. It looked as though Paul

Bunyan had run amok with a giant chain saw. The trees on
the edge of the swath where we stood hadn't been clipped
neatly—they'd been torn up by the roots. Shards of pine and
spruce were littered everywhere. The path itself seemed to
have been randomly sheared, some trees left standing, others
with their upper portions hacked off, still others flattened into
the soft ground. The moon was throwing hard-edged shadows
over the scene, turning it into a convoluted Tolkien land-
scape, a sinister roadway leading to some ghastly destination.
And it was strangely, hauntingly familiar ... Had I seen one
before? Or did I just know, somewhere in the back of my
mind, what would make one ...

"Now what?" asked Georgina.

"We follow it," I said slowly. "This is part of what we came
to find. I'm sure of it."

"I'll tell you one thing," whispered Harry. "They· aren't
strip mining for uranium."

Keeping to the edge of the trees we moved on. As we crept
forward I could feel my brain beginning to put the pieces
together. I had almost all the pieces now, and they were
matching up, logic weaving out of all the random bits we'd
been collecting. And "bit" was the word. In computer par-
lance a "bit" is a single character, the building blocks that
make up a program. Without the proper language, and the
proper sequence of commands, the story remains untold, an
incoherent muddle on a screen or printout, tantalizingly real,
sitting there before your eyes, but still impossible to read.
Now I had a suspicion of the proper language—and I had a
feeling that I didn't want to decipher the story after all.

We found the last clue half a mile later, gleaming in the
dim light from the moon. Harry almost missed it; a square of
burnished metal, etched with words in black: 3-ENG/COMP.
There were two small holes on either side of the tag.

"What is it?" asked Harry, holding it up to the light.

"A label," I said, my voice very flat. "Third Engine Com-
pressor." I took the small piece of metal from him and slipped
it into my pocket.

Georgina had caught my tone. "You know what it means?"
she asked, eyes searching my face.

I didn't want to answer. "Let's keep going," I said.

A hundred yards ahead the trees in front of us ended
abruptly. Harry saw it first and waved us to the ground.

Sinking down to the dank forest floor, we crawled ahead to join him. All of us peered out into the broadened clearing at the end of the rude track we'd been following.

Everything fell into place. In a single instant I had it all.

"Jesus!" whispered Harry.

Moonlight filtered down through the hanging folds of a gigantic camouflage net exactly like the one we'd seen at the Omega installation. This time, though, the netting was hiding more than a forest of pipes and dials. Dozens of small, blue-filtered and hooded spotlights pushed the scene into hideous relief. I felt bile rising in a burning rush at the back of my throat and turned away for a second, squeezing my eyes shut. When I looked again, nothing had changed. Georgina lay beside me, one hand covering her mouth, her eyes wide and staring. Harry Moonblanket looked as though he'd been turned to stone.

"Jesus!" he whispered again.

There were bodies everywhere, or things that looked like bodies. Directly ahead of us, a few yards away, a family sat, still upright in their seats, the chair section perched on a hummock slab of muskeg. Father, mother, and child—once. The man sat, head thrown back against the top of the seat, his mouth opened in a horrible yawning grin. His hands still clutched the buckle of his seatbelt. The child beside him leaned almost sleepily against its mother, head bent to the woman's shoulder at an impossible angle. The mother had no head at all.

Beyond the grisly family grouping I could see other, equally terrible visions of sudden death. Some of the bodies were still strapped in, others had been thrown clear and lay like broken dolls, arms, legs, even whole torsos strewn separately.

Among the corpses lay the debris of the aircraft they had died in: cables and wires; jagged edge chunks of fuselage; a riven section of wing, the massive engine still intact; ruptured suitcases vomiting brightly coloured summer clothes. At the edge of the terrible scar in the land I could see the tail section, its base driven deeply into the earth as though by a gigantic angry fist. The engine pod had split away from under the tall blue fin, its fan cutting through the surrounding trees to lie among the other wreckage a hundred yards away. The big jet had died hard; and so had the people in her.

"Sam!" moaned Georgina. I reached out and tugged her close in beside me, quieting her.

"People," whispered Harry, nodding his head to the left. I followed his glance. He was right. Half a dozen men, eerily dressed in heavy suits and hoods, were picking through the wreckage, reaching down with heavily gloved hands every few seconds, then moving on. One of them carried a long handled device that looked like a metal detector. A few hundred feet behind them, sitting on a cleared patch of ground, were two of the big Sikorskys. Beyond the helicopters, right at the edge of the netting roof, I could make out the rectangular shapes of three small mobile office trailers.

"What do we do?" asked Harry, keeping an eye on the strangely dressed squad of men. "Go back?"

I shook my head. "No. We don't have any evidence. We need proof."

"I'm a witness," said Harry.

"Not good enough," I whispered back. The men were getting closer. I cursed silently. Georgina had lost the camera to Brandt's men back at the Omega operation and we'd never replaced it. The little metal tag wasn't going to be enough, and neither was any kind of testimony Harry Moonblanket could give. The way Llewellyn had set me up I was going to need a lot of credibility to make myself heard.

"We better get our asses back in the woods," said Harry, nodding towards the approaching men. We slipped back, staying on our bellies. I had to drag Georgina; her body was limp, muscles unresponsive. For a moment I thought she'd fainted, but her eyes were still open.

"What the hell are they doing?" asked Harry, his voice low. He kept a wary glance on the edge of the trees.

"Looking for whatever it was they lost," I said. "It's a long story. All I know is they're covering up the fact that she crashed. Christ only knows how they managed it!"

"Big plane," said Harry.

"DC-10," I answered. "And with a belly full of smuggled goods of some kind."

"And that's why they're covering it up?" asked Harry.

I nodded. "In a regular DOT Inquiry the cargo would be revealed," I said softly. "And then the shit would hit the fan."

"They've got weight behind them," murmured Harry. "Those choppers have been getting clearance in and out of Goose. Somebody up high knows what's going on."

"I know," I said, frowning. "That's what scares hell out of me, and that's also why we have to find some pretty strong evidence to hang these people."

"You don't think we should just forget it?" asked Harry. "Maybe you're in too deep."

"No," I said. "I've gone too far with this, seen too much." I jerked my head towards the crash site. "You think those corpses out there would want us to walk away?" I asked.

"I don't think they care much about anything any more," said Harry. "But I guess you're right. So what do we do?"

"Head back to the place where we were at dusk," I instructed. "I don't think she'll be able to get much farther than that tonight." I touched Georgina's arm, wondering whether she'd be able to walk. Her hand clutched at mine.

"I'm staying with you," she said.

I squeezed her hand. "No. Any more than one person trying to get in there and we'd all be dead. I'm not being heroic, I'm just being practical."

"What then?" broke in Harry.

"Tomorrow, head back to the plane. Blaze a trail for me to follow. I'll meet you there by three in the afternoon."

"And if you don't show up?" asked Harry.

"Take off," I said. "When you get back to Goose Bay, write down everything you've seen. Georgina will be able to fill in the blanks. Make half a dozen copies and send them to every major news agency you can think of. And copy this as well." I handed him the metal tag. "It's all we've got."

"I want to stay," said Georgina.

"No way," I said, smiling. "This is Tarzan, remember? I'm not going to get myself killed—and you can do more good putting everything down on paper. If I *do* get caught, then that can be my ace in the hole. Okay?"

"No, it's not okay," she said miserably. "But I'll do it."

I kissed her once, softly. "All right, get going," I whispered.

A few seconds later, they had disappeared into the shadows. I was alone.

Chapter Twenty-three

I shivered in the moonlight that dappled down through the trees. I felt cold—and it wasn't because of the temperature. I dropped to my belly again and crawled to the edge of the forest. The group of oddly garbed men had veered off, picking through another section of the crash site. I had managed to put the scene's horror into a lock-box in my mind, and I felt a hot rush of elation and anger where only hours ago there had been nothing but fear and apprehension. I had reached the source: story's end. Now all I had to do was bring it back to the land of the living.

It wasn't going to be easy. Any kind of compromising evidence was going to be in one of the portable buildings along the fringe of the crash site, and right ahead of them were the choppers. Squinting, I noticed movement in both cockpits. Their cargo doors were open and I could faintly make out the familiar shapes of the stainless steel drums. The choppers were almost ready to go. I checked my watch: 1:00 A.M.

A door opened in the closest of the portable buildings and I saw figures outlined in a flood of yellow light. They headed towards the Sikorskys. Four of them. Two went to work pulling up the metal ramps and shutting the hatches while the other pair began hauling at a box-like piece of equipment a dozen yards away. The two men at the box hooked in a pair of cables and then I heard the faint whine of an electric motor. I saw the cables tighten, arcing up into the camouflage net twenty feet overhead. Slowly, the net began to pull back on itself, leaving a gaping opening, easily big enough for the choppers to take off.

The men finished closing off the cargo doors and then they and the two at the winch climbed aboard the helicopters. There was a dull whirring noise as the pilots began to run up their engines and soon the blades cut in with a clatter. I could feel the blast from the downdraft from my position two hundred yards away and I squinted against the gusting air.

The noise increased as the jets spooled up and then, abruptly, the nearest helicopter lifted shudderingly into the air. It banked slightly, slipping through the gap in the netting, then throbbed away, its engine wailing. A few seconds later the second Sikorsky heaved its seven ton bulk into the air. Then it, too, was gone. The door of the nearest trailer opened and two more figures appeared. They went to the winch machinery and moments later the netting began unfurling, filling the empty space. The men went back into the building, shutting the door behind them.

On the crash site itself the others were still picking over the terrain. They seemed to be concentrating their attention on the man with the detector apparatus, following his erratic route through the debris like bizarre rats behind an equally exotic pied piper. The men trailing were carrying bundles of metal and every so often, at the direction of the man in the lead, they would tamp one into the ground. In the dull-blue light from the floods along the perimeter the markers looked like flags on a snowless slalom course. I waited. After another twenty minutes they completed a full circuit of the site and headed back to the trailer. Obviously, it was a barracks of some kind. They paused at the doorway and slipped out of their suits, depositing them in a large bin to one side of the building. Then they went inside. A few seconds later the floodlights went out and the crash site darkened. I moved farther back into the protective cover of the trees and groped around in my hip pocket for my cigarettes. I lit one, cupping the match flame in my hand, then blowing it out. I held my hand over the glowing end of the cigarette and dragged deeply.

The DC-10 was almost undoubtedly AVTOUR flight 360—the aircraft Sam Underwood had boarded at Heathrow, the same plane that had been reprogrammed in the computers as "flight cancelled," its cargo "not on hand." For some reason the giant jet had crashed, here in the Labrador hinterland. Whatever the flight had been carrying besides its passengers was dangerous—lethally so. The isolated Omega complex suggested that, and so did the kind of suits the squad out on the site had been wearing. Those suits were protection against either toxic chemicals or radiation. I'd seen no sign of chemical burns anywhere. I was willing to bet on radiation.

And that brought the immensity of the situation home.

Aircraft, common carrier passenger flights, had been carrying dangerous materials for years; that was well known, at least to journalists in my field. And they'd caused accidents before, too. In November 1973 a Pan Am Clipper reported a fire soon after takeoff from Kennedy Airport in New York. It was rerouted to Logan International in Boston where it crashed, just short of the runway, exploding on impact. The jet had been carrying more than fifteen thousand pounds of chemicals, including nitric acid, hydrofluoric acid, and one thousand six hundred gallons of methanol. During the inquiry into the crash it was found that none of the packages had been labelled as corrosive or flammable, and some of the crates containing the beakers of acid had accordingly been loaded upside down. It was not an isolated event. After the Logan crash, the Federal Aviation Authority in the US launched a monumental program of spot checks on cargo. Hundreds of prosecutions for illegal shipment of hazardous material resulted after the FAA discovered dangerous cargo in boxes labelled as machine parts, and once even as sanitary pads. The spot checks solved nothing, basically because there is no law in the US or anywhere else in the world forbidding air transport of dangerous goods. There are regulations dealing with the labelling of these goods; and that is the extent of the control.

But nothing I'd ever heard of had been done on the vast scale that I now witnessed on the site of the downed DC-10. Radioactive waste was involved. Tons of it. No wonder AVTOUR could send out flights half empty—the real money was in the illicit cargo it was carrying, and customs was turning a blind eye.

I knew that all of the nuclear nations were faced with a terrible problem: what to do with the high level nuclear waste from their reactors. Evidently, Llewellyn had come up with an answer. They were shipping the stuff in from all over the world, and depositing it at the Omega complex where it could be stored "safely" underground. I had a sneaking suspicion that the rest of the complex at Omega was a reprocessing plant, and that a lot of the waste was being recycled to extract usable fission products. It all made horrifying sense. Governments all over the world, from banana republics to the major powers, had been publicly brooding about the problems of nuclear waste and spending millions of dollars looking for ways to deal with it. One of the solutions proposed had been the burial of high grade wastes in deep holes, preferably in geologically stable areas like the Canadian Shield of northern Ontario and Manitoba. The Americans were thinking about salt mines—but everyone said a long term solution was years in the future. It appeared, however, that the nuclear industry wasn't about to wait. Dealing with waste meant time and energy stolen from expansion. Llewellyn, or whoever Llewellyn represented, had provided a solution. What the public didn't know wouldn't hurt them.

Until now. The discovery of the tragic end of AV360 would blow it all wide open. With the knowledge of the crash and the cargo the flight had been carrying made public, the trail would inevitably lead back to Omega on the Canadian end, and Gambetta in Europe and elsewhere. It was the kind of scandal that toppled governments, and there were a lot of them involved if the locations of AVTOUR and Gambetta branches were any indication of the waste disposal system's scope and range. Germany, France, the UK, Japan: they were all implicated.

And I was right in the middle of it with no place to go. I groaned inwardly. I could find as much documentation as I wanted but it wasn't going to do me much good. If I brought it to the attention of my own government they'd compliment me on my zeal, then put a bullet through my brain. Their system was good enough to somehow deal with the incredible problem of covering up the crash of the Jumbo jet. They weren't about to let a reporter with a hot scoop ruin the whole thing.

I took a last drag on the cigarette, then shredded it, tamping the butt deep into the wet soil.

"Well, screw you," I whispered. I pushed any thoughts of the future aside. There was no time for that now. I had to proceed one step at a time. So what was the next step?

There were three of the portable office trailers. The largest, and closest, seemed to be a barracks. The middle one was windowless; storage maybe? Extra fuel, empty drums for the waste? Then there was the third. It was the smallest, about half the size of the other two. I had seen windows, but they were dark. That could mean either that it was empty, or that it had tightly fitting curtains. After all, there wasn't any light seeping from the barracks trailer.

I made a decision. I'd try the smallest of the three and if I came up empty I could move on to the middle one. Come what may, I wasn't going to try the barracks. I cursed the loss of the camera again. Then I thought it through, and realized that the camera wouldn't have done much good, either. I could have taken photographs anywhere; and pictures can always be faked. It was either hard evidence, or nothing at all.

I crept back to the edge of the trees and peered out onto the crash site again. It was still dark, the details of the deathly gouge in the land thankfully obscured. There was no movement around the trailers. It made sense. Why bother posting guards when you were a hundred miles from the nearest civilization? For the first time I noticed a small radar dish on top of the barracks trailer. Somewhere in that rectangular metal shack a man was at the scope, probably monitoring the immediate area, waiting for the return of the Sikorskys. The dish was motionless so the scanning range was limited; just enough to cover the airspace directly above the crash site and a little on either side.

I lay on the soft earth, the scent of rotting pine needles in my nostrils, and tried to imprint the position of the three trailers in my mind. The simplest route would be to cut right across the crash site, but it was also the most dangerous. If someone happened to come out at the wrong moment I'd be seen. I was going to have to go around the long way. I slipped back until I was out of sight of the clearing, then stood. I began circling around towards the buildings, walking carefully, checking the ground with each step, pausing regularly to listen. It was almost two o'clock before I reached a position I thought was in line with the buildings. I dropped to the ground again and inched forward.

I came out right on the button. I reached the edge of the trees and found myself staring out at the blank rear walls of the three shacks. The two large ones were set close together, no more than ten feet between them. The third was set to one side.

Keeping flat I slid out from under cover of the trees, bellying towards the smaller trailer. I reached it and stopped, letting my breath out slowly and silently. Now what? I thought. I couldn't stay in the open forever, I had to make a move. I peered up at the bare metal wall. There was no rear door. I'd have to take my chances going in the front. I prayed that the door wouldn't be locked. The trailer was raised on concrete blocks so at least I wouldn't have to expose myself by going around the side. I slithered under the building and began to slowly work my way forward.

I wouldn't have noticed it if I hadn't been lying on my back. Halfway under the trailer I caught a glimpse of a square lip about three by three. I crabbed to the side until I was positioned beneath it. It was a hatch, probably used for service connections when that model of trailer was used on a site for an extended period of time. I lifted my hands, splaying the fingers against the cool metal. I pushed. Nothing happened. I pushed again, harder, and I felt the hatch give slightly. I dug my elbows into the damp soil and pressed up as hard as I could. The hatch popped with a loud snapping noise, as something, maybe a bolt, gave inside. I went rigid, listening hard, holding my breath. To my ears it had been as loud as a gunshot, but as the seconds passed I relaxed. No one appeared to investigate. I reached up again and pushed the hatch farther up. It moved back silently on an interior hinge, but I felt a slight resistance. I stuck my head up through the hole and realized what it was.

The hatch *had* been bolted down, but only with a small slide bolt no larger than the kind you'd use on a screen door or a kitchen cabinet. The resistance had come from a rug that had been laid over the hatchway. Whoever lived or worked in the trailer was a bit of a homebody.

The interior of the box-like shack was dark, and obviously vacant. If there'd been anyone inside, the snapping of the bolt would have guaranteed a warm welcome. I got my elbows up over the edge and lifted myself inside. I knelt beside the hatch opening and looked around in the gloom.

The furnishing was sparse but comfortable. There was a metal desk along one wall, and a pair of two-drawer filing cabinets perched on top of it. There was a grouping of folding chairs to one side, and a low box that served as a coffee table. The short wall at the far end was covered with a huge square of paper. I couldn't make out any details in the darkness, but it appeared to be a map—probably a large scale schematic outline of the site. I turned. There was a simple army cot against the other short wall, complete with a metal footlocker at its end. The rug I'd tipped back was nothing more than a square of industrial carpeting. I went to the filing cabinets first, sliding open the drawers as quietly as I could.

The first two were filled with more computer printouts like the ones Llewellyn had been carrying when we crashed outside Alexandria. The other two were much more interesting. They were crammed to overflowing with dozens of pocket filing folders, all neatly labelled with last names. Each one contained personal effects, mostly documents; some had wallets and credit card folders. I flipped through them quickly. I found Sam's right where it belonged, at the back of the second drawer, under the U's. I pulled it out and slid the contents onto the surface of the desk. Wallet, keychain, address book, lighter, his favourite Dunhill cigarette case. I pressed the recessed button on the cigarette case and it opened. There were still seven or eight inside. Something caught in my throat and my eyes blurred for a second; then I closed the cigarette case and slipped it and the lighter into the pocket of my jeans. I put the rest of the stuff back into the folder and replaced it in the filing cabinet. Next, I gave my attention to the desk's single centre drawer. I tugged at it. It was locked.

Getting up, I padded swiftly around the small room, ending up at the footlocker. I went through it and found a short metal shoehorn tucked in beside several pairs of neatly folded green uniforms like the ones the Omega people had been wearing. I spotted a name flash on the pocket and spread the shirt open: LLEWELLYN. With a grim smile, I folded the shirt and put it back into the locker. Now at least I knew whose trailer I was in.

I took the shoehorn back to the desk and poked around until I had it fitted into the crack right above the lock. I pried upward against the desk and the lock snapped. I pulled open the drawer. It was completely empty except for one thing: a large, dark-blue binder. I put it down on the desk, opened it, and peered down at the title page:

ICARUS CONTINGENCY PLAN

Approved: March 20, 1980
Revised: June 30, 1981
Addenda approved: September 8, 1982
Operational Schedule approved: September 8, 1982
Copy #1 of 34

Now I knew what Harry Moonblanket's approach designations stood for: IKE-R-S run together stood for Icarus, the mythical figure who flew too close to the sun using wings attached with wax; DEED-L-S was Daedalus, his father. There was a "copies to" at the bottom of the page. Llewellyn's name was first, circled with a felt pen, and I recognized some of the others; they were the names of the heads of nuclear agencies all over the world. I turned to the next page and began to read; it was an introductory note and I could sense Llewellyn's voice behind the words. This was *his* document, *his* hellish plan.

During early meetings held with yourselves and your representatives, it became clear that above and beyond your reservations concerning the viability of the project as a whole, your most serious concern involved the possibility of an accident. That concern is not an ill-founded one. I doubt that there is any one of you who has not been in the position of dealing with accidental excursions at your own facilities. Our US member has been under attack consistently for several years on this score, as have the members from France, the UK, and Germany. Our Canadian member is also quite disturbed by the possibility of an accident, since the probability of such an event occurring within his country's boundaries is by definition higher than anywhere else.

Statistically, an accident involving one of our carriers is certain to happen. Any system, given a sufficient number of random factors over a long period of time, will fail. This is unavoidable. As chairman and controller of the group, it has been my mandate to establish a counter mode capable of dealing with such an occurrence.

The installation of datalink terminals on all our flights is one method of ascertaining the severity of an accident *while that accident is in progress*. The third officer on each flight has only one function: to update the aircraft's status at ten minute intervals while over sea, and at three minute intervals over land. Since the datalink does not use regular radio channels for transmissions, operational codes can be used freely and all transmissions will remain private. Should an accident occur in mid-flight, we will be advised of the situation immediately. Should the accident develop over water, the flight can be terminated within ninety seconds (see Midflight Terminal Procedures, page 26). In the event of an accident occurring over land, sections 29 through 106 of this contingency plan will come into effect.

Many of you have commented that the addition of passengers on our flights compounds the risks involved should an accident occur. It is my feeling, borne out by statistical surveys of the situation, that passengers are too effective as an operational "blind" to be dispensed with. The problems of passenger fatalities are dealt with between sections 39 and 54 of this manual.

As soon as we are notified that an accident has occurred I shall take immediate command, and all communications dealing with the accident must be routed through my office. Under no circumstances should any of you or your agencies take independent action. I shall be following the Operational Schedule appended to this document and as each element of the matrix is completed you will be notified on an individual basis. Upon completion of the Operational Schedule you will be provided with archival documentation to circumvent the disclosure of any anomalies in the future.

It was signed: Charles Harcourt Llewellyn, Chairman.

I turned to the back of the binder and found the Operational Schedule. It was six pages long, a detailed item by item checklist. Blanks on the inside edges of the pages had been filled in, giving the date of completion for each numbered element. There were only two left open:

84. Stripdown and final cleanup. Inspection. Removal of extraneous material. Remote ignition of site.
85. Public notification of accident on charter return.

The crew I'd seen out on the site had obviously been doing the final inspection. The schedule was almost complete. I checked the calendar on my watch and did some fast calculating. Tomorrow would be the fourteenth day from Sam's takeoff out of Heathrow, the last day of a two week charter. Another AVTOUR flight, maybe the one we'd seen come into

Mirabel, would fly out of New York and with a quick fiddle on the computer keyboard, it would "crash" in Labrador, conveniently bursting into flames—the "remote ignition" referred to in Item 84. By the time anyone from Goose Bay Air-Sea Rescue arrived, the remains of the passengers, dead for two weeks, would be cinders. No autopsies would be performed and the crash investigation, considering the distances and difficulties of working in such a remote area, would be cursory. Llewellyn had probably planted a bogus flight recorder somewhere on the site, artfully depicting a rock solid case of pilot error. Meanwhile, the actual flight out of New York would have landed safely in Europe, switching flight designations en route and popping up on the London Air Traffic Control computers as something altogether different than what it had been at takeoff. With the computer access facilities Llewellyn had in his control it would be easy enough.

It was macabre, but brilliant. Almost every phase of modern air travel was handled by computer, from passenger check-in and ticket purchase, through to takeoff and landing. Radar checks, radio beacons, transponder ID, all of it was computerized. The only human hands and eyes directly involved were those of the actual crews piloting the aircraft, and the harassed and over-worked air traffic controllers. Once a flight was out of a controller's area he forgot about it. He had to if he wanted to keep his sanity.

And the phoney crash would take care of the random factors—the passengers. Friends, relatives, and co-workers would have perfectly acceptable urns of carbonized flesh to mourn over. Except that the dates on all the headstones would be off by fourteen days. I knew that if I read through the sections of the plan on passenger fatalities I'd find detailed instructions for the writing of "I'm fine wish you were here" postcards mailed from Canada and the US. Llewellyn had done exactly that when he'd kidnapped Georgina. Detail work. Monumental, but easy to accomplish with Llewellyn's wide-ranging setup. I was willing to bet that he was responsible for Georgina's phone being out of order during the first critical days after the crash.

It was a perfect plan. Except for me—the fly in the ointment...

"Okay! Let's get the lead out!"

The bellowing voice seemed about a foot away. I froze, my heart racing wildly. Outside I could hear the sound of footsteps banging down the steps of the barracks trailer. I stuffed the binder under my shirt and waited.

"Choppers in ten minutes," roared the bullhorn voice. *"Let's be ready! Go! Go! Go!"*

Whoever was using the loudspeaker had once been a drill sergeant. I tiptoed to the small window beside the door and pulled back the curtain fractionally. The crash site was alive with blue light again, silhouetted bodies running back and forth. At least a dozen men were working away at the poles holding up the camouflage netting, pulling out the cinch pins, allowing the lengths of tubing to telescope in on themselves. Still more were moving across the site itself, dragging large opaque plastic bags on skids. The bags were heavy with sloshing liquid. I watched as the first of the bags were set beside a large piece of the fuselage and then abandoned. I was sure the bags contained high octane aviation fuel. When they were ignited, the fire would incinerate the bags, leaving no trace. With enough bags the crash site could be turned into an inferno, and by the looks of it that's exactly what was intended. The fire would consume everything, removing any evidence. They might even get lucky and start a forest fire, further obscuring their trail. I craned my neck and looked towards the barracks trailer. A squad was already at work tearing it down. If it was anything like the ones I'd seen it wouldn't take long. The portable buildings were designed to be airlifted, and broke down into small components capable of being put into a transport plane or a helicopter like the Sikorsky RH-3. It was time to get moving; someone would be along to clean out Llewellyn's little boudoir and I didn't want to be around when it happened. If they checked the lock on the desk drawer I was in trouble. I eased the curtain down and headed for the hatch.

Which presented a problem. How the hell was I supposed to get the rug back down on my way out? If I left it to one side, the broken latch would stick out like a sore thumb. I stared down at the open hatch. In the distance I could hear the faint throb of the approaching helicopters. I was trapped.

Then, with a sound like the snicking of a rifle bolt sliding home, I heard a key turning in the door behind me.

Chapter Twenty-four

You hear a lot about instinctive reactions. People leaping to save their children, or flinching in the face of a bullet like the famous photo of Lee Harvey Oswald getting it in the guts. In movies, it's usually associated with lightning reflexes and a brain that automatically comes up with the perfect response to a crisis.

If it's true, then I must be the exception that proves the rule because I almost wet my pants when I heard the lock turning. If I had an instinctive reaction it was to fall to the ground in a blind panic, and pray that I had time to get out a few words of abject surrender before my captor blew my brains out.

Somehow I managed to hold my water, but I stayed glued to the floor, bent over the hatch opening, looking back over my shoulder. From then on it was all in slow motion, and I was aware of every tiny movement.

The door swung open and I caught a glimpse of a short, uniformed figure wearing a sidearm. He was into the room before he spotted me. His jaw dropped and then his right arm flew to the holster at his waist. At the same time he half turned to call for help. I pushed off with my bent knee, arms outstretched. One hand managed to snag his holster, the other connected with his chest. We fell in a heap, his outflung arm banging the door shut and cutting off the blue light from outside. We struggled, my hand caught in his belt. I had an advantage of weight and height, but he still managed to get on top of me, and I saw his mouth open again as he prepared to shout. I tore my right hand out of his grasp and did the only thing that would stop him—I jammed it down his throat. There was a searing pain as his teeth bit my fingers. I kept pushing as he gagged, bringing the hand that had been clawing for the holster up to his face, trying to pull my fingers out of his mouth. I jerked my other hand out of his belt and with as much force as I could muster rammed four stiff fingers into his exposed armpit. His teeth loosened on my fingers and he let out a gargling scream, falling backwards. I squirmed out from beneath him and dove for the gun at his belt again. Choking, he managed to roll onto his side, bringing his fist down on the back of my neck like a club. I grunted with pain and lashed out, connecting with my right boot, the hard toe digging into something soft. He doubled into a fetal position and I pushed myself sideways on top of him. I kneed him in the crotch again and then, locking the fingers of both hands together I smashed his face as hard as I could.

Hitting someone in the head is not the smartest thing in the world. It's great if you're wearing ten ounce gloves, but bare knuckled, and with one hand already chewed up, it hurts like hell. As my doubled fist slammed down, I had to bite back a scream. But it worked. Some of the man's teeth splintered, and he gave a wet groan and went limp.

I unlocked my fingers and flexed them. They were operative; more or less. I stayed on top of him, waiting. His mouth was hanging open, filling with blood around the shattered stumps of his teeth; and his face was colouring deeply, open eyes rolling back. I lifted myself off him and rolled his limp form onto one side to keep him from drowning in his own blood. Then I squatted beside him, trying to figure out what to do next. The thunder of the helicopters was quickly filling the air. There was no time for fancy stuff like stripping the man and getting into his uniform. It wouldn't have worked anyway, since I was a good head and shoulders taller than he was. I knew I'd have to go out the way I came in. The state of the desk and the rug on the floor was irrelevant now. The next person who came along was going to find one of his pals bleeding all over the boss's rug and know that all was most definitely not well.

Staggering a little, I stood up and went to the hatch. I felt to make sure the binder was still under my shirt, then eased myself into the hole. I dropped to the ground and lay there for a moment, getting my bearings. The sound of the helicopters was deafening. They had to be right overhead.

I hunkered forward on my elbows and knees, moving painfully to the edge of the trailer. I reached it and paused. Squinting, I could make out the wall of trees twenty feet away. The man with the bullhorn was at it again, his crackling bellow rising above the declining clatter of the choppers, but my mind was too furred with pain and confusion to make out what he was saying. I checked right and left. Nobody. I squirmed out from under the trailer and clambered to my feet. I ran for the trees, making the six or seven yard dash in record time. I crashed into the brush and dropped to the ground as soon as I was a few feet in. I turned to see if anyone had followed me. Still nobody. The landing of the Sikorskys had covered my escape.

But not for long. As soon as they found the unconscious man in Llewellyn's trailer the hue and cry would begin. Almost on cue a whistle began blowing stridently. I got to my feet and lumbered into the bush, branches clawing at my face and tearing at my clothes.

I went about fifty yards and then veered to the right, stumbling over the exposed roots and rock outcroppings in the darkness. A little of the panic was receding and I was thinking again. My trail was going to be easy enough to follow. I'd left enough clues, that was certain. If they couldn't spot the speckles of blood from my gnawed hand, the broken branches and gouges in the earth would lead them to me soon enough. I was in one deep hole and I couldn't see any way out.

To work my way back to the place I'd parted with Harry and Georgina would be suicide—for all of us. I'd told Harry to blaze a trail since I had no compass, and I was sure he'd done a good job. If it was good enough for me to follow, it was good enough for Llewellyn's men. And they had an advantage; I was already exhausted while they were relatively fresh. Heading in any other direction would be equally insane; even if they didn't manage to catch up to me I was doomed. You don't go wandering around in the Labrador bush with no compass, no supplies, and no hope of rescue. I'd be hopelessly lost in a matter of hours.

So what do you do when you can't go forward, and you can't go back? You've got two choices: either you give up and stay where you are, or you do something really crazy, like jump straight up into the air. I decided on the crazy route. I headed in towards the crash site.

I picked my way carefully, trying, this time, not to leave any traces of my passage. I was counting on a few minutes of confusion while they tended to their comrade before the chase really started. I reached the edge of the trees a few minutes later, crawling forward on my belly again.

It looked like an ant colony gone mad. The big barracks trailer was completely down, and men were loading it onto one of the three waiting choppers. The last poles and rolls of camouflage netting were being carted to a second helicopter. On the site itself, a dozen or so men were dropping off more of the big fuel bags. A third group was unbolting the now empty storage shed. There was another milling bunch around Llewellyn's office, arguing, voices raised, arms waving.

Suddenly they stopped yelling and I saw why. A man was climbing down out of the third Sikorsky. One arm was in a sling. I would have recognized him even without the white flutter of bandage at his forehead. It was Brandt.

The stocky, stiff legged man walked across to Llewellyn's office and the clustered men. He brushed past them and went up the short set of steps, disappearing inside. He re-emerged a few seconds later and gave a series of sharp commands. The group formed into a neat parade ground file. He gestured with his free hand, pointing at the woods behind the trailer. Obediently they trotted off. I figured it would take them less than five minutes to pick up my scent. I was going to have to act quickly.

It had to be the helicopters. I knew Brandt wouldn't keep his men out in the bush for long. Llewellyn's schedule didn't leave any room for drawn out searches. I checked my watch. It was almost four. It would be dawn in another hour or so; already the sky was lightening perceptibly.

I studied the three large Sikorskys. Two were parked side by side, close to the spot where the barracks trailer had been. A group of men was already at work unbolting Llewellyn's office and carrying out the furniture, piling it beside the gaping cargo doors of the middle aircraft. The third helicopter, Brandt's, was off to one side, and there was no activity around it. I looked beyond the blunt-nosed machine. Out on the site the last bags had been dropped and some of the men were returning with the empty skids. Others were dismantling the hooded blue spotlights.

Brandt's machine was tempting. There was no one around it, and it was the closest to me of the three. Regrettably, I had to ignore it. By the way things were shaping up, choppers one and two were for equipment, the third would almost certainly be for lifting off the last of the personnel. I might be able to sneak aboard Brandt's chopper, but the chances of being discovered were too great. It was either one or two. I picked two. So far it had only been partially loaded so there might be room for me to squeeze in and lie low without being found. The real difficulty lay in crossing the hundred yards of open ground that stretched between me and it. It might as well have been a hundred miles; the intervening space was a hive of activity. I checked my watch again. Three minutes had passed. If I didn't make a move soon, Brandt's bloodhounds would be right up my tail. I needed a diversion, something to keep the men on the crash site busy while I crossed to the beckoning Sikorsky. It had to be something flamboyant, something they couldn't miss.

Fire. I felt in my pocket and pulled out Sam's lighter. It was a Dunhill, like the cigarette case; gold, inlaid with onyx. I flicked it on. A nice blue flame erupted. I adjusted the flame size to its largest and retreated deeper into the bush. In the distance I could hear Brandt's men crashing around and calling to each other. From the sound of it they were still quite a way off.

I found the stump of a nicely rotting Labrador Pine and tore at the bark, scratching away until I had accumulated a good pile of pulp and some of the soft, tinder dry core. I gathered up as large a pile of twigs as I could find, and added some moss and lichen from the base of another tree for good measure. I laid the whole mess beside the stump with enough space in between to let the fire breathe. If the stump caught well enough the flames would hopefully spread to the surrounding branches of other trees. I flicked on the lighter again and a long tongue of flame sprang up, licking at my makeshift bonfire. I waved the torchlike flame back and forth across the pile, so that it would catch in as many places as possible. "C'mon Sam, let's give 'em hell!" I whispered.

For a moment it seemed as though the fire wouldn't take hold. Suddenly it took off with a great whooshing sound, a blaze sliding up the stump, engulfing it in seconds. Trickles of flame spat out along the surface of the forest floor. Soon a few more trees were going to be ablaze. The funny little cartoon figure on Captain Kangaroo had been right—playing with fire *was* dangerous. And a damn good thing, too. I jammed the lighter back into my pocket and backed quickly away from the hot threat of the flames. I watched for a moment, realizing how effective Llewellyn's gasoline bags would be.

Someone must have seen the fire almost instantly because I heard the booming voice on the bullhorn again. I took one last look at the fire—if anything, it would spread back into the forest towards my pursuers—and began to run, twisting through the trees along the edge of the woods. I ran a few hundred feet and then dropped, elbowing my way to the perimeter of the crash site. I looked out into the open.

The ruse had worked. Everyone had dropped what they were doing and was headed for the crackling flames. Someone jumped down out of Brandt's machine carrying a large cylindrical object—doubtless a fire extinguisher. I could see the crowd, outlined now in the bright, flickering light of the fire. There was no one between me and chopper number two. Everyone's back was to me. I got up and ran.

It was the longest hundred yards of my life. I kept my eyes on the cargo door as I moved with what seemed like agonizing slowness across the open space. My legs pumped. I could feel the blood hammering in my temples. It seemed as though my lungs were going to explode. When I reached the egg crate grillwork of the ramp I took it in three steps without breaking stride, and as I came to the top I threw myself in through the cargo opening in a broad jumper's roll. Landing on the metal floor of the chopper punched my remaining breath away, but I kept on rolling, getting myself as far into the enclosing shadows as I could.

I lay on the rivet studded floor, lungs seared, my breath coming in jagged gasps. I kept my eyes closed and my muscles tensed as I waited for someone to cry out. Nothing happened. I opened my eyes and blinked. I'd managed to roll up against one of the neatly stacked siding panels of the trailer. I sat up and peered down the length of the cargo hold. All the panels had been fitted into pipe enclosures made especially for them. Bits of furniture had been roped to the walls on big cleats, then wrapped with movers' blankets. Efficient to the end. There was plenty of room to make a nest in the rear as long as the chopper didn't take on anybody except the crew in the forward cabin.

I stood up and edged my way around to the side of the cargo doors. I peeked out. The extinguisher seemed to have the fire under control; at least there were no obvious flames that I could see. The man with the bullhorn was ordering people around and they were beginning to disperse, going back to their duties. I slipped back into the cargo hold, working my way as far back as I could. There was nothing to do now but wait. I squeezed in between two rows of panels at the extreme end of the hold beside the narrow toilet enclosure, and settled down on the floor, my back to the wall.

Incredibly, I managed to doze off. When my eyes snapped open it was because I felt the entire body of the chopper moving. The crew was getting on board. I checked my watch, holding the luminous dial up to my eyes. It was four exactly. I'd been asleep for only a few minutes. Up ahead I could hear muffled conversation and then there was a grinding clatter as the cargo door was shut and locked. I heard voices again as the crew ran through the checkout. There was a whine as the pilot hit the ignition switch for the big GE turbines and then the engine caught. Above me, I could feel the steadily increasing vibration as the big four bladed rotors began to spin. The noise grew deafeningly loud, and I sensed the seventy-two foot long beast straining to be away. The pilot let off the rotor brakes and we lurched into the air. As we leaned into the climb my back pressed against the wall, and then I slid forward as we went into the slightly nose down flight mode.

We were on our way back to Goose Bay.

Chapter Twenty-five

The flight back to Goose Bay took a little more than an hour. I spent the time dozing fitfully in my cramped cubbyhole, waking every few minutes, heart pounding. I tried hard to keep my eyes open but it was impossible. I'd been going on all cylinders for almost twenty hours, and my body was taking a break whether I liked it or not. I was totally exhausted. If one of the crew had come back to use the head and seen me I wouldn't have put up a fight. They could have tossed me out of the chopper at ten thousand feet and I probably would have fallen asleep on the way down.

I awoke for the last time at a quarter past five as we banked steeply. The rotor pitch had changed, turning the dull, monotonous thunder of the engines into an insistent wail. We were coming down. Outside I knew the sun would be sneaking up out of the cold Atlantic, turning the purple sky to gold. It was time to move; I didn't want to be found napping in among the trailer panels when they unloaded.

I levered myself up, wincing as I put my weight down onto the pins and needles infesting my lower legs. I waited for a few seconds, letting the numbness subside. I didn't want to stumble; helicopters, even big ones like the Sikorsky, are delicately balanced, suspended like the core of a gyroscope below the twisting gears of the rotor drive. A fall would have alerted the crew instantly. I eased forward, hanging onto the vertical pipes holding up the panels, and reached the toilet cubicle. I checked the dark, narrow aisle leading forward to the cabin bulkhead. A trickle of light was leaking around the cargo door, letting me see that the hatchway through the bulkhead to the cockpit was closed. Gently, I turned the handle on the cubicle and slipped inside, locking it behind me. I sat down in the coffin-sized compartment and waited.

We went through a long, tilting approach and I could visualize the steady descent as we angled in low over the trees bordering the airport plateau. A few minutes later, the chopper angled up, the force of the movement throwing me back, my head slamming painfully into the back wall of the cubicle. We settled downward slowly, swaying from side to side, and then we were down, the back end of the fuselage bouncing gently on the tail wheel shocks. The pilot cut the engines and the rotors slowed, then fell silent. I started to sweat. If one of the crew decided to take a leak I'd had it. I wouldn't have known if someone was approaching the toilet, anyway—my ears were still buzzing from the hour of constant noise. A moment passed, and then I felt the rumbling vibration of the cargo door being pulled back. Someone was climbing up into the cargo hold. As my hearing came back I heard the muffled grating of the loading ramp being lowered, then the pounding of heavy feet. I heard voices, followed by a scraping sound. The panels were being unloaded. I waited, gritting my teeth, eyes tightly shut as the sounds moved down the cargo hold towards the cubicle. I spent the next twenty-five minutes crouched in my tiny dungeon, palpitating with fear.

Finally, they completed the unloading. The ramp was pulled up and once again the cargo door was closed. I waited for another ten minutes, my ear pressed to the cubicle door, listening hard, trying to pick off voices coming from the cabin up ahead. There was nothing but the clicking of the cooling engines somewhere above my head. It looked like we were staying put, for a while anyway.

I took a deep breath and unlocked the door. Still nothing. I pushed it open a fraction of an inch and looked out, peering into the empty, cavernous space. The bulkhead door was wide open, sending long shafts of weak morning light down the length of the hold. The chopper was empty. I eased quickly out into the hold, softly closing the door behind me, and waited a moment, listening. Nothing but silence. I tiptoed forward between the rows of stanchions and stopped at the bulkhead door. Keeping my head down, I went into a crouch and duckwalked into the cockpit. I angled between the two control seats and then raised my head just enough to see over the clutter of instruments on the panel. I looked out onto the landing strip.

It was no part of the Goose Bay Airport I'd ever seen before. According to Harry, the activity had all been on the old, long-abandoned US base. That had to be where we were now.

To the left, less than two hundred feet away, I could see what appeared to be an old hangar, its main doors gaping. The creeping sunlight wasn't very strong but I thought I saw the bulky outline of the big tail-up Caribou Harry had mentioned. Beside the hangar was a low wooden building, set with rows of windows like a barracks. The building was in rough shape—its paint peeling, weeds growing up around it, and bare spots on the roof where shingles had blown off—but there was a light haze of vapour coming up out of a ventilator. It was in use. I looked to the right.

Fifty feet away, looking like a slightly overweight cruise missile, sat a glittering white Hawker Siddeley 125. Above the twin tail mounted engines I picked out the blue and yellow bull's-eye logo of Extran, a big leasing company for executive jets like the 125, working out of Toronto and Montreal. It looked like Llewellyn had picked up some new transportation after the crash of the Beechcraft Duke. The 125 sat alone on the broad stretch of runway. Beyond it there was nothing but a dense wall of trees, the giant triangular patch of brush making up the hub of Goose Bay Airport's three runways. It was also an effective screen, blocking off the view from the main terminal.

I checked my watch again. Ten to six. By now the sun was well up, filling the air with a hazy grey light. I couldn't afford to waste any more time. The other helicopters would be coming in soon, and I didn't want to be around when they landed. The odds were good that as soon as all the choppers were unloaded they'd be flown off somewhere and I wouldn't have the protective cover of the cargo.

I came up with two alternatives: I could try and make it to the hangar building and somehow work my way around it to the edge of the airport plateau; or I could use the Sikorsky itself as cover, and get on board the Hawker Siddeley. Neither choice was particularly appealing. Trying to reach the edge of the plateau meant risking immediate discovery; the barracks building was full of windows and I couldn't see into the hangar well enough to know if there were crews loading the Caribou. On the other hand, I didn't know a hell of a lot about flying a bizjet like the 125. In fact I didn't know anything at all beyond the fact that it had two wings, a rudder, and a tail. I knew that if I tried to take her up I'd blow myself all over the tarmac before I'd gone a hundred yards.

Play at being a stowaway again? I closed my eyes and tried to remember what I knew about the Hawker. Not much. It was a fairly standard executive jet, manufactured in the UK and Canada in conjunction with the Beech Corporation, the same people who made the ill-fated Duke. It used Rolls Royce Viper 524 jet engines and came in a military trainer version as well. Like the Lear, it had gone through its debugging stages long ago. It was a solid, safe, and popular machine.

I'd done tours of Extran jets before, and I knew they pulled out all the stops as far as luxury was concerned. The 125 sitting out there probably had all the options, from doppler radio to a fully equipped bar. If it was like any of the other executive jets it would have a fully enclosed cockpit, roomy seating, a compact but efficient head, and a cloakroom right at the back. The head was out, so if I was going to stow away it would have to be in the cloakroom. The thought of being cooped up in another tiny cubicle, this time with Brandt up front, was enough to send chills down my spine. If I was caught, there wouldn't be any preliminaries. I'd be dead in thirty seconds, and Brandt would enjoy each and every tick of the clock.

Screw it, I thought. Go for the edge of the plateau. I didn't have the guts to face Brandt again. With the decision made, I moved, sliding into the pilot's seat of the Sikorsky and popping the left hand cockpit door. For the first few seconds at least, I'd have the bulk of the big chopper between me and the barracks. The pilot's checklist hung on a clipboard hooked to a stanchion beside the door, and on impulse I slipped it off. If I was going to go, I was going to go in style. I dropped down onto the dew-wet runway, the clipboard in my hand and Llewellyn's binder heavy beneath my shirt. I went around the far side of the high sided machine and began the long walk across the runway to the hangar.

I felt like a novice male stripper on amateur night. The barren stretch of pitted asphalt seemed to stretch endlessly before me. I took the clipboard from under my arm and bent my head to it as I walked, trying to look the part of a concerned maintenance technician. If anybody spotted me and wondered why I wasn't wearing the customary green fatigues, I knew I couldn't keep the bluff up for very long. Another hundred and fifty yards to go; then I'd be in a position between the hangar and the barracks.

I heard a faint drumming noise coming out of the north and I felt the hairs on the back of my neck rise as I recognized the sound. The other helicopters. I bit down on my lip and kept walking, forcing my legs to keep their steady forward march to the safety of the scrub at the edge of the plateau. Seventy yards. The rotor noises from the approaching Sikorskys were distinct now. It sounded like only one of them was coming in. Forty yards. I took a chance and looked up. I found myself staring into the bowels of the hangar. There were seven or eight men that I could see, working by the open cargo doors at the rear of the Short Takeoff and Landing prop-jet. As I looked, one of the men glanced up from his work and saw me. I almost broke into a run but I managed to keep walking. The man resumed his work and I let out a long breath, suddenly realizing that I had the sun almost at my back; to him I'd be nothing but a dark silhouette. Twenty yards and the hammering chatter of the chopper was almost on top of me. I slid my eyes to the right and picked it off, a snub-nosed dot arrowing in low over the barracks building. I had been right; there was only one. Ten yards. On the right there was nothing but the fifty foot high cliff of the hangar wall. To the left, the narrow end of the barracks building. Windowless. My legs mutinied and I took off like a bat out of hell. Half a minute later I had reached the low bushes lining the steeply sloping edge of the plateau. I careened through them, picking up a double pant leg load of burrs, then dropped over the side.

Which was pretty dumb. The slope was at least sixty degrees and I slid a good thirty feet before I managed to dig in my heels and bring myself to a stop just short of an all too solid spur of rock. I flung the clipboard away and continued towards the bottom of the boulder strewn scarp. I reached the base of the plateau, covered from head to toe with dirt. Brushing off what I could, I got to my feet. I put a hand up to my chest—the damning binder was still there. I looked back up the steeply canted rise but there were no curious faces peering over the edge. The sky above was clear as well. Still no sign of the third chopper. I moved away from the plateau, heading into the sparse trees, walking northward at an angle I hoped would eventually bring me around to the rear of the terminal area and the relative sanctuary of Harry Moonblanket's weatherworn office.

I was surprised when I came upon a narrow road less than a quarter of a mile later. It was paved with loose gravel, hardly more than a track. There were no ruts and the road looked as though it hadn't been used for years. I forced myself into a halting trot, each step raising little puffs of dust as I ran.

The road twisted and turned through dozens of gullys, skirting hillocks and outcroppings of rock. For the most part, the track kept fairly close to the base of the plateau except when it bulged to avoid a couple of swampy-looking areas. Every once in a while the surface was split by deeply grooved crevices where the drainage water from the looming cliff on my right had cut into the surface on its way into the muskeg beyond.

After ten minutes of jogging I reached a point where the dirt road joined in a Y with a stretch of two lane blacktop. I recognized where I was. It was the route we'd taken into Happy Valley two days before. One arm of the Y led into the town, the other went up to the terminal. I turned right, heading up the steep grade leading to the airport.

Fifteen minutes later I was letting myself through a rear window into Harry's place. The stale air inside the darkened office smelled as good to me as the finest perfume. Shutting the window behind me, I stumbled across the dark storage area to a doorway. I went through it into the front office and crept up to the front window. There had been no activity around the terminal building when I passed it and the chances that anyone had seen me were slim, but I checked anyway. Everything was quiet. I snapped the venetian blinds closed and sank down onto the worn vinyl couch, breathing a sigh of relief.

Unbuttoning my shirt I eased out the sweat-damp binder and dropped it on the floor. Then I dug into the pocket of my dirt-encrusted jeans and brought out my cigarettes. I looked at them for a moment. It had been Sam's lighter that I'd used to start the fire back at the crash site; I might as well complete the cycle now that I was safe. Scrabbling in another pocket, I brought out Sam's Dunhill case and lit one of the remaining cigarettes. But I only managed to smoke about half of it before exhaustion set in. I stubbed it out and took a last bleary look at my watch. It was almost seven in the morning. I'd told Harry to take off by three in the afternoon if I hadn't shown up. Considering flying time I had about ten hours to wait before they came in. I figured that was just about one tenth the amount of sleep my battered body required. I let myself slide full length along the couch and fell asleep, conjuring up the phantom warmth of Georgina's body beside me.

Chapter Twenty-six

I awoke just after two in the afternoon, still feeling the stiff and aching effects of the past twenty-four hours, but refreshed. I stood up and walked groggily over to the window, opening a couple of slats in the venetian blind and peering out. The sun was shining brightly out of a scattered cloud cover, making me squint. A quarter of a mile away on the tarmac, in front of the terminal building, I could see the Eastern Provincial 727. Generator trucks and fuel bogeys were swarming around her, preparing the mid-size jet for the flight back to Montreal. I felt a tug of excitement. That jet was our pipeline home. According to the schedule I'd glossed over on the flight into Goose Bay, the return flight left at six in the evening. With luck, Georgina and I could be back in the civilized world that night. After that it would be Llewellyn and Brandt on the run, not us. For the first time in days I started feeling optimistic about life. On top of everything else I felt the journalist's relish at having wound up a blockbuster story. I was actually humming under my breath as I puttered around Harry Moonblanket's office, cleaning myself up for the triumphant return. The story of AV360 was going to win me the Governor General's Award and the Pulitzer! By the time I'd washed and shaved I was visualizing myself in Stockholm accepting the Nobel Peace Prize. I'd be a shoo-in for *Time* magazine's Man of the Year.

I found a dried out piece of cheddar and a can of Tab in the bar fridge Harry kept beside the coffee machine—and a well used three-piece suit in a battered government surplus locker. Harry was close enough to my size to ensure a reasonable fit, even though the lime-green disco outfit wasn't quite my style. I grinned in the murky light as I checked myself out in the mirror hung on the locker door. I could imagine Harry dressed to kill on his way to check out the local talent of Happy Valley.

By the time I'd finished off the cheese and drained the can of Tab I was feeling on top of the world. I checked my watch. Three o'clock. Another hour or so and they'd be coming in. I picked the binder up off the floor and settled back down on the couch, lighting a cigarette. I flipped open the binder, bypassing Llewellyn's cold-blooded preface, and began to read.

I had to give him credit—the plan was virtually flawless. Page after page laid out a detailed working plan for covering up the potential crash of an airliner. As I read through it I became more and more horrified, realizing just how simple it really was. Computers were the key; I was willing to lay odds that Llewellyn's background was in that field. He'd recognized the gaping hole in telecommunications and data processing security and he'd taken full advantage of the system's vulnerability. Like anything else, the chain was only as strong as its weakest link. And the weak link was interdependency.

For the most part, people believe what computers tell them. Computers are bigger, smarter, and faster than human beings. The public has long considered computers as entities unto themselves, forgetting that the machines are just that—machines: inert, useless, and absolutely without function. Until people get into the act. People program computers, and people change those programs. When one terminal is linked to another, and the second is in turn linked to a third, you have a symbiotic relationship. Get into one and you can get into them all. You can sidetrack, erase, manipulate, and cover up any amount of information, as long as you know what you're looking for. With a little skill and a personality without ethics like Llewellyn's, all things were possible. It's kind of like getting your hands on the Great Seal of England. No matter how bizarre the request, with the ultimate seal of approval, the request is granted. In today's society the greatest seal of approval comes in the form of memory banks and microchips. The computer and its varied functions are so much a part of day to day life that people take it for granted, accepting anything on a printout or a visual display terminal without question; and that's what Llewellyn had counted on.

The Icarus program was subdivided into a number of parts, the most basic of which was a blocked program he'd inserted into the memory banks of the computer at Heathrow, using the blackmailed assistant general manager, Young, as his access. He could have inserted the program without Young's help, but it would have been slightly more complicated; besides, Young was useful for other things as well. Since the Heathrow computer was connected with the computers used by London Air Traffic Control, and since they, in turn, were tied at various levels with air traffic control computers all over the world—any airport British Airways flew to, Llewellyn could access. The blocked program inserted in the master program lay dormant, never surfacing until the proper bypasses had been coded in. When an AVTOUR flight ran into trouble, the datalink network, with terminals installed in all AVTOUR DC-IO's, would instantly alert Llewellyn's headquarters, automatically tripping a secondary matrix of instructions which would set off the blocked program at Heathrow. Within seconds, the ailing flight would either cease to exist or change its course. Terminals at the arrivals end would show that the flight had been cancelled, while terminals at the departure end would show it either safely arrived or rerouted. With thousands of jets in the air at any one time, no one would be the wiser; and the way Llewellyn had arranged things, people wouldn't even be slightly suspicious. He'd even outwitted the CADIZ network by installing remote transponder beacons at Goose Bay. In the event of a crash such as the one that happened, the beacons would transmit on the downed aircraft's transponder frequency. The CADIZ operators would assume that the aircraft's normal radio was out and that it was using its transponder to ID itself instead.

Piece by piece Llewellyn had constructed a ghost flight in the event of an accident; a ghost in reality, but completely solid as far as the computers were concerned. And it was the computers that counted.

Coping with the passengers was somewhat more complicated, but still relatively easy once the flight itself had been dealt with. The fact that AVTOUR was a charter company made things considerably safer than a normal scheduled flight. Charters require more ticketing information than a scheduled flight, and passengers are locked in to a specific period away from home. In the case of AVTOUR 360 it was fourteen days.

Once again, computers came to Llewellyn's aid. Anyone meeting the non-existent flight could be shown on a video display terminal that the flight had been cancelled. When the friend or relative tried to make contact with the passenger, the passenger's telephone would be out of order. A cable from the passenger would follow shortly, explaining their non appearance, and the problem with the telephone. Sometime within the next two weeks the friend or relative would be notified that the passenger had met with a fatal accident or a heart attack. It was this part of the scenario which had drawn the most criticism from the members of the group; interfamily connections were too complex to eradicate the possibility of someone putting two and two together. In the original Contingency Plan, Llewellyn had used the statistics culled from thousands of charter flights to prove that 93 per cent of people travelling charter were doing so on tours and had no relatives at their point of entry to provide difficulties. In the Revised Plan he had solved the problem completely.

AVTOUR, like any other charter company, offered tour bookings free of charge. Anyone booking onto a flight and *not* requiring hotel or motel accommodation would be informed that there was no room on the flight. The flights would be "pure tourist," without any chance of a slip-up. On an insurance waiver which had to be filled out by each passenger before ticketing, the name, address, and next of kin were designated. In the event of a crash, postcards from the phantom passenger would be sent out, briefly outlining how much fun was being had. Once again, Llewellyn was relying on human nature. You don't really expect to hear from people on holiday.

It was all based on the statistical possibility that the flight would go down over land. There were individual "clean-up" plans for Ireland, Greenland, Labrador, and northern Quebec. If the flight went down over water, the disaster would simply be announced since there was no possibility that the cargo would ever be found. Because approximately 35 per cent of AVTOUR's regular flight patterns went over land, Llewellyn considered the risk worth preparing for, and he had been proved correct.

I closed the binder and lit another cigarette from Sam's case, dragging in the stale smoke and staring up at the ceiling. A single, ominous thought blazed in my brain. Was AVTOUR 360 the first crash that had been dealt with this way? How long had it been going on? I could think of at least a dozen instances when Llewellyn's plan, or one like it, could have been brought into play. I was beginning to realize just how much we were at the mercy of the people who manned the computer centres of the world, or who had access to them. And that access was becoming easier and easier as time went by and more computers were put into regular use.

Computer crime had first come out of the closet in the early seventies and each year the incidence of computer capers had risen—from shaving pennies off people's savings accounts to massive insurance frauds. As far as I knew though, this was the first time a computer crime had included covering up a case of multiple manslaughter. The magnitude of the crime was compounded by the ongoing conspiracy to ship high grade nuclear waste into the country, storing it in an unproven depository system. And how long had *that* been going on? I'd seen a rail spur running into the Omega plant on the map in Pembroke. Waste from the US, brought in with computer altered waybills and manifests? Why not? That was exactly the way the yellow-cake from Port Hope, Ontario, had been shipped down into the US during the Second World War, except then the subterfuge had been an example of patriotism, the fraud perpetrated under that marvellously all encompassing phrase—National Security.

The stuttering growl of an engine pulled me from my reverie. A small plane, and by the sounds of it, taxiing up to Moonblanket Charter Services. I got up and went to the window, parted the slats and looked out. Sure enough, it was the Musketeer. I checked my watch, surprised. It was only three forty-five; they'd made good time. I grinned. Georgina was probably having a fit, wondering what had happened to me. I watched as the weatherbeaten old plane bumped over the uneven asphalt, sunlight bursting on the windscreen.

I stepped away from the window quickly and made for Harry's desk, scooping up the binder as I went. I sat down behind the desk and slid the binder into the drawer. Then I put my feet up and tilted back in the chair, hands locked behind my head, trying to look as nonchalant as possible. I heard the engine rattle to a stop, and a few minutes later the sound of a key turning in the front door. It opened.

And it wasn't Harry Moonblanket.

The man spotted me behind the desk and stopped cold in the doorway, backlit by the hot sun outside. He looked about thirty-five or so, a little on the short side with narrow hips and shoulders. He was wearing a baseball cap tipped back on his head and the same green fatigues I'd seen at Omega and the crash site.

"Who the hell are you?" he asked. He was definitely Canadian, with that unmistakable burr in his voice, the twang of an eastern Ontario native.

"I could ask you the same question," I said, taking my feet off the table. He didn't recognize me, which stood to reason. If he was from the crash site he'd never laid eyes on me before. As far as anyone up there knew I was still somewhere in the bush.

"I'm a friend of Mr. Moonblanket's," he said, the name unfamiliar on his tongue.

I nodded, keeping my eyes on his. As casually as I could I started feeling around in the desk drawer in front of me, looking for something to use against the man. Even a letter opener would have been useful. "That's interesting," I said. "How come you're flying my plane?"

"Your plane?" he asked. He stepped into the office and closed the door behind him. "I thought it was Mr. Moonblanket's plane."

"I'm Harry's partner," I said, watching for a reaction. There was nothing in the centre drawer. I started checking out the file drawer on the left. "It's our plane," I finished.

"Oh," said the man. He was starting to sweat a bit. I hadn't been part of his scenario.

I felt my heart thundering in my chest. What had happened to Georgina and Harry? My hand touched something hard and cool in the bottom of the drawer. I didn't look down. "You haven't answered my question," I said. "How come you're flying the Musketeer?" I felt around in the drawer, letting my fingers trace the outline of whatever it was I'd got hold of.

"Uh, Harry asked me to fly it in for him," said the man nervously. "He's working a charter. Um, fishermen. Two guys. Needed some more supplies."

My fingers curled into a trigger guard. Harry, God bless him, kept a gun in his office. I hefted it. A horse pistol by the feel of it. I didn't waste any time. "You're a liar," I said, hauling out the gun and pointing it at the man. "You work for Brandt!"

The man had frozen, his eyes widening as he stared at the gun. I let my glance drop, checking out what I held in my hand. It was an unbelievable old piece, an honest to God six shooter, bone handles and all. The barrel was dark with age and about a foot long. I wondered what it was loaded with. Probably black powder. It didn't matter, it was doing a terrific job of scaring hell out of the man I was pointing it towards.

"I don't know what you're talking about," he stuttered, his voice beginning to squeak. I raised the barrel slightly, lining it up with the man's head. His hypnotized gaze followed it and he wound up looking at me. I could sense a flutter somewhere around his knees.

"You work for Brandt and Llewellyn," I said matter-of-factly. "You were up at the crash site of AVTOUR 360. I know the whole story."

"You're crazy!" said the man.

I smiled and pulled back the hammer with a nasty double click. The cylinder moved gently around. The gun was ancient, but Harry kept it well oiled. "Maybe you're right," I said. "Maybe I am crazy. Crazy enough to blow your fucking brains out if you don't answer a few questions!"

"What questions?" asked the man.

"The plane," I said. "The Musketeer. Harry and a woman were with it. Where are they now?"

The man blanched. "Harry, he's the Indian guy, right?"

"Right," I said.

The gun weighed about ten pounds. I lifted my other hand to brace it. The man flinched at the movement.

"Harry's dead," he said quickly. "When we found them he put up a fight. Mr. Brandt knew you had to have a plane nearby and the closest place was Shipiskan Lake. We were waiting for them."

"And Harry put up a fight?" I asked.

The man nodded earnestly. "He tried to attack Mr. Brandt. He got shot."

"Harry didn't have a gun. Brandt didn't have to kill him," I said.

"The guy was pretty big," offered the man weakly.

"The woman?" I demanded, my voice tense.

"Brandt flew her in here. She just went out on the 125. That's a—"

"I know what it is," I snapped. "Where are they taking her?"

"I don't know," he said.

I waved the barrel of the revolver slightly. "Bullshit," I said. "Where are they taking her?"

"Honestly, I don't know!" pleaded the man. "They just told me to fly the Indian guy's plane back here, then head over to the base. I'm supposed to be going out on the Caribou."

"Your friends going to miss you?" I asked. "When are you due to take off?" My mind was racing, trying to plot some kind of strategy.

"Sometime this evening. They'll come looking for me if I don't show up." It was almost a threat, the last bit of guts the man had in him. He straightened defiantly.

"I want them to come looking for you," I said, "because you're going to relay a message." I stared at him. "You're going to tell Mr. Brandt to inform his boss that if he hurts the woman I'm going to blow his whole son-of-a-bitching scheme to smithereens. You got that?" The man nodded. "You're going to tell him to get in touch with me at the Lord Elgin Hotel in Ottawa. He can leave a message with a phone number where I can reach him. You still with me?" The man nodded again. "I want a meet," I said. "Sometime soon tomorrow, with the woman. If he doesn't show up I'll let the press have it all. And if he thinks I'm screwing around, you can tell him that I've got his precious copy number one of thirty-four. Okay?"

"Anything you say," said the man, his voice quavering.

"Good. Now turn around."

"What?" asked the man.

"Turn around," I ordered. "Either that or I fire this howitzer after all."

The man did as he was told. I got up carefully and skirted the desk, keeping my eyes on the back of his head. He was shaking like a leaf. I kept the revolver centred on his back and my finger tight on the trigger. He felt me coming up behind him and I could see the corded tendons in his neck going taut. He knew what was coming. With a quick movement I flipped the gun around, holding it by the long barrel, and brought the butt down behind his left ear, just like they tell you to do in the James Bond books. Surprisingly, it worked. The butt connected with a wet thudding sound and the man fell like a stone. I reversed the gun again and pointed it at the back of his head as I bent down beside him. I checked his pulse. Nice and steady. I jammed the pistol into the waistband of my pants and looked around the office, finally resorting to the cords from the venetian blinds. I tied the man up tightly, running the rope from his ankles back around to his neck to make sure he didn't struggle too much. I checked my watch. Ten past four. I just had time to get back to the motel room in Happy Valley, pick up the money and my other things, and make it back to the terminal for the Eastern Provincial flight to Montreal. I dragged the man's limp body back into the rear of Harry's storeroom and covered him up with some old burlap bags I found. I wanted them to take as long as possible finding him.

Finally, I went back out to the front office. I tugged the revolver out of my pants, flipping open the cylinder before I put it back in the drawer. I looked down through six empty sockets. Through all of that the gun had never been loaded.

Harry was as careful with his weapons as with his aircraft. I
retrieved the binder containing the Icarus Contingency Plan
from the desk and headed for the door. As I went out I felt
my mouth working into a tight-lipped grin. If Brandt gave
me the slightest chance, I promised myself I'd give Harry
Moonblanket fair value for the life he'd lost.

Chapter Twenty-seven

I arrived in Ottawa at ten o'clock after cooling my heels at
Dorval waiting for a connection. There are always a few
brown uniformed RCMP officers hanging around an airport,
but there seemed to be more than usual that night so I
resisted the urge to rent a car from one of the booths across
the narrow concourse from the baggage collection area.
Llewellyn's setup with the heroin could easily have resulted
in an all-points for me, and by this time he'd have added
Henri's credit cards to the scenario. I made a bee line for the
main doors and hoisted myself into the same rattletrap airporter
bus Georgina and I had ridden in a few days before. None of
the loitering mounties gave me a second look, even in
Harry's dayglo suit.

I rode the bus down the dark Airport Parkway into the
centre of the city and got off at the Lord Elgin, a ponderous
old hotel on the boulevarded street of the same name that
runs south away from Confederation Square. I checked in,
using my own name, and took the elevator up to my room. As
soon as the bellhop left, a dollar richer, I turned around and
left the hotel again, using the stairs and exiting through the
side door onto Slater Street, across from the pale office
building rectangle of the National Gallery. I turned right onto
Elgin Street again and headed south to Laurier Avenue. It
was one of those nights in Ottawa where the lack of sun has
no effect on the temperature or the humidity. The air was
flat, calm, and sweltering. By the time I'd gone a block I felt
as though I'd spent two weeks in a steam bath.

I crossed Elgin at Laurier and continued south, passing
Ottawa Teachers College then turning onto Lisgar Street.
The red neon sign on top of the Park Lane Hotel shimmered

in the heat haze a few blocks away. I headed for it, going through the glass doors a couple of minutes later and into the welcome coolness of its air-conditioned lobby. I signed in at the desk, and for the second time in less than half an hour, I followed a bellhop. This time I stayed. The phoney check-in at the Lord Elgin would enable me to receive telephone messages there, and the real check-in at the Park Lane would keep me safe from anything Llewellyn might have up his sleeve—like an early morning visit from Brandt. I dropped my bag on the bed and yawned hugely. My body was craving another dose of sleep like the one I'd had in Harry's office earlier in the day, but the night wasn't over yet. If I was going to beard the lion in his den (as Georgina had put it), I had to be ready. I sat down on the bed, fighting off the urge to lie prone, and picked up the telephone book. I looked up the number I wanted and dialled, keeping my fingers crossed. It rang half a dozen times and I'd almost given up hope when there was a double click as the connection was made.

"What?" said the clipped voice. I smiled, relieved. It was Dennis Mackay, Ottawa Bureau Chief for United Press International. He'd been my boss during my sojourn in the nation's capital.

"Dennis, Peter Coffin."

There was a long, long pause. Finally he spoke again, his normally precise and faintly mechanical voice hesitant. "Hello Peter, what are you doing in town?"

"Tying up the biggest story you ever heard of," I said, hoping to pique his interest. Dennis Mackay cared about only three things in life: good grammar, double Scotches in the Press Club, and getting his hands on hard news.

"What kind of story?" he asked.

"I can't go into details, I don't want anyone else involved, not yet at least. It's too dangerous," I said slowly.

"Does it have anything to do with your in absentia dope bust?" he asked.

"That was a setup," I said.

"That's what they all say, Peter." Dennis was fifty-five years old, had three daughters, and believed that marijuana invariably caused rape. We'd argued a lot in my time in Ottawa, but there had always been an underlying feeling of mutual respect. It looked as though the respect had faded.

"It's true, Dennis. It's a frame, to discredit me. The people I'm after would do anything to kill the story."

"So tell me about it," he said. "Tell me why I've had the RCMP in my office twice so far asking questions about you."

"I don't want you involved," I said. "People have already died because of this thing."

"Very considerate of you, Peter," he said dryly. "What do you want from me?"

"Help," I said.

"What kind?" he asked. "I'm not about to spirit you out of the country, you know, and from the sound of it, that's the only kind of help that would do you any good right now."

"I want access to the bureau," I said. "Now, tonight. I need an hour at one of the terminals."

"Why?" he asked.

"I can't tell you," I pleaded. "Just trust me. I'll give you an exclusive when the story breaks."

"You'll give me five to ten in Joyceville Penitentiary for aiding and abetting a wanted criminal," he said.

I took a deep breath and let it out slowly. "Dennis, I absolutely guarantee that I'm not involved in anything like the RCMP have told you."

"Scout's honour?" he said sourly.

"No," I said. "Just my own. That should be enough."

There was another long silence. I could see his lined Scot's face considering the situation. "All right," he said finally. "I'll help. But by God, if you've been lying to me..."

"I haven't," I said quickly. "You won't regret this."

"I hope not," he said.

I asked him to meet me at the East Block gate on Parliament Hill. He told me twenty minutes, and true to his word, he was there. He took me up to the UPI office in the National Press Building on Wellington, almost directly opposite the Peace Tower, and left me alone with the terminal in his office. I finished just after midnight, thanked him again, and we parted. He went back to his home and family, and I went back to my hotel room. I spent the next two hours drawing diagrams on hotel stationery, filling in the next step in my plan. I was going to need a weapon, just in case. By three o'clock I'd done as much as I could and I collapsed onto the bed, leaving a call with the wake-up service to ring me at eight.

* * *

The jarring clamour of the telephone beside my bed rescued me from a sleep filled with nightmares about Georgina. I came awake groggily, blinking in the flood of sunlight from the floor to ceiling windows at the end of the room. I answered the wake-up call with a gummy mutter and got up. By nine I'd showered, put on Harry's wrinkled suit, and eaten a light breakfast in the hotel snackbar. It was time to go shopping.

Canada doesn't have the most stringent gun control laws in the world, but they're stiff enough to keep you from walking into a sporting goods store and out again with a pistol in your pocket. If I was going to meet Llewellyn armed, I'd have to work for it. I stepped out of the air-conditioned sanctuary of the hotel into the brilliant sun and choking heat of the Ottawa summer, hailed a cab, and told him to take me to the Byward Market. The driver dropped me on the corner of Sussex Drive and York Street and I began poking around. Things had changed since I'd last been there.

Once upon a time the market was a haven for drunks, Ottawa's tiny community of worn out hookers, and pawn shop devotees. The buildings were dark and sour with age, and on a Saturday the narrow streets around the ancient market building were full of vegetable stalls and live meat sold off the back of rusted out Ford pick-ups. It was a section of the city the Tourist and Convention Bureau preferred to ignore in its brochures.

Time had obviously pressed on, and by the looks of things property values had skyrocketed. It was amazing what a bit of sandblasting and a lot of money could do. Someone had decided that the Byward Market had "potential," and they'd done a terrific job realizing it. The drunks and hookers were nowhere to be seen. The fat old Italian women digging into barrels of olives and whacking watermelons had been replaced by Calvin Klein jeans examining the watermarks on old prints while their unisex mates haggled over handmade wooden toys in the mini-boutiques that filled the old market hall.

The beer halls and dry good warehouses had been replaced with architects' offices and restaurants specializing in "surf-n-turf" and Muzaked *Sgt. Pepper's Lonely Hearts Club Band.*

The old pawn shops sold organically dyed wool, macramé kits, and unpasteurized honey. It was as though all the dreams of the sixties and seventies had been preserved forever beneath a doublethick coat of plastic varnish. I eventually found what I wanted in the Outdoors Department of the Hudson's Bay store on Freiman Street.

It was a hammerless slide-action AR-7 Explorer, a .22 calibre survival rifle with an eight shot clip and a fourteen-inch barrel. The rifle disassembled, fitting neatly into the extra long butt. The whole thing didn't weigh more than three pounds. According to the salesman it even floated. I bought the gun and a box of Remington .22 long rifle mushroom bullets. I also bought a box of 12-gauge shotgun shells filled with number six shot. Then I moved on to the Hardware Department. I bought a hacksaw, a small vise, a fine tooth file, three rolls of electrician's tape, a one pound box of Plaster of Paris, and a jar of quick setting latex compound. I took my packages and left the department store, crossing Freiman Street to the Sir-Plus army surplus store I'd spotted on my way into the Bay. There I bought a flat steel throwing knife, a navy flare pistol, and an old Canadian Army field jacket, the kind with loose sleeves and two big pockets in the front. Loaded up to my chin I took a cab back to the hotel. I dumped everything on the bed and looked at my watch. It was eleven o'clock—time to phone the Lord Elgin and check if I had any messages.

I did; one, from a Mr. Llewellyn requesting that Mr. Coffin call as soon as possible. I jotted down the number Llewellyn had left, broke the connection and dialled. He picked it up on the first ring. His voice sounded tinny and I could hear distant machine-like sounds.

"Mr. Llewellyn," I said, "So glad you called."

"Irritating to the end, I see," he replied. "I understand you think we can come to some kind of arrangement, yes?"

"Do you have Georgina?"

"I do."

"Unharmed?"

"Entirely."

"Prove it," I said. I could hear the faint sound of his breathing.

"That is impossible at the moment," he said slowly.

"Then no deal," I answered.

"Mr. Coffin, please," he murmured, "let us be serious. You have something I want, I have something you want. I wouldn't be so foolish as to tell you she was unharmed if that were not the case. I kept the young woman alive precisely because I expected something like this when Brandt informed me that you had not been caught. I assure you, Miss Underwood is alive and well. For the moment."

"And so am I," I said. "Not that you haven't tried to change that situation a couple of times."

"Let us get to the point, yes? I assume you wish to make an exchange. My document for the woman."

"Right," I said.

"And your silence concerning this affair."

"I don't have much choice do I?" I snapped back. "Without that binder of yours I can't prove anything."

"Exactly."

"Can you fix the dope charge?"

"It shouldn't present a problem. I can do it almost immediately."

"Then do it," I said. "That's part of the deal. I get clear, you get clear."

"Agreed."

"So how do we swing it?" I asked. The tough part.

"I beg your pardon?"

"The exchange, damn it, how do we make the exchange." I was getting nervous. For all I knew Llewellyn was having the call traced, though I doubted it. Even with all the cooperation in the world it takes a lot longer than anyone thinks to trace a telephone call.

"I don't believe we can come to any agreement over the telephone," he said after a moment. "I suggest we meet."

"And have you put me away? Forget it."

"A public place."

"Where?"

"The choice is yours," he said smoothly.

I thought about it, then decided to let him pick the spot. I wanted to give him as much rope as possible—put his mind at ease. "No," I said, "you pick the spot."

There was another pause, and then he answered. "The National Aeronautical Collection. Do you know where that is?"

"The old Rockcliffe Air Base? Yes, I know where it is, out on the eastern edge of the city, Manor Park or something."

"I believe so, yes. The collection is held in three of the old hangars. Numbers 66, 67, and 68. The numbers are clearly written on each building. I suggest hangar 68; we should be able to remain relatively anonymous there."

"When?" I asked.

"As soon as possible, yes? An hour?" If snakes could talk they'd sound like him.

I glanced at the mound of packages on the bed at my side. "Three o'clock," I said. That would give me lots of time to put together my little arsenal. I could sense Llewellyn's hesitation on the other end of the line; he was obviously trying to figure out why I wanted so much time.

"Agreed," he said at last. "Three o'clock."

"Right," I said. "And Mr. Llewellyn?"

"Yes?"

"If Georgina has been even slightly harmed I'll have your balls for bookends, you understand?"

I hung up and started unwrapping the goodies.

The AR-7 was first. I took it, the vise, and the hacksaw over to the desk by the window. I attached the vise to the desk and then snapped off the butt plate of the rifle, slipping out the breech, barrel, and magazine. I wrapped a wash cloth around the barrel. I clamped the cloth covered length of blue steel into the jaws of the vise and started cutting, chewing through the barrel about three inches ahead of the trigger guard. When I had the barrel cut down, I removed the shortened mechanism from the vise, exchanging it for the butt. I sawed off the entire shoulder rest and four inches of the grooved barrel support, leaving me with a rough pistol grip. I locked the magazine into the lower part of the breech and fitted the entire firing mechanism onto what was left of the butt. The result was a decidedly ugly handgun with a six-inch barrel. It was also very awkward to hold. No matter how I grasped the curved grip I couldn't get my finger around the trigger without the thing wobbling. But I'd expected that. I got out the Plaster of Paris and the latex compound.

I mixed up half the box of plaster, using a cardboard ice-bucket as a container. According to the instructions, the plaster set fully within an hour. I gave it half that long, then took out a handful of the semi-solid muck and wrapped it around the pistol grip, taking care to ensure that I got lots of it up over the end of the breech. I let it set a little more and then I removed the homemade contraption from the vise. I put my hand around the plaster covered grip and squeezed, shaping the plaster to my hand and giving me enough body to let my finger get at the trigger. I carried it back to the vise and clamped it in, barrel first this time. When the plaster had set completely, I opened up the latex compound and brought the wide-mouthed jar up under the grip, dipping the whole thing in, then removing it. Except for a few drips at the bottom the grip was completely coated in a layer of dull-red rubber, sealing the plaster. If it worked out the way I figured, the plaster and latex would give me a solid grip on the ersatz pistol as well as keeping the whole thing from blowing up in my hand. I left the rubber to dry and started work on the flare gun.

A flare gun like the one I'd picked up at the surplus store looks like a primitive kind of blunderbuss pistol—which is exactly what it is. Flare pistols have a wide, slightly flared barrel without any kind of rifling. The chamber is tooled to take a standard issue phosphorous flare, which is exactly the same size as a 12-gauge shotgun shell. The firing pin is little more than a sharpened extension of the hammer mechanism. I cracked open the box of shotgun shells and slipped one into the breech of the flare pistol just to be sure. It fit perfectly. I slid it out again and got out the file and the electrician's tape. I filed the pin a bit sharper to guarantee that the primer would be touched off, then wound the thin tube of the barrel with the tape. Flares have a low grade primer about one tenth as strong as the charge in a shotgun shell. I didn't want the thing exploding in my face when I pulled the trigger. If I was lucky, the tape would give the barrel enough extra strength to keep it intact for at least one shot. I hefted the thing in my hand. The smooth bore and short barrel meant that the shot would begin to disperse almost as soon as it left the end of the gun. It was useless for any kind of accurate aiming but anything within twenty feet would be turned into hamburger. I put the newly created shotgun-pistol aside and went back to the vise. The mutated AR-7 was dry. I lifted it carefully out of the vise and set it down, then I fetched the box of .22 cartridges and spilled them out onto the desk. Lightly clamping each one lead up into the vise, I started dum-dumming the bullets. The small oily noses of the cartridges were already pinholed, but I needed something more than the mushroom effect the puckered bullets would give. A mushroom shell expands when it hits its target, its end flattening out and tumbling through tissue erratically. The deeper the hole or notch, the more the bullet flattens on contact. Using the hardened steel of the one piece throwing knife, and the side of the file as a mallet, I took the notch halfway down the bullet, making sure I didn't distort the actual curvature of the lead. When I'd done enough for a full magazine I stopped. I took what was left of the electrician's tape and wound it tightly around the bare metal haft of the throwing knife. I put on the field jacket, and dropped the flare pistol and a handful of shells into one pocket and the rubber gripped AR-7, fully loaded, into the other. The pockets bulged slightly, but not enough to make anyone too suspicious. I found a couple of rubber bands around some pamphlets in the desk drawer and slid them over my arm, making a clumsy restraint for the knife. I checked myself in the mirror and winced. The field jacket with Harry's bright-green suit pants made me look like an escapee from a mental institution. I shrugged at my image. To hell with it; GI Joe was ready for action.

Chapter Twenty-eight

I managed to get a car after all, from a place called Rent-A-Wreck on Gladstone, a street in the Italian-Lebanese neighbourhood on the fringes of Centretown, Ottawa's urban core. The car was a 1969 fire-engine red Austin Mini, its roof painted like the Union Jack. The front end of the tiny car looked as though it had gone through at least a score of resurrections, and I had a suspicion the vehicle had been used in the Winter Races held on the frozen Ottawa River. At $6.95 a day, insurance extra, all cash and no questions asked, I wasn't going to argue. I didn't care as long as the thing ran, which it did.

In fact it ran surprisingly well. Once upon a time someone with grease under his nails had bored out the cylinders and done something to the carburettors while he was at it. Mini's

are responsive beasts right off the assembly line, anyway—
this one handled like a formula I racer. It also burned oil like
a truck and rattled like an old lady on her last legs. But I was
mobile.

The Big Ben replica on the top of the Peace Tower was
showing two-thirty as I went around Confederation Square
and then turned off onto Sussex Drive. I followed the wide
street along the cliffed edge of the Ottawa River in light
traffic, taking the sharp turn past the dark stone fortress of
the Royal Canadian Mint on the tail of a Piccadilly Tours
double decker on its way to show the tourists the Prime
Minister's residence. I beat them to it, turning past the stone
wall and gate entrance with its red-coated Mountie guards.
Postcard stuff. What the tourists in the bus behind me
wouldn't know was that duty in front of the PM's during the
summer, like duty on Parliament Hill, was a punishment
detail. Doing an eight hour shift in those uniforms during
boiling temperatures, hounded by Instamatic-toting ladies
from Des Moines, or Red Deer, Alberta was pure torture. I
geared down and fed the growling car into the S curves of
Rockcliffe Park.

A few minutes later I came out of the trees and onto the
flat plain of the Mile Circle, a sightseeing parkway that
arched around a hundred acre pasture left undeveloped for
no particular reason that I could see. The parkway ended on
the edge of Manor Park, a large mid-fifties suburb.

I skirted the subdivision, heading east on Eastbourne
Avenue past the RCMP training centre, then turned north
onto St. Laurent Boulevard, following the pot-holed road up
to the corner of Hemlock. Ahead and to the right I could see
the tree fringed grounds of Beechwood Cemetery; to the left
the dead flat expanse of the old Rockcliffe Air Base. I turned
down between a Dairy Queen and a pizza parlour, following
the gradual incline to the chain link fence surrounding the
base. The big green signs were enough to give me a severe
case of déjà vu. It was almost like coming home. Unauthorized
Entry Prohibited...Canadian Forces Base Ottawa (North)...I'd
learned to read from signs like that. Another, smaller sign
pointed away from the clustered buildings of the military
reservation and down to the vacant crisscross of runways and
taxi-lanes: National Aeronautical Collection/Rockcliffe Flying
Club. I went left, following the signs.

The airport had been abandoned in the mid-sixties, the Ottawa squadrons moving to new quarters at Uplands, beside the civilian airport. All that was left were the three big hangars housing the collection, and the army base on the scarp above. I vaguely remembered schemes for using the old runways, schemes ranging from a drag race setup to pastures for the RCMP Musical Ride horses, but nothing had ever happened. The only flying activity was from the flying club on the far side of the airport.

I turned onto one of the taxi-lanes, now being used as an access road, and headed for the hangars. I passed Number 66 and Number 67, pulling up in the shadow of Number 68. I checked my watch. Five to three. There were no other cars around. I levered myself out of the car and squinted in the harsh sunlight. Sitting mournfully between hangar 67 and 68 was a Viscount prop jet in the colours of Trans Canada Airways, the original Air Canada. The red flash trim was faded to pink, the aluminum body was pitted, and half the windows were broken. Nevertheless, some prescient bureaucrat had made sure the broken bird was securely chained to the asphalt of the parking lot.

I lit a cigarette from a fresh pack of Camels and stood there, smoking and looking out across the empty airfield. On the far side, half a mile to the north, I could see a couple of Cessnas getting ready for takeoff. Other than that there was nothing. A light breeze off the river beyond the hazy shapes of the flying club hangars riffled my hair. My mouth had gone dry and the cigarette tasted terrible. I dropped it, grinding the butt out with my heel.

I knew perfectly well that Llewellyn was a liar. The meeting was a trap, it had to be. But *he* knew *I* knew, and that scared me. The only way I was going to get Georgina was by force; Llewellyn would be prepared for it. And there would be no mistakes this time. This was it—the finale, the shootout at the OK Corral. The only questions remaining were who were the Clantons and who were the Earps?

I checked my watch again. Three on the nose. I took my last look at the sun and crossed to the side door of the hangar. I stepped inside, blinking in the dim light of the interior.

The desk beside the door on the left was empty. The

commissionaire was gone. I let my hands drop into my pockets and went down two steps into the hangar.

The building was a good three hundred feet long and half as wide. Overhead, the ceiling was a maze of cream coloured girders, hung regularly with big industrial pan-lights. The only other illumination came from the windows on the main doors that took up the length of the hangar on the far side. The grey enamelled floor in between was crammed full of airplanes.

Right in front of me was a replica of the Silver Dart, the Kitty Hawk type biplane that had been the first aircraft flown by a British Subject, J.A.D. McCurdy, from the frozen surface of a lake in Nova Scotia, February 1909. Beyond it I could see at least twenty other vintage planes, but no sign of Llewellyn. I frowned. It wasn't like the son-of-a-bitch to be late. I wandered through the collection, the hands in my pockets wrapped around the shotgun-pistol and the AR-7.

A Neuiport 17 biplane; Raymond Colishaw's Black Maria Sopwith triplane; the remains of a corrugated aluminum Junkers J-1. At any other time I would have been fascinated by the array of aircraft. Now I could feel the sweat trickling down the short hairs at the back of my neck. Where the hell was he? Suddenly a door slammed and I heard the echo of advancing footsteps. I ducked under the wing of the decrepit Junkers and scanned the floor. I spotted a well shined pair of brogues heading towards me. I stood up. Llewellyn came around the tail of a big Curtiss Seagull floatplane and stopped. He was dressed for business: dark suit, white shirt, and tie. He was also carrying a cane—the only sign that the crash of the Duke had done him any harm. I let my fingers curl around the trigger of the AR-7, the latex coated butt clammy against my palm.

"Mr. Coffin," he said. The jet hair neatly combed above the hard-lined face gave him the look of a hideously realistic ventriloquist's dummy. He stepped forward, leaning lightly on the cane.

"Mr. Llewellyn," I answered, listening to the faint echo of my voice return from the girders overhead.

Llewellyn took another step. We were still a good twenty feet apart. "You have done extraordinarily well, Mr. Coffin," said Llewellyn, his mouth moving in a taut parody of a smile. "You are to be complimented on your tenacity once again."

"Where is Georgina?" I asked.

Llewellyn shook his head wearily. "In time, Mr. Coffin, in due time. We have other things to discuss first." He waved his cane lightly, pointing to the aircraft around us. "Shall we view the collection as we talk? I believe you know quite a lot about airplanes."

"You might say that."

"Shall we?" he offered, again. We moved slowly along the wide aisles, still keeping at least ten feet between us.

"You know I have the Contingency Plan?" I said.

He nodded, staring up at the mottled, night-black shape of a big German AEG bomber from the First World War. "Yes, I am aware of that, Mr. Coffin. I may assume that you have read it through, yes?"

"Yes." We went around a banner pinned with squadron badges from the RCAF and found ourselves at the rear of a Noorduyn Norseman, one of the first real bush planes used in Canada. We ducked under the high wing and turned down another aisle. I started to get fidgety; why was Llewellyn going over the obvious? I felt like a fly swan-diving into a spider's web.

"I suppose that I may also assume you have the document in a safe place?"

"Safer than you could ever imagine," I answered.

"Is an explanation in order?" he asked.

I shrugged. "Sure," I said, "why not? It should do your heart good to know I've used a familiar tool of yours."

"Yes?"

"Computers," I said. "I've got the original stashed and about a thousand copies spread out all over the world. As of six o'clock this evening."

"Fascinating," said Llewellyn. We went between an Aeronca C-2 and a Stitts Playboy, two tiny sport planes from the fifties, then stopped under the looming nose of a Lockheed 12-A, one of the first twin engine passenger planes to fly in Canada.

"I figured I needed a bit of insurance, so I transcribed the whole thing onto a United Press International Terminal. A blocked program just like yours. It's set to feed onto the world wire with a triple A priority the first time one of the guys at the bureau keys in a dateline after 6:00 P.M."

"Bad luck for me."

"It wasn't luck," I said. "Sam got in touch with me for exactly those reasons."

Llewellyn put 'on one of his pseudo smiles again. "Of course, it's all for naught you realize, yes?"

"Why?" I said.

"Because the system is not yours. It is mine." He shifted slightly, easing the cane forward. I tensed, feeling metaphorical doors closing all over the place. "You assume that the press is inviolate. It is not. Not its telecommunications network at any rate. Your program will never be utilized I am afraid. You may well have a blocked program on the UPI terminal, but I assure you that I and my colleagues can get past the block, or failing that, simply tap into the UPI line and erase anything held in storage. Quite simple, yes? We shall find the original eventually, and you will have nothing, Mr. Coffin, nothing at all." He straightened, a piercing gleam in his eye, then slowly lifted his cane into the air, raising it over his head.

Danger is like sex—it leaves you in a state of heightened awareness. The minute his cane moved, so did I. I noticed his eyes swivelling back as he lifted the ebony stick and I followed his glance as I dropped to the floor, digging into my field jacket. There was a flash of movement from the cockpit of the old Lockheed and I understood what the meandering walk had been in aid of. The squat shape of a silencer poked out of the side window of the cockpit. I dragged out the shotgun-pistol, hauled back the stiff hammer and jerked the trigger, pointing the bell-nosed barrel in the direction of the cockpit fifteen feet above my head.

The windscreen disintegrated, and so did the shotgun-pistol. It literally flew apart, bits of metal and melting tape flying in all directions. It felt as though the explosion had broken my wrist. There was a hammering whine as a bullet from the weapon in the cockpit splattered against the concrete floor a foot away from my head. I rolled, trying to get myself under the nose. Vaguely I saw Llewellyn limping away in the direction of the emergency exit one hundred feet distant. I managed to unlimber the AR-7 and get a shot off, but it was too late. I hadn't had any small arms practice in years and I went wide, the shot hitting a heating pipe yards away from his retreating figure. Then he was through the door and gone. I got to my knees and looked up at the metal underbelly of the Boeing, wondering if it was worth taking a shot up through the floor of the plane. I decided against it. I crept back farther under the fuselage and waited. Listening, I could catch dull scraping noises from the aircraft's interior.

The Lockheed 12-A was a larger version of that company's Model 10-A Electra. It first flew in 1935, seating six passengers with a two man crew. It had six large windows over the low slung wings, and two doors just aft, one on each side.

Whoever my unseen assassin was, he'd probably figured on getting me with one shot. Failing, he was now trapped inside the aircraft as effectively as I was pinned beneath it. Stalemate. If I ran he'd pot me through the window. If he tried getting out I'd nail him coming through one of the doors. Meanwhile, Llewellyn was getting away and that didn't mean anything good for Georgina. I couldn't afford to wait. I was going to have to make the first move.

I got up into a crouch and pressed my ear to the silver metal skin of the plane. Now I could hear the movement clearly—he was coming down the cabin towards the door. I edged along until I was positioned just past the wings and waited. There was a scuffling noise and then a harsh metallic sound. I saw the shadow of the port side door opening. Then there was silence. The open door was bait. If I stuck my head up I knew I'd find myself looking down his silencer. I squeezed my eyes shut, trying to put myself in his place. How would he do it? Prone, standing, crouched? The best position would be a squat over the doorsill, the gun pointing down, probably held in both hands.

And that left his back exposed. I shifted as quietly as I could, getting to my feet on the starboard side. I could just reach the latch on the oval door. I grasped the handle in my left hand and pulled down slightly. There was no resistance. I took a deep breath, held it, and tugged on the handle, pulling the door open.

He was a classic target—the broad back outlined in the far doorway. He had turned partially at the sound behind him and I saw his face as my finger tightened on the trigger of the AR-7. It was Brandt, his right cheek and eye pulped and bleeding; it looked as though the shotgun-pistol had done some good after all. The notched bullet took him under the arm as he raised it to fire, and the impact of the dum-dum threw him backwards out of the port side door, his single muffled shot clanging up into the roof of the Lockheed. I crabbed under the plane and reached him just as he was getting up on his knees. He still had the gun in his hand. I didn't hesitate at all. I pulled the trigger again, hitting him in his good eye. His skull seemed to swell for an instant and then his brains were all over the floor. I stared down at his sprawled body. It wouldn't bring back Sam or Harry Moonblanket, but at least now they had company. I took off after Llewellyn.

By the time I got out of the hangar he was already halfway across the large field, limping through the grass in between the runways. In the distance I could see the hot sun winking off the high tail of a small bizjet taxiing steadily in his direction. The 125.

I hesitated. It was a hundred yards to the Mini, but if I didn't go for it Llewellyn would be at the Hawker before I could reach him on foot. Even limping he still had too much of a lead. I sprinted for the car.

I reached it, lungs burning, and threw myself behind the wheel. I wasted precious seconds scrabbling for the keys and then I was off, running the car through the gears mercilessly, keeping the gas to the floor even when I clutched. The little shoebox of an automobile rocketed onto the taxi-way and then hit the grass as I slewed to intercept Llewellyn. The front wheel drive stuck like glue. I hit a narrow gully and jumped it, feeling something give in the engine compartment as we bottomed and then bounced up, slicing through a chicken wire fence on the far side of the ditch. The slowly moving Hawker rolled towards Llewellyn on the runway, the gangway door behind the cockpit gaping open, waiting for him. I slid the car left, leading Llewellyn's fleeing figure like a clay pigeon at a trap shoot. The movement put me directly in the path of the oncoming jet, and above the whine of the Mini's sewing machine motor I could hear the roar of the Hawker's rear mounted engines reversing thrust. The Mini was small, but it was enough of an obstacle to stop the jet. The Hawker slowed even more, then stopped as the pilot figured out what his next move should be. I kept on going, keeping the accelerator to the floor.

Llewellyn and I reached the jet within seconds of each other. I pulled to a scorching halt and jumped out of the car as he began climbing the ladder.

He'd reached the top of the steps as I hit the bottom. I tugged the AR-7 out of my pocket and waved it at him crazily.

He struggled with the door controls, trying to raise the gangway with me on it, screaming at the pilot in the cockpit to take off. The pilot did as he was told and I felt the stairway lurch as the plane began to move, veering slightly to avoid the Mini. The gangway began to vibrate, twisting under my feet, jerking crazily, almost tumbling me off. I hung on desperately, the furious wash of air over the wings tugging at my clothes and the engine wail threatening to burst my eardrums. I felt my stomach drop and looked down for an instant. We were in the air. I felt another lurch, this time in the stairs. Llewellyn had managed to get the hydraulics working, even with my weight on the gangway. The pilot trimmed up and we went into a climb, the sudden acceleration throwing me against the handrail. The rate of climb increased sharply and I lost my footing, both legs dangling into space while the furious slipstream pried at my aching hands and arms. I felt the railing slipping out of my grasp so I released the pistol. It spun out of sight behind me and I took a firmer grip, dragging my legs up against the howling jetstream, wedging one foot onto the stairs at the far side of the gangway. Three more steps and I'd be even with Llewellyn, who was still trying to manhandle the door closed. The few feet seemed infinitely far apart; my hands would lose their hold long before I got to him.

Out of the corner of my eye I saw the ground below and gagged, almost fainting. We were at least a thousand feet above the steel-grey waters of the Ottawa River, and still climbing. I tore my eyes away, struggling to jack myself up another step. I looked up just in time to see Llewellyn's foot coming down on my head.

I jerked my head to one side and the foot passed my right ear and connected with my shoulder. The hammering air tore the scream away and I suddenly found myself hanging by one hand. I lunged upward trying to regain my hold as Llewellyn's knee bent for a second and final kick. There was no way to avoid it. And then I spotted a second pair of legs behind his. A woman's legs. Georgina.

She must have got him in the small of the back because his body arched at the waist as he flipped out the doorway over my head. I ducked as his shadow loomed over me. I caught a single glimpse of his face, features twisted into a mask of paralyzing horror as his brain sent one last message, telling him what was going to happen next. Then he was gone. The next thing I knew Georgina's hands were under my arms, dragging me into the Hawker's cabin. I fell into the aircraft, sobbing for breath, Llewellyn's screaming death burning like a vision in my mind. An instant later and it might have been me doing the long dive down to the ground.

"Are you all right?" yelled Georgina, pulling me farther into the aircraft and away from the half-opened door.

I nodded, still trying to catch my breath. I struggled to my feet and discovered that I was shaking all over. Fingers quivering, I reached up the sleeve of my jacket and brought out the throwing knife. I looked forward to the closed door into the cockpit and tightened my grip on the tape covered haft of the blade. I didn't think the pilot would give us any problem. He'd land when and where I told him to.

Still shaking, I staggered to the doorway, Georgina's arm firm around my waist. I edged across the opening and looked down. We had moved away from the river, climbing above the dense forest of Gatineau Park. I closed my eyes as the shock rolled over me in waves. It was over.

Icarus had fallen.

Appendix A

AER LINGUS (Ireland)
AEROLINEAS ARGENTINA (Argentina)
AIR CANADA (Canada)
AIR FRANCE (France)
AIR INDIA (India)
AIR NEW ZEALAND (New Zealand)
ALIA (Jordan)
ALITALIA (Italy)
ALLEGHENY AIRLINES (USA)
AMERICAN AIRLINES (USA)
AUSTRIAN AIRLINES (Austria)
AVNA (South Africa)
BRANIFF INTERNATIONAL (USA)
BRITISH AIRWAYS (UK)
BRITISH CALEDONIAN (UK)
CP AIR (Canada)
CRUZEIRO (Brazil)
DELTA AIRLINES (USA)
EASTERN AIRLINES (USA)
EASTERN PROVINCIAL (Canada)
EAST WEST AIRLINES (Australia)
EL AL (Israel)
FINNAIR (Finland)
IBERIA (Spain)
JAL (Japan)
KLM ROYAL DUTCH (Netherlands)
LUFTHANSA (Germany)
NATIONAL (USA)
OLYMPIC (Greece)

PIA (Pakistan)
QANTAS (Australia)
SABENA (Belgium)
SAS (Denmark, Norway, and Sweden)
SWISSAIR (Switzerland)
TAP (Portugal)
TURK HAVA YOLLARI (Turkey)
TWA (USA)
UNITED AIRLINES (USA)
UTA (France)
VARIG (Brazil)
VIASA (Venezuela)

Appendix B

Following the accident at the Three Mile Island nuclear facility in Harrisburg, Pennsylvania, three flatbed trucks carrying highly radioactive waste from the reactor were turned away from the Nuclear Waste Repository at Barnwell, South Carolina because the levels of radiation were too high. The trucks then began an odyssey across the heartland of America, looking for a place to get rid of the dangerous material. They eventually found it at the Hanford Richland Waste Repository in eastern Washington state, more than two thousand miles away. The route taken by the trucks was Interstate 80, a public highway. During the trip no authorities in the towns the trucks passed through were notified; and during the period in which the trucks were travelling, officials from the Federal Department of Health had no idea where the shipments were. Neither did any of the nuclear regulatory agencies in the US.

The shipment of radioactive cargo presents a direct threat to the general public, exposing large numbers of people to the risk of radiation poisoning. Between 1971 and 1978, the US Department of Transport reported three hundred and sixty-nine "incidents" involving radioactive cargoes. About one third of these resulted in spillage of the materials concerned.

Since there are no government monitoring systems for transportation of radioactive materials in the US, Canada, the UK, or Europe, the companies concerned are on an "honour" system to ensure that the packages are properly and safely constructed. A survey of the honour system by the Los Alamos Scientific Labs, a research facility in New Mexico, found 1,141 "occurrences" out of 2,593 shipments. The "occurrences" ranged from no labels on packages to broken

274

security seals, improper seals, levels of radiation higher than indicated, and apparently deliberate mislabelling of packages.

Various assessments have been made regarding damage caused by a major radioactive cargo mishap; the average appears to be in the region of two to three billion dollars for a large scale accident involving spent fuel or plutonium in a major urban area. This estimate does not take into consideration sociological, political, or economic costs associated with such an accident. Some idea of the scope of an accident involving radioactive materials can be gathered from the Mississauga chlorine gas accident that took place outside Toronto in 1979. That railway accident resulted in the evacuation of almost half a million people, almost all of whom returned to their homes within a week or so of the accident. Had the tank cars involved been carrying high grade nuclear waste, the results would have been catastrophic.

There are dozens of different types of radioactive shipments. They have varying levels of hazard, and are shipped for a variety of purposes. Almost all of these shipments are made by private common carriers—private firms that deal with freight trains, trucks, ships, cargo aircraft, and passenger airlines.

In the US and Canada roughly 50 per cent of radioactive shipments go by truck. Cargo aircraft account for 13 per cent, and passenger airlines carry 30 per cent. Rail and water transport account for the rest. In other words, a third of the radioactive material shipped is transported in the bellies of aircraft carrying unsuspecting passengers. Legally, pilots have to be informed of what they are carrying, but considering the number of mislabelling "occurrences" uncovered by the Los Alamos group it would be impossible for a pilot, or even the airline itself, to know what was being transported.

The number of shipments of radioactive material is steadily increasing, rising from 200,000 shipments in 1961 to 2.5 million shipments in 1975. By 1985 the number is expected to be in the range of five million shipments per year. The number of radiation accidents has also increased from twenty-six reported in-transit mishaps per year between 1971 through 1974, to an average of sixty-seven accidents per year in the period between 1975 through 1978.

ABOUT THE AUTHOR

CHRISTOPHER HYDE established his reputation as a writer of potent thrillers with *The Wave*, which sold nearly 200,000 copies worldwide. He has been a broadcast journalist for most of his working life, specializing in intelligence, military technology, and the environment. Hyde lives in seclusion on Prince Edward Island, working on a series of forthcoming novels. He rarely flies, if ever, and prefers to travel by train if at all possible.